CAUGHT IN A STORY:
Contemporary Fairytales and Fables

Christine Park was born and brought up in Sussex. After completing an MA at the University of Sussex, she worked in a variety of jobs, principally in publishing and as a literary agent. She has published two novels, *Joining the Grown-ups* and *The Househusband* and co-edited *Close Company*, stories of mothers and daughters. She has led workshops in both England and Canada and taught courses in editing at Bristol University and the Universities of British Columbia and Simon Fraser in Vancouver, where she is currently living and working on a third novel.

Caroline Heaton was born in Aldershot and grew up in North London. After qualifying as a professional librarian, she worked briefly in Sheffield before taking a degree in English at Birmingham University. She has been a reader for Methuen Children's Books, a freelance reviewer for a number of publications, including *City Limits* and *British Book News*, and co-edited *Close Company*. She currently works for Ealing Libraries.

CAUGHT IN A STORY:

Contemporary Fairytales and Fables

edited by

Christine Park
and
Caroline Heaton

VINTAGE

VINTAGE

20 Vauxhall Bridge Road, London SW1V 2SA

London Melbourne Sydney Auckland
Johannesburg and agencies throughout the world

First published by Vintage, 1992

1 3 5 7 9 10 8 6 4 2

Phototypeset by Intype, London

Printed and bound in Great Britain by
Cox & Wyman Ltd, Reading

ISBN 0 09 986420 7

For Lloyd and Cortes
alive with fairytales

To my mother, who is so courageously writing her story,
and to David, who helped me to write mine

CONTENTS

Preface   ix

Introduction   xi

A MODERN FAIRYTALE Gabriel Josipovici   1

A TALE ABOUT SOUP Annie Dillard   9

THE STORY OF THE ELDEST PRINCESS A.S. Byatt   12

Extract from THE MIDNIGHT LOVE FEAST
Michel Tournier   29

PIERROT OR THE SECRETS OF THE NIGHT
Michel Tournier   43

THE SHARING OF BREAD Clarice Lispector   55

ISIS IN DARKNESS Margaret Atwood   58

WHEN THE LIGHTS RETURN Ben Okri   82

GRAFFITI Julio Cortazar   108

A TALE ABOUT FIRE AND KNOWLEDGE Péter Nádas   113

THE OTHER BOHEMIA Michael Bracewell   123

A CLEAN SHEET Tatyana Tolstaya   143

HOW I FINALLY LOST MY HEART Doris Lessing   163

THE FISH-SCALE SHIRT Ruth Fainlight   175

BLUE-BEARDED LOVER Joyce Carol Oates   182

SECRET OBSERVATIONS ON THE GOAT-GIRL
Joyce Carol Oates   185

ANNINA Helen Dunmore   189

ONE BEAR John Berger   199

THE PROSPECT FROM THE SILVER HILL Jim Crace   203

AIR RIDE from IS BEAUTY GOOD Rosalind Belben   213

THE SECRET MIRACLE Jorge Luis Borges   216

THE STONE DOOR Leonora Carrington   223

Notes on the Authors   288

Acknowledgements   293

PREFACE

In 1988, while I was on Cortes Island in British Columbia, I attended a workshop given by the American poet, Robert Bly, and his Jungian therapist wife, Ruth. The telling and re-enacting of fairytales ran as a central thread through their work. By that time I had already taken part in other gatherings where the oral tradition of sharing fairytales was being revived and I was surprised at the profound effect these stories had on me, linking me to the fantasy figures of my childhood; revealing a literary vein as rich and relevant, now, as ever before.

Returning to England I was eager to write in this form myself, drawing on aspects of my own life but setting them within the framework of the traditional fairytale. I also became intrigued by the work of other living writers who were using and transforming aspects of the fairytale. In this way the idea of a collection evolved.

Approaching Caroline Heaton, my co-editor for *Close Company*, I felt optimistic that she would be fired by equal enthusiasm, knowing that, since childhood, the literature of the fairytale had been a central influence on her reading and thought. So the anthology is a culmination of our joint interests.

CHRISTINE PARK

When I was a child, I devoured fairytales, fantasy and magic stories of all kinds – or they devoured me, swallowing me whole, like Jonas's whale and bearing me off to strange underworld caverns, returning me at length, dazed and transported. I can still hear my father's voice intoning *Three Billy Goats Gruff* and it was his impassioned love of books, which first imbued me with a sense of the value of literature. But although his bookshelves contained volumes of history, philosophy and the Classics, he was no novel-reader. It was this which led him to say gently one day, when he caught me reading yet another magic tale: 'Fairytales are all very well, but you should read other books, too.' The implication was 'proper' books, books that would help in the serious business of life.

I could not have told him so, but that is what they were doing, helping me with the business of my life and child world. And, quite apart from this, what riches they were in themselves, with such a satisfying form and structure, with seductive rhythms and refrains, peopled so fantastically and yet bounded so securely. Later, as an adult, my fascination with the form deepened when I discovered critics and psychologists whose work explored the meaning and value of fairytales. It has been a great delight to re-enter this world through the work of the contemporary writers in this collection, and to sense its enduring power in the modern world.

CAROLINE HEATON

INTRODUCTION

A collection enables stories to be read again, read afresh and to be put into a particular context that provokes broader questions; that is part of the fun of a book like this. The questions raised by *Caught in a Story* are to do with the very nature of the modern fairytale.

In approaching writers initially, we described the essence of the fairytale as we then saw it. Yet what we found was that many of the richest, most powerful stories we received departed radically from our brief prescription: Joyce Carol Oates's *Blue-Bearded Lover* and *Secret Observations on the Goat-Girl*, Margaret Atwood's *Isis in Darkness*, John Berger's *One Bear* and Péter Nádas's *A Tale About Fire and Knowledge*, amongst them.

Other stories we discovered, such as Jim Crace's *The Prospect From the Silver Hill*, Rosalind Belben's *Air Ride* (an extract from her novel *Is Beauty Good*), Ben Okri's *When the Lights Return*, linked with those we had received by a thread both as fragile and as sturdy as the cotton umbilical cord which connects the Thumbelina child to her mother in Helen Dunmore's *Annina*. For all their fierce individuality they draw on a similar subterranean source; yet many are not fairytales in the strictest sense. Rather they are fables, allegories, meditations, brothers and sisters to the fairytale, whose use of fantasy, a dipping into a common well of archetypal symbol and imagery suggests they are members of the same family.

The stories share a concern with some of the most urgent political, personal and social questions of our time, addressed through symbol and metaphor; their sidelong glance sometimes revealing more than direct scrutiny through realism alone. Some, like Doris Lessing's *How I Finally Lost My Heart*, and Tatyana Tolstaya's *A Clean Sheet*, start from a realistic base, but rapidly depart from it into realms of fantasy and magic, if not outright fairytale. Many of them reveal elements and echoes of the traditional fairytale, embedded in the narrative like so many fragments; as if the old form has fractured under immense pressure, but can be discerned in outline through its remains.

The way the writers use echoes, hints, allusions to fairytales appears representative of the present time where knowledge is so often culled from a multiplicity of sources. Tension between the desire to pattern and the seeming impossibility of patterning, in an age where the old certainties have died, informs the structure and often the subject matter of many of the tales. Some mourn and strain after a sense of lost wholeness; others allude to the fairytale as a way of hinting at its re-discovery, or even briefly recreating it for the space of the story, like Annie Dillard's *A Tale About Soup*, in which a whole sense of community is created through the shared meal.

Rosalind Belben in *Air Ride* has her tuba player saying: 'Hasn't it always been so? Innumerable messages throughout history, that never quite arrive. In the mountains we hear one another, and what do we do? We call back, we are drunk on the sound of our own voices, how they carry, and for practical purposes the carrying is of use. If we speak only of goats, if we pass the time of day, that's fine. In the world there are bigger messages, and our failing to listen, to understand, makes great nanny-goats of all of us.' The stories in this collection, distant descendents of the traditional tale, appear to us part of the attempt to listen, to attend to those 'bigger messages' and to bring them to others' attention through the universal language of the fairytale and the fable, translated into modern terms.

If fragmentation is one distinguishing mark, so too is the modern tale's alertness to the world in which it is constructed. Gabriel Josipovici's protagonist, at the end of *A Modern Fairytale*, says that we ' . . . must never forget that fairytales can occur, even in our modern world . . . But we must also never forget that fairytales exist in a context which is not that of fairytales. There will always be fairytales as long as there are human beings, but we must never forget that all fairytales exist in a context of pain and loss and failure and death.' His tale tells of a Jewish boy who escapes concentration camp and survives several years in the forest, fed and nurtured by 'the people on the margins', to arrive safely in Israel. There, in a scene reminiscent of a traditional fairytale, he finds his father in an orchard picking fruit. But there is no 'happily ever after' ending, for the boy's mother remains lost, and this is not the painless disappearance of classic fairytales, where characters emerge and vanish according to the dictates of the narrative. Josipovici, on the contrary, uses his *A Modern Fairytale* to raise uncomfortable questions: if loss is the counterpoint to gain in his hero's personal story, so it is in the history of the 'fairytale' country, miraculously cultivated and flowering, in which he finds peace – a home-land, perhaps, at the cost of others' displacement.

This thrust informs many of the stories, where we are denied the traditional sense of completion. Is this, too, a sign of the times that the tales engage most readily with the teachings of the journey, rather than the finality of arrival? Helen Dunmore's *Annina*, for example, ends at the point where most conventional tales would begin. Concentrating on the inner world of the mother, it hints at her spiritual travail and half-concluded quest, which becomes the motive force in preparing and propelling her daughter towards the threshold of her own journey. Joyce Carol Oates' *Secret Observations on the Goat-Girl* portrays the narrator as groping at truths just beyond her grasp. Whether or not she will succeed in coming to full awareness is left uncertain, the author denying us the luxury of assurance.

A.S. Byatt's *The Story of the Eldest Princess* involves the bucking of another tradition in the heroine's refusal to take the prescribed path. Recognizing that we are all 'caught in a story' the eldest princess determines she will at least decide for herself what type of story it is – similarly, in John Berger's *One Bear*, the protagonist turns to a book to read the end of his story. A.S. Byatt's princess gains a sense of personal destiny through her creative disobedience. But what are we to make of her mentor, the old woman, seemingly embodying wisdom, who assures her that the natural calamity, which her quest was to have reversed, is not the tragedy it appears? Are we to think that personal transformation makes the troubled outer world a benign place, or that we can only control our perception of it? Perhaps the emphasis of the story reminds us that we must determine our own course before we can effect change in the world, and that if we do our success will resonate – hence the younger princess is able to conclude the quest.

The setting of the stories is of crucial importance, with nature very often providing a challenging or healing part in the protagonist's journey. At one end of the spectrum we have John Berger's *One Bear*, which can be read as the embodiment of the human relationship with nature, as well as with the primitive forces within us. The chained bear reflects the process of 'civilization'. Once freed through the transformative act of dance he is at first a threatening, then ultimately a liberating force. In the final scene the protagonist is aware of the bear's huge silent steps and reflects ' . . . in that soundlessness we might find a peace.' The mystery and imperative of communication, whether through speech or silence, is a theme which pervades many of these stories. The communication beyond ordinary speech John Berger conjures is perhaps akin to that alluded to in Rosalind Belben's tale: the profound truths, the bigger messages awaiting a listener.

Nature itself, together with its creatures, can be both message and messenger, as in Tolstaya's *A Clean Sheet*. Often the message consists of a warning, which we heed or not, like the woodland creatures' humorous rendering of the woodcutter's song in A.S. Byatt's *The Story of the Eldest Princess*, which reveals his true nature, or the implicit message of the distant stars in *The Blue-Bearded Lover* which the wife absorbs unconsciously. In *A Clean Sheet*, Tolstaya's political and personal allegory, the protagonist Ignatiev's despair at his poverty-stricken existence is so burdensome – he and depression 'spend hours in silence holding hands' – that a friend advises him to have his heart cut out. Then moments before the operation, Ignatiev notices outside the window 'the warm, already dusty leaves of the luxurious linden splashed, whispered, conspired about something. . . . a wonderful, happy, warm summer secret . . . ' But the joyous camaraderie of the trees seems to exclude him. If their laughter contains knowledge of his fate, it isn't anything that he is able to grasp, already set as he is on his desperate course.

In Michel Tournier's *Pierrot or The Secrets of the Night* the natural setting provides a redemptive message and it is this which reunites the lovers. The beauty of the sudden snowfall restores Columbine's appreciation of the 'real, profound colours' of Pierrot's world which she has abandoned for Harlequin's 'artificial, superficial colours'. She can now accept the reality beneath appearances and the true warmth of Pierrot's universe as he describes it: ' "My night isn't black, it's blue. And it's a blue you can breathe. My oven isn't black, it's golden. And it's a gold you can eat".' Here the internal movement is towards completion, acceptance of opposites: her day, his night, her sun, his moon; even the inclusion of Harlequin the interloper, as he is invited into the bakery to share the pastry Columbine. The delightful culminating image of Columbine's enjoyment as she eats the replica of herself contrasts with Ignatiev's isolation, in *A Clean Sheet*, as he watches the trees.

Community is a theme running through many of these stories. In both Clarice Lispector's *The Sharing of Bread* and the extract from Michel Tournier's *The Midnight Love Feast*, a shared meal turns into a joyous celebration of companionship, following initial alienation. Some wayfarers find help within the fairytale forest: A.S. Byatt's princess enjoys a sense of community with the creatures in the woods; Josipovici's young boy is sustained by 'the gypsies, the horse-thieves, the prostitutes, the very old mad people in the villages of the forests.' On the other hand, Jim Crace's company agent's deep affinity with nature separates him from the community of cruder mineral prospectors. And many of the tales illustrate the suffering that arises when individuals are at war with their community, when the wider society is troubled. Cortazar's hero, for example, in *Graffiti*, nurses a stubborn hope so long as he sees his scribbled drawings echoed, answered by a kindred spirit. But when the authorities imprison and torture his fellow painter, there is: ' . . . no mirror any more, only a hollow to hide in . . . '

Food is an important symbol in these tales, often the rustic food of fairytales: bread, fruit, milk . . . 'as if it had crossed a rocky desert with the goats' in *The Sharing of Bread*, 'rosy apples, enormous yellow carrots, round tomatoes with their skins ready to burst . . . ' Food can represent basic sustenance, but also connection, caring, generosity of spirit. The Goat-girl in Joyce Carol Oates' tale symbolically offers her rejected 'twin' a piece of her own birthday cake. Reconciliation between the three characters in *Pierrot* comes through the creation of the brioche Columbine. The vision of the mysterious host in Annie Dillard's *A Tale About Soup* infuses that of the guest until he sees the oceans, the fields, the rivers, the kitchen gardens, the sources of each of the ingredients that have gone into the soup and in so doing recognises the beauty and richness of the world. On the other hand, where Richard in Margaret Atwood's *Isis in Darkness* is only able to offer his alter-ego, Selena, a token cup of coffee when she is desperate for sustenance and help, this appears an ironic comment on the emotional poverty of his life.

The combination of the magnificent fish 'medianoche' in the extract from Tournier's *The Midnight Love Feast*, accompanied by the telling of fairytales, has such a transformative effect on the formerly disaffected hosts that by the end of the night they no longer wish to part. Tournier's original treatment of the themes of disillusionment, the power of the fairytale, communication and silence, links it closely with other tales in the collection, particularly those by Okri, Atwood and Tolstaya.

The theme of what gets communicated, handed on, handed down, handed out, reverberates through the collection. Many of the stories are about having voice to record, create, enact; or lacking it. And voice can be one of the gifts that we are given at the outset of the fairytale journey. It is also linked with the idea of memory: the loss of memory will be part of the price Ignatiev pays in *A Clean Sheet* for his new-found assurance. Blood, too, can be linked with memory. The blood on the key in *Blue-Bearded Lover* is the link with Bluebeard's former wives, carrying with it an implicit message; part of the heritage which the new girl-friend rejects, to her cost.

Communication through art, on the other hand, can be a form of private subversion, as it is for Cortazar's defiant hero in *Graffiti*. Art is often a secret source of courage, as in Borges's *The Secret Miracle*, where the writer facing execution longs for a reprieve long enough to complete his play. It can also be a way of sustaining the individual's vision. Both Okri's song-writer, and Atwood's bohemian poet are ultimately compromised, defeated, but something of the true romance and integrity of their attempt mesmerises others.

Michael Bracewell's *The Other Bohemia* and Péter Nádas's *A Tale About Fire and Knowledge* show the failure of culture and communication in differently corrupted societies. Bracewell's ironic vision is of a mythical 'old Bohemia', in Eastern Europe, once 'the home of all the Arts' now a uniformly prosperous, but spiritually impoverished land. Nádas takes a cool look at his native Hungary under the old regime. In a story redolent of both Orwell and Kafka, he examines the very nature of reality for the inhabitants of a country where language is tainted at its very source. In this society uneasily bound by denial there are ' . . . self-sacrificing individuals, who, in the interest of complete and perfect equality . . . had to remain more equal than others . . . these were none other than the news announcers', whose ability to relay disingenuous information is raised to the level of an art. It is only when one of the most gifted makes a near-truthful slip that the fabric of distortion is rent apart.

The sculptor-dancer of Michel Tournier's extract from *The Midnight Love Feast* raises the question of art's relationship to temporality. His solution to an art which seeks to defy time and death is to create sand-sculptures: '. . . the great moment was the return of the tide and the terrible ceremony of the destruction of the work . . . "My sand sculptures live," he declared, "and the proof of this is that they die".'

Fairytale time, though, can be many-layered and capable of expansion and contraction. The year's reprieve given to the protagonist in *The Secret Miracle* takes only two minutes of real time. Conversely, the bear of Berger's story has been chained 'for centuries' and man and bear inhabit a continuous present until the dance which precipitates the march of time and a new relationship.

Time may also assume the properties of dream, unfolding to reveal parallel universes and a multiplicity of viewpoints. In *The Stone Door*, Leonora Carrington's rich, surreal novella, dream-time interpenetrates real time; the unnamed heroine returns night after night in dream to seek her lost counterpart, the Wandering King of the Jews, but they meet in the time that is also the course of his real-life's journey. The story constantly opens out to reveal new levels of meaning. As it moves backwards and forwards in time Carrington dramatizes the self's impetus to fullest development, without which, she writes, it is 'a pitiful and incomplete creature'. The woman's integration of her masculine side and the man's integration of the feminine is portrayed through symbols taken from astrology, alchemy and ancient hermetic teachings.

In Okri's equally powerful *When the Lights Return*, Ede's inability to tolerate his girlfriend's vulnerability or to recognise her illness appears symptomatic both of his own soul-sickness and of the malaise afflicting his country. In rejecting her he seeks to suppress a side of himself which may become permanently inaccessible. Maria tries to warn him: ' " . . . if you ignored me, and never saw me again, then you would have killed me. ... And if you really loved me, and if later you want to talk to me, you would have to wake me from death ..." ' Ede's nightmare journey through the 'Phantasmagoria' of the decaying city, with its overcrowding, dust, noise like 'terrible music ... fashioned out of the extremes of human chaos', to reach her sick-bed, indicates the degree to which life is out of balance.

' "Even our seas have gone mad" she said, referring to the items of sacrifice that had been washed up on the beach like rejected prayers.

' "These are new times," Ede remembered saying, "We need new skins to cope. New songs".'

Warnings of one kind or another echo in many of the tales, where the pysche remains at war with itself. While Okri's story suggests one scenario, in which individuals and an entire society alike are imbued with a corruption of the spirit and ' ... the lights are out', Joyce Carol Oates explores the malaise within a family. Through the ambiguous figure of the goat-girl she hints at family secrets, ill-suppressed. The power of this delicate, uneasy tale lies in its symbolic reach, seeming to tap deep into the unconscious and to summon up both darkness and the redemptive powers available to conquer it.

Both Ruth Fainlight's *The Fish-Scale Shirt* and A.S. Byatt's *The Eldest Princess* reflect the current preoccupation with the theme of female quest. Here the heroine is, post-modern fashion, only too conscious of fairytale convention and the fun of both stories lies in its subversion. What happens when the frog does not turn into a prince; or when the princess leaves the alotted path? *Blue-Bearded Lover*, on the other hand, in ironically depicting the dangers of a too-acquiescent feminine obedience, neatly upends the original tale.

Even in these modern tales nothing is as it seems, any more than in the traditional fairytale. Despite the upheavals of this century and our contemporary scepticism, the redemptive and transformative powers are as alive in the pages of this collection, as in the collections of old. And this is surely heartening. Borges's tale illustrates the redemptive power of prayer, Lispector's, the power of sharing bread. Cortazar conjures the vitality that comes from finding a fellow traveller. Doris Lessing in *How I Finally Lost My Heart* points to the central theme of all fairytales: the transformative power of the heart. In her warm, witty story a leaden heart, like that in *A Clean Sheet*, is causing grief. But plucked out and covered in foil, it eventually becomes a gift. In this, as in all fairytales, there is never just one path to travel, our own choices constantly open up new ways. And though we may be 'caught in a story' it may also be a story which we have the power to re-write.

We hope this collection will be every bit as intriguing, thought-provoking and delighting as the gift of the heart in Doris Lessing's tale was to its recipient in the London tube.

CHRISTINE PARK and CAROLINE HEATON

A MODERN FAIRYTALE

GABRIEL JOSIPOVICI

ONCE UPON A time there was a little boy who lived in a
land of reeds. Wherever you went the great river or one of
its tributaries was always close at hand. But though the river,
which had its source far away in the Mountains of the West,
had almost reached its destination in the vast inland sea as
it passed through the land of reeds, the land was so flat and
so interspersed with streams that no-one who lived there had
ever seen the sea.

The little boy lived in a big house with his father and
mother and many servants, for his father was one of the
richest men in the land. He had grown rich by bringing the
railway to the land of reeds, and every year the family would
pack their bags and board one of the trains for which his
father had been responsible and travel in great luxury to the
big city which had once been the capital of an Empire. There
they would stay in a splendid hotel and his father would take
him to concerts and to cafés and to see the horses in the
famous riding school. Once men went on pilgrimages to holy
shrines, his father would say, now they go on pilgrimages to
the shrine of culture.

The little boy had a nurse from the village, whom he loved,
and a tutor from the big city, whom he hated. The tutor was
there to teach him history and geography and the language
of the city, and no-one in the big house was allowed to speak
the language of the grandparents or the language of the
village, though the nurse whispered it to him on their walks
along the river banks. You must grow up speaking the true

1

language of civilization, his father told him. That is the language of the great poets and you must never forget that it is the culture of the great poets to which you belong.

But one day the visits to the great city stopped. Uncle, father's brother, came to stay, and he could hear him and his father shouting in the library and sometimes his mother shut herself up in her room for the whole day and when she came down he could see that she had been crying. Then Uncle went away and shortly after that men in uniform, speaking the language of the great poets, came and took them away. Though the little boy clung to his mother they separated them and took his mother in one car and put him and his father in another. They were men in a hurry. They drove the little boy and his father to the station and put them in a train that was waiting. This was not at all a luxury train such as the one they took when they went to the big city, but a train crowded with people who spoke the language of the grandparents. Where are we going? the little boy asked. Where is Mother? But all his father would say was, I cannot believe it, I cannot believe it.

After a long journey the little boy and his father were taken from the train with all the other people crowded in there and pushed into a courtyard. Everybody was crying and the men in uniform were shouting orders which nobody understood and beating people with their guns. But after a while life settled down to a routine. It was very different from life in the big house. Everybody slept together in one huge room which smelt so bad you wanted to be sick. The only food was a thin soup and occasionally a small piece of stale bread. The men in uniform shouted all the time and beat the people. Every morning before the sun was up everybody had to get up and dress and go down in long rows to the quarry. You did not get back from the quarry till the sun had set. Your hands and back hurt so much from the quarry that you could not sleep, and people cried in the dark and cursed in the language of the grandparents.

The little boy decided to escape. He stepped out of the line as they were going down to the quarry and hid behind a tree. Then, when the guards had passed and no-one seemed to have noticed, he began to run. He ran for a long time, his heart pounding in his chest, and the taste of blood in his mouth, but no-one shouted and no-one came after him. Night fell and he stumbled and hurt his leg. So he crawled under a bush and went to sleep.

The next day it was raining. The little boy ate some berries from a tree and went on walking as fast as he could. His only thought was to keep moving. Once he came within sight of a village, but although he was hungry he skirted round it, keeping to the forest, and went on walking. That night he slept in the forest, covering himself with leaves, but the next morning he had terrible pains in his stomach and he found it almost impossible to get up. He knew he would have to get food that day even if it meant having to talk to people. And, soon enough, he heard the sound of farm animals and of people at work in the fields. He heard them shouting to each other and he remembered the language of the village he had been forbidden to speak and knew he would have to speak it now or his life would be over.

When he reached the village – it was no more than a poor collection of houses and huts lining a dirt track – his heart was pounding. But he felt so weak he knew there was no alternative. He knocked at a door and when an old woman opened he asked her, in the language his nurse had whispered to him as they walked along the river banks, whether she might have a crust of bread for him. He did not understand the stream of words that issued from her mouth but stood, looking at her, until her face grew blurred and he felt himself falling.

He did not entirely lose consciousness but he kept his eyes shut tight as the voices rose and fell around him and many hands picked him up and laid him on a couch. Then he opened his eyes and saw them all looking at him and said again, in the language of his nurse, Bread, bread. The old woman who had opened the door brought him bread and milk and the others watched as he ate. They asked him questions but an instinct told him not to answer even those he could understand. So he closed his eyes again and fell into a heavy sleep.

When he woke up he did not at first know where he was. He thought he was in his room in the big house and then all the events of the past few months came rushing back into his mind and he grew very still. He listened but there was not a sound in the house. He got up and found that he was still dressed, though someone had taken off his shoes and put them at the foot of the couch. He put them on, listening out for any noises, but the house was silent. He went to the door and listened again, then opened it and found himself in a hall with another door in front of him. He opened that and peered out into the street but the village seemed to be deserted. Even the old woman must be down in the fields, he thought. He ran quickly along the track and soon found himself in the forest again.

After that he planned more carefully. He went into the villages to beg for food and went back into the forest as soon as he could. He knew that one point in his favour was that he looked more like the village children than like the other children with whom he had been shut up. His face was round, his skin blackened by the days in the quarry, his eyes twinkling. If I don't talk much I may be able to get away with it, he thought.

– How terrible it must have been, someone would usually say at this point when, many years later, a famous writer now, and living in another country, speaking another language, he would tell audiences round the world about his childhood. – How dreadful to be a child alone in those forests with your life threatened at any moment.

– You know, he would say, the twinkle still bright in his eye, it was not terrible. Perhaps to think about it is terrible, but when you are living something then you are just living it. And when you are a child it is perhaps easier. You do not think too much. You live one day and then you live another day. You are not anxious about the day after that.

– But how did you survive? he would be asked.

– I survived, he would say. For three years. Maybe four. And then I was found by the other army and I travelled with them. It was there I learned to smoke, he would say, laughing. From the age of twelve I was smoking cigarettes. That is not

4

good for the health, but when you are young you do not know any better. Last year I was in hospital for my chest and I had to stop.

– And you wandered like that, all that time? he would be asked.

– You know, he would say, his eyes twinkling, I am one of the luckiest people in the whole world. When you are small, he would say, then you don't want to go to school. You don't want to sit and read books all day long. You want to be free and to be out in the woods and the fields. And that is what happened to me. I had the best education anybody could have, he would say. The people I met on my travels, they were the people on the margins, the gypsies, the horse-thieves, the prostitutes, the very old mad people in the villages of the forests. They gave me food, sometimes clothes, and they told wonderful stories. Wonderful stories. What more could a child want? And then, when I was older and I wanted to study, I was able to go to University and listen to the very greatest, to many famous names who had come to the new country and wished to be of service to it. What better education could there be?

– If I was Minister of Education, he would say, his eyes bright, then I would insist that everybody should have the education that I had. But how would that be possible?

– And what happened after the other army found you? someone would ask.

– You know, he would say, after many months I got to the South, to the land of the sun. There was a group of us. A priest took us in. He was sorry for us and he took us in and fed us and looked after us. He taught us how to say prayers. He wanted us to become priests too and we didn't know any better, we liked him, we were willing to do as he said. And then one day a man came and he called us together and he explained to us who and what we were. So we left the priest and went with him and waited on the beaches for a boat to come and take us to the new country. We waited for a long time but in the end a boat came and we were taken on board.

– That was the time they were attacking those boats, he

5

said, to stop them getting to their destination. But I got there. Some of my friends did not get there, they were drowned in the boats that were sunk, but I was fortunate and I got there.

– After I had been in the new country for a year, he said, I suddenly could not do anything any more and I could not speak to people any more. I looked at my hands and I did not know they were my hands. I looked at my face in the mirror and I could not understand how it was my face. But then slowly I recovered and I began to be able to speak to the people around me and to do the things I had to do. When I looked at my hands they were still strange to me but I knew that they were mine.

– After that, he said, I went to school and learned the language of the new country and then I went to the University and after that I got married and had my children. Of course there were the wars, he said. I fought in three wars. In the first, after ten days learning how to fire a rifle, we were told we would have to take back a fortress on the top of a bare hill that the enemy had captured. Everybody could see that it was suicide. If you left the cover of the trees and started to climb the hill you were completely exposed, and they had machine-guns in the fortress, we knew that because they were our machine-guns which they had captured. So we knew that once we left the cover of the trees and started up the hill it was only a matter of minutes before our lives would end. But we were soldiers and we had to obey orders. If someone thought it would help for us to be killed like that then we had to be killed. But fortunately, he said, just before the order to advance was given another message came from head-quarters and we were told to retreat instead. So again I survived.

After a little while, as he seemed disinclined to continue, someone said: – May I ask whether you ever heard what happened to your father?

– Every week, he said, from the time I arrived, I looked in the papers where they have a list of the people who have arrived in the country. I did not expect to see his name but I looked. Every week. Like a ritual. And one day I was looking and I saw his name. The names were printed very

6

small and all close together because so many people were arriving in those days, so my eye went past it, but my brain told me to stop. I went back slowly over the list and there was his name. There are not many with our name, he said, but it was quite possible of course that it was not him. I made enquiries and they told me where this person with this name had been sent on his arrival. So I went and I asked and they looked at the list and then at another list and they said, He is in the orchard. So I went to the orchard, there were many trees and in each tree was a man, up in the branches, picking the fruit. So I went from tree to tree looking up to see if I recognized the man up there. And finally I came to a tree and I looked up and there was my father.

In the silence that followed someone said: – It's really like a fairytale, your life.

– You see, he said, and his eyes twinkled more than ever, it is a fairytale, but it is a modern fairytale. Why? For two reasons. One is that my own life has been like a fairytale, but I cannot forget that my mother disappeared. She disappeared and many others with her. If this was a traditional fairytale, he said, this would not have happened, and even if perhaps it had happened I would have no memory of it. But I will always have the memory. I cannot forget it. So it is a fairytale but it is a modern fairytale.

– The other reason, he said, is that the new country, in which I live and whose language I speak and in whose language I write and where by the grace of God I have become a well-known writer, so that I am invited here to talk to you and my good friend the cultural attaché looks after me and brings me here and my other good friends make me welcome in their beautiful flat and you are invited here to listen to me – this country too is like a fairytale. Fifty years ago it did not exist and now there are cities and orchards and schools and universities and printing presses and here children can be brought up in safety and happiness and in their turn bring up their children. It is a miracle. It is a fairytale. But it too is a modern fairytale. Because here too there is something we cannot forget. We cannot forget that before we came this land was not empty. We cannot forget that there were people

7

here with houses and villages and their own language and their own stories and their own memories. And if we wanted to forget they would not let us forget, for they cannot forget that they have lost fields and houses and fathers and husbands and sons. I do not say it is our fault. I do not say they are blameless. I only say they cannot forget and they will not let us forget. So it is a fairytale but it is a modern fairytale.

– You see, he said, we must never forget that fairytales can occur, even in our modern world. For if we forget this then we will cease to be human beings. But we must also never forget that all fairytales exist in a context which is not that of fairytales, a context of pain and loss and failure and death. There will always be fairytales as long as there are human beings, he said, but we must never forget that all fairytales exist in a context which is not that of fairytales. And now I see that food and drink have been prepared by our kind hostess, so let us eat and refresh ourselves so that tomorrow we may be ready to go out and face another day.

A TALE ABOUT SOUP

ANNIE DILLARD

ONCE THERE WAS a great feast held in a banquet hall of such enormous proportions that you could not believe men built such a thing. Two thousand chandeliers hung from the ceiling; lumber cut from all the world's forests made the vast and parti-coloured floor. Great loose areas of the hall were given to various activities: there were dances and many kinds of gaming; a corner was devoted to the sick and injured, and another to the weaving of cloth. Children chanted rhymes wherever they gathered, and young men sought pretty girls in greenhouses or behind the damask hanging of booths and stalls.

The feast lasted all night long. Guests sat at a table as long as a river that stretched down the middle of the hall. No one cloth could cover such a table, nor could one centrepiece suffice. So the table was decorated in hundreds of different themes, with different combinations of colours and kinds of tableware, with various carved figures and various drinks, and with lively musicians in costume playing to each set of guests a special music.

There was only a single course served to the guests, but that was a soup made of so many ingredients it seemed to contain all other dishes. The soup was served continuously, all night long, and there were so many guests that all the places at the table were always taken, and the benches always full, when the servants ladled the soup into the endlessly decorated array of metal, glass, wood, and pottery bowls.

Now, the host of this feast was a young man of tremendous

9

wealth and power who stood behind a curtain on a balcony above the great hall, and watched the guests as they ate and drank at the long table. He thought: 'All night long people have been eating as much soup as they wanted, and then coming back to the table for more. It is good that they enjoy themselves. But not one person has seen or really understood the excellence of that soup.'

So the host parted the curtain a crack more and let his gaze fall. It fell directly on an old man who happened to be sitting at the table in his line of vision, looking about and thinking of nothing at all. At once the old man felt an overwhelming sense of power, an impact as if his spirit had been struck broadside and wakened to a flood of light. He bowed his head and saw, through charged eyes, his bowl of soup that had come alive and was filled to endless depths with wonderful things.

There were green fields in his soup bowl, with carrots growing, one by one, in slender rows. As he watched, transfixed, men and women in bright vests and scarves came and pulled the carrots, one by one, out of the soil, and carried them in baskets to shaded kitchens, where they scrubbed them with yellow brushes under running water. He saw white-faced cattle lowing and wading in rivers, with dust on the whorled and curly white hair between their ears. He saw tomatoes in kitchen gardens set out as seedlings by women in plaid shirts and by strong-handed men; and he watched the tomatoes as, before his eyes, the light from the sun blew each one up like a balloon. Cells on the root hairs of beans swelled and divided, and squashes grew spotted and striped in the fall. Wine aged in caves, and the barrel-maker went home to his wife through sunlight and shade.

He saw the ocean, and he seemed to be in the ocean himself, swimming over orange crabs that looked like coral, or off the deep Atlantic banks where whitefish school. Or again he saw the tops of poplars, and the whole sky brushed with clouds in pallid streaks, under which wild ducks flew with outstretched necks, and called, one by one, and flew on.

All these things the old man saw in his soup. Scenes grew in depth and sunlit detail under his eyes, and were replaced by ever more scenes, until, with the flight of wild ducks, the worlds resolved into one blue sky, now streaked, now clear, and, at last, into soup again, dark soup, fragrant in its bowl. The host had let the curtain fall shut.

The man blinked and moved his head from side to side. 'I see now,' he said to himself, 'that this is truly an excellent soup, praise God.' And he ate his bowlful, and joined the dancers in a daze, a kind of very energetic daze.

THE STORY OF THE ELDEST
PRINCESS

A.S. BYATT

ONCE UPON A time, in a kingdom between the sea and the mountains, between the forest and the desert, there lived a King and Queen with three daughters. The eldest daughter was pale and quiet, the second daughter was brown and active, and the third was one of those Sabbath daughters who are bonny and bright and good and gay, of whom everything and nothing was expected.

When the eldest Princess was born, the sky was a speedwell blue, covered with very large, lazy, sheep-curly white clouds. When the second Princess was born, there were grey and creamy mares' tails streaming at great speed across the blue. And when the third Princess was born, the sky was a perfectly clear plane of sky-blue, with not a cloud to be seen, so that you might think the blue was spangled with sun-gold, though this was an illusion.

By the time they were young women, things had changed greatly. When they were infants, there were a series of stormy sunsets tinged with sea-green, and seaweed-green. Later there were, as well as the sunsets, dawns, where the sky was mackerel-puckered and underwater-dappled with lime-green and bottle-green and other greens too, malachite and jade. And when they were moody girls the green colours flecked and streaked the blue and the grey all day long, ranging from bronze-greens through emerald to palest opal-greens, with hints of fire. In the early days the people stood in the streets and fields with their mouths open, and said oh, and ah, in tones of admiration and wonder. Then one day a small girl said to her mother that there had been no blue at all for three days now, and she wanted to see blue again. And her mother told her to be sensible and patient and it would blow over, and in about a month the sky was blue, or mostly blue, but only for a few days, and streaked, ominously, the people now felt, with aquamarine. And the blue days were further and further apart, and the greens were more and more varied, until a time when it became quite clear that the fundamental colour of the sky was no longer what they still called sky-blue, but a new sky-green, a pale flat green somewhere between the colours which had once been apple and grass and fern. But of course apple and grass and fern looked very different against this new light, and something very odd and dimming happened to lemons and oranges, and something more savage and hectic to poppies and pomegranates and ripe chillies.

The people, who had at first been entranced, became restive, and, as people will, blamed the King and the Queen for the disappearance of the blue sky. They sent deputations to ask for its return, and they met and muttered in angry knots in the Palace Square. The royal couple consulted each other, and assured each other that they were blameless of greening, but they were uneasy, as it is deep in human nature to suppose human beings, oneself or others, to be responsible for whatever happens. So they consulted the chief ministers, the priests, and a representative sample of generals, witches and wizards. The ministers said nothing could be done, though a contingency-fund might usefully be set up for when a course of action became clear. The priests counselled patience and self-denial, as a general sanative measure, abstention from lentils, and the consumption of more lettuce. The generals supposed it might help to attack their neighbours to the East, since it was useful to have someone else to blame, and the marches and battles would distract the people.

The witches and wizards on the whole favoured a Quest. One rather powerful and generally taciturn wizard, who had interfered very little, but always successfully, in affairs of

State, came out of his cavern, and said that someone must be sent along the Road through the Forest across the Desert and into the Mountains, to fetch back the single silver bird and her nest of ash-branches. The bird, he added, was kept in the walled garden of the Old Man of the Mountains, where she sipped from the crystal fountain of life, and was guarded by a thicket of thorns – poisonous thorns – and an interlaced ring of venomous fiery snakes. He believed that advice could be sought along the way about how to elude their vigilance, but the only advice he could give was to keep to the Road, and stray neither in the Forest, nor in the Desert, nor in the rocky paths, and always to be courteous. Then he went back to his cavern.

The King and Queen called together the Council of State, which consisted of themselves, their daughters, the chief minister and an old duchess, to decide what to do. The Minister advised the Quest, since that was a positive action, which would please the people, and not disrupt the state. The second Princess said she would go of course, and the old duchess went to sleep. The King said he thought it should be done in an orderly manner, and he rather believed that the eldest Princess should go, since she was the first, and could best remember the blue sky. Quite why that mattered so much, no one knew, but it seemed to, and the eldest Princess said she was quite happy to set out that day, if that was what the council believed was the right thing to do.

So she set out. They gave her a sword, and an inexhaustible water-bottle someone had brought back from another Quest, and a package of bread and quails' eggs and lettuce and pomegranates, which did not last very long. They all gathered at the city gate to wish her well, and a trumpeter blew a clear, silver sound into the emptiness ahead, and a minister produced a map of the Road, with one or two sketchy patches, especially in the Desert, where its undeviating track tended to be swallowed by sandstorms.

The eldest Princess travelled quickly enough along the Road. Once or twice she thought she saw an old woman ahead of her, but this figure vanished at certain bends and slopes of the path, and did not reappear for some time, and then only briefly, so that it was never clear to the Princess whether there was one, or a succession of old women. In any case, if they were indeed, or she was indeed, an old woman, or old women, she, or they were always very far ahead, and travelling extremely fast.

The Forest stretched along the Road. Pale green glades along its edges, deeper rides, and dark tangled patches beyond these. The Princess could hear but not see, birds calling and clattering and croaking in the trees. And occasional butterflies sailed briefly out of the glades towards the Road, busy small scarlet ones, lazily swooping midnight blue ones, and once, a hand-sized transparent one, a shimmering film of wings with two golden eyes in the centre of the lower wing. This creature hovered over the Road, and seemed to follow the Princess for several minutes, but without ever crossing some invisible barrier between Forest and Road. When it dipped and turned back into the dappled light of the trees the Princess wanted to go after it, to walk on the grass and moss, and knew she must not. She felt a little hungry by now, although she had the inexhaustible water-bottle.

She began to think. She was by nature a reading, not a travelling princess. This meant both that she enjoyed her new striding solitude in the fresh air, and that she had read a great many stories in her spare time, including several stories about princes and princesses who set out on Quests. What they all had in common, she thought to herself, was a pattern in which the two elder sisters, or brothers, set out very confidently, failed in one way or another, and were turned to stone, or imprisoned in vaults, or cast into magic sleep, until rescued by the third royal person, who did everything well, restored the first and the second, and fulfilled the Quest.

She thought she would not like to waste seven years of her brief life as a statue or prisoner if it could be avoided.

She thought that of course she could be very vigilant, and very courteous to all passers-by – most eldest princess's failings were failings of courtesy or over-confidence.

There was nobody on the Road to whom she could be

courteous, except the old woman, or women, bundling along from time to time a long way ahead.

She thought, I am in a pattern I know, and I suspect I have no power to break it, and I am going to meet a test and fail it, and spend seven years as a stone.

This distressed her so much that she sat down on a convenient large stone at the side of the road and began to weep.

The stone seemed to speak to her in a thin, creaking, dry sort of voice. 'Let me out', it said. 'I cannot get out.' It sounded irritable and angry.

The Princess jumped up. 'Who are you?' she cried. 'Where are you?'

'I am trapped under this stone,' buzzed the voice. 'I cannot get out. Roll away the stone.'

The Princess put her hands gingerly to the stone and pushed. Pinned underneath it, in a hollow of the ground was a very large and dusty scorpion, waving angry pincers, and somewhat crushed in the tail.

'Did you speak?'

'Indeed I did. I was screaming. It took you an age to hear me. Your predecessor on this Road sat down just here rather heavily when I was cooling myself in this good crack, and pinched my tail, as you see.'

'I am glad to have been able to help,' said the Princess, keeping a safe distance.

The Scorpion did not answer, as it was trying to raise itself and move forwards. It seemed to move with pain, arching its body and collapsing again, buzzing crossly to itself.

'Can I help?' asked the Princess.

'I do not suppose you are skilled in healing wounds such as mine. You could lift me to the edge of the Forest where I might be in the path of someone who can heal me, if she ever passes this way again. I suppose *you* are tearing blindly along the Road, like all the rest.'

'I am on a Quest, to find the single silver bird in her nest of ash-branches.'

'You could put me on a large dock-leaf, and get on your way, then. I expect you are in a hurry.'

The Princess looked about for a dock-leaf, wondering

whether this irascible creature was her first test, which she was about to fail. She wiped up another tear, and plucked a particularly tough leaf, that was growing conveniently in reach of the Road.

'Good,' said the fierce little beast, rearing up and waving its legs. 'Quick now, I dislike this hole extremely. Why have you been crying?'

'Because I am not the princess who succeeds, but one of the two who fail and I don't see any way out. You won't force me to be discourteous to you, though I have remarked that your own manners are far from perfect, in that you have yet to thank me for moving the stone, and you order me here and there without saying "please", or considering that humans don't like picking up scorpions.'

She pushed the leaf towards it as she spoke, and assisted it onto it with a twig, as delicately as she could, though it wriggled and snapped furiously as she did. She put it down in the grass at the edge of the Forest.

'Most scorpions,' it observed, 'have better things to do than sting at random. If creatures like you stamp on us, then of course we retaliate. Also, if we find ourselves boxed in and afraid. But mostly we have better things to do.' It appeared to reflect for a moment. '*If* our tails are not crushed,' it added on a dejected note.

'Who is it,' the Princess enquired courteously, 'who you think can help you?'

'Oh, she is a very wise woman, who lives at the other side of the Forest. She would know what to do, but she rarely leaves home and why should she? She has everything she might want, where she is. If you were going *that* way, of course, you could carry me a little, until I am recovered. But you are rushing headlong along the Road. Good-bye.'

The Princess was rushing nowhere; she was standing very still and thinking. She said:

'I know that story too. I carry you, and ask you, but will you not sting me? And you say, no, it is not in my interest to sting you. And when we are going along, you sting me, although we shall both suffer. And I ask, why did you do that? And you answer – it is my nature.'

17

'You are a very learned young woman, and if we *were* travelling together you could no doubt tell me many instructive stories. I might also point out that I *cannot* sting you – my sting is disabled by the accident to my tail. You may still find me repugnant. Your species usually does. And in any case, you are going along this road, deviating neither to right nor left. Good-bye.'

The Princess looked at the Scorpion. Under the dust it was a glistening blue-black, with long arms, fine legs and complex segments like a jet necklace. Its claws made a crescent before its head. It was not possible to meet its eye, which was disconcerting.

'*I* think you are very handsome.'

'Of course I am. I am quick and elegant and versatile and delightfully intricate. I am surprised, however, that you can see it.'

The Princess listened only distractedly to this last remark. She was thinking hard. She said, mostly to herself:

'I *could* just walk out of this inconvenient story and go my own way. I *could* just leave the Road and look for my own adventures in the Forest. It would make no difference to the Quest. I should have failed if I left the Road and then the next could set off. Unless of course I got turned into stone for leaving the Road.'

'I shouldn't think so,' said the Scorpion. 'And you could be very helpful to *me*, if you chose, and I know quite a few stories too, and helping other creatures is always a good idea, according to them.'

The Princess looked into the Forest. Under the green sky its green branches swayed and rustled in a beckoning way. Its mossy floor was soft and tempting after the dust and grit of the Road. The Princess bent down and lifted up the Scorpion on its leaf and put it carefully into the basket which had contained her food. Then, with a little rebellious skip and jump, she left the Road, and set out into the trees. The Scorpion said she should go south-west, and that if she was hungry it knew where there was a thicket of brambles with early blackberries and a tree-trunk with some mushrooms, so they went in search of those, and the Princess made her mouth black without *quite* assuaging her hunger.

They travelled on, and they travelled on, in a green-arched shade, with the butterflies crowding round the Princess's head and resting on her hair and shoulders. Then they came to a shady clearing, full of grassy stumps and old dry roots, beneath one of which the Princess's keen eye detected a kind of struggling and turbulence in the sand. She stopped to see what it was, and heard a little throaty voice huskily repeating:

'Water. Oh, please, water, if you can hear me, water.'

Something encrusted with sand was crawling and flopping over the wiry roots, four helpless legs and a fat little belly. The Princess got down on her knees, ignoring the angry hissing of the Scorpion. Two liquid black eyes peered at her out of the sandy knobs, and a wide mouth opened tremulously and croaked 'Water' at her. The Princess brought out her inexhaustible water-bottle and dropped drops into the mouth and washed away the crust of sand, revealing a large and warty green and golden toad, with an unusual fleshy crest on its head. It puffed out its throat and held up its little fingers and toes to the stream of water. As the sand flowed away, it could be seen that there was a large bloody gash on the toad's head.

'Oh, you are hurt,' cried the Princess.

'I was caught,' said the Toad, 'by a Man who had been told that I carry a jewel of great value in my head. So he decided to cut it out. But that is only a story, of course, a human story told by creatures who like sticking coloured stones on their heads and skins, and all I am is flesh and blood. Fortunately for me, my skin is mildly poisonous to Men, so his fingers began to itch and puff up, and I was able to wriggle so hard that he dropped and lost me. But I do not think that I have the strength to make my way back to the person who could heal me.'

'We are travelling in her direction,' said the Scorpion. 'You may travel with us if you care to. You could travel in this Princess's luncheon-basket, which is empty.'

'I will come gladly,' said the Toad. 'But she must not suppose I shall turn into a handsome Prince, or any such

19

nonsense. I am a handsome Toad, or would be, if I had not been hacked at. A handsome Toad is what I shall remain.'

The Princess helped it, with a stick, to hop into her lunch-basket, and continued on through the Forest, in the direction indicated by the Scorpion. They went deeper and darker into the trees, and began to lose sense of there being paths leading anywhere. The Princess was a little tired, but the creatures kept urging her on, to go on as far as possible before night fell. In the growing gloom she almost put her foot on what looked like a ball of thread, blowing out in the roots of some thorny bushes.

The Princess stopped and bent down. *Something* was hope-lessly entangled in fine black cotton, dragging itself and the knots that trapped it along in the dust. She knelt on the Forest floor and peered, and saw that it was a giant insect, with its legs and its wing-cases and its belly pulled apart by the snarled threads. The Princess, palace-bred, had never seen such a beast.

'It is a Cockroach,' observed the Scorpion. 'I thought cock-roaches were too clever and tough to get into this sort of mess.'

'Those threads are a trap set by the Fowler for singing birds,' observed the Toad. 'But he has only caught a giant Cockroach.'

The Princess disentangled some of the trailing ends, but some of the knots cut into the very substance of the creature, and she feared to damage it further. It settled stoically in the dust and let her move it. It did not speak. The Princess said:

'You had better come with us. We appear to be travelling towards someone who can heal you.'

The Cockroach gave a little shudder. The Princess picked it up, and placed it in the basket with the Scorpion and the Toad, who moved away from it fastidiously. It sat, inert, in its cocoon of black thread and said nothing.

They travelled in this way for several days, deeper into the Forest. The creatures told the Princess where to find a variety of nuts, and herbs, and berries, and wild mushrooms she would never have found for herself. Once, a long way off, they heard what seemed to be a merry human whistling, mixed with bird cries. The Princess was disposed to turn in its direction, but the Scorpion said that the whistler was the Fowler, and his calls were designed to entice unwary birds to fly into his invisible nets and to choke there. The Princess, although she was not a bird, was filled with unreasoning fear at this picture, and followed the Scorpion's instructions to creep away, deeper into the thornbushes. On another occasion, again at a distance, she heard the high, throaty sound of a horn, which reminded her of the hunting-parties in the Royal Parks, when the young courtiers would bring down deer and hares and flying fowl with their arrows, and the pretty maidens would clap their hands and exclaim. Again she thought of turning in the direction of the sound, and again, the creatures dissuaded her. For the poor Toad, when he heard the note of the horn, went sludge-grey with fear, and began to quake in the basket.

'That is the Hunter,' he said, 'who cut at my crest with his hunting-knife, who travels through the wood with cold corpses of birds and beasts strung together and cast over his shoulder, who will aim at a bright eye in a bush for pure fun, and quench it in blood. You must keep away from him.' So the Princess plunged deeper still into the thornbushes, though they were tugging at her hair and ripping her dress and scratching her pretty arms and neck.

And one day at noon the Princess heard a loud, clear voice, singing in a clearing, and, peering through a thornbush, saw a tall, brown-skinned man, naked to the waist, with black curly hair, leaning on a long axe, and singing:

> Come live with me and be my love
> And share my house and share my bed
> And you may sing from dawn to dark
> And churn the cream and bake the bread
> And lie at night in my strong arms
> Beneath a soft goosefeather spread.

The Princess was about to come out of hiding – he had such a cheery smile, and such handsome shoulders – when a dry little voice in her basket, a voice like curling wood-shavings rustling, added these lines:

And you may scour and sweep and scrub
With bleeding hands and arms like lead
And I will beat your back, and drive
My knotty fists against your head
And sing again to other girls
To take your place, when you are dead.

'Did you speak?' the Princess asked the Cockroach in a whisper. And it rustled back:

'I have lived in his house, which is a filthy place and full of empty beer-casks and broken bottles. He has five young wives buried in the garden, whom he attacked in his drunken rage. He doesn't kill them, he weeps drunken tears for them, but they lose their will to live. Keep away from the Woodcutter, if you value your life.'

The Princess found this hard to believe of the Woodcutter, who seemed so lively and wholesome. She even thought that it was in the creatures' interest to prevent her from lingering with other humans, but nevertheless their warning spoke to something in her that wanted to travel onwards, so she crept quietly away again, and the Woodcutter never knew she had heard his song, or seen him standing there, looking so handsome, leaning on his axe.

They went on, and they went on, deeper into the Forest, and the Princess began to hunger most terribly for bread and butter, touched perhaps by the Woodcutter's Song. The berries she ate tasted more and more watery and were harder and harder to find as the Forest grew denser. The Cockroach seemed inanimate, perhaps exhausted by its effort at speech. The Princess felt bound to hurry, in case its life was in danger, and the other creatures complained from time to time of her clumsiness. Then, one evening, at the moment when the sky was taking on its deepest version of the pine-green that had succeeded dark indigo, the Scorpion begged her to stop and settle down for the night, for its tail ached intolerably. And the Toad added its croaking voice, and begged for more water to be poured over it. The Princess stopped and washed the Toad, and arranged a new leaf for the Scorpion, and said:

'Sometimes I think we shall wander like this, apparently

going somewhere, in fact going nowhere, for the rest of our days.'

'In which case,' rasped the Scorpion, 'mine will not be very long, I fear.'

'I have tried to help,' said the Princess. 'But perhaps I should never have left the Road.'

And then the flaky voice was heard again.

'If you go on, and turn left, and turn left again, you will see. If you go on now.'

So the Princess took up the basket, and put her sandals back on her swollen feet, and went on, and left, and left again. And she saw, through the bushes, a dancing light, very yellow, very warm. And she went on, and saw, at a great distance, at the end of a path knotted with roots and spattered with sharp stones, a window between branches, in which a candle burned steadily. And although she had never in her cossetted life travelled far in the dark, she knew she was seeing, with a huge sense of hope, and warmth and relief, and a minor frisson of fear, what countless benighted travellers had seen before her – though against midnight blue, not midnight-green – and she felt at one with all those lost homecomers and shelter-seekers.

'It is not the Woodcutter's cottage?' she asked the Cockroach. And it answered, sighing, 'No, no, it is the Last House, it is where we are going.'

And the Princess went on, running, and stumbling, and hopping, and scurrying, and by and by reached the little house, which was made of mossy stone, with a slate roof over low eaves and a solid wooden door above a white step. There was a good crisp smell of woodsmoke from the chimney. The Princess was suddenly afraid – she had got used to solitude and contriving and going on – but she knocked quickly, and waited.

The door was opened by an old woman, dressed in a serviceable grey dress, with a sharp face covered with intricate fine lines like a spider's web woven of her history, which was both resolute, thoughtful, and smiling. She had sharp green eyes under hooded, purple lids, and a plaited crown of wonderful shining hair, iron-grey, silver and bright white woven together. When she opened the door the Princess almost fainted for the wonderful smell of baking bread that came out, mingled with other delicious smells, baked apples with cinnamon, strawberry tart, just-burned sugar.

'We have been waiting for you,' said the Old Woman. 'We put the candle in the window for you every night for the last week.'

She took the Princess's basket, and led her in. There was a good log fire in the chimney, with a bed of scarlet ash, and there was a long white wooden table, and there were chairs painted in dark bright colours, and everywhere there were eyes, catching the light, blinking and shining. Eyes on the mantelpiece, in the clock, behind the plates on the shelves, jet-black eyes, glass-green eyes, huge yellow eyes, amber eyes, even rose-pink eyes. And what the Princess had taken to be an intricate coloured carpet rustled and moved and shone with eyes, and revealed itself to be a mass of shifting creatures, snakes and grasshoppers, beetles and bumblebees, mice and voles and owlets and bats, a weasel and a few praying mantises. There were larger creatures too – cats and rats and badgers and kittens and a white goat. There was a low, peaceful, lively squeaking and scratching of tiny voices, welcoming and exclaiming. In one corner was a spindle and in another was a loom, and the old lady had just put aside a complicated shawl she was crocheting from a rainbow-coloured basket of scraps of wool.

'One of you needs food,' said the Old Woman, 'and three of you need healing.'

So the Princess sat down to good soup, and fresh bread, and fruit tart with clotted cream and a mug of sharp cider, and the Old Woman put the creatures on the table, and healed them in her way. Her way was to make them tell the story of their hurts, and as they told, she applied ointments and drops with tiny feathery brushes and little bone pins, uncurling and splinting the Scorpion's tail as it rasped out the tale of its injuries, swabbing and stitching the Toad's wounded head with what looked like cobweb threads, and unknotting the threads that entwined the Cockroach with almost invisible hooks and tweezers. Then she asked the

24

Princess for her story, which the Princess told as best she could, living again the moment when she realized she was doomed to fail, imitating the Scorpion's rasp, and the Toad's croaking glup, and the husky whisper of the Cockroach. She brought the dangers of the Forest into the warm fireside, and all the creatures shuddered at the thought of the Hunter's arrow, the Fowler's snare and the Woodman's axe. And the Princess, telling the story, felt pure pleasure in getting it right, making it just so, finding the right word, and even – she went so far – the right gesture to throw shadow-branches and shadow-figures across the flickering firelight and the yellow pool of candlelight on the wall. And when she had finished there was all kinds of applause, harmonious wing-scraping, and claw-tapping, and rustling and chirruping.

'You are a born storyteller,' said the old lady. 'You had the sense to see you were caught in a story, and the sense to see that you could change it to another one. And the special wisdom to recognize that you are under a curse – which is also a blessing – which makes the story more interesting to you than the things that make it up. There are young women who would never have listened to the creatures' tales about the Woodman, but insisted on finding out for themselves. And maybe they would have been wise and maybe they would have been foolish: that is *their* story. But you listened to the Cockroach and stepped aside and came here, where we collect stories and spin stories and mend what we can and investigate what we can't, and live quietly without striving to change the world. We have no story of our own here, we are free, as old women are free, who don't have to worry about princes or kingdoms, but dance alone and take an interest in the creatures.'

'But—' said the Princess, and stopped.

'But?'

'But the sky is still green and I have failed, and I told the story to suit myself.'

'The green is a very beautiful colour, or a very beautiful range of colours, I think,' said the old lady. 'Here, it gives us pleasure. We write songs about greenness and make tapestries with skies of every possible green. It adds to the beauty of the newt and the lizard. The Cockroach finds it restful. Why should things be as they always were?'

The Princess did not know, but felt unhappy. And the creatures crowded round to console her, and persuade her to live quietly in the little house, which was what she wanted to do, for she felt she had come home to where she was free. But she was worried about the sky and the other princesses. Then the Cockroach chirped to the old lady:

'Tell us the rest of the story, tell us the end of the story, of the story the Princess left.'

He was feeling decidedly better already, his segments were eased, and he could bend almost voluptuously.

'Well,' said the old lady, 'this is the story of the eldest Princess. But, as you percipiently observe, you can't have the story of the eldest, without the stories of the next two, so I will tell you those stories, or possible stories, for many things may and do happen, stories change themselves, and these stories are not histories and have not happened. So you may believe my brief stories about the middle one and the youngest or not, as you choose.'

'I always believe stories whilst they are being told,' said the Cockroach.

'You are a wise creature,' said the Old Woman. 'That is what stories are for. And after, we shall see what we shall see.' So she told

The brief story of the second Princess

When the second Princess realized that the first was not returning, she too set out, and met identical problems and pleasures, and sat down on the same stone, and realized that she was caught in the same story. But being a determined young woman she decided to outwit the story, and went on, and after many adventures was able to snatch the single silver bird in her nest of branches and return in triumph to her father's palace. And the old wizard told her that she must light the branches and burn the bird, and although she felt very uneasy about this she was determined to do as she should, so she lit the fire. And the nest and the bird were consumed, and a new glorious bird flew up from the conflagration, and swept the sky with its flaming tail, and everything was blue, as it had once been. And the Princess became Queen when her parents died, and ruled the people wisely, although they grumbled incessantly because they missed the variety of soft and sharp greens they had once been able to see.

The brief story of the third Princess

As for the third Princess, when the bird flamed across the sky, she went into the orchard and thought, I have no need to go on a Quest. I have nothing I must do, I can do what I like. I have no story. And she felt giddy with the empty space around her, a not entirely pleasant feeling. And a frisky little wind got up and ruffled her hair and her petticoats and blew bits of blossom all over the blue sky. And the Princess had the idea that she was tossed and blown like the petals of the cherry-trees. Then she saw an old woman, with a basket, at the gate of the orchard. So she walked towards her and when she got there, the Old Woman told her, straight out,

'You are unhappy because you have nothing to do.'

So the Princess saw that this was a wise old woman, and answered politely that this was indeed the case.

'I might help,' said the Old Woman. 'Or I might not. You may look in my basket.'

In the basket were a magic glass which would show the Princess her true love, wherever he was, whatever he was doing, and a magic loom, that made tapestries that would live on the walls of the palace chambers as though they were thickets of singing birds, and Forest rides leading to the edge of vision.

'Or I could give you a thread,' said the Old Woman, as the Princess hesitated, for she did not want to see her true love, not yet, not just yet, he was the *end* of stories not begun, and she did not want to make magic Forests, she wanted to see real ones. So she watched the old lady pick up from the grass the end of what appeared to be one of those long, trailing gossamer threads left by baby spiders travelling on the air in the early dawn. But it was as strong as linen thread, and as fine as silk, and when the Old Woman gave

27

it a little tug it tugged tight and could be seen to run away, out of the orchard, over the meadow, into the woods and out of sight.

'You gather it in,' said the Old Woman, 'and see where it takes you.'

The thread glittered and twisted, and the Princess began to roll it neatly in, and took a few steps along it, and gathered it, and rolled it into a ball, and followed it, out of the orchard, across the meadow, and into the woods, and . . . but that is another story.

'Tell me one thing,' said the eldest Princess to the Old Woman, when they had all applauded her story. The moon shone in an emerald sky, and all the creatures drowsed and rustled. 'Tell me one thing. Was that you, ahead of me in the road, in such a hurry?'

'There is always an old woman ahead of you on a journey, and there is always an old woman behind you too, and they are not always the same, they may be fearful or kindly, dangerous or delightful, as the road shifts, and you speed along it. Certainly I was ahead of you, and behind you too, but not only I, and not only as I am now.'

'I am happy to be here with you as you are now.'

'Then that is a good place to go to sleep, and stop telling stories until the morning, which will bring its own changes.'

So they went to bed, and slept until the sun streaked the apple-green horizon with grassy-golden light.

Extract from

THE MIDNIGHT LOVE FEAST

MICHEL TOURNIER

HE: IT WAS a bright September morning after an equinoctial tide which had given the bay a devastated, frantic, almost pathetic air. We were walking along a shore sparkling with mirrors of water which made the flatfish quiver; a shore strewn with unusual shell-fish – whelks, cockles, ormers, clams. But we weren't in the mood for fishing, and spent most of our time looking over towards the south coast, which was shrouded in a milky fog. Yes, there was mystery in the air, almost tragedy, and I wasn't particularly surprised when you drew my attention to two human bodies clasped in each other's arms and covered in sand, about a hundred metres away. We immediately ran up to what we took to be drowned corpses. But they weren't drowned corpses covered in sand. They were two statues sculpted in sand, of strange and poignant beauty. The bodies were curled up in a slight depression, and encircled by a strip of grey, mudstained cloth, which added to their realism. One thought of Adam and Eve, before God came and breathed the breath of life into their nostrils of clay. One also thought of the inhabitants of Pompeii whose bodies were fossilized under the hail of volcanic ash from Vesuvius. Or of the men of Hiroshima, vitrified by the explosion of the Atom Bomb. Their tawny faces, spangled with flakes of mica, were turned towards each other and separated by an impassable distance. Only their hands and legs were touching.

We stood for a moment in front of these recumbent figures, as if at the edge of a newly-opened grave. At this moment a strange sort of devil suddenly emerged from some invisible hole, barefoot and stripped to the waist, wearing frayed jeans. He began a graceful dance, making sweeping arm movements. which seemed to be greeting us, and then to be bowing to the recumbent figures as a preliminary to picking them up and raising them to the heavens. The deserted, slack-water shore, the pale light, this couple made of sand, this dancing madman – all of these things surrounded us with a melancholy, unreal phantasmagoria. And then the dancer came to a standstill, as if suddenly in a trance. After which he bowed, knelt, prostrated himself before us, or rather – as we realized – before an apparition that had loomed up behind us. We turned round. To the right, the Tomberlaine rock was emerging from the haze. But most impressive, suspended like a Saharan mirage above the clouds, was the pyramid of the abbey of Mont-Saint-Michel, with all its glistening pink rooftiles and glinting stained-glass windows.

Time had stopped. Something had to happen to restart it. It was a few drops of water tickling my feet that did it. A foam-capped tongue licked my toes. Listening carefully, we could hear the incessant rustling of the sea that was stealthily creeping up on us. In less than an hour this immense area, now laid bare to the wind and sun, would be returned to the glaucous, merciful depths.

'But they'll be destroyed!' you exclaimed.

With a sad smile the dancer bowed, as a sign of approval. Then he sprang up and mimed the return of the tide, as if he wanted to accompany it, encourage it, even provoke it by his dance. African sorcerers do much the same when they want to induce rain or drive out demons. And the sea obeyed, first flowing round the edges of the depression in which the couple were lying, then finding a breach that allowed through an innocent trickle of water, then two, then three. The joined hands were the first affected and they disintegrated, leaving in suspense stumps of amputated wrists. Horrified, we watched the capricious and inexorable dissolution of this couple which we persisted in feeling to be human, close to us, perhaps premonitory. A stronger wave broke over the woman's head, carrying away half her face, then it was the man's right shoulder that collapsed, and we thought them even more touching in their mutilation.

A few minutes later we were obliged to beat a retreat and abandon the sand basin with its swirling, frothy eddies. The dancer came with us, and we discovered that he was neither mad nor dumb. His name was Patricio Lagos and he came from Chile, more precisely from Chiloe Island, where he was born, which is off the south coast of Chile. It is inhabited by Indians adept in exploiting the forests. He had studied dancing and sculpture at the same time, in Santiago, and had then emigrated to the Antipodes. He was obsessed by the problem of time. Dance, the art of the moment, ephemeral by nature, leaves no trace and suffers from its inability to become rooted in any kind of continuity. Sculpture, the art of eternity, defies time by seeking out indestructible materials. But in so doing, what it finally finds is death, for marble has an obvious funerary vocation. On the Channel and Atlantic coasts, Lagos had discovered the phenomenon of tides governed by the laws of astronomy. Now the tide gives a rhythm to the shore dancer's games, and at the same time suggests the practice of ephemeral sculpture.

'My sand sculptures live,' he declared, 'and the proof of this is that they die. It's the opposite of the statuary in cemeteries, which is eternal because it is lifeless.'

And so he feverishly sculpted couples in the wet sand just uncovered by the ebbing tide, and both his dancing and his sculpture stemmed from the same inspiration. It was important that his work should be finished at the very moment of slack water, for this must be a parenthesis of rest and meditation. But the great moment was the return of the tide and the terrible ceremony of the destruction of the work. A slow, meticulous, inexorable destruction, governed by an astronomical destiny, and which should be encircled by a sombre, lyrical dance. 'I celebrate the pathetic fragility of life,' he said. That was when you asked him a question of prime importance to us, which he answered in what I considered an obscure, mysterious way.

SHE: Yes, I raised the question of silence. Because according

31

to our customs, dance is accompanied by music, and in one way it is only music embodied, music made flesh. So there was something paradoxical and strange about the dance he was performing in silence round his recumbent sand-figures. But he unreservedly rejected the word silence. 'Silence?' he said, 'but there *is* no silence! Nature detests silence, as she abhors a vacuum. Listen to the shore at low tide: it babbles through the thousands of moist lips it half-opens to the skies. *Volubile.* When I was learning French, I fell in love with that graceful, ambiguous word. It is another name for bindweed, whose fragile, interminable stem twines round the sturdier plants it comes across, and it finally chokes them under its disordered profusion studded with white trumpets. The rising tide too is voluble. It entwines the chests and thighs of my clay lovers with its liquid tentacles. And it destroys them. It is the kiss of death. But the rising tide is also voluble in the childish babble it whispers as it flows over the ooze. It insinuates its salty tongues into the sands with moist sighs. It would like to speak. It is searching for its words. It's a baby burbling in its cradle.'

And he stayed behind and left us, with a little farewell wave and a sad smile, when we reached the beach.

HE: He's a bit mad, your sculptor-dancer, but it's true that by crossing Normandy from east to west, by emigrating from the pebbles of Fécamp to the sands of Mont-Saint-Michel, we changed ocean sounds. The waves on the shores of the Pays de Caux smash thousands of stones in a rocky pandemonium. Here, the tide murmurs as it advances with seagull's steps.

SHE: This false silence hasn't been good for you. In Fécamp I loved a taciturn man. You despised all the conventional chit-chat with which human relations surround themselves. Good-morning, good-evening, how are you, very well, and you? what filthy weather . . . You killed all that verbiage with a stern look. Here, you have become uncommunicative. There are grunts in your silences, grumbles in your asides.

32

HE: Just a moment! I never despised 'what filthy weather!' I don't think it's a waste of time to talk about the weather. It's an important subject to seamen. For me, weather reports are lyric poetry. But that's just it. The words we use ought to accord with the sky and the sea. The words appropriate to Fécamp don't correspond to the air in Avranches. Here there is something like a soft, insidious appeal, a demand that I don't know how to satisfy.

SHE: Here we are separated by an immense shore of silence, to which every day brings its low tide. The great logorrhoea of May 1968 made me dream of laconic wisdom, of words that were weighed, and rare, but full of meaning. We are sinking into an oppressive mutism that is just as empty as the student verbosity.

HE: Make up your mind! Nowadays you never stop reproaching me for my silence. No attack is too aggressive for you, no matter how hurtful it might be.

SHE: It's to get a rise out of you. I want a crisis, an explosion, a domestic scene. What is a domestic scene? It's the woman's triumph. It's when the woman has finally forced the man out of his silence by her nagging. Then he shouts, he rages, he's abusive, and the woman surrenders to being voluptuously steeped in this verbal downpour.

HE: Do you remember what they say about the Comte de Carhaix-Plouguer? When they're in company, his wife and he look as if they are the perfect couple. They exchange as many words as are necessary not to arouse curiosity. Though not one more, it's true. Because it's only a façade. Having discovered that his wife was unfaithful to him, the Count communicated his decision never again to talk to her when they were alone – and that was the last time he spoke to her. The extraordinary thing is that in spite of this silence, he managed to have three children with her.

SHE: I have never been unfaithful to you. But I would like to remind you that you sometimes don't even grant me the minimum of words necessary not to arouse people's curiosity. On Sundays, we usually lunch together in a restaurant on the coast. There are times when I am so ashamed of our silence that I move my lips soundlessly, to make the other customers think I'm talking to you.

HE: One morning, while we were having breakfast . . .

SHE: I remember. You were deep in your newspaper. You had disappeared behind the newspaper, which you were holding up like a screen. Could anyone be more boorish?

HE: You pressed the playback button on a little tape recorder you had just put down on the table. And then we heard a chorus of wheezing, rattling, gurgling, puffing and blowing and snoring, all of it orchestrated, rhythmic, returning to the point of departure with a reprise of the whole gamut. I asked you: 'What's that?' And you answered: 'It's you when you're asleep. That's all you have to say to me. So I record it.' 'I snore?' 'Obviously you snore! But you don't realize it. Now you can hear it. That's progress, isn't it?'

SHE: I didn't tell you everything. Incited by you, by your nocturnal snoring, I made enquiries. There is always an old student lying dormant in me. I discovered a science, rhonchology, a definition of nocturnal snoring. This is it: 'Respiratory sound during sleep, caused at the moment of inhalation by the vibration of the soft palate, due to the combined and simultaneous effect of the air entering through the nose and the air being drawn through the mouth.' There. I might add that this vibration of the soft palate is very similar to that of the sail of a boat when it's flapping in the wind. As you see, in both cases it's something to do with air.

HE: I appreciate this nautical aside, but I might remind you that I have never worked on a sailing boat.

SHE: As for the cures suggested by rhonchology, the most

34

radical is tracheotomy; that's to say, opening an artificial orifice in the trachea so that breathing may be carried on outside the normal nasal passages. But there is also uvulo-palato-pharyngo-plastic-surgery – u.p.p.p.s. to initiates – which consists in resecting part of the soft palate including the uvula, so as to limit its vibratory potential.

HE: Young men ought to be told what they're letting themselves in for when they get married.

SHE: And vice versa! How could a girl ever suspect that the Prince Charming she loves makes a noise like a steam engine at night? Nevertheless, when she spends night after night by the side of a heavy snorer, she works out a rather bitter philosophy for herself.

HE: What does this rhonchological philosophy say?

SHE: That a couple is formed slowly over the years, and that with time the words they exchange take on increasing importance. At the beginning, deeds are enough. And then their dialogue becomes more extensive. It has to become deeper, too. Couples die from having no more to say to each other. My relations with a man are at an end on the evening when, coming back to him from a day spent elsewhere, I no longer want to tell him what I have done, or to hear him tell me how he has spent those hours away from me.

HE: It's true that I was never talkative. But it quite often happens that you interrupt one of my stories because it doesn't interest you.

SHE: Because you've already told it a hundred times.

HE: You made a diabolical suggestion on that subject one day, and I'm still wondering whether you were being serious. You suggested that I should number my stories. From then on, instead of telling you one from beginning to end with all the subtleties of the good story-teller, I should simply state

35

its number, and you would understand at once. If I said 27, you would remember the story of my grandmother's dog which came aboard my trawler by mistake and returned to Fécamp a military hero. 71, and we would both have thought silently of the fidelity of those two gulls I saved and fed on one boat, and which knew how to find me on another vessel. 14, and my grandfather's odyssey during his one and only visit to Paris would have come to mind. So don't reproach me for my silence any more!

SHE: I know all your stories, and I even tell them better than you do. A good story-teller must be able to ring the changes.

HE: Not absolutely. Repetition is part of the game. There is a narrative ritual which children, for instance, respect. They are not concerned with novelty; they insist on the same story being told in the same words. The slightest change makes them leap up in indignation. In the same way, there is a ritual of daily life, of weeks, seasons, feast-days, years. A happy life is one that can cast itself in these moulds without feeling confined.

SHE: You're wrong to think that my idea of numbering your stories was only aimed at silencing you. I could just as well have used it to get you to talk. I would simply have said: 23. And you would straightaway have told me how you lived under siege in Le Havre from September 2nd to 13th, 1944. But I ask myself, honestly: would I have the heart to listen to the same story told indefinitely in the same words? Would I have the childlike imagination needed for that?

HE: I'm quite sure you would. You're lying, or you're lying to yourself. And there's the other point of view: mine. There's a certain, very dangerous concept which is quite likely to kill off the dialogue between a couple: the concept of the *innocent ear*. If a man changes his woman, he does so in order to find in the new woman an innocent ear for his stories. Don Juan was nothing but an incorrigible braggart, *un hâbleur* – a word of Spanish origin meaning a glib talker. A woman

36

only interested him for the length of time – short, alas, and increasingly short – that she had faith in his *hâbleries*. If he detected the shadow of a doubt in her gaze, it cast a glacial chill over his heart and his genitals. And then he would leave, he would go off to look elsewhere for the exquisite, warm credulity that alone gave their true weight to his *hâbleries*. All this proves the importance of words in the life of a couple. And anyway, when one of the two sleeps with a third person, we say that he 'deceives' the other, which is to situate his betrayal in the domain of language. A man and a woman who never lied to each other and who immediately confessed all their betrayals would not be deceiving one another.

SHE: No doubt. But that would be a dialogue of cynics, and the wounds they inflicted on each other in the name of transparency would quite soon part them.

HE: Then people should lie?

SHE: Yes and no. Between the obscurity of lying and the transparency of cynicism, there is room for a whole range of light and shade in which the truth is known but not discussed, or else is deliberately ignored. In company, courtesy doesn't allow certain truths to be uttered bluntly. Why shouldn't there also be courtesy between couples? You're deceiving me, I'm deceiving you, but we don't want to know about it. The only valid intimacy is of a twilight nature. 'Pull down the shade a little,' as the charming Paul Géraldy said.

HE: Between couples, perhaps, but certainly not between women. There, the crudest cynicism is calmly displayed. Ladies, amongst yourselves, you are appalling gossips! I was waiting at the hairdresser's one day, on the side marked 'Gentlemen', which was only separated from the ladies' salon by a half-partition. I was staggered by the complicity that united stylists, manicurists, shampoo girls and clients in a generalized babble in which the most intimate secrets of bodies and couples were laid bare without the slightest discretion.

37

SHE: And men in the company of other men keep such things to themselves, I suppose?

HE: More than you think. More than women do, in any case. Masculine vanity, which is generally so ridiculous, imposes a certain reticence on them in such matters. For instance, we aren't too fond of talking about our illnesses.

SHE: It's true that 'intimate secrets', as you so delicately put it, don't amount to much for men. Everything always comes down to figures, with them. So many times or so many centimetres. Women's secrets are far more subtle and obscure! As for our complicity, it's a complicity of the oppressed, and hence universal, because women are everywhere subjected to men's whims. No man will ever know the depth of the feeling of complicity that can unite two women, even when they are perfect strangers to each other. I remember a visit to Morocco. I was the only woman in our little group. As so often in the South, we were approached by a very young boy who spontaneously invited us to come to his house for tea. The father received us, surrounded by his sons – three or four of them, I don't remember exactly. The youngest one must just have learnt to walk. There was a blanket over a doorway which no doubt led to the bedrooms. Every so often it moved surreptitiously, and a black eye could be seen peeping through. The mother, the daughters, the grandmother, the mother-in-law, confined to the inner rooms, were waiting, listening, spying. I remember the way the women had protested when a running-water tap was installed in their houses. For them, that was the end of their trips to the village fountain, and of the long, delightful chats with the other women that these trips occasioned. When we left, I passed a girl on her way home. She smiled at me alone, because I was the only woman, and there was a world of warm fraternity in that smile. And when I say fraternity, I ought rather to say sorority, but the word doesn't exist in French.

HE: Perhaps because the thing itself is too rare to deserve a name.

SHE: It's principally because it's men who construct language. In a strange novel called *The Miracle of the Women's Island*, Gerhart Hauptmann invents his own version of the Robinson Crusoe story. He imagines that after a steamer has been shipwrecked, lifeboats exclusively occupied by women are cast up on a desert island. The result is a women's republic of about a hundred citizenesses.

HE: It must be hell!

SHE: Not at all. Quite the contrary! It's the great sorority. The idea Hauptmann champions is that if women fall out with one another, it's the fault of men. It is men who are the great sowers of discord among sisters, even among the sisterhood of nuns, whose shared confessor is a disruptive influence.

HE: Is that the miracle?

SHE: No. The miracle is that one day, after years of living in their happy sorority, one of the women discovers that she is inexplicably pregnant.

HE: The Holy Ghost, no doubt.

SHE: Everything might still be all right if she had given birth to a daughter. But the malignancy of fate saw to it that she had a son. The knell of the women's island had tolled. The virile virus was about to do its devastating work.

HE: In short, since you and I have the misfortune to belong to opposite sexes, since we have no more to say to each other, the only thing left for us to do is to separate. Let's at least do so with a flourish. We'll get all our friends together for a late-night dinner.

SHE: A *medianoche*, as the Spaniards call it.

HE: We'll choose the shortest night of the year so that our guests will leave as the sun is rising over the bay. We'll serve nothing but the produce of my foreshore fishing.

SHE: We'll talk to them, they'll talk to us, it will be a great palaver about the couple and love. Our *medianoche* will be a midnight love feast and a celebration of the sea. When all our guests have had their say, you will tap your knife on your glass and solemnly announce the sad news: 'Oudalle and Nadège are separating because they don't get on any more. Sometimes they even have words. Then a disagreeable silence surrounds them . . . ' And when the last guest has gone, we'll put a notice on the front door: FOR SALE, and we too will go our different ways.

* * *

And so it was. Invitations were sent out for the summer solstice to all Nadège and Oudalle's friends. Nadège reserved all the rooms in the three hotels in Avranches. Oudalle, with two of his fishing friends, prepared a memorable banquet of foreshore fish.

It was still light when the first guests arrived. These were the ones who had had the farthest to travel, as they had come all the way from Arles. Then, almost immediately, their nearest neighbours rang the bell, and it was half an hour before the next influx arrived. More and more came, all through the night, in a constant balletic flow of cars, just as Nadège and Oudalle had wished, for they hadn't prepared a formal dinner round a table but a permanent buffet from which all the guests could help themselves no matter when they arrived. To start with, there was poached crab, a consommé of mussels with croûtons, and smoked eel. Then hermit-crabs flambéed in whisky, and smoke-dried sea urchins. In keeping with tradition, they waited for the twelfth stroke of midnight to serve the *plat de résistance* – lobster Pompadour garnished with sea cucumbers. Then the night continued with octopus with paprika, paellas of cuttlefish, and a fricassee of wrasse. With the first glimmers of dawn the guests were brought ormers in white wine, sea-anemone fritters, and scallops in champagne. Thus, it was a true marine *medianoche* with neither vegetables, fruit nor sugar.

A group of guests had gathered on the high terrace whose piles reached out onto the shore itself. Neither Nadège nor Oudalle could have said whose idea it was to tell the first story. That one was lost in the night, as no doubt were the second and the third. But surprised by what was taking place in their house, they saw to it that the subsequent narratives were recorded and preserved. There were thus nineteen, and these narratives were sometimes tales which began with the magical and traditional 'once upon a time', and sometimes short stories told in the first person, slices of life that were often raw and sordid. Nadège and Oudalle listened, astonished by these imaginary constructions they saw being built in their own house and which vanished as soon as the last word was uttered, giving way to other, equally ephemeral descriptions. They thought of Lagos's sand statues. They followed the slow work this succession of fictions was accomplishing in them. They had the feeling that the short stories – grimly realistic, pessimistic and demoralizing – were tending to further their separation and the break-up of their marriage, whereas on the contrary the tales – delectable, warm-hearted and tender – were working to bring them together. And while the short stories had at first commanded more attention by their weighty, melancholy truth, as the night wore on the tales gained in beauty and in strength, and finally reached the point of radiating an irresistible charm. In the first hours, Ange Crevet, the humiliated child full of hatred, Ernest the poacher, the suicidal Théobald, and Blandine's frightful father, and Lucie, the woman without a shadow, and a few others – all this grey, austere crowd exuded an atmosphere of morose hatred. But soon Angus, King Faust the Wise Man, Pierrot with his Columbine, Adam the dancer and Eve the perfumed lady, the Chinese painter and his Greek rival, formed the scintillating procession of a new, young and eternal wedding. And it was above all the last tale, the one about the two banquets, that rescued, so it seemed, daily conjugal life by elevating the actions repeated every day and every night to the level of a fervent, intimate ceremony.

The solstice sun was setting the silhouette of Mont-Saint-Michel aglow when the last guest stood up to take his leave after having told, to his hosts alone, the most beautiful tale no doubt ever invented. The incoming tide was flowing under the open-work floor of the terrace. The shellfish caressed by the waves opened their valves and let out the mouthful of water they had been retaining during the arid hours. The thousands upon thousands of parched throats on the foreshore filled themselves with the briny fluid and began to whisper. The shore was stammering in search of a language, as Lagos had understood so well.

'You didn't stand up, you didn't tap your glass with your knife, and you didn't announce the sad news of our separation to our friends,' said Nadège.

'Because the inevitability of our separation no longer seems so obvious to me since all those stories have entered my head,' Oudalle replied.

'What we lacked, in fact, was a house of words to live in together. In former times, religion provided couples with an edifice that was at the same time real – the church – and imaginary, peopled with saints, illuminated with legends, resounding with hymns, which protected them from themselves and from outside aggression. We lacked this edifice. Our friends have provided us with all the materials for it. Literature as a panacea for couples in distress . . . '

'We were like two carps buried in the mud of our daily life,' Oudalle concluded, ever true to his halieutic metaphors. 'From now on we shall be like two trout quivering side by side in the fast-flowing waters of a mountain stream.'

'Your seafood *medianoche* was exquisite,' Nadège added. 'I appoint you the head chef of my house. You shall be the high priest of my kitchens and the guardian of the culinary and manducatory rites that invest a meal with its spiritual dimension.'

PIERROT OR THE SECRETS OF THE NIGHT

MICHEL TOURNIER

TWO LITTLE WHITE houses stood opposite each other in the village of Pouldreuzic. One was the laundry. No one could remember the real name of the laundress, for everyone called her Columbine because of her snowy-white dress which made her look like a dove. The other house was Pierrot's bakery.

Pierrot and Columbine had grown up together on the benches of the village school. They were so often together that everyone imagined that later they would marry. And yet life had separated them, when Pierrot had become a baker and Columbine a laundress. Inevitably, a baker has to work at night, so that the whole village may have fresh bread and hot croissants in the morning. A laundress works during the day, so that she can hang out her linen in the sun. Even so, they might have met at twilight, in the evening when Columbine was getting ready to go to bed and Pierrot was getting up, or in the morning when Columbine's day was starting and Pierrot's night was ending.

But Columbine avoided Pierrot, and the poor baker was eating his heart out with sorrow. Why did Columbine avoid Pierrot? Because her former schoolmate reminded her of all sorts of unpleasant things. Columbine only liked the sun, the birds, and the flowers. She only blossomed in the summer, in the daylight. Whereas the baker, as we have said, lived mostly at night, and for Columbine night was only darkness peopled by terrifying beasts like wolves and bats. And then

43

she preferred to close her door and her shutters, to snuggle up under her duvet and go to sleep. But that wasn't all, because Pierrot's life was spent between two other, even more alarming darknesses, that of his cellar and that of his oven. Who knew whether there weren't rats in his cellar? And isn't there an expression: 'as dark as an oven?'

It must be admitted, though, that Pierrot looked the part. Perhaps because he worked at night and slept during the day, he had a round, pale face which made him look like the full moon. His big, watchful, astonished eyes gave him the appearance of an owl, as did his loose, baggy clothes, white with flour. Pierrot was shy, taciturn, loyal and reticent. He preferred the winter to the summer, solitude to company, and rather than speak – which he found difficult, and wasn't very good at – he preferred to write, which he did by candle-light, with an enormous pen, addressing long letters to Columbine which he never sent, as he was sure she wouldn't read them.

What did Pierrot write in his letters? He tried to disabuse Columbine. He explained to her that the night wasn't what she thought.

Pierrot knew the night. He knew that it isn't a black hole, any more than his cellar and his oven were. At night, the river sings more loudly and more clearly, and it scintillates with thousands and thousands of silvery scales. The foliage that the tall trees shake against the dark sky is all sparkling with stars. The night breezes are more profoundly imbued with the smell of the sea, of the forest and of the mountain than are the day's effluvia, which are impregnated with the work of men.

Pierrot knew the moon. He knew how to look at it. He could see that it isn't just a white disc as flat as a plate. Because he looked at it so carefully and with such affection, he had been able to see with the naked eye that it has con-tours, that it is actually a ball – like an apple, like a pumpkin; – and moreover, that it is not smooth but nicely sculpted, modelled, undulating – like a landscape with its hills and its valleys, like a face with its wrinkles and its smiles.

Yes, Pierrot knew all that, because of his dough which,

44

after he had kneaded it for a long time and secretly impregnated it with yeast, needed two hours to rest and rise. Then he went out of his bakehouse. Everyone was asleep. He was the clear conscience of the village. He walked through all its streets and alleyways, his big, round eyes wide open while the others were asleep, the men, women and children who, when they awoke, would eat the hot croissants he had made for them. He passed under Columbine's closed windows. He had become the village's night watchman, Columbine's protector. He imagined the young girl sighing and dreaming in the moist whiteness of her big bed, and when he raised his pale face to the moon, he wondered whether that soft, round shape floating above the trees in a shroud of fog was that of a cheek, a breast, or, better still, a buttock.

No doubt everything could have gone on like this for a long time if, one fine summer's morning, a funny sort of vehicle, completely covered in flowers and birds and pulled by a man, had not made its entrance into the village. It was something between a caravan and a fairground stall, because on the one hand it was quite clear that you could shelter and sleep in it, and on the other hand it glistened with bright colours, and gaudily-painted curtains floated all around it like flags. On top of the vehicle was a glossy sign:

HARLEQUIN
House Painter

The man – lithe, vivacious, with rosy cheeks and curly red hair – was dressed in a kind of leotard composed of little motley diamonds. There were all the colours of the rainbow in it, plus a few more, but none of the diamonds was either black or white. He stopped his cart in front of Pierrot's bakery and pursed his lips in disapproval as he examined its bare, dull façade which bore only these two words:

PIERROT BAKER

He rubbed his hands with a confident air, and began to knock on the door. It was broad daylight, as we have said, and

45

Pierrot was fast asleep. Harlequin had to drum on the door for a long time before it opened to reveal a Pierrot who was paler than ever and tottering with fatigue. Poor Pierrot! He really did look like an owl, all white, dishevelled, bewildered, his eyes blinking in the merciless summer light. What was more, before Harlequin had even had time to open his mouth, a great burst of laughter rang out behind him. It was Columbine, who was watching the scene from her window, with a heavy iron in her hand. Harlequin turned round, saw her, burst out laughing in his turn, and Pierrot found himself alone and sad in his lunar clothing confronted by those two children of the sun, brought together by their common gaiety. Then he lost his temper and, his heart aching with jealousy, he slammed the door in Harlequin's face and went back to bed, but it is highly unlikely that he got back to sleep very quickly.

As for Harlequin, he crossed the street to the laundry, where Columbine had disappeared. He looked for her. She reappeared, but at another window, then disappeared again before Harlequin had time to get close. It looked as if she was playing hide-and-seek with him. Finally the door opened, and Columbine came out carrying a huge basket of clean linen. Followed by Harlequin, she went into her garden and began to hang her linen out to dry. It was white linen, exclusively. As white as Columbine's dress. As white as Pierrot's costume. But Columbine never exposed her white linen to the moon, only to the sun, the same sun that makes every colour shine, in particular those of Harlequin's costume.

Harlequin, the glib talker, held forth to Columbine. Columbine answered him. What did they say to each other? They talked about clothes. Columbine about white clothes. Harlequin about coloured clothes. For the laundress, white went without saying. Harlequin did his best to put colours into her head. He was quite successful, at that. It is since this famous encounter in Pouldreuzic that we have seen the market in white goods swamped by mauve napkins, blue pillowslips, green tablecloths and pink sheets.

When she had hung her linen out in the sun, Columbine went back into the laundry. Harlequin, who was carrying the empty basket, offered to repaint the façade of her house. Columbine accepted. Harlequin went to work at once. He dismantled his caravan and used the bits and pieces to erect a scaffold over the front of the laundry. It was as if the dismantled caravan had taken possession of Columbine's house. Harlequin nimbly jumped up on to his scaffolding. With his multicoloured leotard and his crest of red hair, he looked like an exotic bird on its perch. And as if to stress the resemblance, he sang and whistled with gusto. From time to time Columbine's head came out of the window, and they exchanged jokes, smiles and songs.

Harlequin's work took shape very quickly. The white façade of the house disappeared under a multicoloured palette. There were all the colours of the rainbow plus a few more, but neither black, nor white, nor grey. But above all there were two of Harlequin's inventions that would prove, if necessary, that he was really the most enterprising and most insolent of all house painters. In the first place, he painted a life-sized portrait of Columbine on the wall, in which she was carrying her linen basket on her head. But that wasn't all. Instead of painting this Columbine in her usual white clothes, Harlequin gave her a dress consisting of little multicoloured diamonds, just like his leotard. And there was also something else. True, he had repainted the word LAUNDRY in black letters on a white background, but after it, in letters of every colour, he had added: DYERS! He had worked so fast that everything was finished by the time the sun went down, although the paint was still far from dry.

The sun went down, and Pierrot got up. The little basement window in the bakery began to glow with warm reflected light. An enormous moon was floating like a milk-white balloon in the phosphorescent sky. Soon Pierrot came out of his bakehouse. At first, all he saw was the moon. He felt very happy. He ran towards it, waving his arms in adoration. He smiled at it, and the moon smiled back at him. Actually, they were like brother and sister, with their round faces and their diaphanous clothes. But Pierrot twirled and danced with such verve that he caught his feet in the paint pots littering the ground. He bumped into the scaffolding erected over Columbine's house. The shock roused him from his dream. What was going on? What had happened to the laundry? Pierrot didn't recognize that motley façade, and especially that Columbine dressed like Harlequin. And that barbarous word coupled with the word laundry: DYERS! Pierrot was no longer dancing, he was flabbergasted. The moon in the sky grimaced in distress. So Columbine has allowed herself to be seduced by Harlequin's colours! So she dresses like him now, and instead of washing and ironing fresh white linen, she's going to soak old clothes in vats full of messy, nauseating, artificial colours.

Pierrot went up to the scaffolding. He touched it with disgust. Above, a window was lit up. Scaffolding is a terrible thing, because it allows people to look through windows on upper floors and see what's going on in the bedrooms! Pierrot climbed up on to one plank, then on to another. He approached the lighted window. He darted a glance through it. What did he see? We shall never know! He leapt back. He had forgotten that he was perched on a scaffold three metres above the ground. He fell. What a tumble! Was he dead? No. He stood up painfully. Limping, he went back into the bakery. He lit a candle. He dipped his big pen in the inkwell. He wrote a letter to Columbine. A letter? No, just a brief message, but he put all the truth he knew into it. He went out again, envelope in hand. Still limping, he hesitated, and looked around for a moment. Then he decided to fasten his message to one of the uprights of the scaffolding. Then he went home. The basement light went out. A big cloud came along and masked the sad face of the moon.

A new day began under a glorious sun. Harlequin and Columbine came dashing out of the laundry-dyers, holding hands. Columbine wasn't wearing her usual white dress. She was in a dress made of little coloured diamonds, diamonds of every colour, but none of them black or white. She was dressed like the Columbine Harlequin had painted on the façade of her house. She had become a Harlequina. How happy they were! They went dancing round the house together. Then Harlequin, still dancing, began to do something strange. He dismantled the scaffolding erected against

Columbine's house. And at the same time he reassembled his funny sort of vehicle. The caravan took shape again. Columbine tried it out. Harlequin seemed to take it for granted that they were going to leave. Because the painter was a real nomad. He lived on his scaffolding as a bird lives on a branch. There was no question of his staying on. And anyway, he had nothing more to do in Pouldreuzic, and all the magic of the countryside was beckoning.

Columbine seemed quite willing to leave. She put a little bundle in the caravan. She closed the shutters of her house. There she was, with Harlequin in the caravan. They were on their way. But not yet. Harlequin got out again. He had forgotten something. A notice, which he painted with sweeping gestures, and then hung on the house door:

CLOSED ON ACCOUNT OF HONEYMOON

This time, they could go. Harlequin harnessed himself to the caravan and began to pull it along the road. Soon, the countryside surrounded them and gave them a festive welcome. There were so many flowers and butterflies that it looked as if the scenery had put on a Harlequin costume.

Night fell over the village. Pierrot ventured out of the bakery. Still limping, he went over to Columbine's house. Everything was shut up. Suddenly he saw the notice. It was so hideous, he couldn't even read it. He rubbed his eyes. He had to bow to the evidence, though. So, still hobbling, he went back into his bakehouse. He soon came out again. He too had his notice. He hung it on his door, and then slammed it shut. It read:

CLOSED ON ACCOUNT OF A BROKEN HEART

The days went by. Summer was coming to an end. Harlequin and Columbine were still travelling. But they were not as happy as before. More and more often it was Columbine who pulled the caravan along, while Harlequin rested in it. Then the weather began to break. The first autumn rains pattered down over their heads. Their beautiful motley costumes began to fade. The trees turned red, then lost their leaves. They crossed forests full of dead wood, ploughed fields that were brown and black.

And then one morning – what a sensation! All night long the sky had been full of fluttering snowflakes. When day broke, snow was covering the whole countryside, the road, and even the caravan. It was the great triumph of white, Pierrot's triumph. And as if to crown the baker's revenge, that evening an enormous silvery moon floated above the icy landscape.

Columbine thought more and more frequently about Pouldreuzic, and also about Pierrot, especially when she looked at the moon. One day a little piece of paper found its way into her hand, she didn't know how. She wondered whether the baker had come by recently and left this message. In actual fact, it was the one in which he had put all the truth he knew, and fastened to one of the uprights of the scaffolding, which had become a piece of the caravan. She read:

Columbine!

Don't abandon me! Don't let yourself be seduced by Harlequin's artificial, superficial colours! They are toxic, evil-smelling colours, and they chip. But I too have my colours. Only they are real, profound colours.

Listen carefully to these marvellous secrets:

My night isn't black; it's blue. And it's a blue that you can breathe.

My oven isn't black, it's golden. And it's a gold that you can eat.

The colour I make rejoices the eye, but it's also thick, substantial, it smells good, it's warm, it's nourishing.

I love you, and I'm waiting for you.

Pierrot

A blue night, a golden oven, real colours that can be breathed and eaten – so that was Pierrot's secret? In this icy landscape that resembled the baker's costume, Columbine pondered and wavered. Harlequin was asleep in the back of the caravan, not giving her a thought. Quite soon she would once again have to put on the harness which bruised her shoulder and chest, and pull the vehicle along the frozen road. Why?

50

If she wanted to go home, what was there to keep her with Harlequin now that his beautiful, sunny colours, which had seduced her, had faded? She jumped out of the vehicle. She gathered up her bundle, and off she went with a light step in the direction of her village.

She walked, and walked, and walked, did little Columbine, whose dress had lost its brilliant colours, although it hadn't become white. She fled through the snow which made a faint frou-frou under her feet and floated around her ears: flight-frou-flight-frou-flight-frou . . . Soon she saw in her mind's eye a whole lot of words beginning with F, ferocious words forming up into a grim army: frost, flint, famished, folly, fantom, frailty. Poor Columbine nearly collapsed, but luckily a whole swarm of words also beginning with F, friendly words, came to her rescue, as if they had been sent by Pierrot: furnace, fumes, fortitude, flower, fire, flour, flame, feast, fairyland . . .

At last she came to the village. It was the middle of the night. Everything was asleep in the snow. White snow? Black snow? No. Because she had come closer to Pierrot, Columbine now had eyes to see: the night is blue, the snow is blue, that's obvious. But it isn't the garish, toxic, Prussian blue that Harlequin had a whole potful of. It's a luminous, living blue of lakes, glaciers and the sky, a blue that smells good, and that Columbine breathed deeply into her lungs.

She came to the fountain, imprisoned in ice, then to the old church, and here were the two little houses facing each other, Columbine's laundry and Pierrot's bakery. The laundry was in darkness and seemingly dead, but there were signs of life in the bakery. The chimney was smoking, and through the bakehouse window a flickering, golden light fell on the snow that lay on the pavement. To be sure, Pierrot had not been lying when he wrote that his oven was not black but golden!

Columbine stopped, bewildered, outside the little window. She felt she would like to crouch down in front of that glowing mouth breathing out warmth and a heady fragrance of bread. She didn't dare, though. But suddenly the door opened, and Pierrot appeared. Was it by chance? Had he

51

sensed his friend's arrival? Or was it simply that he'd seen her feet through the basement window? He held out his arms to her, but just as she was going to throw herself into them he took fright, stepped aside, and led her down into his bakehouse. Columbine felt she was entering a tender refuge. How comforting it was! The oven doors were closed, yet the fire inside was so lively that the heat came oozing out of all sorts of nooks and crannies.

Pierrot, huddled in a corner, drank in this fantastic apparition with wide-open eyes: Columbine in his bakehouse! Columbine, hypnotized by the fire, looked at him out of the corner of her eye and thought that this kind-hearted Pierrot, there in the shadows, with the big white folds of his costume and his lunar face, did indeed look very much like a night bird. He ought to have said something to her, but he couldn't, the words stuck in his throat.

Time went by. Pierrot lowered his eyes on to his kneading trough, where the big round knob of golden dough was resting. Golden-blonde and soft, like Columbine . . . While the dough had been dormant in the wooden kneading trough for two hours, the yeast had done its vivifying work. The oven was hot. It would soon be time to put the dough into it. Pierrot looked at Columbine. What was Columbine doing? Exhausted by her long walk, cradled in the gentle heat of the bakehouse, she had fallen asleep on the flour bin in a posture of delightful abandon. There were tears in Pierrot's eyes as he looked at his friend who had come to take refuge with him to escape a dead love and the rigours of the winter.

Harlequin had painted a portrait of Columbine-Harlequina in a motley costume on the laundry wall. Pierrot had an idea. In his own fashion he would sculpt a Columbine-Pierrette in his brioche dough. He went to work. His eyes kept darting from the sleeping girl to the knob lying in the trough. His hands would have liked to caress the sleeper, of course, but to create a Columbine out of dough was almost as good. When he thought his work was complete, he compared it with his living model. Obviously the dough-Columbine was a bit pale. Quick, into the oven!

The fire roared. There were now two Columbines in Pierrot's bakehouse. At this moment a few timid knocks on the door woke up the living Columbine. Who is it? For all answer a voice was suddenly heard, a voice made weak and sad by the night and the cold. But Pierrot and Columbine recognized the voice of Harlequin, the mountebank singer, although he no longer had – far from it! – his triumphant accents of the summer. What was he singing, this shivering Harlequin? He was singing a song which has since become very well-known, but whose words cannot be understood by anyone who doesn't know the story we have just related:

> Au clair de la lune,
> Mon ami Pierrot!
> Prête-moi ta plume
> Pour écrire un mot.
> Ma chandelle est morte,
> Je n'ai plus de feu.
> Ouvre-moi ta porte,
> Pour l'amour de Dieu!

For, among his paint pots, poor Harlequin had found the message Columbine had left behind, thanks to which Pierrot had persuaded her to come back to him. And so this glib talker was able to measure the power sometimes possessed by people who write, especially when they also own an oven in the wintertime. And he was naïvely asking Pierrot to lend him his pen and his firelight. Did he really believe he had any chance of thus winning Columbine back?

Pierrot felt sorry for his unhappy rival. He opened his door to him. A pitiable, colourless Harlequin dashed over to the oven whose doors were still oozing warmth, colour, and a lovely smell. How comforting it was at Pierrot's!

The baker was transfigured by his triumph. He made great sweeping gestures, amplified by his long, floating sleeves. With a theatrical flourish, he opened both doors of his oven. A wave of golden light, of feminine warmth and of the delicious smell of pastry flooded over the three friends. And then, with a long wooden shovel, Pierrot slid something out of the oven. What was it? *Who* was it, rather! A girl made of golden crust, steaming and crunchy, who resembled

Columbine like a sister. She was no longer the flat Columbine-Harlequina, daubed in gaudy artificial colours on the façade of the laundry, she was a Columbine-Pierrette, modelled in brioche dough with all the contours of life, her round cheeks, her high, rounded bust, and her lovely, firm little buttocks.

Columbine took Columbine in her arms, at the risk of burning herself.

'How lovely I am, how good I smell!' she said.

Pierrot and Harlequin watched this extraordinary scene in fascination. Columbine put Columbine down on the table. Gently, greedily, with both hands, she separated Columbine's brioche breasts. She plunged an avid nose, a quivering tongue into the mellow gold of the cleavage. With her mouth full, she said:

'How tasty I am! You too, my darlings, taste her, eat this good Columbine! Eat me!'

And they tasted, they ate the warm Columbine, who melted in their mouths.

They looked at each other. They were happy. They wanted to laugh, but how can you laugh when your cheeks are bulging with brioche?

THE SHARING OF BREAD

CLARICE LISPECTOR

IT WAS SATURDAY and we had been invited to lunch out of a sense of obligation. But we were all much too fond of Saturday to go wasting it in the company of people whom we did not care for. Each of us had experienced happiness at some time or other and had been left with the mark of desire. As for me, I desired everything. And there we were, trapped, as if our train had been derailed and we had been forced to settle down among perfect strangers. No one there cared for me and I did not care for them. As for my Saturday – it swayed outside my windows in acacias and shadows. Rather than spend it badly, I preferred to hold it in my clenched fist, where it could be crumpled like a handkerchief. Waiting for lunch to be served, we half-heartedly drank a toast to the health of resentment: tomorrow it would be Sunday. I have no desire to be with you, our gaze was saying without any warmth, as we slowly blew smoke from our dry cigarettes. The avarice of refusing to share our Saturday eroded little by little and advanced like rust, until any happiness would have been an insult to a greater happiness.

Only the mistress of the household did not appear to save her Saturday in order to exploit it on a Thursday evening. But how could this woman, whose heart had experienced other Saturdays, have forgotten that people crave more and more? She did not even betray impatience with this heterogeneous gathering in her home, daydreaming and resigned, as if waiting for the next train to leave, any train – rather than remain in that deserted railway station, rather than have to restrain the horse from bolting furiously to join more and more horses.

We finally moved into the dining room for a lunch without the blessing of hunger. When taken by surprise, we came face to face with the table. This could not be for us . . .

It was a table prepared for men of good will. Who could the expected guest be who had simply failed to turn up? But it was we ourselves. So that woman served the best no matter the guest? And she was content to wash the feet of the first stranger. We watched, feeling uneasy.

The table had been covered with solemn abundance. Sheaves of wheat were piled up on the white table-cloth. And rosy apples, enormous yellow carrots, round tomatoes with their skins ready to burst, green marrows with translucent skins, pineapples of a malign savageness, oranges golden and tranquil, gherkins bristling like porcupines, cucumbers stretched tight over watery flesh, red, hollow peppers that caused our eyes to smart – were all entangled in moist whiskers of maize, as auburn as if bordering human lips. And the berries of the grape. The purplest of the grapes that could barely wait to be pressed. Nor did they mind who pressed them. The tomatoes were circular for no one: for the atmosphere, for the circular atmosphere. Saturday belonged to anyone who cared to turn up. The oranges would sweeten the tongue of the first person to arrive. Beside the plate of each unwanted guest, the woman who washed the feet of strangers had placed – even without choosing or loving us – a sheaf of wheat, a bunch of fiery radishes, or a crimson slice of water-melon with its merry seeds. All dissected by the Spanish acidity visible in the green lemons. In the earthenware jugs there was milk, as if it had crossed a rocky desert with the goats. Wine that was almost black after being thoroughly trampled shuddered in the clay vessels. Everything was set before us. Everything cleansed of perverse human desire. Everything as it really is, and not as we would wish it to be. Simply existing and intact. Just as a field exists. Just as the mountains exist. Just as man and woman exist, but not those of us who are consumed by greed. Just as Saturday exists. Simply existing. It exists.

On behalf of nothing, it was time to eat. On behalf of no one, it was good. Without any dream. And on a par with day, we gradually became anonymous, growing, rising, to the height of possible existence. Then, like the landed aristocracy, we accepted the table.

There was no holocaust: everything there was anxious to be eaten just as we were anxious to eat it. Saving nothing for the following day, there and then I offered my feelings to that which aroused those feelings. It was a feast for which I had not paid in advance with the suffering of waiting, the hunger that comes as we bring the food to our lips. For now we felt hungry, an all-consuming hunger which embraced the entire spread down to the crumbs. Those who drank wine kept a watchful eye on the milk. Those who slowly sipped milk could taste the wine that the others were drinking. Just outside, God among the acacias. Acacias which existed. We ate. Like someone giving water to a horse. The carved meat was shared out. The friendly exchanges were homely and rustic. No one spoke ill of anyone because no one spoke well of anyone. It was a harvest reunion and a truce was declared. We ate. Like a horde of living creatures, we slowly covered the earth. As busy as someone who cultivates existence, and plants, and reaps, and kills, and lives, and dies, and eats. I ate with the honesty of the man who does not belie what he is eating; I ate the food and not its name. God was never so possessed by what He is. The food was saying, brusque, happy, austere: eat, eat and share. Everything there was mine, it was my father's table. I ate without affection, I ate without the passion of mercy. Without offering myself to hope. I ate without any longing whatsoever. And I was wholly deserving of that food. For I cannot always be my brother's keeper, just as I can no longer be my own keeper, for I have ceased to love myself. Nor do I wish to form life because existence already exists. It exists like some territory where we all advance. Without a single word of love. Without a word. But your pleasure comprehends mine. We are strong and we eat. For bread is love among strangers.

Isis in Darkness

Margaret Atwood

HOW DID SELENA get here? This is a question Richard is in the habit of asking himself, as he sits at his desk again, shuffling his deck of filing cards, trying again to begin. In a way it's the main question: because she was then, and remains, altogether improbable, an anomaly for her time and place. Or as the new physics would say: a singularity.

Richard has a repertoire of answers. Sometimes he pictures her drifting gently down towards the mundane rooftops of late-fifties Toronto in a giant balloon made of turquoise and emerald-green silks, or arriving on the back of an outsized and resplendant red-gold bird, like the ones on Chinese tea-cups. At other times he sees her landing from a transparent spacecraft, a time-warp traveller *en route* from Venus or Pluto, where there are other beings like herself, all female. An airy tourist who'd got off at the wrong stop and found herself dismayed and disoriented, stranded in the land of a sluggish, earthclogged race, a thick waterlogged language. On other days, darker ones like this Thursday – Thursday, he knows, was a sinister day in her calendar – she winds her way through a long series of underground tunnels encrusted with blood-red jewels and with arcane, brightly-painted inscriptions that glitter in the light of torches. For years she walks, her garments – garments, not clothes – trailing, her face intent, her eyes fixed and hypnotic, wending her way from past ages lost in the confusing fogs of time, for she is one of those cursed with an unending life; walks until she reaches, one moonlit night (midnight, of course; full moon, of course) the iron-grilled door of the Petrowski tomb, which is real, though dug improbably into a hillside near the entrance to the also-real Mount Pleasant Cemetery.

(She would love that intersection of the specific, the banal even, with the numinous, the visionary. She once said that the universe was a doughnut. She named the brand.)

The lock splits. The iron gate swings open. She emerges, raises her arms towards the suddenly-chilled moon. The world changes.

There are other plots. It just depends which mythology he's cribbing from.

A factual account exists. She came from the same sort of area that Richard came from himself: old pre-Depression Toronto, strung out along the lakeshore south of the Queen streetcar tracks, a region of small vertical houses with peeling woodwork and sagging front porches and dry, mangy lawns. Not quaint in those days, not renovated, not desirable. The sort of constipated lower-middle-class white-bread ghetto he'd fled as soon as he could, because of the dingy and limited versions of himself it had offered him. Her motivation was perhaps the same. He likes to think so.

They'd even gone to the same constricting highschool, though he'd never noticed her there. But why would he? He was four years older. By the time she'd come in, a spindly, frightened Grade Niner, he'd been almost out the door, and none too soon for him. He couldn't imagine her there; couldn't imagine her sauntering along the same faded green hallways, banging the same scratched lockers, sticking her gum underneath the same cage-like desks.

She and the highschool would have been destructive opposites, like matter and anti-matter. Every time he placed her mental image beside that of the school, one or the other of them exploded. Usually it was the school's.

Selena was not her real name. She had simply appropriated it, as she'd appropriated everything else that would help her to construct her new preferred identity. She'd discarded the old name, which was *Marjorie*. Richard has learned this by

59

mistake, in the course of his researches, and has tried in vain to forget it.

The first time he saw her is not noted on any of his filing cards. He only makes notes of things he is not otherwise likely to remember.

It was in 1960 – the end of the fifties or the beginning of the sixties, depending on how you felt about zero. Selena was later to call it 'the white-hot luminous egg/from which everything hatches,' but for Richard, who at the time was slogging through *Being and Nothingness*, it signalled a dead end. He was in his first year of graduate school, on a meagre grant eked out by the marking of woefully-written under-graduate essays. He was feeling jaded, over-the-hill; senility was rapidly approaching. He was twenty-two.

He met her on a Tuesday night, at the coffee house. *The* coffee house, because as far as Richard knew there was not another one like it in Toronto. It was called *The Bohemian Embassy*, in reference to the anti-bourgeois things that were supposed to go on in there, and to a certain extent did go on. It sometimes got mail from more innocent citizens who had seen the listing in the phone book and thought it was a real embassy, and were writing about travel visas. This was a source of hilarity among the regulars, of whom Richard was not quite one.

The coffee house was on a little cobbled sidestreet, up on the second floor of a disused warehouse. It was reached by a treacherous flight of wooden stairs with no bannister; inside, it was dimly-lit, smoke-filled, and closed down at intervals by the fire department. The walls had been painted black, and there were small tables with checked cloths and dripping candles. It also had an espresso machine, the first one Richard had ever seen. This machine was practically an icon, pointing as it did to other, superior cultures, far from Toronto. But it had its drawbacks. While you were reading your poetry out loud, as Richard sometimes did, Max behind the coffee bar might turn on the machine, adding a whooshing, gurgling sound effect, as of someone being pressure-cooked and strangled.

Wednesdays and Thursdays were folk-singing, the weekends were jazz. Richard sometimes went on these nights, but he always went on Tuesdays, whether he was reading or not. He wanted to check out the competition. There wasn't a lot of it, but what there was would surely turn up at The Bohemian Embassy, sooner or later.

Poetry was the way out then, for young people who wanted some exit from the lumpen bourgeoisie and the shackles of respectable wage-earning. It was what painting had been at the turn of the century. Richard knows this now, although he did not then; though he doesn't know what the equivalent is at the moment. Film-making, he'd guess, for those with intellectual pretensions. For those without, it's playing the drums in a group, a group with a disgusting name such as *Animal Fats* or *The Living Snot*, if his twenty-seven-year-old son is any indication. Richard can't keep close tabs though, because the son lives with Richard's ex-wife. (Still! At his age! Why doesn't he get a room, an apartment, a job, Richard finds himself thinking, sourly enough. He understands, now, his own father's irritation with the black turtle-necks he used to wear, his scruffy attempts at a beard, his declamations, over the obligatory Sunday-dinner meat and potatoes, of *The Waste Land*, and, later and even more effectively, of Ginsberg's *Howl*. But at least he'd been interested in *meaning*, he tells himself. Or words. At least he'd been interested in words.)

He'd been good with words, then. He'd had several of his poems published in the university literary magazine, and in two little magazines, one of them not mimeographed. Seeing these poems in print, with his name underneath – he used initials, like T.S. Eliot, to make himself sound older – had given him more satisfaction than he'd ever got out of anything before. But he'd made the mistake of showing one of these magazines to his father, who was lower-middle-management with the Post Office. This had rated nothing more than a frown and a grunt, but as he was going down the walk with his bag of freshly-washed laundry, on his way back to his rented room, he'd heard his old man reading one of his free-verse anti-sonnets out loud to his mother, sputtering with mirth, punctuated by his mother's disapproving, predictable voice: 'Now, John! Don't be so hard on him! He's only a boy!'

The anti-sonnet was about Mary Jo, a chunky, practical girl with an off-blonde pageboy who worked at the library, and with whom Richard was almost having an affair. 'I sink into your eyes,' his father roared. 'Old swamp-eyes! Cripes, what's he gonna do when he gets down as far as the tits?'

And his mother, acting her part in their ancient conspiracy: 'Now, John! Really! Language!'

Richard told himself severely that he didn't care. His father never read anything but the Readers' Digest and bad paperback novels about the war, so what did he know?

By that particular Tuesday Richard had given up free verse. It was too easy. He wanted something with more rigour, more structure; something, he admits to himself now, that not everybody else could do.

He'd read his own stuff during the first set of the evening, a group of five sestinas followed by a vilanelle. His poems were elegant, intricate; he was pleased with them. The espresso machine went off during the last one – he was beginning to suspect Max of sabotage – but several people said 'Shhh.' When he'd finished there was polite applause. Richard sat back down in his corner, surreptitiously scratching his neck. The black turtle-neck was giving him a rash. As his mother never ceased telling anyone who might be interested, he had a delicate skin.

After him there was a straw-haired older woman poet from the West Coast who read a long poem in which the wind was described as blowing up between her thighs. There were breezy disclosures in this poem, off-handed four-letter words; nothing you wouldn't find in Alan Ginsberg, but Richard caught himself blushing. After her reading this woman came over and sat down beside Richard. She squeezed his arm and whispered, 'Your poems were nice.' Then, staring him straight in the eye, she hitched her skirt up over her thighs.

This was hidden from the rest of the room by the checked tablecloth and by the general smokey gloom. But it was a clear invitation. She was daring him to take a peek at whatever moth-eaten horror she had tucked away in there.

Richard found himself becoming coldly angry. He was supposed to salivate, jump her on the stairway like some deranged monkey. He hated those kinds of assumptions about men, about dipstick sex and slobbery, pea-brained arousal. He felt like punching her. She must have been at least fifty.

The age he now is himself, Richard notes dejectedly. That's one thing Selena has escaped. He thinks of it as an escape.

There was a musical interlude, as there always was on Tuesdays. A girl with long straight dark hair parted in the middle sat on a high stool, an autoharp across her knees, and sang several mournful folksongs in a high, clear voice. Richard was worrying about how to remove the woman poet's hand from his arm without being ruder than he wanted to be. (She was senior, she'd published books, she knew people.) He thought he might excuse himself and go to the washroom; but the washroom was just a cubicle that opened directly onto the main room. It had no lock, and Max was in the habit of opening the door when you were in there. Unless you turned out the light and pissed in the dark, you were likely to be put on exhibit, brightly-lit as a Christmas creche, hands fumbling at your crotch.

He held a knife against her breast,
As into his arms she pressed,
sang the girl. *I could just leave*, thought Richard. But he didn't want to do that.

Oh Willy Willy, don't you murder me,
I'm not prepared for eternity.
Sex and violence, he thinks now. A lot of the songs were about that. We didn't even notice. We thought it was art.

It was right after this that Selena came on. He hadn't seen

her in the room before. It was as if she'd materialized out of nowhere, on the tiny stage, under the single spotlight.

She was slight, almost wispy. Like the singer, she had long dark hair with a centre part. Her eyes were outlined in black, as was becoming the fashion. She was wearing a long-sleeved, high-necked black dress, over which was draped a shawl embroidered with what looked like blue and green dragon-flies.

Oh jeez, thought Richard, who like his father still used the laundered blasphemies of the schoolyard. *Another jeezly poetess. I suppose now we'll have more pudenda*, he added, from his graduate-school vocabulary.

Then the voice hit him. It was a warm, rich voice, darkly spiced, like cinnamon, and too huge to be coming from such a small person. It was a seductive voice, but not in any blunt way. What it offered was an entrée to amazement, to a shared and tingling secret; to splendours. But there was an undercurrent of amusement too, as if you were a fool for being taken in by its voluptuousness; as if there were a cosmic joke in the offing, a simple, mysterious joke, like the jokes of children. As if you were being promised the nectar of the gods, but would find it served to you in a broken doll's teacup, under the front porch, by a dirty-faced angel with scraped knees.

Yes. But an angel.

What she read was a series of short connected lyrics. *Isis in Darkness.* The Egyptian Queen of Heaven and Earth was wandering in the underworld, gathering up the pieces of the murdered and dismembered body of her lover Osiris. At the same time, it was her own body she was putting back together; and it was also the physical universe. She was creating the universe by an act of love.

All of this was taking place, not in the ancient Middle Kingdom of the Egyptians, but in flat, dingy Toronto, on Spadina Avenue, at night, among the darkened garment factories and delicatessens and bars and pawnshops. It was a lament, and a celebration. Richard had never heard anything like it.

He sat back in his chair, fingering his patchy beard, trying as hard as he could to find this girl and her poetry trivial, overdone and pretentious. But he couldn't manage it. She was brilliant, and he was frightened. He felt his own careful talent shrivelling to the size of a dried bean.

The espresso machine did not go on once. After she'd finished there was a silence, before the applause. The silence was because people didn't know what to make of it, how to take it, this thing, whatever it was, that had been done to them. For a moment she had transformed reality, and it took them a breath to get it back.

Richard stood up, pushing past the bared legs of the woman poet. He didn't care any more who she might know. He went over to where Selena had just sat down, with a cup of coffee brought to her by Max.

'I liked your poems,' he managed to get out.

'Liked? Liked?' He thought she was making fun of him, although she wasn't smiling. '*Liked* is so margarine. How about *adored*?'

'Adored, then,' he said, feeling like an idiot twice over – for having said *liked* in the first place, and for jumping through her hoop in the second. But he got his reward. She asked him to sit down.

Up close her eyes were turquoise, the irises dark-ringed like a cat's. In her ears were blue-green earrings in the shape of scarabs. Her face was heart-shaped, her skin pale; to Richard, who had been dabbling in the French Symbolists, it evoked the word *lilac*. The shawl, the darkly-outlined eyes, the earrings – few would have been able to pull it off. But she acted as if this was just her ordinary getup. What you'd wear any day on a journey down the Nile, five thousand years ago.

It was of a piece with her performance – bizarre, but assured. Fully achieved. The worst of it was that she was only eighteen.

'That's a lovely shawl,' Richard attempted. His tongue felt like a beef sandwich.

'It's not a shawl, it's a table-cloth,' she said. She looked down at it, stroked it. Then she laughed a little. 'It's a shawl *now*.'

Richard wondered if he should dare to ask – what? If he could walk her home? Did she have anything so mundane as a home? But what if she said no? While he was deliberating, Max the bullet-headed coffee hack walked over and put a possessive hand on her shoulder, and she smiled up at him. Richard didn't wait to see if it meant anything. He excused himself, and left.

He went back to his rented room and composed a sestina to her. It was a dismal effort; it captured nothing about her. He did what he had never before done to one of his poems. He burnt it.

Over the next clutch of weeks Richard got to know her better. Or he thought he did. When he came into the coffee house on Tuesday nights, she would greet him with a nod, a smile. He would go over and sit down, and they would talk. She never spoke about herself, her life. Instead she treated him as if he were a fellow professional, an initiate, like herself. Her talk was about the magazines by which her poems had been accepted, about projects she'd begun. She was writing a verse play for radio; she would be paid for it. She seemed to think it was only a matter of time before she'd be earning enough money to live on, though she had very little conception of how much *enough* would be. She didn't say what she was living on at the moment.

Richard found her naive. He himself had taken the sensible course: with a graduate degree he could always make an income of some sort in the academic saltmines. But who would pay a living wage for poetry, especially the kind she wrote? It wasn't in the style of anyone, it didn't sound like anything else. It was too eccentric.

She was like a child sleepwalking along a roof-ledge ten stories up. He was afraid to call out in warning, in case she should wake, and fall.

Mary Jo the librarian had phoned him several times. H[e] put her off with vague mumbles about overwork. On th[e] rare Sunday when he still turned up at his parents' house to do his laundry and eat what his father called a decent meal for once, he had to endure the pained scrutiny of his mother. Her theory was that he was straining his brain, which could lead to anaemia. In fact he was hardly working at all. His room was silting up with unmarked, overdue student papers; he hadn't written another poem, another line. Instead he went out for gummy egg sandwiches or glasses of draft beer at the local beverage room, or to afternoon movies, sleazy double features about women with two heads or men who got changed into flies. Evenings he spent at the coffee house. He was no longer feeling jaded. He was feeling desperate.

It was Selena who was causing this desperation, but he had no name for why. Partly he wanted to get inside her, find that innermost cave where she hid her talent. But she kept him at a distance. Him, and in some way, everyone else.

She read several times. The poems were astonishing again, again unique. Nothing about her grandmother, or about snow, or about childhood; nothing about dying dogs, or family members of any kind. Instead there were regal, tricky women, magical, shapeshifting men; in whom, however, he thought he could recognize the transposed outlines of some of the regulars from the Bohemian Embassy. Was that Max's white-blonde bullet head, his lidded ice-blue eyes? There was another man, a thin intense one with a moustache and a smouldering Spanish look that set Richard's teeth on edge. One night he'd announced to the whole table that he'd caught a bad case of crabs, that he'd had to shave himself and paint his groin blue. Could that be his torso, equipped with burning wings? Richard couldn't tell, and it was driving him crazy.

(It was never Richard himself though. Never his own stubby features, his own brownish hair and hazel eyes. Never even a line, about him.)

He pulled himself together, got the papers marked, finished off an essay on the imagery of mechanism in Herrick that he needed in order to haul himself safely from this academic year into the next one. He took Mary Jo to one of the

Tuesday poetry evenings. He thought it might neutralize Selena, like an acid neutralizing an alkali; get her out of his head. Mary Jo was not impressed.

'Where does she *get* those tatty old clothes?' she said.

'She's a brilliant poet,' said Richard.

'I don't care. That thing looks like a table-cloth. And why does she do her eyes in that phoney way?'

Richard felt this like a cut, like a personal wound.

He didn't want to marry Selena. He couldn't imagine marriage with her. He could not place her within the tedious, comforting scenery of domesticity: a wife doing his laundry, a wife cooking his meals, a wife pouring his tea. All he wanted was a month, a week, a night even. Not in a motel room, not in the back of a car; these squalid venues left over from his fumbling youth would not do. It would have to be somewhere else, somewhere darker and infinitely more strange. He imagined a crypt, with hieroglyphics; like the last act of *Aida*. The same despair, the same exultation, the same annihilation. From such an experience you would emerge reborn, or not at all.

It was not lust. Lust was what you felt for Marilyn Monroe, or sometimes for the strippers at the Victory Burlesque. (Selena had a poem about the Victory Burlesque. The strippers, for her, were not a bunch of fat sluts with jiggling, dimpled flesh. They were diaphanous; they were surreal butterflies, emerging from cocoons of light; they were splendid.)

What he craved was not her body as such. He wanted to be transformed by her, into someone he was not.

By now it was summer, and the university and the coffee house were both closed. On rainy days Richard lay on the lumpy bed in his humid, stifling room, listening to the thunder; on sunny ones, which were just as humid, he made his way from tree to tree, staying in the shade. He avoided the library. One more session of sticky near-sex with Mary Jo, with her damp kisses and her nurse-like manipulations of his body, and especially the way she sensibly stopped short of anything final, would leave him with a permanent limp.

'You wouldn't want to get me knocked up,' she would say, and she was right, he wouldn't. For a girl who worked among books, she was breathtakingly prosaic. But then, her *forte* was cataloguing.

Richard knew she was a healthy girl with a normal out-look. She would be good for him. This was his mother's opinion, delivered after he'd made the mistake – just once – of taking her home with him to Sunday dinner. She was like corned beef, cottage cheese, cod-liver oil. She was like milk.

One day he bought a bottle of Italian red wine and took the ferry over to Ward's Island. He knew Selena lived over there. That at least had been in the poems.

He didn't know what he intended to do. He wanted to see her, take hold of her, go to bed with her. He didn't know how he was going to get from the first step to the last one. He didn't care what came of it. He wanted.

He got off the ferry and walked up and down the small streets of the Island, where he had never been. These were summer homes, cheap and insubstantial, white clapboard or pastel, or sided with insulbrick. Cars were not permitted. There were kids on bicycles, dumpy women in swimsuits taking sunbaths on their lawns. Portable radios played. It was not what he'd had in mind as Selena's milieu. He thought of asking someone where she lived – they would know, she'd stand out here – but he didn't want to advertise his presence. He considered turning around, taking the next ferry back.

Then, off at the end of one of the streets, he saw a minute one-storey cottage, in the shade of two large willows. There had been willows in the poems. He could at least try.

The door was open. It was her house, because she was in it. She was not at all surprised to see him.

'I was just making some peanut butter sandwiches,' she said, 'so we could have a picnic.' She was wearing loose black cotton slacks, Oriental in tone, and a sleeveless black top. Her arms were white and thin. Her feet were in sandals; he looked at her long toes, with the toenails painted a light peach-pink. He noted with a wrench of the heart that the nail-polish was chipped.

'Peanut butter?' he said stupidly. She was talking as if she'd been expecting him.

'And strawberry jam,' she said. 'Unless you don't like jam.' Still that courteous distance.

He proffered his bottle of wine. 'Thanks,' she said, 'but you'll have to drink it all by yourself.'

'Why?' he said. He'd intended this to go differently. A recognition. A wordless embrace.

'If I ever started I'd never stop. My father was an alcoholic,' she told him gravely. 'He's somewhere else, because of it.'

'In the Underworld?' he said, in what he hoped was a graceful allusion to her poetry.

She shrugged. 'Or wherever.' He felt like a dunce. She went back to spreading the peanut butter, at her diminutive kitchen table. Richard, wrung dry of conversation, looked around him. There was only the one room, sparsely furnished. It was almost like a religious cell, or his idea of one. In one corner there was a desk with an old black typewriter, and a book-shelf made of boards and bricks. The bed was narrow and covered with a swathe of bright-purple Indian cotton, to double as a sofa. There was a tiny sink, a tiny stove. One easy chair, Sally Ann issue. A braided, faded rug. On the walls there were no pictures at all.

'I don't need them,' she said. She'd put the sandwiches into a crumpled paper bag and was motioning him out the door.

She led him to a stone breakwater overlooking the lake, and they sat on it and ate the sandwiches. She had some lemonade in a milk bottle; they passed it back and forth. It was like a ritual, like a communion; she was letting him partake. She sat cross-legged, with sunglasses on. Two people went by in a canoe. The lake rippled, threw off glints of light. Richard felt absurd, and happy.

'We can't be lovers,' she said to him after a time. She was licking jam off her fingers. Richard jolted awake. He had never been so abruptly understood. It was like a trick; it made him uncomfortable.

He could have pretended he didn't know what she was talking about. Instead he said, 'Why not?'

'You would get used up,' she said. 'Then you wouldn't be there, later.'

This was what he wanted: to be used up. To burn in divine conflagration. At the same time, he realized that he could not summon up any actual, carnal desire for this woman; this *girl* sitting beside him on the breakwater with her skinny arms and minimal breasts, dangling her legs now like a nine-year-old.

'Later?' he said. Was she telling him he was too good to be wasted? Was this a compliment, or not?

'When I'll need you,' she said. She was stuffing the waxed-paper sandwich wrapping into the paper bag. 'I'll walk you to the ferry.'

He had been circumvented, outmanoeuvred; also spied on. Maybe he was an open book and a dolt as well, but she didn't have to rub it in. As they walked, he found himself getting angry. He still clutched the wine bottle in its liquor-store bag.

At the ferry dock she took his hand, shook it formally. 'Thank you for coming,' she said. Then she pushed the sun-glasses up onto her hair, giving him her turquoise eyes full-force. 'The light only shines for some,' she said, kindly and sadly. 'And even for them it's not all the time. The rest of the time you're alone.'

But he'd had enough of gnomic utterances for one day. 'Theatrical bitch,' he told himself on the ferry.

He went back to his room and drank most of the bottle of wine. Then he phoned Mary Jo. When she'd negotiated her way as usual past the snoopy landlady on the ground floor and arrived on tiptoe at his door, he pulled her inside roughly and bent her backwards in a tipsy, mocking embrace. She started to giggle, but he kissed her seriously and pushed her onto the bed. If he couldn't have what he wanted he would

71

at least have something. The bristles of her shaved legs rasped against him; her breath smelled like grape bubble-gum. When she began to protest, warning him again of the danger of pregnancy, he said it didn't matter. She took this as a marriage proposal. In the event, it was one.

With the arrival of the baby his academic work ceased to be a thing he did disdainfully, on suffrance, and became a necessity of life. He needed the money, and then he needed more money. He laboured over his PhD. thesis, on cartographic imagery in John Donne, interrupted by infant squalling and the dentist's-drill whine of the vacuum cleaner, and by the cups of tea brought to him by Mary Jo at inappropriate moments. She told him he was a grouch, but since that was more or less the behaviour she expected from husbands she didn't seem to mind. She typed his thesis for him and did the footnotes, and showed him off to her relatives, him and his new degree. He got a job teaching composition and grammar to veterinary students at the agricultural college in Guelph.

He did not write poetry any more. Some days he hardly even thought about it. It was like a third arm, or a third eye that had atrophied. He'd been a freak when he'd had it.

Once in a while though he went on binges. He would sneak into bookstores or libraries, lurk around the racks where the little magazines were kept; sometimes he'd buy one. Dead poets were his business, living ones his vice. Much of the stuff he read was crap and he knew it; still, it gave him an odd lift. Then there would be the occasional real poem, and he would catch his breath. Nothing else could drop him through space like that, then catch him; nothing else could peel him open.

Sometimes these poems were Selena's. He would read them, and part of him – a small, constricted part – would hope for some lapse, some decline; but she just got better. Those nights, when he was lying in bed on the threshold of sleep, he would remember her or she would appear to him, he was never sure which; a dark-haired woman with her arms upstretched, in a long cloak of blue and dull gold, or of feathers, or of white linen. The costumes were variable, but she herself remained a constant. She was something of his own, that he had lost.

He didn't see her again until 1970, another zero year. By that time he'd managed to get himself hired back to Toronto, to teach graduate-level Puritan literary theory and freshman English at a new campus in the suburbs. He did not yet have tenure: in the age of publish-or-perish, he'd published only two papers, one on witchcraft as sexual metaphor, the other on *The Pilgrim's Progress* and architecture. Now that their son was in school Mary Jo had gone back to cataloguing, and with their savings they'd made a down-payment on a Victorian semi-detached in the Annex. It had a small back lawn, which Richard mowed. They kept talking about a garden, but there was never the energy.

At this time Richard was at a low point, though it was Mary Jo's contention that he was always at a low point. She fed him vitamin pills and nagged him to see a shrink so he could become more assertive, though when he was assertive with her she would accuse him of throwing his patriarchal weight around. He'd realized by now that he could always depend on her to do the socially correct thing; at the moment she was attending a women's consciousness-raising group and was (possibly) having an affair with a sandy-haired, pasty-faced linguist at the University whose name was Johanson. Whether it existed or not, this affair suited Richard, in a way: it allowed him to think badly of her.

It was April. Mary Jo was at her women's group or screwing Johanson, or possibly both; she was efficient, she could get a lot done in one evening. His son was staying overnight with a friend. Richard was supposed to be working on his book, the book that was going to do it for him, make his name, get him tenure: *Spiritual Carnality: Marvell and Vaughan and the 17th Century*. He'd hesitated between *carnal spirituality* and *spiritual carnality*, but the latter had more zing. The book was not going all that well. There was

73

a problem of focus. Instead of rewriting the second chapter again, he'd come downstairs to rummage in the refrigerator for a beer.

'And tear our pleasures with rough strife, Thorough the iron gates of life, Olay!' he sang, to the tune of *Hernando's Hideaway*. He got out two beers and filled a cereal bowl with potato chips. Then he went into the living-room and settled into the easy chair to slurp and munch, flipping through the channels on the television set, looking for the crassest, most idiotic thing he could find. He badly needed something to sneer at.

This was when the doorbell rang. When he saw who it was he was very glad he'd had the sense to click off the item he'd been watching, a tits-and-bums extravaganza posing as a detective show.

It was Selena, wearing a wide-brimmed black hat and a long black knitted coat, and carrying a battered suitcase. 'May I come in?' she said.

Richard, amazed and a little frightened, and then suddenly delighted, stood back to let her in. He'd forgotten what delight felt like. In the last few years he'd given up even on the little magazines, preferring numbness.

He didn't ask her what she was doing at his house, or how she'd found him. Instead he said, 'Would you like a drink?'

'No,' she said. 'I don't drink, remember?' He did remember then; he remembered her tiny house on the island, in every clear detail: the pattern of small gold lions on the bedspread, the shells and round stones on the windowsill, the daisies in a jam jar. He remembered her long toes. He'd made a fool of himself that day, but now she was here it no longer mattered. He wanted to wrap his arms around her, hold her closely; rescue her, be rescued.

'Some coffee would be nice though,' she said, and he led her to the kitchen and made her some. She didn't take off her coat. The sleeves were threadbare; he could see the places where she'd stitched over the ravelled edges with mending wool. She smiled at him with the same acceptance of him she'd always shown, taking for granted that he was a friend and equal, and he was ashamed of the way he'd spent the last ten years. He must be absurd to her; he was absurd to himself. He had a paunch and a mortgage, a bedraggled marriage; he mowed the lawn, he owned sports jackets, grudgingly he raked the autumn leaves and shovelled the hackneyed winter snow. He indulged his own sloth. He should have been living in an attic, eating bread and magotty cheese, washing his one shirt out at night, his head incandescent with words.

She was not noticeably older. If anything she was thinner. He saw what he thought was the fading shadow of a bruise over her right cheekbone, but it could have been the light. She sipped at her coffee, fiddled with the spoon. She seemed to have drifted off somewhere. 'Are you writing much?' he said, seizing on something he knew would interest her.

'Oh yes,' she said brightly, returning to her body. 'I have another book coming out.' How had he missed the first one? 'How about you?'

He shrugged. 'Not for a long time.'

'That's a shame,' she said. 'That's terrible.' She meant it. It was as if he'd told her someone she'd known had died, and he was touched. It wasn't his actual poems she was regretting, unless she had no taste at all. They hadn't been any good, he knew that now and certainly she did too. It was the other poems, the ones he might have written, if. If what?

'Could I stay here?' she said, putting down her cup.

Richard was taken aback. She'd meant business with that suitcase. Nothing would have pleased him more, he told himself, but there was Mary Jo to be considered. 'Of course,' he said, hoping his hesitation hadn't shown.

'Thank you,' said Selena. 'I don't have anywhere else right now. Anywhere safe.'

He didn't ask her to explain this. Her voice was the same, rich and tantalizing, on the edge of ruin; it was having its old devastating effect on him. 'You can sleep in the rec room,' he said. 'There's a sofa that folds out.'

'Oh good.' She sighed. 'It's Thursday.' Thursday, he recalled, was a significant day in her poetry, but at the time he couldn't remember whether it was good or bad. Now he knows. Now he has three filing cards with nothing but Thursdays on them.

When Mary Jo got home, brisk and defensive as he'd decided she always was after furtive sex, they were still sitting in the kitchen. Selena was having another cup of coffee, Richard another beer. Selena's hat and mended coat were on top of her suitcase. Mary Jo saw them and scowled.

'Mary Jo, you remember Selena,' Richard said. 'From the Embassy?'

'Right,' said Mary Jo. 'Did you put out the trash?'

'I will,' said Richard. 'She's staying overnight.'

'I'll put it out myself then,' said Mary Jo, stomping off towards the glassed-in back porch where they kept the garbage cans. Richard followed her and they fought, at first in whispers.

'What the hell is she doing in my house?' Mary Jo hissed.

'It's not just your house, it's my house too. She's got nowhere else to go.'

'That's what they all say. What happened, some boyfriend beat her up?'

'I didn't ask. She's an old friend.'

'Look, if you want to sleep with that weird flake you can do it somewhere else.'

'As you do?' said Richard, with what he hoped was bitter dignity.

'What the hell are you talking about? Are you accusing me of something?' said Mary Jo. Her eyes were bulging out, as they did when she was really angry and not just acting. 'Oh. You'd love that, wouldn't you. Give you a voyeuristic thrill.'

'Anyway I'm not sleeping with her,' said Richard, reminding Mary Jo that the first false accusation had been hers.

'Why not?' said Mary Jo. 'You've been letching after her for ten years. I've seen you mooning over those stupid poetry magazines. *On Thursdays you are a banana,*' she intoned, in savage mimicry of Selena's deeper voice. 'Why don't you just screw her and get it over with?'

'I would if I could,' Richard said. This truth saddened him.

'Oh. Holding out on you? Tough shit. Do me a favour, just rape her in the rec room and get it out of your system.'

'My, my,' said Richard. 'Sisterhood *is* powerful.' As soon as he said it he knew he'd gone too far.

'How dare you use my feminism against me like that?' said Mary Jo, her voice up an octave. 'That is so cheap! You always were a cheap little prick!'

Selena was standing in the doorway watching them. 'Richard,' she said, 'I think I'd better go.'

'Oh no,' said Mary Jo, with a chirpy parody of hospitality. 'Stay! It's no trouble! Stay a week! Stay a month! Consider us your hotel!'

Richard walked Selena to the front door. 'Where will you go?' he said.

'Oh,' she said, 'there's always somewhere.' She stood under the porch light, looking up the street. It *was* a bruise. 'But right now I don't have any money.'

Richard dug out his wallet, emptied it. He wished it was more.

'I'll pay you back,' she said.

If he has to date it, Richard pinpoints this Thursday as the day his marriage was finally over. Even though he and Mary Jo went through the form of apologizing, even though they had more than a few drinks and smoked a joint and had dislocated, impersonal sex, nothing got fixed. Mary Jo left him soon after, in quest of the self she claimed she needed to find. She took their son with her. Richard, who hadn't paid that much attention to the boy, was now reduced to nostalgic, interminable weekends with him. He tried out several other women, but couldn't concentrate on them.

He looked for Selena but she'd disappeared. One magazine editor told him she'd gone out west. Richard felt he'd let her down. He had failed to be a place of refuge.

Ten years later he saw her again. It was 1980, another year

of the nothing, or of the white-hot egg. He notes this coincidence only now, laying out the filing cards like a fortune-teller across the surface of his particle-board desk.

He'd just got out of his car, having returned through thickening traffic from the university, where he was still clinging on by his fingernails. It was mid-March, during the spring melt, an irritating and scruffy time of year. Mud and rain and scraps of garbage left over from the winter. His mood was similar. He'd recently had the manuscript of *Spiritual Carnality* returned to him by a publisher, the fourth rejection. The covering letter informed him that he'd failed to sufficiently problematize the texts. On the title page someone had written, in faint, semi-erased pencil, *fatuously romantic*. He suspected that shrike Johanson, who was one of their readers, and who'd had it in for him ever since Mary Jo had left. After a brief interval of firm-chinned single coping, she'd moved in on Johanson and they'd lived together for six months of *blitzkrieg*. Then she'd tried to hit him up for half the value of his house. Johanson had been blaming this on Richard ever since.

He was thinking about this, and about the batch of student papers in his briefcase: James Joyce from a Marxist perspective, or garbled structuralism seeping in from France to dilute the student brain yet further. The papers had to be marked by tomorrow. He had a satisfying fantasy of laying them all out in the muddy street and running over them with his car. He would say he'd been in an accident.

Coming toward him was a short thickish woman in a black trenchcoat. She was carrying a large brown tapestry bag; she seemed to be looking at the numbers on the houses, or possibly the snowdrops and crocuses on the lawns. Richard did not understand that it was Selena until she'd almost passed him.

'Selena,' he said, touching her arm.

She turned up to him a blank face, the turquoise eyes dull. 'No,' she said. 'That's not my name.' Then she peered more closely. 'Richard. Is that you?' Either she was feigning pleasure, or she really felt it. Again, for him, there was a stab of unaccustomed joy.

He stood awkwardly. No wonder she'd had trouble recognizing him. He was prematurely grey, overweight; Mary Jo had told him, on the last, unpleasant occasion on which he'd seen her, that he was slug-coloured. 'I didn't know you were still here,' he said. 'I thought you'd moved out west.'

'Travelled,' she said. 'I'm through with that.' There was an edge to her voice he'd never heard before.

'And your work?' he said. It was always the thing to ask her.

'What work?' she said, and laughed.

'Your poetry.' He was beginning to be alarmed. She was more matter-of-fact than he'd ever known her to be, but somehow this struck him as crazy.

'Poetry,' she said with scorn. 'I hate poetry. It's just this. This is all there is. This stupid city.'

He went cold with dread. What was she saying, what had she done? It was like a blasphemy, it was like an act of desecration. Though how could he expect her to maintain faith in something he himself had so blatantly failed?

She'd been frowning, but now her face wrinkled in anxiety. She put a hand on his arm, stood on tiptoe. 'Richard,' she whispered. 'What happened to us? Where did everyone go?' A mist came up with her, an odour. He recognized sweetish wine, a whiff of cat.

He wanted to shake her, enfold her, lead her to safety, wherever that might be. 'We just changed, that's all,' he said gently. 'We got older.'

'Change and decay in all around I see,' she said, smiling in a way he did not like at all. 'I'm not prepared for eternity.'

It wasn't until she'd walked away – refusing tea, hurrying off as if she couldn't wait to see the last of him – that he realized she'd been quoting from a folk-song. It was the same one he'd heard sung to the autoharp in the coffee-house, the night he'd first seen her, standing under the single spotlight in her dragonfly shawl.

That, and a hymn. He wondered whether she'd become what his students called 'religious.'

Months later he heard she was dead. Then there was a piece in the paper. The details were vague. It was the picture that caught his eye: an earlier picture of her, from the jacket of one of her books. Probably there was nothing more recent, because she hadn't published anything for years. Even her death belonged to an earlier time; even the people in the small closed world of poetry had largely forgotten about her.

Now that she's dead, however, she's become newly respectable. In several quarterly reviews the country has been lambasted for its indifference towards her, its withholding of recognition during her lifetime. There's a move afoot to name a parkette after her, or else a scholarship, and the academics are swarming like botflies. A thin volume has appeared, of essays on her work, shoddy stuff in Richard's opinion, flimsy and superficial; another one is rumoured to be in the offing.

This is not the reason Richard is writing about her, however. Nor is it to cover his professional ass: he's going to be axed from the university anyway, there are new cutbacks, he lacks tenure, his head is on the block. It's merely because she's the one thing left he still values, or wants to write about. She is his last hope.

Isis in Darkness, he writes. *The Genesis*. It exalts him simply to form the words. He will exist for her at last, he will be created by her, he will have a place in her mythology after all. It will not be what he once wanted: not Osiris, not a blue-eyed god with burning wings. His are humbler metaphors. He will only be the archaeologist; not part of the main story, but the one who stumbles upon it afterwards, making his way for his own obscure and battered reasons through the jungle, over the mountains, across the desert, until he discovers at last the pillaged and abandoned temple. In the ruined sanctuary, in the moonlight, he will find the Queen of Heaven and Earth and the Underworld lying in shattered white marble on the floor. He is the one who will sift through the rubble, groping for the shape of the past. He is the one who will say it has meaning. That too is a calling, that also can be a fate.

He picks up a filing card, jots a small footnote on it in his careful writing, and replaces it neatly in the mosaic of paper he is making across his desk. His eyes hurt. He closes them and rests his forehead on his two fisted hands, summoning up whatever is left of his knowledge and skill, kneeling beside her in the darkness, fitting her broken pieces back together.

WHEN THE LIGHTS RETURN

BEN OKRI

EDE HAD BEEN singing at a poorly attended concert when the power failed. The hotel didn't have any electric generators. The audience shouted for their money to be returned, then they left in disgust. In the darkness Ede saw the luminous white dress of his girlfriend floating up to him. He heard her sad voice say:

'The third time in one night.'

'I don't think they liked my song, Maria.'

She laughed gently.

After a while she said she didn't feel well.

'It's the blackout,' he said absent-mindedly. 'It makes you feel weird at first.'

With the microphone in his hand he stared into the haze of darkness. Her eyes glowed like that of a cat. He put the microphone back on the stand and paid her no further attention. While he joined the musicians in clearing up the instruments she sat in a corner of the stage, feverish in the dark. He didn't notice her again till the hotel manager went around with a lamp and saw her asleep on the floor. Ede woke her up, lifted her into a taxi, and took her home. He was irritated with her that night, and because he was irritated with her he didn't notice that she had begun to change.

He avoided her for a while. He began to think of her as being too soft, too frail, a bit of a spoil-sport. He managed to blame her for the failure of his last concert. He even began to contemplate finding another woman. But when she came to see him, after a week's lack of contact, and after the lights had returned, she looked so beautiful and her eyes were so sad that he forgot all about his petty irritations. Without asking how she was, or whether she was feeling better, he locked the door and began to kiss her. She pushed him away. He held her hands and stared at her. She trembled slightly. Her hands were soft and her palms were damp; beads of sweat glistened under her nose. He made her lie down on the bed. Then he took off her shoes and made her face him.

'I want to watch television,' she said.

'Watch my eyes.'

She smiled. Stealthily, as if he didn't want to disturb her acquiescence, he moved his fingers up her legs. He began to play with her when she sneezed.

'Have you got a cold?'

'I just sneezed.'

'Maybe someone is calling your name.'

'Who?'

'I don't know.'

He went on playing with her warm thighs. She stiffened. He had encountered her wetness. It always came as a surprise.

'You're tickling me.'

He tickled her some more. Then he took off her silk blouse and her skirt and threw them on the armchair. His breathing became laboured. He waited for her protestations.

'What about your mother?' she asked, in a new voice.

Ede lived with his mother in the two small rooms.

'I knew you would bring up something.'

'Well?'

'She's gone to our town people's meeting.'

'So?'

'She'll be gone a long time.'

Maria paused, then asked:

'What if someone comes to visit her?'

'It's okay.'

'What about the door?'

'It's fine.'

She stared at him. Her eyes glowed. When she laughed Ede took a deep breath before burying his face between her breasts.

83

'It's good to be alive,' he said with a sentimental quaver in his voice.

'Who disputed it?'

'No one.'

They were silent. Gently, she caressed his hair. Then she held onto him with such loving strength that he felt his sudden hardness.

'What if I don't want to?' she said, drawing back a little.

'Then you will be surprised.'

'By what?'

'By yourself.'

'Seriously, Ede, what if for no reason I don't want to?'

'What?'

'Seriously.'

'Do you want to kill me?'

'Be serious.'

'Well, I'll be utterly frustra . . . '

Then it happened again, suddenly, without warning, invading their lives. Every day, once, twice, often uncountably, the lights went, plunging everything into darkness, releasing an obsessional tide of heat and sweat and incomprehension.

In the darkness Ede felt the mood change. Maria's body burned beside him. He got up and lit a candle. Maria's face was pale. Her lips trembled. Sweat broke out on her forehead. She had a frightened expression in her eyes. When he started to climb back into bed she pushed him off and got dressed.

'What's the matter?'

'I've got to go.'

'Why?'

'I'm going.'

'Is it because of the light? It'll be back soon.'

'I'm going.'

'Why?'

'Nothing.'

'Why are you so strange all of a sudden?'

'I'm scared.'

'Of what?'

'Nothing.'

He tried to persuade her to stay, but he felt no conviction.

Maria's beauty took on a single-minded and uncanny concentration.

'Alright!' he said angrily, 'if you want to go then go!'

Galvanized by the new tone in his voice, she dressed hurriedly. The mosquitoes whined around her. The heat seemed to be rising. If he had looked carefully at her face in the candle-light he would have seen how curiously disturbed she was. But he only noticed what he took to be her indifference. When she was fully dressed she turned her impenetrable eyes to him and said:

'Are you going to see me off?'

Frustrated, unable to understand why she suddenly broke off the mood of the evening, he stayed silent. Holding her head high, she swept up her handbag and left the room. Then he lost his temper, shouting at her incoherently, calling her names. It was very dark in the corridor. Outside, he heard others shouting as well: some at their wives, some at their children, others seemed to shout at the air, as if to register the existence of their protest.

The other voices rose to him, but he drummed on with his insults, hoping that he might get a response out of her, hoping to whip up the sort of confrontation that only an instantaneous reconciliation could resolve. But she didn't rise to his baits. When they passed a stall with kerosene light he saw a shadow on her face, but he didn't recognize it. And when they got to the main road he had aggravated the situation so badly that when a taxi came along all he could do was stare at her threateningly. Before she got into the taxi, she said:

'Don't be bad to me.'

'And why not?'

'Why?'

Without meaning to, without resisting it, irritated by the darkness, he said:

'You're too much trouble. Too frail. Always ill. Too coy. You're not really interested. I don't want to see you again.'

She stared at him. The impatient taxi-driver blasted his horn.

'I don't,' Ede said, with too much feeling, and with some inexplicable satisfaction.

Maria opened the car door and, with the candle-lights reflected in her eyes, said:

'If you do that, if you ignored me and never saw me again, then you would have killed me.'

She looked almost demonic, almost possessed. She continued:

'And if you really love me, and if later you want to talk to me, you would have to wake me up from death. Can you do that?'

Ede didn't understand her. He was quite startled. Without saying another word she disappeared into the taxi. And the taxi, with no back-lights, disappeared into the darkness.

Three weeks passed, and he refused to see her. The blackout had persisted. His mother had kept asking about Maria's absence and he had kept on lying that everything was fine. Then one day, after he had finalized the date of a recording session, and finished a day's work in the office, he had come home bound nerve and brain in exhaustion, when it occurred to him that she was passing completely out of his life. He sat on the armchair, thinking about Maria. He shut his eyes and tried to sleep. The candle flame kept twisting. Mosquitoes whined in his ears. With his eyes shut he saw the candle's shape as an agonized dancer, oily with sweat.

He stank. The mosquitoes and the gnats tormented him. Exhausted from another day's work, flattened by the abnormal efforts of struggling for a bus, dulled by the persistence of the heat waves, he felt as if a hand had wiped clean the slate of his emotions. He gave up the chair and fell asleep on the floor. While he slept he had an unaccountable dream in which Maria stepped out of a mirror. There was an aureole round her head which blinded him momentarily. When he saw her face he was surprised that it had changed to the colour of alabaster. Her eyes were dark holes. Her teeth fell out of her mouth, one by one, as he gazed at her. He woke up suddenly with a sadness like lead in his stomach.

The candle had burned low. He did not feel rested. On the contrary, he felt more drained. He sat up on the floor and could not breathe for the heat. He wished the mosquitoes would spare him for an hour so he might regain the energy he had yielded to the heat, the dust, and the fray. He hoped – and in reality he dared not hope – that the lights would return. He got up and was wiping his face with a towel when he thought he saw Maria at the door. He went out. The corridor was dark and empty. He came back in and resumed sleep. He dreamt again about Maria. She was walking upside-down, in a world of mirrors, naked.

'Why are you walking like that?' he asked.

'Sing for me,' she said.

'Why?'

'Delay what I'm going through.'

'I can't sing till the lights return.'

She laughed. Then he saw her clearly. Flowers grew from her ears. When her head moved he noticed that bats had matted themselves tightly to her hair. He screamed and the bats flew into his eyes. He woke up, soaked in sweat.

'Oh God!' he said, as a queer premonition passed through him.

He got up and lit another candle and blew the old one out. He sat on the chair and wondered how it was that he hadn't seen Maria for three weeks. He felt ashamed of himself. Three weeks! His shame grew so much that he blamed her entirely for the frustrations of the day. He blamed the traffic jams on her. He blamed her for the loss of three shirt buttons during the struggle for buses on his way to work. He managed to blame her for the electric failures.

The candle-flame elongated the scuttling wall-geckos, enlarged the cobwebs. With the heat conquering his consciousness, he decided to go and see Maria, sweating as he was, and to confront her with her handiwork. Releasing himself from his obduracy, Ede got dressed. He left a note for his mother, which read: 'I've gone to see Maria. Will not be long.' He blew out the candle. In the darkness he felt suddenly that his neglect of Maria had gone too far and was now beyond redemption. He left the room key under the doormat, for his mother to find. Then he went through the corridor and out into the compound.

The street had been waiting for him.

In a patch of wasteland, in front of the houses, people were burning piles of rubbish and years of hoarded junk. It was the latest act of desperation. Ede had seen how the long absence of electricity had begun to generate new tensions. The twigs of the fire flared up and brightened the hungry faces of the children. Ede looked over the marshland with its high grasses and its solitary stunted tree. At the edge of the marshland there was a school building whose compound was also used as an abattoir. Ede watched the restless goats that were tied to the school wall. Then he saw that the fire had begun to burn the stunted tree. The animals fought against the ropes. The tree had no leaves and at night he had often seen roosters curled up, asleep, on the bare branches.

Ede passed the fire and the burning tree. The crowd watched the consummation in silence. There were solitary candle-lights at the house fronts, as if the city were keeping vigil. When he got to the main road, to catch a taxi, he saw the city's usual traffic jams. The cars were motionless. Ede waited for an empty taxi. And while he waited he chided himself. What was wrong with him? Who did he think he was? He was fully aware of how fortunate he had been to have met Maria in the first place. He was even more fortunate that she was also interested in him, when there were so many other musicians and men who out-dazzled him with their wealth, their success, their status. So why didn't he treat Maria a little better? Why had he begun to take her so much for granted? He smiled: he knew. It was the arrogance and the perversity that comes with small successes. He had recently brought out his first album, which was well received, and which was selling well. He had been interviewed on television and occasionally someone had recognized him in the streets. But more than all that, more than the small pleasures of bending her to his will, he had begun to feel possessed by a new energy, by the certainty that there are powers in the air, in the lungs of the transformant, which could clean the rust out of living, and tune up the spirit's unfettered will.

He waited for fifteen minutes, but the traffic jam didn't ease. He decided to walk all the way to Maria's place, to her bungalow sinking in the depths of the Munshin ghetto. And as he began to walk he had a vision of her face as it had been three weeks ago: pale and beaded with sweat along the nose. He found it curious that he was beginning to remember things about her face which he hadn't paid attention to at the time. He felt he had done her a great injustice and was overcome with the exaggerated anxiety that if he didn't hurry she might just start going out with the first considerate man that came along.

He passed a prophetess who uttered her visions in the dust-laden street. She carried a placard which read: 'THE WAGES OF VANITY IS DEATH.' Outside the hut of a sorcerer two men were in the grip of hallucinations. There was a white chicken, wildly flapping, in the hands of one of the men. The two men danced towards Ede, chattering and gnashing their teeth, their raving a kind of invasion. When Ede went past them they sang after him. He crossed the bus-stop and tried to avoid the beggars, who looked as if they had all the world's afflictions septic on their bodies. They were vengeful wraiths who clung to him, dragged at his hands, tugged at his shirt-sleeves, entreating for money. He gave them nothing. He pushed them away and they limped behind him, pleading. On the face of one of the beggar-girls he saw the face of Maria. He saw her as she was one day at the bus-stop when she dipped into the bus fray and emerged screaming, crushed on all sides by the violence of the struggle. She was going home after a visit to his place. He had watched her, amazed that the ferocities of ordinary city existence didn't squash her altogether.

There were cockchaffers in the evening light. The darkness had increased and the inhabitants of the city moved through veils of dust. He passed a crowd of people who stood staring at the road, as if a wondrous and terrible thing were about to happen. He passed children who played hopscotch, surrounded by gutters.

The cockchaffers, weaving in the air, formed clouds over the rubbish heaps along the road. And over the mighty rubbish mound of the market they made such shrill noises that Ede gritted his teeth.

Maria's face came to him again when he got to an intersection where the soldiers were in an electric frenzy. The noise of cars, of human voices, of music from record shops, was quite incredible. It was as if a nameless instrument, whose terrible music is fashioned out of the extremes of human chaos, were being strained to cracking point. The shops, which sold trinkets, bales of cloth, plastic basins, and all manner of artefacts, glittered in the dust of kerosene lamps and the pale orange of electric generators.

He remembered her face when he last made love to her on the settee. She always behaved as if there were something intrinsically wrong about love-making. She had to be endlessly coaxed and she had to be made to feel as if she were not responsible for the act, or for her own enjoyment of it. Strange girl, Ede thought. She always bit her lower lip when she was really enjoying herself. She bit it hard, half-tormented, half-ecstatic.

He came to the hut of a fortune-teller and an interpreter of dreams. He wanted to go in, but he was scared of the visions they might evoke, the requests for spiritual appeasement they might make, if he told them about his dreams.

Further on Ede was surprised to see Maria sleepwalking. He had seen her sleepwalking before, but seeing her in public, crossing the road, frightened him. She seemed completely unmindful of the roaring traffic. He crossed the road after her and he had to run because an articulated lorry shot past, ignoring the soldiers. He pursued her, touched her on the shoulders, and when she turned to face him he could have fainted. It wasn't her. It was a blind woman with milky eyes. Ede staggered away, confused, mumbling. Then he stopped to recover from the shock.

The electric frenzy of the soldiers reached him. They

directed the traffic with manic gestures. They stopped cars, flogged drivers, and thrashed motorcyclists on the back. While Ede stood in the midst of the cacophony he heard a tune so familiar that he held his breath. It was his album. He breathed more easily. He listened to his music, blaring out of a record shop, with a smile on his face. He anticipated a phrase, but it never came. The record was cracked and it seemed the record shop owner wasn't around. Hearing his record stuck in a groove annoyed him. He frowned and made an angry gesture. Then he noticed that one of the soldiers directing the traffic had been staring at him with an intense look in his eyes. It struck Ede that he had been absent-mindedly staring at the soldier. He started to move away, but the soldier left off directing the traffic and came over. His whip dangled behind him. When he spoke Ede thought he saw cockchaffers leaping from his mouth.

'Why are you making faces at me, eh?' the soldier asked.

Ede made incoherent noises.

'You don't like the way I do my job, eh?' continued the soldier, his whip dangling.

Ede didn't speak.

'What were you looking at?'

'Me? Nothing.'

'I am a corporal, you know.'

'I know,' Ede said.

'Are you trying to be clever?'

'No.'

'Follow me to the station!'

'Why?'

'I said FOLLOW ME!'

Ede had no real reason to be scared, but the corporal stared at him, sweating, his eyes red. His uniform stank faintly of urine.

'Why? What have I done?'

'Shut up!' the corporal shouted.

'Why?'

'I say SHUT UP!' the corporal said, spraying Ede's face with spittle.

Ede wiped away the saliva and backed off slowly. A

woman came out of a shed and poured a bucketful of slime-water on the road. Car horns clashed in the air. A group of traditional musicians, beating on little drums with their fingers, came towards them. They sang very sadly. When they went past them, Ede – who had often contemplated adapting traditional music for modern purposes – found a possibility for escape. Before he could act the corporal thrashed him on the back.

'STUPID RAT! WHO ARE YOU TO REPLY TO ME WHEN I TALK!' foamed the corporal, lifting the whip again.

Ede didn't wait for a second thrashing. He snatched the whip, pushed the corporal, and ran into the procession of musicians. The corporal slipped on the slimy water and fell. He clawed up some chicken intestines on the road, mistaking them for his whip, and gave chase.

The poor musicians sang of corrupt governments, of bad roads, and of electric failures, when the corporal lashed out at one of their faces with the chicken intestines. Ede, in his attempts to get away, narrowly missed falling into a manhole. He slipped across the road and hid beneath the flyover, where the tethered goats moved restlessly in the darkness.

He smelt urine. Human and animal urine.

The mallams and goatherds were asleep on their mats.

Cloaked in darkness, he watched the musicians shouting at the corporal, pushing him angrily. It was only after the corporal disappeared into the manhole that Ede realized he had witnessed a tiny nemesis. Laughing, he went out through the other side of the flyover. He crossed the road and pushed on. He held his head low, ready, as he passed through the invisible gateway and into the infernal ghetto of Munshin.

Ede found himself continually moving against the flowing crowds of people. Beggars streamed towards him. Groups of praise-singers, who make their living by flattering influential citizens, poured past him. 'I should write a song in praise of Maria,' he thought, as he remembered the first time he went to visit her at the office. Her desk was near the window and it was a hot day. The sun beat mercilessly on her, and yet she remained conscious of her beauty and the difference it made. She was the most challenging woman he had ever met.

She always eluded him somehow, as if she were enveloped in a haze, slightly beyond comprehension. It made him hungry to think of her.

He bought some sand-roasted nuts. Two articulated lorries thundered past. The fumes they left behind made him feel sick, unable to breathe; the clouds of dust in the air made him thirsty. He stopped off at a kiosk and bought a bottle of Fanta. The woman selling had a big fleshy face and a frame made massive by the quantity of wrappers she had round her. She talked a lot while he drank. She said the government deliberately created blackouts so that ordinary people would have to bribe officials at the board. He was a quarter-way through the Fanta when she added that it was really because the government despised its own people, that they wanted citizens to walk off into the wild roads, and to disappear into open drains and manholes. Halfway through the Fanta, she changed her entire theory. She said the electric failures existed because of the lucrative business in generators.

'Most of the military governors own the companies,' she said, laughing.

The immensity of her body shook with her laughter. A generous face, Ede thought. He laughed as well, infected by her good humour. But then, turning serious, she said:

'It's not a laughing matter.'

He still laughed.

'A child in the compound died because of this.'

He finished the Fanta and paid. She threw his change on the counter.

'I'm sorry to hear that, madam,' he said.

She scowled at him.

'Sorry for yourself.' Then, with an antagonistic expression on her face, she added:

'And who is your madam, eh?'

The kerosene lamp shone on her forehead. Still a generous face, Ede thought as he plunged on through the unending marketplace.

93

Two vultures circled in the sky. At first he was not sure. He passed the corpse of a grown man on a heap of rubbish beside the road. The body was half-covered with yam peelings and the rotting intestines of cows and goats. People stood around watching the corpse as if it would suddenly get up and do something extraordinary. Ede felt he had seen the dead man before. He wasn't sure. The corporal? It couldn't be. The flies were busy in the half-darkness. Ede pushed through the crowd, picked up a stick, and began to rake off the entrails on the dead man's body. The stench of the rubbish made him feel ill. He was about to pull the body off the heap when he noticed that the dead man's eyes were open. They stared at him. A lizard ran across the dead man's face and suddenly he moved. The crowds of people ran. They fled across the road and overturned stalls in their haste to escape. Ede staggered backwards, with the light of clarity coming and going like a loose connection in his head. The dead man stood up and, fixing Ede with a burning stare, said:

'First they shat on us. Now we shit on ourselves.'

Ede didn't know where to run. The dead man came slowly towards him, bringing an immense variety of smells. Ede moved backwards. The dead man stopped. Then he lifted his right hand up, with one finger pointing at the sky, like a demented preacher, and said, in a voice of monstrous power:

'REVOLT!'

At that moment Ede became aware that the heat was unbearable. The air didn't move. The crowds forced their ways on, pushing past Ede, till he was caught in the stream of confused movements that carried him away from the dead man and his sermon.

The midges came to him in the heat. The wind blew gently. He remembered Maria's depressions. He remembered how she looked when she returned from work, her face worn and crinkled with dust. He remembered when she fell into her curious obsession with death. She began to pore over the obituary notices, commenting on how many pages of the newspapers they took up. She kept drawing his attention to

94

the news stories of accidents on the roads, armed robberies, contract killings, ritual murders, military executions at the beach.

The midges flew into his nose and he had to blow hard into his handkerchief to get them out. He realized, for the first time, how hard it must have been for Maria all along. She used to cry because she could have got a particular job or promotion if only she had less respect for her body. As he approached the bottleneck of a crowd fighting to get through a narrow space ahead, he remembered how odd she became when the lights went. It disturbed him that he was never aware of the precise moment when she started to become afraid of the darkness. Things she had said started to come back to him. How she out-stared a snake in the backyard. How the soldiers would stop buses and commandeer a woman at the slightest whim. How one day, as she was daydreaming in the office, three male-spirits came in through the walls and, with their heads facing backwards, tried to force her to make love to them.

The world wants to eat up her beauty, he thought, as he got to the crowded narrow space. The trouble was caused by a woman's stall. It was the largest for miles around. It had chaotic displays of aluminium buckets, calendars, basins, statuettes, masks and lamps. For people to get past the tight space between stall and road there would have to be some kind of order. But the crowd jostled and struggled. Squashed on all sides, Ede decided that he had suffered enough for one day. He tried to turn and go back home, with the intention of seeing Maria another day, when he realized that going back was worse than going forward. A girl howled in the crowd. Ede fought his way through and emerged with his body drenched in sweat.

Passing a shop that sold imitation ancestral carvings, Ede remembered something strange Maria had said: that a man in the office had sworn to make her his woman, even if it meant using sorcery. Suddenly, as if the confusions of the city were making him hallucinate, he began to see Maria everywhere. He caught her face fleetingly on the faces of old women. He saw her in the eyes of women flashing by on the backs of motorcycles. He thought he saw her from behind, her head and shoulders disappearing into the marketplace.

He went down several crossroads, jumped over gutters to avoid the indifferent truck-pushers, and caught flies in his ears as he listened to the music from the numerous record shops. It occurred to him that when chaos is the god of an era, clamorous music is the deity's chief instrument. He didn't fully understand the thought, but it illuminated why he felt drawn to music that had clear, burning melodic lines like forces of nature. He remembered the last time he went to the beach with Maria.

'Even our seas have gone mad,' she said, referring to the items of sacrifice that had been washed up on the beach like rejected prayers.

'These are new times,' Ede remembered saying. 'We need new skins to cope. New songs.'

'We need new nervous systems,' she had added, laughing.

He heard her laughter through the window. As he hurried on to her room he found his anticipation not only intact, but multiplied by all the obstacles. A wondrous feeling kindled in him at the sound of her. He knocked. A man he had never seen before opened the door.

'Yes, who are you looking for?'

Ede peered into the room. A group of old men and women stood round the bed.

'Maria. Is she in?'

'Who are you?'

'Me?'

'Yes, you.'

The man who had opened the door was cross-eyed and his face was covered in a complicated net of wrinkles.

'My name is Ede . . . '

Then Maria, in a weak voice, called him in. Ede walked into a sorrowful atmosphere. He stood with the people gathered round the bed. Maria, her face paler than ever, was covered up to her neck with a white cloth. She had a red head-tie on. Her eyes were feverish. She looked unbearably lean, her features had narrowed, her eyes were larger. There were the smells of carbolic, incense, and animal sacrifice in the room. The old women kept touching her and mumbling prayers under their breath. The old men looked on with inexplicable sadness in their eyes. A beautiful little girl sat on the bed beside Maria. She had been crying. Maria's eyes kept shutting slowly and opening suddenly. When it looked as if she had fallen asleep the people gathered round her began to leave. The mother of the little girl had to carry her away because she didn't want to leave Maria. Ede could still hear the little girl crying outside. The seven candles fluttered in a corner of the room. Soon Ede was the only person left. He sat down on the bed. Maria opened her eyes wide and said:

'I have been thinking about you.'

Then she shut her eyes again.

'What's wrong?'

'Nothing.'

'What do you mean? Something's wrong.'

'I'm fine.'

There were several bottles of medicine on the table beside her bed. Around the room, as if a herbalist had visited, there were basins of herbal waters with barks and leaves floating in them. There were jujus on all four walls and there was another one on the awning above the door. He had never seen them in Maria's room before.

'I am ashamed and sorry about the way I behaved the last time I saw you.'

The kerosene lamp gave off black smoke. Grotesque shadows stalked the room. Mosquitoes whined. It was hot and stuffy, but Maria did not sweat.

'This mad city has been throwing obstacles in my path, delaying me from reaching you. It took me more than three hours to get here. But how are you, my sweet Maria?'

'I've been looking death in the face,' she said.

'What's been wrong?'

97

'No one knows. My uncle, the herbalist, thinks I was poisoned or bitten by a snake.'

'A snake? Come on!'

'I don't know. I've been feeling faint. I passed out for two days. I haven't been able to eat, to walk, or do anything. This is the first day I've been able to talk to anyone.'

'Take it easy,' he said, touching her forehead. He felt the boiling heat of her skin.

'They finally sacked me at the office,' she continued. 'I got the letter yesterday, a week after it had been sent. Where have you been all this time?'

'I have been very stupid. I deserve to be punished. I have missed you so much. I'm sorry.'

'Save your sorrow for yourself,' she said, her face brightening. 'I've been throwing up at least twice a day. My head feels like a wizard's drum. What can I do with your sorrow? I might have died while you stayed away.'

'Look, don't be too hard on me.'

'Why not?'

'You don't know how much I've suffered getting here today.'

'So what? I make that journey every day. Every single day. On my way back from work. You're not the only one who suffers, you know.'

Ede looked at her lean face, her shining eyes, and a sudden feeling made him start to cry. She did not hold him or console him. She watched him with bright, pitiless eyes. When he managed to pull himself together he asked:

'How are you feeling now?'

'Fine.'

'I mean really.'

'I'm really fine.'

She had addressed him like a stranger. There was no special affection in her voice. He stared at her. She stared at the ceiling.

'I dreamt that you had died,' he said.

She shivered.

'I haven't yet.'

'I took it to mean that you had stopped loving me.'

98

'You never know.'

'Have you?'

She shut her eyes. They were silent. Then she said:

'I dreamt that market-women stoned you to death.'

'Don't say such things.'

'And in the dream I had to die for both of us to come back to life.'

'You're frightening me.'

She looked at him as if she had never seen him before.

'Are you strong enough to walk?' he asked, changing the subject.

'Why?'

'It's hot in here. Let's go for some fresh air.'

'Have you got a basin?'

'What for?'

'To catch it in.'

'What?'

'Nothing.'

He watched her for a long moment. Then he drew closer to her. She smiled.

'So long as you don't mind getting what I've got.'

'Come on, Maria.'

He kissed her passionately. She did not respond. Her lips were warm. She shivered again and pushed him away.

'I thought I would never see you again.'

'Impossible.'

'It's only when you want something that I see you anyway.'

'You're wrong,' he said, feeling transparent and ashamed. 'Do you want something to drink?'

'No thanks.'

'I'm a bad host today.'

'Don't worry.'

'In one of my dreams a goat spoke to me with your voice.'

He looked at her, baffled.

'In another dream you sat in a dark room, singing. No one was listening to you except me.'

He sighed.

'Have you written any new songs?'

He wanted to tell her of the song he intended to write in praise of her, but he decided to keep it a secret.

'Yes. I'm writing a song about a burning tree,' he lied.

After he had said it he realized that it was a good idea.

'So what about a burning tree?'

'They burnt one near our house.'

'The city is burning.'

'You should have seen the tree.'

'You should have seen what I saw.'

'What?'

'It's nothing.'

He kissed her again.

'Let's go out,' he said.

'I can't go far.'

'Let's go for a short walk.'

While she considered it, he swept the covering off her. She was half-naked underneath. Her stomach had shrunken. His eyes were hungry.

'Do you want to eat up a sick woman?'

He kissed her stomach and smelt the warm herbal essences of her skin. She held his head to her full breasts. He kissed them and she moaned. Then she got out of bed and tied the white sheets round herself. Her bones creaked.

'I sound like an old woman,' she said, laughing.

She brushed her teeth, got dressed, and powdered her face. When she had finished she said:

'I am ready. If I fall you must catch me. I don't want to drown in a gutter.'

He put his arm supportively round her. They went out into the courtyard. In the street, she said:

'The air is bad.'

They passed huts and stalls. She began to talk feverishly, the words moving in and out of focus:

'One night, about three weeks ago, I went out to the toilet. I saw a man with three heads sitting outside the toilet door. I asked who he was and he spoke to me with your voice. I was scared. When he spoke all of his six eyes shone at me in the dark. Then I heard something hissing. I felt something touch my leg. I ran inside and knocked on people's doors

100

and came back out with a lamp and a knife. But the man had disappeared. I told people what I saw and we searched the compound and we found nothing. When I went to work the next day that man I told you about, who threatened me with sorcery, was sitting on my desk. He left, but whenever he saw me he smiled strangely. When I came back from work that day I fell ill. Just like that. I couldn't sleep unless there was light around. Why didn't you come and see me all this time?'

He had no excuse, except vanity. They walked on. She continued.

'And all this time I've been having strange dreams. Prophets run after me, singing. One-legged visionaries hallucinate around me. I saw strange tall women dressed in black pouring salt out of bags. They poured it out until they had made a white mound. Then they began to scoop the salt back into the bags. When they had done that they tipped it all out again. I saw dead bodies getting out of their graves and walking around the market places. They bought garri and kola nuts and stared at people. I was at the sea and you were a bird that was flying away. Are you?'

Half afraid, half embarrassed, Ede laughed. The Maria he thought he knew had transformed into something different, had entered into an incomprehensible mist. A curious energy emanated from her face. It was as if the illness had sharpened her spirit.

'I'm dying,' she said.

Ede held her hand.

'Nonsense. Don't talk like that.'

They walked in silence.

'Let's go back,' she said, after a while. 'I am not strong enough.'

They turned and started to go back.

'Why don't you sing for me?'

He did.

He had never sung for anyone in the streets before. He sang of the bicycle-repairer who had crazy dreams of riding on the sea. He sang of friends who died in the Civil War, of mad soldiers and hungry policemen, of children who grow leaner, of buildings in the city that were sinking into the earth. He sang of love, his love for Maria, her love for the world. He got carried away with his improvisations and sang loudly, outdoing the record shops and the bellowing hawkers. She touched him on the arm and said:

'It's alright.'

He sang on. Then she added:

'Or do you think you are Orpheus?'

He stopped singing.

Near the house they encountered Maria's uncle, the herbalist. He had a green feather in his hair and a red cloth round his waist. He had a handsome young boy, an acolyte, with him.

'Go in and rest for your next treatment,' he said sharply to Maria.

They went into the room. Maria got into bed and kept looking at Ede as if she wanted him to be daring. But when he touched her thighs she looked towards the door and said:

'In this heat even the mosquitoes are jealous.'

He lay quietly with her on the bed. He listened to her thinking aloud about getting a new job, living a new life. The heat made him drowsy. He slept for a while, his head on her chest. Her irregular breathing lifted his head and lowered it. Then suddenly she woke him up.

'A spirit entered the room just now. It's been staring at me.'

'Where?'

She pointed in the direction where the seven candles burned in the corner. He saw nothing. He sat up. One of the candles went out.

'Are you tired?' she asked.

'I love you,' he said.

'That's what politicians say to the people.'

'I'm going to stay with you tonight and forever. I will never leave you. And when you are better I would like you to be my wife.'

She giggled and then she fell silent.

'Did you hear me?'

She stayed silent. Then her lips began to quiver. Her limbs trembled. Her eyes opened wide and she stared fixedly ahead of her, at something quite specific but invisible.

'Are you alright?'

Her trembling grew worse. She clung on to him and dug her nails into his arms as she stared straight ahead. The bed began to vibrate. Tears rolled down her face. Ede, worried, shook her. She screamed so piercingly that Ede was momentarily deafened. When he recovered she had got out of bed and was running about the room, cowering against the wall, fighting out against an invisible thing that seemed to bear down on her.

Ede ran over to her, but she ran away from him, as if he had become her antagonist. He caught her, held her, and pinned her down on the floor. She kicked and scratched and fought at him. In an uncanny, guttural voice, she shouted:

'Leave me! Go away! Don't come back!'

She fought wildly and drew blood from his neck. Terrified, Ede called her uncle. When he entered the room she became still. Ede carried her to the bed. She looked pale, her eyes were shut, and she seemed asleep. Her uncle began a preparation of herbal treatment. After a while Maria opened her eyes and stared at Ede sadly.

'Go,' she said. 'I don't want you to see me like this.'

'No, I'm not leaving. I'm staying here tonight.'

'What about your mother? Won't she be worried about you?'

'Just rest,' he said, 'and don't worry about anything.'

There were knocks on the door.

'Go now!'

'No.'

'I will come and see you.'

'When?'

'When I can.'

The door opened and Maria's relatives came in. They brought with them an air of mourning. They came into the room and gave Ede rough looks, as if he were intruding, or as if he were in some way responsible for Maria's condition. When they came in he got up from the bed and stood feeling isolated, unwanted. Maria beckoned him. He went over and she said, in a whisper:

'What made you think I would wait for you, anyway?'

'I don't understand.'

'You treat me so badly.'

'Forgive me.'

'You better go before my relatives make you feel unwanted.'

He hovered over her, but she didn't say anything else. Her eyes had become lifeless. He wasn't sure if she had fallen asleep or passed into a coma. Then her lips moved. He leant over.

'I might be yours forever,' she said, weakly.

Then she fell still. He shook her.

'Don't!' her uncle said sternly.

Ede waited, but Maria didn't move.

'It's time for you to go,' her uncle added.

Without knowing what he was doing Ede got up, greeted everyone mechanically, and stumbled out into the courtyard. He passed the handsome young acolyte. As he drew away from Maria's place, confused, he thought he heard her voice ringing in laughter into the yellow dust of the night air.

She's a strange girl, he thought. He passed children playing at street corners. He took short cuts through the backs of houses and leapt over gutters of stagnant water. She really is a strange girl, he kept thinking as he wound his way back to the main road. A three-headed man outside the toilet? What did she smoke? He smiled as he remembered one morning when he had woken early and had heard a goat being slaughtered at the abattoir opposite their house. At the time he thought a woman was being murdered. He raised an alarm. The compound people had asked him the same question. What did you smoke?

As he came to the crowded marketplace he made out numerous heads floating above the blue haze of dust and darkness. People were still pouring back from their late jobs or visits. Hawkers called out their wares. He heard cries of 'Thief' in the depths of the market. The cries circled the air, shouts followed, then the cries died down. He passed a stall where a man with matted hair was preaching. People around warned one another to watch their pockets, that preachers were often allied with thieves.

Then suddenly a weight of sadness came over Ede. For a moment his eyes clouded and in the ethereal mist Maria came to him, luminous in a white dress. When his eyes cleared he felt different. He felt that something had fallen out of his life. Then he began to see Maria everywhere. She transformed into an owl that was flying away. She became a cat. She turned into a dog that followed him barking. He saw her dark eyes in the eyes of chickens and goats. Dogs looked at him mournfully. He got the curious feeling that she was watching him from all the eyes of the animals, old men, and children. Beautiful young girls stared at him as if they knew. As he pushed through a crowd he heard a voice far behind him call out:

'Ede! Ede!'

He tried to stop, but the crowd pushed him on. He didn't hear the voice again. Jostled and pushed, wherever he looked he saw, as if in a multiplying mirror, Maria disappearing and passing out of focus. Then he heard something being shouted, being echoed all around the marketplace in a cacophony of ecstatic voices:

'The lights have returned!'

The houses, the stalls with electric bulbs, the shops, all suddenly lit up. It was as if the city had woken from sleep. Ede joined in the cheering. He felt as if a burden had fallen from him. He felt freed from a mysterious pestilence.

At the bottleneck in front of the madam's shop the excitement about the lights turned into commotion. The crowd pushed and struggled, their faces defined in new energies. There was confusion everywhere; people seemed to be running in all directions. After a while Ede realized that the commotion was caused by the movement of cattle being driven towards the corral. He also soon realized that he was trapped between the moving hulks of cattle and the immovable wall of the crowd. Then he heard someone close by call out:

'Ede! Ede!'

He looked round and saw the handsome acolyte in the crowd, separated from him by the moving cattle. When Ede saw the boy, he knew.

'Maria . . .' the boy shouted, and made a hopeless gesture.

Ede stood confused. He turned and stumbled sideways. He tried to reach the acolyte but he found himself struggling against the grain of the crowd. Someone pushed him. He fell. The crowds, in their hysteria, swept over him. When he got up he felt as if his joints had been wrenched out of their sockets.

'Ede! Ede!' the boy called. 'Stay there. I am coming over.'

But Ede couldn't stand still. He staggered and tripped on the wares of the madam's stall. As he got up he saw Maria standing over him. Then she disappeared and in her place was a midget-girl, with an old body, a young face, and a weird growth of beard. The midget-girl pointed at him and shouted something. She began to jump up and down, pointing excitedly. A moment later Ede heard what she was shouting:

'Djrunk! Djrunk!'

As Ede got up the wares of the stall, the masks, the plates, the trinkets, seemed to cling to his hands.

'Djrunk! Thief!'

The last word went round, and grew in volume. The crowd turned on him. Ede tried to escape, but the market-women caught him and set upon him with sticks and stones. The blood flowed over his face and the lights of the world went out slowly in his eyes. The acolyte arrived too late.

Deep in the marketplace, amid all the cacophony, a woman sang in a voice of agonized sweetness. In Ede's street the electric bulbs swayed in the breeze. The dogs barked at the dust. The wind sighed over the rooftops. Neighbours were quiet, and couples had made up their quarrels. Ede's mother stayed up that night, listening to the frogs croaking all over the marshland.

GRAFFITI

JULIO CORTAZAR

SO MANY THINGS begin and perhaps end as a game, I
suppose that it amused you to find the sketch beside yours,
you attributed it to chance or a whim and only the second
time did you realize that it was intentional and then you
looked at it slowly, you even came back later to look at it
again, taking the usual precautions: the street at its most
solitary moment, no patrol wagon on neighbouring corners,
approaching with indifference and never looking at the graffiti face-on but from the other sidewalk or diagonally, feigning interest in the shop window alongside, going away
immediately.

Your own game had begun out of boredom, it wasn't really
a protest against the state of things in the city, the curfew, the
menacing prohibition against putting up posters or writing on
walls. It simply amused you to make sketches with coloured
chalk (you didn't like the term graffiti, so art critic-like) and
from time to time to come and look at them and even, with
a little luck, to be a spectator to the arrival of the municipal
truck and the useless insults of the workers as they erased the
sketches. It didn't matter to them that they weren't political
sketches, the prohibition covered everything, and if some
child had dared draw a house or a dog it would have been
erased in just the same way in the midst of curses and threats.
In the city people no longer knew too well which side fear
was really on; maybe that's why you overcame yours and
every so often picked the time and place just right for making
a sketch.

You never ran any risk because you knew how to choose well, and in the time that passed until the cleaning trucks arrived something opened up for you like a very clean space where there was almost room for hope. Looking at your sketch from a distance you could see people casting a glance at it as they passed, no one stopped, of course, but no one failed to look at the sketch, sometimes a quick abstract composition in two colours, the profile of a bird or two entwined figures. Just one time you wrote a phrase, in black chalk: *It hurts me too.* It didn't last two hours, and that time the police themselves made it disappear. Afterward you went on only making sketches.

When the other one appeared next to yours you were almost afraid, suddenly the danger had become double, someone like you had been moved to have some fun on the brink of imprisonment or something worse, and that someone, as if it were of no small importance, was a woman. You couldn't prove it yourself, but there was something different and better than the most obvious proofs: a trace, a predilection for warm colours, an aura. Probably since you walked alone you were imagining it out of compensation; you admired her, you were afraid for her, you hoped it was the only time, you almost gave yourself away when she drew a sketch alongside another one of yours, an urge to laugh, to stay right there as if the police were blind or idiots.

A different time began, at once stealthier, more beautiful and more threatening. Shirking your job you would go out at odd moments in hopes of surprising her. For your sketches you chose those streets that you could cover in a single quick passage; you came back at dawn, at dusk, at three o'clock in the morning. It was a time of unbearable contradiction, the deception of finding a new sketch of hers beside one of yours and the street empty, and that of not finding anything and feeling the street even more empty. One night you saw her first sketch all by itself; she'd done it in red and blue chalk on a garage door, taking advantage of the worm-eaten wood and the nail heads. It was more than ever she – the design, the colours – but you also felt that that sketch had meaning as an appeal or question, a way of calling you. You came back at dawn, after the patrols had thinned out in their mute sweep, and on the rest of the door you sketched a quick seascape with sails and breakwaters; if he didn't look at it closely a person might have said it was a play of random lines, but she would know how to look at it. That night you barely escaped a pair of policemen, in your apartment you drank glass after glass of gin and you talked to her, you told her everything that came into your mouth, like a different sketch made with sound, another harbour with sails, you pictured her as dark and silent, you chose lips and breasts for her, you loved her a little.

Almost immediately it occurred to you that she would be looking for an answer, that she would return to her sketch the way you were returning now-to yours, and even though the danger had become so much greater since the attacks at the market, you dared go up to the garage, walk around the block, drink endless beers at the café on the corner. It was absurd because she wouldn't stop after seeing your sketch, any one of the many women coming and going might be her. At dawn on the second day you chose a grey wall and sketched a white triangle surrounded by splotches like oak leaves; from the same café on the corner you could see the wall (they'd already cleaned off the garage door and a patrol, furious, kept coming back), at dusk you withdrew a little, but choosing different lookout points, moving from one place to another, making small purchases in the shops so as not to draw too much attention. It was already dark night when you heard the sirens and the spotlights swept your eyes. There was a confused crowding by the wall, you ran, in the face of all good sense, and all that helped you was the good luck to have a car turn the corner and put on its brakes when the driver saw the patrol wagon, its bulk protected you and you saw the struggle, black hair pulled by gloved hands, the kicks and the screams, the cut-off glimpse of blue slacks before they threw her into the wagon and took her away.

Much later (it was horrible trembling like that, it was horrible to think that it had happened because of your sketch on the grey wall) you mingled with other people and managed to see an outline in blue, the traces of that orange colour

110

that was like her name or her mouth, her there in that truncated sketch that the police had erased before taking her away, enough remained to understand that she had tried to answer your triangle with another figure, a circle or maybe a spiral, a form full and beautiful, something like a yes or an always or a now.

You knew it quite well, you'd had more than enough time to imagine the details of what was happening at the main barracks; in the city everything like that oozed out little by little, people were aware of the fate of prisoners, and if sometimes they got to see one or another of them again, they would have preferred not seeing them, just as the majority were lost in the silence that no one dared break. You knew it only too well, that night the gin wouldn't help you except to make you bite your hands with impotence, cry, crush the pieces of coloured chalk with your feet before submerging yourself in drunkenness.

Yes, but the days passed and you no longer knew how to live in any other way. You began to leave your work again to walk about the streets, to look fleetingly at the walls and the doors where you and she had sketched. Everything clean, everything clear; nothing, not even a flower sketched by the innocence of a schoolboy who steals a piece of chalk in class and can't resist the pleasure of using it. Nor could you resist, and a month later you got up at dawn and went back to the street with the garage. There were no patrols, the walls were perfectly clean; a cat looked at you cautiously from a door-way when you took out your chalk and in the same place, there where she had left her sketch, you filled the boards with a green shout, a red flame of recognition and love, you wrapped your sketch in an oval that was also your mouth and hers and hope. The footsteps at the corner threw you into a felt-footed run, to the refuge of a pile of empty boxes; a staggering drunk approached humming, he tried to kick the cat and fell face down at the foot of the sketch. You went away slowly, safe now, and with the first sun you slept as you hadn't slept for a long time.

That same morning you looked from a distance: they hadn't erased it yet. You went back at noon: almost inconceivably it was still there. The agitation in the suburbs (you'd heard the news reports) had taken the urban patrols away from their routine; at dusk you went back to see that a lot of people had been seeing it all through the day. You waited until three in the morning to go back, the street was empty and dark. From a distance you made out the other sketch, only you could have distinguished it, so small, above and to the left of yours. You went over with a feeling that was thirst and horror at the same time; you saw the orange oval and the violet splotches where a swollen face seemed to leap out, a hanging eye, a mouth smashed with fists. I know, I know, but what else could I have sketched for you? What message would have made any sense now? In some way I had to say farewell to you and at the same time ask you to continue. I had to leave you something before going back to my refuge where there was no mirror any more, only a hollow to hide in until the end in the most complete darkness, remembering so many things and sometimes, as I had imagined your life, imagining that you were making other sketches, that you were going out at night to make other sketches.

A TALE ABOUT FIRE AND KNOWLEDGE

PÉTER NÁDAS

ONE HOT SUMMER night Hungary was set on fire at all four corners by unknown persons for no apparent reason under unknown circumstances. All we know is that the fire started at Agfalva in the west, at Tiszabecs in the east, at Nógrádszakáll in the north, and at Kübekháza in the south. The stubble and the fields made dry by the drought were burning, and shortly after midnight the fire reached the first houses of the villages. Even the most gentle and innocent of breezes blowing across the borders at Agfalva from the west, at Tiszabecs from the east, at Nógrádszakáll from the north, and at Kübekháza from the south was driving the flames towards the interior of the country. Unaware of all this, Budapest was asleep.

Although it was announced as the seventh item in the morning news that comprehensive fire-drills were being held in the western, eastern, northern and southern counties, from this insignificant news item every Hungarian knew that the event was significant.

Although everybody knew that the news item meant something different from what it meant, everybody pretended not to know what it meant. For example, in the Hungarian language of the times, significant meant insignificant and insignificant meant significant, though these words had not completely lost their original meanings either, and therefore there could be no public agreement as to how to define them.

113

There was merely a tacit agreement to define what non-existent public agreement could not mean.

If the words, through some happy coincidence, might have lost their original meanings, they would have acquired new ones, which however was inconceivable without first making individual knowledge public, without a new public agreement. For this reason then, almost every word of their language meant something different from what it meant according to their individual knowledge or their common non-knowledge, and they had to try to work out the meanings of words sometimes on the basis of the speaker's position, and sometimes on the basis of the new sense relative to the original. And if a word had apparently lost its meaning, since it could not be understood either on the basis of its sense or the speaker's position, then this impossibility acquired a more profound meaning than if the word had actually meant something. Words with incomprehensible meanings in the language of the Hungarians referred to the deep human community, of which, otherwise, they were not allowed to think. In thinking about nothing, people thinking in other languages can inevitably think of something, whereas people thinking in Hungarian must overcome the apparently insuperable historical task of not thinking of anything when they think about nothing and of not thinking of something that might lead their thinking somewhere when they think about something.

Though this strange way of using language did not make their communication easier, the basic principle of their communication was not to make their individual knowledge public – and in this they had a great deal of practice. During the last century and a half of their history they had come to realize that it is only shared ignorance that can protect them from individual follies of any kind; so, if they do not share their individual knowledge, they cannot commit follies jointly either, follies which would breed in them hatred against each other or against others. This was the way they reasoned. And the logic of their reasoning, no matter how complicated it may appear to be, had not proved to be faulty in handling their individual or common fate, for they remained Hungarians by virtue of their sharing this logic which excludes the sharing of knowledge, and, therefore, from the point of view of their survival not only had their logic not been useless but, on the contrary, it had become the only and exclusive precondition for it. However, what is a useful implement in a gale should not necessarily be useful in a fire as well.

If a ship is into a storm, the sails are usually taken in; however, the wind may create such conditions in which the proper thing to do is to let out all the sails. If, on the other hand, fire breaks out on board, in battling with the all-consuming flames, it makes little difference whether the sails are taken in or let out.

Thus the logic of their behaviour, thinking, and use of language possessed a feature which can be deemed neither mistaken nor faulty and which it is perhaps more accurate to perceive as a failing that is inherent to each ambiguous thing. Insofar as the basic principle of their communication with each other had become the idea of not making their individual knowledge public – since it was this obsessive insistence on a tacit agreement through which they have been able to preserve their national unity – it had to follow, as regards the individual, that each Hungarian assumes that every other Hungarian knows what he does and knows it equally well, though they are not in a position to determine what they do and do not know. However, since they can rely only on constant, mutual assumptions, assumptions that enable them to search for the meanings of words by ignoring their meanings, all they can jointly know is that they all have to rely on assuming things of which either they do not know individually or cannot know individually what it is they do not know jointly.

In this rather delicate situation the inhabitants of the country nevertheless remained unified in that no one tried to put out the fire. By their lack of action, which obviously concerned the fire, they preserved their unity in such a way that they were all thinking about the meaning of fire – and who would not consider thinking a form of action? Of course, there was disagreement as regards the meaning of fire, but there was no need to exchange opinions about it, if for no other reason than that everyone justifiably assumed that the others knew just as well as he did that it does not mean what it means. And if fire does not mean fire, then either it is superfluous to worry about it, or it can only be a fire which is not burning, or the really burning question is whether fire means water. Those who approached the issue from the aspect of the sense of the word had inevitably to think of water, and those who approached it from the aspect of the speaker's position were unable to reach such a conclusion. While the former thought in reality a major flood was threatening the country, the latter thought instead of trying to raise fake fires. For if there can be fires which do not burn things, then likewise we can have fake fires which do burn things, and this is no less dangerous than the fire which really means flood.

By the afternoon this collective non-knowledge of the individual knowledge of serious danger had produced an atmosphere of tension, which in other languages even today is referred to as the tension of responsibility felt for the fate of one's nation. But not for the Hungarians of that time. For no matter what they thought individually, there was no one who could not smell the pungent smell of smoke. But in case they talked about it at all, they were jointly of the opinion that a big storm was about to break out because the skies were black, although they knew individually that neither a flood nor a fake fire emits smoke, and that for the same reason neither can give rise to a storm. But then there was more about the events on the evening news.

In order to gain a more precise understanding of the events, we should also say more about those respectable women and honourable men for whom the public announcement of the news which serves the common good had not simply been a profession but also a style of life, making demands on their bodies and souls alike. For in those years Hungarians had become uniform in their thinking, behaviour and consequently their physical appearance to such a degree that it was almost impossible for them to distinguish themselves from others. For example, one characteristic they possessed was that they were born as adults, and since there was nothing to grow up to, they remained children. There was no need for schools any more. As an adult, anyone could lecture anyone about anything, for there was no one who did not remain a child, but on the other hand as a child anyone could learn from anything, for there was no one who could have become an adult. And if it happened that there was no one around to lecture, then one could lecture himself, for it had become a common and inalienable trait of all Hungarians that as children they were no longer aware of what they knew as adults. In this domain of equality, however, there were self-sacrificing individuals who, in the interest of perfect and complete equality, had to remain more equal than others.

We should brand as malicious and misleading all those irresponsible assumptions that it was the women and men governing the country who could be identified as these more equal individuals. At the present state of scientific research, we do not have any evidence to show that the women and men governing the country had ever shared their individual knowledge with anyone. This they did not do either among themselves or with others and, as a consequence, there was merely a formal distinction between those Hungarians who were well-acquainted with public affairs and those who were not. While the Hungarians who were not familiar with the public affairs of the country obstinately insisted – precisely because of this unfamiliarity – upon the tacit agreement undertaken in their own individual interest that they could not make their own individual knowledge public under any circumstances, those familiar with the public affairs of the country obstinately insisted – precisely because of their familiarity with public affairs – upon the tacit agreement undertaken in the public interest that it was only the common non-knowledge of things that could ensure the individual knowledge of which one could be aware. While the former pretended not to have individual knowledge of things – merely common non-knowledge of them – the latter pretended that their common non-knowledge was their individual knowledge. And this was reasonable indeed. For how could those unfamiliar through no fault of their own with

117

public affairs make their individual knowledge a part of public thinking, and how could those familiar through no fault of their own with public affairs not make common non-knowledge the essence of individual thinking. Hence, in this respect we can certainly regard the situation as one in which those who governed and those who were governed were essentially equal. Those who governed could not restrict those who were governed in their freedom of individual knowledge, but neither could those who were governed restrict those who governed in their freedom of common non-knowledge. In the Hungary of those times, anyone could do what he did not know, and everyone could publicly think of this what they did not think. And if the Hungarians had not plunged their country into the chaos of final destruction with their noble and appealing ignorance, this was only because there were among them individuals more equal than themselves. These individuals were none other than the news announcers.

Hungarian announcers were the spitting image of other Hungarians and yet when they began to speak they differed from them in every way. They resembled every other Hungarian in that they were also the happy combination of child and adult, but whereas the ordinary Hungarian could at best lecture some Hungarians about the state of the world, the announcers were in a position to lecture each and every Hungarian except themselves about this. Their self-instruction could not have been effective in any case because they differed from the rest of the Hungarians in that, while the other Hungarians could interpret the news to their own liking, the announcers had to pretend against their liking that they did not understand a word of what they said to the others. They were spirited in teaching, dispirited in learning. For if they were individuals who could not understand a word of what they said – since they were not individuals – then they could be the best, indeed the shining examples of the common non-knowledge which was shared by all Hungarians. And if one can represent something which is shared by all, doesn't this provide more than enough grounds for being spirited individually as well?

118

As regards teaching no one could be more adult than they were, since they lectured everyone, but no one could be more childish than they were either, since they could not learn even from their own words. For had they pretended to understand what they said, everyone would have thought they were fools, since they presumed to understand something that was in reality unintelligible. So they could not do this. But then this is a good enough reason for anyone to be dispirited.

But their unique popularity could not be called into question for still other reasons. In those times, Hungarians made use of a mere three words in their speech, words which derived from the domain of basic life functions but which had lost their original meaning. One word denoted action, the second the object of action, and the third word was used as a substitute for all possible adjectives and adverbs. Not only would we commit an act of indecency but we would also overburden the present scholarly paper if we said more about these words here. However, there is a circumstance that we cannot leave unmentioned. It is that the announcers as individuals also used the same three words for the purposes of everyday speech, though as soon as they appeared in public they began to use a language no one spoke. And this was regarded as a multiply ambiguous circumstance by all Hungarians. Above all, it meant that there existed a common language which did not exist and, on the other hand, it reminded them that something like this not only had been in existence but, in addition, can be brought into existence if public agreement can be arrived at through some lucky coincidence.

On that hot summer night, when the larger part of the country was already in flames, an especially popular female announcer was reading the news, a woman whose voice had a sweetly maternal quality. It is no exaggeration to say that she was the most equal even among the more equal among equals. Throughout the past century and a half in the history of the Hungarians there was no buoyantly joyful or mournfully stormy event of which it was not her who informed them, and thus the grateful inhabitants of the country could not help but enthrone her in their hearts. Her exceptional popularity was due to an exceptional personality trait of hers for which others longed ardently but in vain, and which they could only imitate at most. For her personality was split not into two, as was the case with all the rest or ordinary Hungarians, but into three by schizophrenia, and she was not only capable of reading a text of which she apparently did not understand a word with the deepest conviction and utmost empathy, but through her emphases she in part indicated to the others how they should interpret the unintelligible words from the viewpoint of common non-knowledge, and she in part indicated from the viewpoint of their individual knowledge what it is that they should not understand those things to mean, things that do not really make sense anyway. This woman was an oracle and a fount of knowledge.

I have to begin with a dramatic announcement, she said in her cloudless voice, addressing those who could still hear her, and as her face lit up with the irresistible charm of her ripe womanhood, her words stuck in her throat as though she said one of those ordinary words she was wont to use. She knew very well that her countrymen understood unspoken words even better because they understand not only what a word does not mean but also what it means relative to a situation. And then, from the viewpoint of individual knowledge, in anticipation of the words referring to common non-knowledge-words that were about to leave her fine lips glittering with irony, her eyes began to blaze. Though there are all sorts of rumours, she said, according to which the country is burning, it can be stated with certainty, on the basis of information from the most reliable sources, that everything is quiet and life is going on as normal nationwide. No one had allowed themselves to be misled. People are frying their fish for dinner at the small street-stands, the little bear in the evening TV cartoon for children is brushing his teeth as usual, and the machine-heart of the discos will also start beating soon. She made these announcements in a voice filled with gentleness and with eyes dimmed by real tears. Those who do not believe it, she said, bridling up her head with death-defying courage, can take a look around. She did not risk too much. In the Hungarian language of the times, a request meant a statement, of course, so not even those Hungarians who were still in a position to look around actually did look around. The beautiful woman did not say anything about the alleged fire-drills in the remainder of the announcement, and neither did she explain the spreading of the rumours with the usual hysteria-provoking propaganda campaign of the enemy news media, but as the possible source of the news she referred, accompanying what she said with a belittling smile for all credulous minds, to a circumstance that in the past few days during the normal annual inventory certain maps had indeed been set on fire at their four corners in the National Cartographical Institute.

At this point, however, she made an irredeemable mistake. The sheet of paper in front of her read that the long invalid maps of the country had been set on fire, but instead she said that the long invalid country's maps had been set on fire. And this really almost meant what it did.

Forks stopped in midair and so did the knives in the hands of the Hungarians who were still alive. In their gaping mouths the parsleyed boiled potatoes, the pickled cucumber, and the roasted parson's nose remained unchewed. Every single person gaped into space, every single person was silent. And this had created a silence that, regardless of how anyone had looked at the situation previously, no one could help not noticing. No word is more powerful than collective silence. Every Hungarian had to notice it at the same time, and through this happy coincidence their knowledge about silence also became common. The windows were open.

Everyone could hear his own silence, which did not differ in any way from that of the person next door. Silence does not disturb silence. And since everyone had more than one neighbour, it was only inevitable that the neighbours felt within themselves the same silence that they felt in others. The silence of one Hungarian became the silence of another. The silence became so widespread that there was no saying which silence belonged to whom, though everyone, invariably, belonged to himself.

Deep down in their common silence they could all hear

the sound of the blaze. Only sound disturbs silence. But no one spoke. For from that time on, luckily for all of us, what anyone knew was in no way different from what the others could also think.

As long as there is water in the wells.

Translated by Zoltán Kövecses

THE OTHER BOHEMIA

MICHAEL BRACEWELL

ONE EVENING, NOT so very long ago, three young men from England were dining at a restaurant in Rome. They were feeling very pleased with themselves: firstly, because the dinner was so good, and there was plenty of it; secondly, because they knew themselves to be young, and rich, and clever (a constellation of blessings which seldom fails to induce a sense of well-being); and thirdly (quite simply) because they were in Rome, and Rome (in their opinion) was the home of all Art, and all Civilization, and consequently well-suited (as a rendezvous) to their high opinion of themselves.

They were discussing the futility of Life.

'In the Arts,' (said Hugo, an Urban Anthropologist whose little pamphlet on 'Decay as Metaphor: Towards A New Perspective' had created quite a stir) 'there is nothing left to achieve. Computerate brokerage, with all its limitless power to redefine a culture according to the skill and ingenuity of its operatives, now far exceeds (as a means by which we describe ourselves) the dismal efforts of painters and sculptors and all their little ideas. We ought, by rights, to call a halt to Art, and concentrate upon Economics, for there is great wisdom to be found there.' His two friends (prompted by loyalty and the arrival of the fish course) nodded sadly in agreement.

'You're quite right' replied William, who was a Cultural Theorist, and whose newspaper column ('No Prisoners') was syndicated across three continents. 'But perhaps you are miss-

123

ing a vital point: we can still copy the Great Artists; indeed, we can improve – with our technology – upon their ideas. Think of the Plaza Centre in Nottingham. Is it not . . . ' (and here he gesticulated towards the Pantheon, which was visible from their table) ' . . . much better, as a building, than the original structure upon which it is based?' The three young men all glared at the Pantheon for a moment, and then William continued: 'But I agree with your fundamental point: all artistic invention, carried out in our culture, is quite nugatory; we would do better to concentrate upon developing, cerebrally, the infinite power of Science.' The young men were then silent for a while, and all around they could hear the sounds of an evening in Rome: traffic roared in the distance as the drivers raced one another up and down the main streets; a fountain splashed nearby; groups of young people met one another with shouted greetings; a young man started to sing a facetious song to his girlfriend.

Finally, as cheese and fruit were brought to the table, Charles (the third of the young Englishmen, and a man who had brought the sensitivity of conceptual sculpture to the medium of Soap Opera) cleared his throat to speak: 'As for me, I regret the absence of Love. I look everywhere for Love . . . ' (and here his voice trembled a little) ' . . . but all I see are worn-out passions and the formulae of the seducer. We may pretend that we have hearts, and great desires, but all we really possess are replications of Love from a vast amorous mythology. We have learned our lines – that is all – and our ability to love is based entirely upon our individual talents as actors. It is very sad.'

The evening was so beautiful, and the square in which the young men were dining was so magnificent, and so crowded with glorious statues, and so filled with vibrancy and romance, that fairly soon they all felt quite dizzy with the sense of how right they were to see no meaning in Life. The busy waiter (who was quite beside himself with worry as he tried to serve eight tables simultaneously) brought the young men their coffee and fine brandy.

'Perhaps,' said William, 'we ought to go on a further journey together, and visit some country where we can really feel the Soul – as opposed to the past achievements – of Art. Perhaps, then, we would stop feeling so sad. I suggest . . . ' (and here he raised his glass) ' . . . that we travel to Bohemia, in the North, for there we shall find the Spirit of Art – not simply some museum of old relics which, although beautiful, merely inspire regret.'

'I find your suggestion tasteless,' replied Hugo. 'We all know that Bohemia, in the sense which you refer to it, is now nothing more than a part of Czechoslovakia, and to suggest that we will find any happiness *there* is both wrong and offensive. Besides,' (he added), 'we would look like tourists.'

'But that's where you're wrong,' said William. 'There is another Bohemia – I have the details back at the hotel – and it is a place where no advanced, North European intellectual has set foot for many hundreds of years. It is a wonderful place, quite untouched by the polluting energy of sophistication and computers, and it is – I assure you – the very cradle of all Passion, and all Art. It is like Sixteenth Century Venice, or Versailles during the reign of the Sun King; really – it's super.'

'Is there Love there?' asked Charles, sadly.

'It is the true birthplace of Love!'

And so, when they had finished their meal, the three young Englishmen returned to their hotel on the Via Veneto, and stayed up until dawn making plans for their journey.

From the airport, at least, there was little to be seen of Bohemia which looked particularly interesting. The sky was white and the air was tepid. A faint smell of cooked vegetables seemed to carry on the listless breeze.

'Don't worry,' said William, enthusiastically. 'They always build national airports on the outskirts of the dullest suburbs; think of Heathrow, or de Gaulle, or, indeed, of the Fiumicino and Ciampino airports at Rome; everything will be alright once we get to the city.' And so they set off, walking three abreast, through the terminal buildings (which were, thought

125

Hugo, amongst the most uninspired of Communications and Transfer structures he had ever seen) in search of a taxi.

The taxi rank was, frankly, a disgrace. Four battered saloon cars, each unwashed, and each attended by a dozing driver, stood in a shabby row to one side of a closed kiosk. There was no one to ask and nowhere to sit down. William marched up to the first taxi and rapped on the window. 'Excuse me,' (and here it should be pointed out that all three of the young men were fluent in most modern languages, to say nothing of the various sub-dialects of same) 'I was wondering if you could take us to the city? We have some luggage as well.' The driver looked up, and then he gave a heavy sigh.

'To the city?' His tone was one of long-sufferance.

'Anyone would have thought,' whispered Charles to William, as the driver, with many grumbles and pauses for thought, loaded their bags into the car, 'that we had asked him to take us to the moon. There appear to be no other customers, I see no evidence of his having a private income, and I would have thought, therefore, that he would have been grateful for our fares.' William agreed. Once inside the taxi there was another long wait whilst the driver struggled first with the handbrake and then with the gears. Having rushed forward two metres the car then stopped, gave a rasping cough of exhaust, and finally shuddered into silence once more.

'Problem?' enquired William, brightly. The driver shrugged, removed the keys from the ignition, and then, very slowly, got out of the car again.

'It's never really worked properly,' he said, 'I suppose that I could have got it mended, but . . .' (and he scratched the side of his nose as he searched for the correct phrase) '. . . to be honest I couldn't really be bothered. I'll tell you what: you unload your bags and I'll get one of the other drivers to take you into town.' And he went to wake up the driver in the next taxi.

Finally on their way, William attempted conversation with the new driver.

'Your colleague seemed rather down in the dumps. Is he

always like that?' Now it was the turn of the new driver to shrug. 'Well,' he said, 'some days he is, and some days he isn't. It depends.'

'Depends on what?'

'Oh. You know – this and that.' Quite exhausted, or so it seemed, by the effort of this statement, the driver lapsed into silence once more. Meanwhile, the three young travellers studied the country around them. The taxi was moving very slowly, and so this was quite easy to do. Having passed through mile upon mile of flat, brown fields, the road was now running in a straight line between rows of bungalows. They were quite nice bungalows, such as one might see on the south coast of England, but other than that there was nothing to be said of them. Neat little gardens (each containing a few tulips, and a small, ornamental pond) stood before each of the houses, and here and there, dressed in dull but presentable clothes, pedestrians with shopping bags were making their way home.

'This must be the new part of town?' enquired Hugo, hopefully.

'It's newer than some of the other bits I suppose,' replied the taxi driver, slowing down to allow a group of sturdy and disconsolate school children to cross the road.

'I hope that you'll forgive me for asking,' said William, 'but how would you describe the state of your national economy? Have you, for instance, enough to eat? Are there frequent power cuts, or breakdowns in the television broadcasts?'

'No. I don't think so. We're perfectly well provided for in those departments.' Charles took up the questioning: 'Are you under police surveillance? Do you have a free press? Is there evidence of martial law or an infringement of Human Rights?'

'Not that I've heard of,' (the taxi was now rumbling down a broad, cobbled boulevard which was lined with large, but essentially plain, mansion blocks). 'In fact,' (and here the driver glanced out of the window with a complacent lifting of the shoulders) 'I think that everyone's pretty well off – on balance, all things taken into consideration . . . '

127

'So why,' demanded Hugo, his exasperation finally getting the better of him, 'does everything, and everyone, look so, well, fed up?'

'Oh, I don't know,' said the taxi driver, and dropped the three friends outside a tall, modern building which had the word 'Hotel' written in lights above its porch.

The hotel was as dull as the taxi ride. Its brown corridors were lined with orange carpets, the lift seemed to take an eternity to arrive, and in the third-floor ice-making machine (so Hugo noticed) there was a cobweb and a discarded bow-tie. Once inside their separate rooms, the three young men all started talking to themselves: 'I don't know,' muttered Hugo, 'A real waste of time and money *this* little trip is turning out to be. I've never seen such a tedious country. And after all that talk in Rome about "The Soul of Art" and "The Birthplace of Love". It's enough to make you weep . . .'

In the room next door, as he struggled with the tea-making facilities, William was feeling guilty. 'I really don't understand it,' he said to himself, 'My research was, I'm certain, quite accurate, and yet Bohemia makes Croydon look thriving and cosmopolitan. There is no evidence of oppression, or injustice, and yet the people here are most definitely monotonous and downcast. What on earth must Hugo and Charles be thinking? I'd better wait for a little while before I discuss the situation with them.' And thinking along these lines he went to stare out of the window. On the street below an endless stream of casually dressed and mournful pedestrians were mooching up and down.

Charles, by the time that William and Hugo called for him, was, quite literally, sobbing with boredom. 'I just don't think that I can stand it,' he howled. 'There are precisely two television channels: "Hobbies" and "News"; my mini-bar contains tomato juice, tomato juice and a pale yellow beer; the soap in the bathroom is neither coloured, nor shaped, nor scented. A little while ago a woman rang me up and asked, in the flattest, most unappealing way, whether or not I'd like her to "show me a good time". When I replied that I thought prostitution was both wrong and offensive, she said that she supposed I was quite right really, and that it

128

didn't honestly matter much anyway, she was just asking . . .'

'We must get to the bottom of this,' said William. 'Either Bohemia is very different to what we might imagine, or something, here, is seriously wrong.'

And so they set off to explore.

It was a depressed trio who sat down to their boiled beef and mashed turnip in the hotel dining room that night. A slow, tuneless little melody was playing from concealed speakers. A xylophone stood unattended in one corner. The wooden chairs were upholstered in a dreary brown fabric which nearly made Charles cry again. When the waitress uncorked the wine there was no encouraging 'pop', and the contents of the bottle seemed to pour forth in a manner which was both sluggish and bad tempered.

The dining room, however, was full. Quiet couples and sober family groups were eating their meals in a steady, dismal sort of way, and the conversation which hovered above the tables was never broken by either loud voices or laughter. On the walls there were large pictures of flowers, and in the little alcoves pink candles gave off a feeble light.

'This is the most boring country I've ever visited,' said Hugo, finally.

'We've been all around the town,' continued Charles, 'and we couldn't find any art at all – not even a Folk Museum.'

'I vote that we try and find someone in authority,' said William, who had already made some notes in his room for a new pamphlet which he intended to call: 'Bohemia? Towards a New Perspective.' He was particularly proud of the question mark.

At that moment, a silver-haired gentleman, dressed in a smart dinner suit, and wearing a decoration in his buttonhole, came up to the young men and bowed gravely. Fearing, perhaps, that he had been mistaken for a waiter, he then introduced himself in the most courteous manner imaginable:

'I hope,' he began, 'that you will forgive my intruding upon your private dinner, but I could not help but overhear your conversation just now. I have the honour to be the First

Minister of Bohemia, and perhaps, if you will permit me to place my limousine and my services at your disposal, I shall be able to go some way to answering your questions about my country. It is many, many years since we have received any visitors from England, and I would hate you to leave Bohemia without having heard some explanation for the dullness which surrounds you. If you would care to meet me outside the hotel when you have finished your meal, I shall be most happy to guide you personally around our city, and to offer some information which might be of interest to you.' This offer was eagerly accepted.

A little while later, just as a luke-warm shower was beginning to blow across the empty streets, the three friends met the First Minister beside his limousine. The chauffeur, needless to say, was gazing ahead of himself with such glazed and unblinking eyes that at first the travellers thought that he had died. This was not, however, the case. Prompted by a sharp command from his employer, the driver opened the car door and the three friends got in with the First Minister. Soon they were driving down the dark and dismal streets.

'As you can see,' began their guide, 'there is little, here, to catch the eye or remind the tourist of Bohemia's glorious past. Our city functions well – as does our country as a whole – but all in all it is a drab and gloomy place. The citizens, too,' (and here he pointed to a small group of men who were sitting in attitudes of immense boredom outside a forlorn-looking café) 'are dispirited and colourless. It has been this way for as long as anyone can remember. Generation after generation have grown up in Bohemia, envied by the outside world as the inheritors of a unique and passionate culture, but in reality, as I'm sure that your studies here have revealed, there is not one spark of wit or enthusiasm from one end of the country to the other.'

'But why?' asked William, 'Can you not oblige us with a rational explanation for this lack-lustre attitude? Are there no examples of your great Art and Love of Life to be seen anywhere? What can you possibly mean?'

The First Minister gave a deep sigh. 'Hundreds of years ago,' he said, as the car crawled passed an Electricity Show-

130

room, 'Bohemia was the home of all the Arts. It was as though, in some strange way which was the wonder of the Northern Hemisphere, our country had been granted far, far more than its fair share of Artists and Lovers and Poets. Our national sensibility was almost too acute; we could not produce the most mundane object, or utter the dullest platitude, without our creating something quite special, and wholly precious. The most tedious of laws turned to poetry when dictated by our Statesmen, and as for the Music and the Painting – well! we scarcely knew what to do with it all. Our tremendous culture, needless to say, became both envied and legendary. In fact, by the time that your country was entering into its Industrial Revolution, a great deal of our National Treasure (and, I might add, National Pride) had already been plundered or copied into illegibility.'

'Inter-cultural exploitation,' muttered Hugo, nodding wisely, 'the ultimate destruction of the original signifier – terrible.'

'Quite so,' said the First Minister, 'As you say, terrible. Anyway, by the end of the Eighteenth Century, Bohemia was little more than the root of an adjective–'

'"Bohemian",' said the three friends in unison.

'– and the country itself was a cultural desert, worn out by the endless need to supply the rest of the world with artistic concepts. Indeed, as can happen to individual artists, Bohemia had become . . . ' (and here his voice sank to a fearful whisper) ' . . . *self-conscious* . . . ' The three friends gasped in horror.

By now the limousine had passed through the part of the city which the travellers had already seen, and was entering a strange new neighbourhood. Here the buildings were ancient, and imposing. Vast pediments spanned rows of Corinthian columns, curious onion-shaped domes gleamed beneath the moon, and here and there, just visible by the light of flaring torches, exquisite tiled façades, lined with tall Moorish windows, could be seen stretching off into the distance. As the limousine was drawing to a halt beside a huge marble piazza, the First Minister continued his story: 'After a little while, the people of Bohemia were gripped by

131

The Great Boredom; nowhere, not even Holland, had ever experienced such tedium. It was like slow death. In 1916, when the rest of the world was ensnared in a terrible war, advancing Prussian troops found Bohemia too dreary to occupy. In the 1940s, when no Bohemian newspaper had reported a Human Interest story for as long as anyone could remember, rumours that a woman in a distant Bohemian province had blushed sent reporters from all over the country hurrying to her house, so rare was such an emotion. It transpired, unfortunately, that the woman in question had merely stood too close to her stove whilst boiling dishcloths. And now I will ask you to follow me, but please, I beg you, in the name of tact and decency, no photographs.' And the little party got out of the car and gazed upon Old Bohemia.

For a long while the friends were speechless. Never had they seen such magnificence. 'It is as though,' said Charles, dreamily, 'the Byzantine had wed the Rococo . . . '

'Yes, yes!' sniffed the First Minister, quite overcome himself, 'But, please, follow me.' He led his guests down a broad, perfectly carved flight of stairs, and then, before they had even had time to gasp at the towering Classical and Allegorical statues, ushered them towards a pair of huge bronze doors. 'Fifteenth Century,' he snifled, fumbling with some keys, 'nothing to rival the workmanship in the whole of Europe or Asia . . . ' Hugo ran his finger along the carved beard of a bronze lion. 'Such vigour,' he murmured, 'such delicacy, and yet – such strength . . . '

By now the three friends were quite incapable of giving voice to their admiration for all that they saw. Following the First Minister into the enormous building, and hearing the vast bronze doors boom shut behind them, all that they could do was adjust their eyes to the light (the place was lit by a long row of elegant candelabra, each arm of which was a sonnet in silver) and prepare themselves for even further splendours. The hall in which they were standing (so William guessed) was at least the size of St. Peter's. But what was its function? It was not, most definitely, a Church, but on the other hand it appeared to have a Sacred air. The central aisle which stretched out before them (and oh, the glory of the encaustic tiling: gold, and white, and blue, with crimson and indigo motifs) was lined with statues of ancient Kings and Queens, their noble faces caught in the glow of the candles, and their regal brows imperious and stern. The heavy smell of incense pervaded, but there was neither a choir nor an altar.

'What, exactly, is this place?' gasped Charles, resorting to Rationalism.

'It is the Treasure House,' replied the First Minister, 'But, oh alas! It no longer contains any treasure; just a few old statues and gold plate. The spirit of the place – the Spirit of Bohemia – was taken away long ago . . . ' And here the poor man broke down in floods of tears. The three friends, quite aghast at the succession of incidents which had befallen them, were, for a moment, uncertain how best to proceed. After a little while, however, William spoke for the group. 'See here,' he said, 'Not only are we Englishmen, we are also Cultural Theorists, and if you will stop crying,' (here he offered the First Minister a large white handkerchief) 'and tell us what to do, we will do our level best to restore Bohemia to rights. We ask for nothing in return, and we will respect your wishes in every respect should you desire to remain nationally segregated from the Northern Alliance. No one, not even our Editors, will be told of this adventure – on that you have our word!'

'Oh, thank you! Thank you!' said the First Minister, 'If you will just allow me to recover myself . . . ' He blew his nose noisily, and for some minutes (or so it seemed) the echoes of his exertion raced up and down the long, shadowy hall. Once the last sniff had died away, the First Minister (recomposed, and assuming once more his role of guide and historian) continued: 'Long, long ago, before even this place was built, the Ancient Kings of Bohemia brought with them to this country three Sacred Gifts. These gifts were, I suppose, in the language of modern essayists, little more than primal symbols, but whatever their scientific validity they seemed to exert a certain power over the Kingdom. Indeed, for many centuries the people of Bohemia believed that the great Art and Spirit of our country was derived from them.'

'But what were these gifts – I mean, these primal symbols?' asked Hugo.

'I shall show you where they were kept,' replied the First Minister, 'and you shall be the first strangers to be granted this great honour.' Picking a candle from the nearest candelabra, the First Minister began to make his way down the dark side aisle of the Treasure House. Enormous shadows appeared to leap before him, and every now and then, in the passing light, a massive frieze or a towering sculpted figure would suddenly become visible. The smell of incense was by now quite overwhelming. The three friends almost tiptoed behind their guide.

Soon they were faced by a broad curtain of ancient brocade. Delicate embroidery, in silver thread, gleamed in the candlelight.

'There!' said the First Minister, and drew back the curtain with a flourish. Peering into the darkness, and almost falling over one another in their excitement, the travellers soon discerned three vessels of curious shape. These looked rather like urns. They were made of the finest china, and their proportions, whilst elegant, were also somewhat bizarre. The first urn was extremely small, and upon its side was painted a weeping face. It was perhaps the most beautiful face that Charles had ever seen. His throat tightened, his chin trembled, and he asked the First Minister: 'Whose is the beautiful face? And what do you keep in the urn?'

'The face,' replied the First Minister, 'is the face of an ancient Bohemian Princess. All our Princesses, including Her Royal Highness Princess Cherry – the present King's young daughter – are blessed with these lovely features. In the urn itself,' he continued, 'we used to keep The Tear – which was the first Gift – but that, I am afraid, was stolen long ago. The urn is now quite dry . . . ' The candle guttered, and he turned to the second vessel. This looked rather like a violin case, and was carved out of sky-blue marble, with gay garlands of flowers and fruit. 'Here,' said the First Minister, 'is where we used to keep the second Gift, which was – The Laugh.' He lifted the lid. 'Now, as you can hear, it is quite silent . . . ' The three friends shuffled their feet, and didn't know quite what to say. 'Finally,' said the First Minister, holding the candle a little higher so that they could all see, 'here is where we used to keep the third Gift, which was The Heart . . . ' And he showed them a pathetic little bed, with a tiny pillow upon it carved out of sapphire. 'The Heart has gone;' (the First Minister began to weep again) 'and The Laugh has gone; and The Tear has gone. All stolen, or lost, long ago . . . ' He sat down upon a little stone bench and wept profusely. 'Poor Bohemia!' he wailed, 'A country doomed to endless Boredom, and tedium without end, and all for the want of three little gifts . . . Oh dear, oh dear . . . ' He really was quite inconsolable. 'It is particularly sad at the moment,' he gulped, 'because next month sees the coming of age of Princess Cherry, and without The Tear or The Laugh or The Heart there will be neither Love nor Art nor Joy to celebrate her birthday . . . Only twenty-one years old,' he sobbed, 'and her party will be such a dreary affair. If the King wasn't so bored himself he'd be quite distraught, I'm sure of it; and The People you know, they feel it too – the endless dullness of life in Bohemia. Soon we'll just be machines: an efficient economy based upon a few mineral deposits and the production of natural gas; and once we were the spiritual envy of the world. Oh dear, oh dear . . . '

'Take us to your bored King!' said William, firmly. 'We will restore your country to rights!'

'Will you really?' said the First Minister, his gratitude prompting even further emotion. 'We'd have done it ourselves years ago, only who would have taken us seriously?'

The following day, true to their word, the three friends (or rather, The Three Heroes, as they now liked to think of themselves) drove through the monotonous city to the King's palace.

They found the King watching a television programme about small-gauge railways. The First Minister coughed discreetly: 'Sire,' he began, 'here are the three Cultural Theorists who have offered to help our Kingdom. They merely await your final authorization and instructions before they leave

135

on their quest.' The King turned off the television set and regarded the trio glumly. 'Ah,' he said, 'You must be the travellers?' Ideologically opposed to acts of obeisance, the three friends made various signs of acknowledgement. 'Are you aware,' the King continued, 'that each of the Gifts – which, we might add, we are extremely grateful to you for offering to find – must be, above all else, sincere? This is to say: the Tear must be a genuine tear, shed with genuine emotion; the Laugh must be a real laugh, provoked by honest merriment . . . '

'And what about the Heart?' asked William, fearing the worst.

'Ah. The Heart is a different matter, for the Heart is a symbol of Love. That,' (he added graciously) 'is a problem which you must solve for yourselves. And now – have you met my daughter, Her Royal Highness, The Princess Cherry?' He beckoned to an equerry who had been staring dully into space, his eyes quite rigid within their sockets, and immediately the throne room doors swung open. There, standing before the three friends, was the most beautiful girl that any of them had ever seen. All the romance of her glorious ancestry was in her face: her eyes were dark and shining, her skin was pale and flawless, her mouth was a drooping bow of deepest red and her hair (cut short, and parted at the side in a most charming way) was black and lustrous. She was tall, and elegant, and except for the rather tired manner in which she moved she was altogether quite wonderful. She was wearing a short black dress (in the height of fashion) and the movement of her limbs, as she strolled casually to greet the young men, appeared dangerously sensual.

From that moment on, Charles was in love. 'Forgive me!' he burst out, 'But unless I have some hope to cherish I may fail in my part of the quest. You are,' (and here he addressed the Princess) 'quite simply the woman of my dreams. I love you, and only you, and if I return successful from my journey will you please consider marrying me?' The Princess (stifling a yawn) looked Charles up and down and then said: 'Alright. On one condition: if you can bring back The Gifts in time for my birthday party; and if The Gifts return my enthusiasm for life to me, and I see you through the eyes of love – then we can get engaged. Is it agreed?'

'Gladly!' gushed Charles, and kissed Cherry's outstretched hand.

'Well that's that then,' said the King. 'Return with The Gifts in time for my daughter's birthday party and both she – and we – shall be extremely grateful to you.'

'I should add, Sire,' concluded William, 'that I feel it somewhat negligent of you to have lost your cultural bearings. Would it be possible – should we return The Gifts – for one or all of us to remain in your country in order to write a small volume about this most interesting state of affairs?'

'If you want,' said the King, and then, with a wave of the hand, he dismissed them.

For the next three weeks the three friends were busily engaged in their individual tasks. It fell to Hugo, the Urban Anthropologist, to find and secure The Laugh. Sitting in a hotel room in Paris, he pondered long and hard on how best to achieve his goal. The French (he had supposed) were by rights a cheerful nation, and it would be (he thought) merely a question of waiting until he could capture a deep Gallic chortle.

Several days passed. The streets were wet and windy; the cafés were filled with bad tempered citizens. Worst of all the Welsh had just beaten France at Rugby, and as a consequence nobody was feeling very bright. In fact, when Hugo telephoned William to report on his progress, he felt rather ashamed.

'I've never known the French to be like this,' he said, 'All they do is just gloom, gloom, gloom, all day – really, it's worse than Bohemia!'

'Why don't you show the chambermaid your collection of ties?' suggested William, 'I'm sure that to a fashion conscious country they'd at least raise a smile . . . '

'Well, get back in the knife drawer Miss Sharp!' retorted Hugo, but he thought that he'd try the plan anyway.

The following morning, when the maid brought in his coffee and rolls, Hugo asked for her advice on neckware. 'How about this one?' he roguishly enquired, displaying a knitted cravat which was embroidered with little pigs; 'Or this one?' – he held up a fluorescent kipper tie. 'I could wear it on my head . . . ' he suggested, 'Or I could fasten it . . . ' The sight of Hugo wearing his bow tie back to front proved irresistible to the maid. No sooner had she let out a joyous giggle than Hugo had trapped the sound in his sponge bag. After the maid had left the room, he could see the laugh quietly chuckling to itself, and causing the bag to bounce about a little on the bathroom shelf. 'A marvellous laugh.' said Hugo, as he packed it carefully into his case. 'The very essence of merriment.'

Over in Vienna, William was tracking a tear. This proved to be a harrowing business. He had no wish to return with a wholly tragic tear, but on the other hand he didn't want something which was merely sentimental. Bereavements and divorces were therefore unsuitable. In desperation he sat for some hours in the Café Koliniska, where groups of young people were known to meet and tryst. He was just beginning to feel rather sick (having eaten more cream than seemed either wise or healthy) when he espied out of the corner of his eye a sad young girl who was sitting alone at a table. Putting himself into the hands of Fate he wandered over to talk to her. 'Excuse me, sad girl,' he said, 'may I be of any assistance?' The girl looked up at him. Her big eyes were filled with tears. 'Splendid!' thought William, 'Now to get hold of one of them . . . ' He continued: 'Please forgive my intruding, and I mean you no harm, but I couldn't help noticing that you are upset. Perhaps I can help?' For a little while the girl merely carried on crying. Finally she spoke: 'It is the rock concert,' she said, 'over at the stadium. All of my friends are going but I can't . . . '

'Why not?'

'My Saturday job boss has just sacked me because I was late back from lunch. Now my boyfriend is angry because he thinks that I won't come to the concert, and all my friends believe that I have plenty of money; and now no one will like me any more . . . Oh dear, oh dear . . . '

'I'll tell you what,' said William, 'Are you really, sincerely, sad – or are you just feeling sorry for yourself?' At this the

138

girl exploded into further tears: 'Now you don't like me either! And you don't even know me!'

'Look down there,' said William, and he pointed out of the window to a very old woman, dressed in rags, who was sitting by the busy road and talking to herself. 'Imagine being like that,' he continued, 'imagine *her* being sad about a rock concert . . . ' The girl looked, gulped a little, and then, quite angry, said: 'Oh why did you have to make it worse . . . The poor old woman; I see her every day, always the same . . . ' And she started crying again.

'Well,' said William, 'Oh! There's something on your cheek . . . ' (he removed a perfectly formed tear with a leaf from one of the plastic roses on the table). 'That's life I suppose . . . ' And then he left the café, carefully transferring the girl's tear into a little pill box. He had left behind, on the table, enough money – and more – for the girl to go to the concert. Waiting around the corner, he watched for her to come out. After a little while she did, and gave all the money to the old lady who was sitting by the road. 'Now I know,' said William to himself, as he hurried along, 'that I have got the right sort of tear.'

In Liverpool, Charles was distraught. He had no idea what kind of heart he was meant to find, and was beginning to panic. Eventually, by dint of discussing the matter with a love-lorn youth in a hamburger bar, he hit upon the idea of simply buying the Princess a sentimental satin heart, and inscribing it with his love for her. After all (he reasoned) if his love was true then the heart would be a sincere symbol of Love itself. If he was wrong, and merely obsessed with romance, then the whole quest would fail accordingly. Determined by faith in his emotions, he went into a corner newsagent and bought a pink, satin heart. Upon this he wrote: 'To My Dear Princess Cherry. With Undying Love, Charles . . . ' And then he put it in a box.

Soon the three friends were back in Bohemia. Flushed with triumph, and feeling even more pleased with themselves than they had been in Rome, they were quite unaware of the curious manner in which their adventure would end.

* * *

The Princess Cherry's birthday party was, quite understandably, an odd affair. The whole Court, and all the important Officers of Bohemia, had dragged themselves apathetically to the Treasure House. Even the King looked rather fed up. Standing amidst the splendours of Ancient Bohemia, some twiddling their thumbs, and others whistling tunelessly under their breaths, the gathered guests were indeed uninspiring to look upon. Princess Cherry, dressed in Royal Blue, and looking (to Charles) even more beautiful than before, was idly twirling one strand of her fringe about her little finger. She was gazing at the floor whilst she did this, and if she hadn't been so beautiful she really would have looked rather stupid. But at least she'd thrown away her chewing gum.

At precisely ten o'clock in the morning, and to a rather half-hearted fanfare, the three friends advanced with the New Gifts.

'My friends!' said the King, 'Have you been successful on your mission of mercy?' William stepped forward: 'I hope so, Sire,' he said.

'Then proceed.'

One by one, and beneath the rather cynical gaze of the Court, the three travellers made their way to the Sacred Vessels. First of all, and with due care, Hugo poured the maid's laugh into its allotted urn. As he did so, and as a refreshing ripple of merriment could be felt blowing around the Treasure House like a cool breeze, the expressions on the Bohemians' faces suddenly came to life. The King gave a healthy snort, like someone waking up on the first day of their holiday; the Courtiers all turned to one another and started exchanging friendly jokes; and then the Princess smiled! It was like the sun coming out. No other words can describe it.

Then William came forward, and clutching the fragile tear (which he shielded with his hand) he stepped up to The Tear's urn. At the moment it fell into place there was a beautiful chime, like that of a gently knocked crystal glass, and immediately (once more) the audience in the Treasure House underwent a sudden transformation. Warmth, friendliness and sympathy flowed through them. They gasped as though

140

they were seeing the magnificence around them for the first time. Some wept openly, but with relief, and joy. 'We have been in the dark for so long!' cried the King. And the Princess smiled again, and looked at Charles most tenderly.

Prompted by this look, and quite certain now of success, Charles carried the satin heart to its bed of sapphire. He gently laid it down, and then, with a lover's deportment, stepped forward to Princess Cherry. She opened her arms to receive him, and raised her lovely face to accept his kiss. For Charles, in his happiness and triumph, it was a moment of exquisite stillness . . .

'My children!' said the King, and raised his arms in blessing. The Court beamed.

There was then a pause, such as follows the drinking of a toast, during which everyone was silent and the lovers – fondly holding hands – turned to face their well-wishers. A faint tinkling sound, like that of little bells being tickled by a breeze, rang around the Treasure House. Charles smiled, squeezing Cherry's hand, but then there was another sound, this time far louder, like the noise of paving stones cracking – a horrible sound. The Court looked about themselves nervously, and the King, equally alarmed, signalled to his guards to investigate the disturbance. No sooner had he issued this command than a low, swelling tone, frightening in its volume, rose up from a mysterious source to cause even further panic. It was as though all the Sacred Gifts were suddenly filling the vast hall with deafening music: a symphony of heavenly noise, too loud to bear, was starting to swirl between the statues and roar up and down the aisles. In the twinkling of an eye, before anyone could defend themselves, the sound could be felt as well; it began to buffet and strangle the assembled audience, pummelling their senses and forcing them to the ground.

Charles held Cherry as close to himself as he could. He could hear her crying beneath the din, and feel her body jolting, as though to harsh blows. William and Hugo had flattened themselves against pillars – it appeared as though

141

all chaos had been released. The Courtiers were shouting and crying, but none of them could move. 'It's the Gifts!' wailed the First Minister, reeling past with his fists pressed to the side of his head. 'We cannot stop them . . . They are too strong for us now!' He looked up, his eyes filled with bewilderment and sorrow: 'Would it have been better,' he gasped, 'to die of boredom?' And then the poor man sank to the ground.

After what seemed to be an eternity, the Treasure House was still once more. On the faces of the dead Courtiers were fixed expressions of utmost grief or joy. The King himself was lying across the marble steps with a look of terrible longing in his eyes. A noise like thunder, or the last notes of a swollen chorus, finally echoed away. Looking about themselves, and dusting down their suits with their hands, William and Hugo saw Charles. He was holding the lifeless Princess in his arms, and sobbing as though his heart would break.

His friends could not console him.

A CLEAN SHEET

TATYANA TOLSTAYA

HIS WIFE FELL asleep the minute she lay down on the sofa in the nursery: nothing wears you out as much as a sick child. Good, let her sleep there. Ignatiev covered her with a light blanket, stood around, looked at her open mouth, exhausted face, the black roots of her hair – she had stopped pretending to be a blonde a long time ago – felt sorry for her, for the wan, white, and sweaty Valerik, for himself, left, went to bed, and lay sleepless, staring at the ceiling.

Depression came to Ignatiev every night. Heavy, confusing, with lowered head, it sat on the edge of the bed and took his hand – a sad sick-nurse for a terminally ill patient. And they spent hours in silence, holding hands.

The house rustled at night, shuddered, lived. There were peaks in the vague din – a dog's bark, a snatch of music, the thud of the lift going up and down on a thread – the night boat. Hand in hand with depression, Ignatiev said nothing: locked in his heart, gardens, seas, and cities tumbled; Ignatiev was their master, they were born with him, and with him they were doomed to dissolve into non-being. My poor world, your master has been conquered by depression. Inhabitants, colour the sky in twilight, sit on the stone thresholds of abandoned houses, drop your hands, lower your heads: your good king is ill. Lepers, walk the deserted streets, ring your brass bells, carry the bad tidings: brothers, depression is coming to the cities. The hearths are abandoned and the ashes are cold and grass is growing between the slabs where the bazaar was once boisterous. Soon the low red

143

moon will rise in the inky sky, and the first wolf will come out of the ruins, raise its head and howl, sending a lone call on high, into the icy expanses, to the distant blue wolves sitting on branches in the black groves of alien universes.

Ignatiev did not know how to cry, and so he smoked. The light glowed in tiny toy flashes of summer lightning. Ignatiev lay there, depressed, tasting tobacco bitterness and knowing that in it was truth. Bitterness, smoke, a tiny oasis of light in the dark – that was the world. On the other side of the wall the plumbing rumbled. His earthy, tired, dear wife slept under a torn blanket. White Valerik was restless – thin, sickly shoot, pathetic to the point of spasms – rash, glands, dark circles under his eyes. And somewhere in the city, in one of the brightly lit windows, unfaithful, unsteady, evasive Anastasia was drinking wine with someone else. Look at me . . . but she just laughs and looks away.

Ignatiev turned on his side. Depression moved closer to him and flung up her ghostly sleeve – a line of ships floated up. The sailors were drinking with the locals in taverns, the captain had stayed late on the governor's veranda (cigars, liqueurs, pet parrot), the watchman had left his post for a cockfight and to see the bearded woman at the motley side-show; the painters quietly slipped themselves, a night breeze came up, and the old sailing ships, creaking, left the harbour for points unknown. Sick children, small, trusting boys, sleep soundly in their berths; they snuffle, holding a toy tight in their fists; the blankets slip off, the empty decks sway, the flock of ships sails with a soft splash into the impenetrable dark, and the wake spreads out on the warm black surface like an arrow.

Depression waves a sleeve and spreads out a boundless stony desert – hoarfrost shining on the cold rocky plain, stars frozen indifferently, the white moon indifferently drawing circles, the steadily stepping camel's bridle jangles sadly, a rider draws near, wrapped in chilled striped cloth of Bukhara. Who are you, rider? Why have you dropped your reins? Why have you wrapped up your face? Let me loosen your stiff fingers. What is this, rider, are you dead? . . . The rider's mouth gapes, a bottomless pit; his hair is tangled, and deep

144

sorrowful gutters have been etched in his cheeks by tears flowing for millennia.

A flutter of the sleeve. Anastasia, floating lights over a swamp. What was that slurp in the thicket? Don't look back. A hot flower beckons you to step on the springy brown hummocks. A thin, impatient fog moves about, sometimes lying down, sometimes hanging over the kindly beckoning moss: the red flower floats, winking through the white clumps: *come here, come here.* One step – that's not scary, is it? One more step – you're not afraid, are you? Shaggy heads stand in the moss, smiling, winking. A noisy dawn. Don't be afraid, the sun won't rise. Don't be afraid, we still have the fog. Step. Step. Step. Floating, laughing, the flower flashes. Don't look back! I think I'll get it. I *do* think I'll get it. I will. *Step.*

'Oo-oo-oo,' came a groan from the next room. Ignatiev pushed through the door in a bound and rushed to the crib – what's the matter, what is it? His wife jumped up, confused, and they began jerking at Valerik's sheets and blanket, getting in each other's way. Just to do something, to act! The little white head tossed and turned in its sleep, muttered, *ba-da-da, ba-da-da.* Rapidly muttering, pushing them away with his hands; then he calmed down, turned, settled down . . . He went off into his dreams alone, without his mother, without me, down the narrow path under the pines.

'What's the matter with him?'

'Another fever. I'll sleep here.'

'I've already brought you a blanket. I'll get you a pillow.'

'He'll be like that till morning. Shut the door. If you want to eat, there are some cheese dumplings.'

'I'm not hungry. Get some sleep.'

Depression was waiting, lying in the wide bed, moved over, made room for Ignatiev, embraced him, put her head on his chest, on the razed gardens, the dried-up seas, the ashen cities.

But not everything was killed: towards morning, when Ignatiev slept, Life came out of the dugouts; it pulled apart the burned logs and planted small seedlings: plastic primroses, cardboard oaks; hauled building blocks to erect temporary shelter, filled the seas with a watering can, cut pink bug-eyed crabs out of oilcloth, and with an ordinary pencil drew the dark, convoluted line of the surf.

After work, Ignatiev did not go straight home, but drank beer with a friend in a little cellar bar. He always hurried to get the best spot, in the corner, but rarely succeeded. And while he hurried, avoiding puddles, speeding up, patiently waiting for the roaring rivers of cars to pass, behind him, merging into the crowd of people, depression hurried; now and then, her flat, dull head appeared. There was no way he could get away from her, the doorman let her into the cellar bar, too, and Ignatiev was happy if his friend also came early. Old friend, school friend: he waved to him from afar, nodding, smiling gap-toothed; his thinning hair curled over his old, worn jacket. His children were grown up. His wife had left him a long time ago and he didn't want to remarry. Everything was just the opposite with Ignatiev. They would meet joyously and part irritated, unhappy with each other, but the next time it would start all over again. And when his friend, panting, made his way through the arguing tables, and nodded to Ignatiev, then deep in Ignatiev's chest, in his solar plexus, Life raised its head and also nodded and waved.

They ordered beer and pretzels.

'I'm in despair,' Ignatiev said. 'I'm desperate. I'm confused. It's all so complicated. My wife is a saint. She quit her job, she spends all her time with Valerik. He's ill, he's ill all the time. His legs don't work well. He's just this tiny little candle stump. Barely burning. The doctors give him jabs, he's afraid. He screams. I can't stand hearing him scream. The most important thing for him is home care and she kills herself. She's killing herself. But I can't go home. Depression. My wife won't even look me in the eye. And what's the point? Even if I read *The Old Man and the Turnip* to Valerik at bedtime, it's still depressing. And it's a lie; if a turnip is stuck in the ground, you can't get it out. I know. Anastasia . . . I call and call, she's never home. And if she is home, what can we talk about? Valerik? Work? . . . It's bad, you know, it gets me down. Every day I promise myself: tomorrow I'll wake up a new man, I'll perk up, I'll forget Anastasia, make a pile of money, take Valerik down south . . . Do up the apartment, start jogging in the morning . . . But at night, I'm depressed.'

'I don't understand,' his friend would say. 'What are you making this into such a big deal for? We all live pretty much the same way, what's the problem? We all manage to live somehow.'

'You don't understand. Right here' – Ignatiev pointed to his chest – 'it's alive, and it hurts.'

'You're such a fool,' his friend said, and picked his teeth with a wooden match. 'It hurts because it's alive. What did you expect?'

'I expected it not to hurt. It's too hard for me. Believe it or not, I'm suffering. And my wife is suffering, and so is Valerik, and Anastasia must be suffering and that's why she unplugs the phone. And we all torment one another.'

'You're a fool. Just don't let yourself suffer.'

'I can't help it.'

'You're a fool. Big deal, the world-class sufferer! You just don't want to be hale and hearty, you don't want to be master of your life.'

'I'm at the end of my tether,' Ignatiev said, clutching his hair and staring at his foam-flecked mug.

'You're an old woman. You're wallowing in your invented suffering.'

'No, I'm not an old woman. And I'm not wallowing. I'm ill and I want to be well.'

'If that's the case, you should know: the diseased organ has to be amputated. Like an appendix.'

Ignatiev looked up, shocked.

'What do you mean?'

'I just told you.'

'Amputated in what sense?'

'Medically. They do that now.'

His friend looked around, lowered his voice, and explained: there's an institute near Novoslobodskaya, and they operate on it; of course, it's still semi-official for now, it's done privately, but it's possible. Of course, you have to make it worth the surgeon's while. People come out completely renewed. Hadn't Ignatiev heard about it? It's very widespread in the West, but it's still underground here. Has to be done on the sly. Bureaucracy.

Ignatiev listened, stunned.

'But have they at least . . . experimented on dogs?'

His friend made circles near his ear.

'You're really nuts. Dogs don't have it. They have reflexes. Remember Pavlov?'

'Oh, yes.'

Ignatiev thought a bit. 'But it's horrible!'

'There's nothing horrible about it. The results are excellent: the mental processes become much sharper. Will power increases. All those idiotic, fruitless doubts end for ever. Harmony of body and, uh, brain. The intellect beams like a projector. You set your goal, strike without missing, and grab first prize. But I'm not forcing you, you know. If you don't want treatment, stay ill. With your glum expression. And let your women unplug the phone.'

Ignatiev did not take offence, he shook his head: those women . . .

'Ignatiev, for your information, what you tell a woman, even if she's Sophia Loren, is: shoo! Then they'll respect you. Otherwise, you don't count.'

'But how can I say that to her? I worship her, I tremble . . .'

'Right. Tremble. You tremble, I'm going home.'

'Wait! Stay a bit. Let's have another beer. Listen, have you seen any of these . . . *operated* people?'

'Certainly.'

'How do they look?'

'How? Like you and me. Better. Everything's just fine with them, they're successful, they laugh at fools like us. I have a friend, we were at college together. He's become a big shot.'

'Could I have a look at him?'

'A look? Well, all right, I'll ask. I don't know if he'd mind. I'll ask. Although, what's it to him? I don't think he'll refuse. It's no big deal!'

'What's his name?'

It was pouring. Ignatiev walked through the city in the evening; effervescent red and green lights replaced each other, flickering on the streets. Ignatiev had two kopeks in his hand, to call Anastasia. A Zhiguli drove right through a puddle on purpose, splashing Ignatiev with murky water, splattering his trousers. Things like that happened frequently to Ignatiev. 'Don't worry, I'll have that operation,' thought Ignatiev, 'buy a car, and I'll splash others. Revenge on the indifferent for humiliation.' He was ashamed of his base thoughts and shook his head. I'm really sick.

He had a long wait at the phone booth. First a young man whispered smiling into the phone. Somebody whispered back a long time, too. The man ahead of Ignatiev, a short, dark man, banged his coin against the glass: have a heart. Then he called. Apparently he had his own Anastasia, but her name was Raisa. The short man wanted to marry her, insisted, shouted, pressed his forehead against the cold telephone.

'What's the problem?' He couldn't understand. 'Can you please explain what the problem is? What more could you want? Tell me! Just tell me! You'll be rolling ... ' – he switched the receiver to his other ear – 'You'll be rolling in clover! Go on. Go on.' He listened a long time, tapping his foot. 'Why, my whole apartment is covered with rugs. Yes. Yes.' He listened a long time, grew bewildered, stared at the phone with its dialling tone, left with an angry face, with tears in his eyes, walked into the rain. He didn't need Ignatiev's sympathetic smile. Ignatiev crawled into the warm inside of the booth, dialled the magical number, but crawled out with nothing: his long rings found no response, dissolved in the cold rain, in the cold city, beneath the low, cold clouds. And Life whimpered in his chest until morning.

N. received him the next week. A respectable establishment with lots of name plates. Solid, spacious corridors, carpets.

A weeping woman came out of his office. Ignatiev and his friend pushed the heavy door. N. was an important man: desk, jacket, the works. Just look, look! A gold pen in his pocket, and look at the pens in the granite slab on his desk. Look at the desk calendars. And a fine cognac behind the square panes of his cupboard – well, well!

His friend explained their visit. He was visibly nervous: even though they had been at college together, all those pens . . . N. was clear and precise. Get all possible analyses. Chest X-rays – profile and frontal. Get transferred to the institute by your local hospital, without making a fuss, put down the reason: For *tests*. And at the institute, go to Dr Ivanov. Yes, Ivanov. Have one hundred and fifty roubles ready in an envelope. That's basically it. That's what I did. There may be other ways, I don't know.

Yes, quick and painless. I'm satisfied.

'So, they cut it out?'

'I'd say, take it out. Extract it. Clean, hygienic.'

'And afterwards . . . did you see it? After the extraction?'

'What for?'

N. was insulted. Ignatiev's friend kicked him: indecent questions!

'Well, to know what it was like,' Ignatiev said embarrassedly. 'You know, just . . . '

'Who could possibly be interested in that? Excuse me . . .' N. lifted the edge of his cuff: a massive gold timepiece was revealed. With an expensive strap. Did you see, did you notice? The audience was over.

'Well, what did you think?' His friend peered into his face as they walked along the embankment. 'Are you convinced? What do you think?'

'I don't know yet. It's frightening.'

Headlights splashed in the black river waves. Depression, his evening girlfriend, was creeping up on him. Peeking out from behind the rain gutter-pipe, running across the wet pavement, blending into the crowd, watching constantly, waiting for Ignatiev to be alone. Windows were lighting up, one after another.

'You're in bad shape, Ignatiev. Decide. It's worth it.'

'I'm scared. This way I feel bad, the other way I'm scared. I keep thinking, what happens later? What comes after? Death?'

'Life, Ignatiev! Life! A healthy, superior life, not just chicken scratching. A brilliant career. Success. Sport. Women. Free of complexes and neuroses! Just look at yourself: what are you? A wimp. Coward! Be a man, Ignatiev! A man! That's what women want. Otherwise, what are you? Just a rag!'

Yes, women. Ignatiev pictured Anastasia and felt lonely. He remembered her last summer, leaning towards a mirror, radiant, plump, her reddish hair tossed back, putting on carrot-coloured lipstick, pouting her lips in a convenient cosmetic position, talking in spurts, with pauses.

'I doubt. That you're. A man. Ignatiev. Because men. Are. Decisive. And-by-the-way-change-that-shirt-if-you-have-any-hopes-at-all.' And her red dress burned like a flower dipped in love potion.

And Ignatiev was ashamed of his tea-coloured short-sleeved silk shirt, which used to belong to his father. It was a good shirt, long-wearing; he had got married in it and had welcomed Valerik home from the hospital in it. But if a shirt stands between us and the woman we love, we'll burn the shirt – even if it's made of diamonds. And he burned it. And it helped for a short while. And Anastasia loved him. But now she was drinking red wine with others and laughing in one of the lit windows of this enormous city, he didn't know which one, but he looked for her silhouette in each. And – not to him, but to others, shifting her shoulders under the lace shawl, on the second, seventh, sixteenth floor – she was saying her shameless words: 'Am I really *very* pretty?'

Ignatiev burned his father's tea-coloured shirt; its ashes fall on the bed at night, depression sprinkles him with it, softly sowing it through half-shut fists. Only the weak regret useless sacrifices. He will be strong. He will burn everything that erects obstacles. He'll grow into the saddle, he'll tame the evasive, slippery Anastasia. He will lift the clay-like, lowered face of his beloved, exhausted wife. Contradictions won't tear him apart. The benefits will balance clearly and

151

justly. Here is your place, wife. Reign. Here is your place, Anastasia. Rule. And you: smile, little Valerik. Your legs will grow strong and your glands will stop swelling, for Papa loves you, you pale city potato seedling. Papa will be rich, with lots of pens. He will call in expensive doctors in gold-rimmed glasses with leather cases. Carefully handing you from one to the other, they will carry you to the fruity shores of the eternally blue sea, and the lemony, orangey breeze will blow the dark circles away from your eyes. Who's that coming, tall as a cedar, strong as steel, with his step springy, knowing no shameful doubts? That's Ignatiev. His path is straight, his income high, his gaze confident. Women watch him pass. Shoo! . . . Down a green carpet, in a red dress, Anastasia floats towards him nodding through the fog, smiling her shameless smile.

'I'll at least get started on the paperwork. That takes ages,' Ignatiev said. 'And then I'll see.'

Ignatiev's appointment was for eleven, but he decided to go early. A summer morning chirped outside the kitchen window. Water trucks sprayed brief coolness in rainbow fans, and Life cheeped and hopped in the tangled tree branches. Behind his back, sleepy night seeped through the netting, whispers of depression, foggy pictures of misery, the measured splash of waves on a dull deserted shore, low, low clouds. The silent ceremony of breakfast took place on a corner of the oilcloth – an old ritual whose meaning is forgotten, purpose lost; what remains is only the mechanical motions, signs, and sacred formulas of a lost tongue no longer understood by the priests themselves. His wife's exhausted face was lowered. Time had long since stolen the pink flush of youth from the thousand-year-old cheeks and their branched fissures. . . . Ignatiev raised his hand, cupped it, to caress the parchment tresses of the beloved mummy – but his hand encountered only the sarcophagus's cold. Frozen cliffs, the jangle of a lone camel's bridle, the lake, frozen solid. She did not lift her face, did not lift her eyes. The mummy's wrinkled brown stomach: dried up, sunken, the sliced-open rib cage filled with balsamic resins, stuffed with dry tufts of herbs; Osiris is silent. The dry limbs are tightly bound with linen strips marked with blue signs: asps, eagles, and crosses – the sneaky, minuscule droppings of ibis-headed Toth.

You don't know anything yet, my dear, but be patient: just a few more hours, and the shackles will burst and the glass vessel of despair will shatter into small, splashing smithereens, and a new, radiant, shining, glorious Ignatiev will appear to the boom and roll of drums and the cries of Phrygian pipes, wise, intense, complete; will arrive riding on a white elephant on a rug-covered seat with coloured fans. And you will stand at my right, and on my left – closer to the heart – will stand Anastasia; and white Valerik will smile and reach out, and the mighty elephant will kneel and gently wing him in his kind, ornamented trunk, and pass him to Ignatiev's strong arms, and Ignatiev will raise him above the world – the small ruler, intoxicated by heights – and the exulting nations will cry: *ecce homo!* Behold the ruler from sea to sea, from edge to edge, to the glowing cupola, the blue curving border of the gold-and-green planet earth.

Ignatiev arrived early, the hallway outside the office was empty, there was only a nervous blond man hanging around, the one with the ten o'clock appointment. A pathetic blond with shifty eyes, biting his nails, nibbling his cuticle, stoop-shouldered; sitting down, then jumping up and examining closely the four-sided coloured lanterns with edifying medical tales: 'Unwashed Vegetables Are Dangerous.' 'Gleb Had Toothache.' 'And the Eye Had To Be Removed' (If thine eye offend thee, pluck it out). 'Give the Dysentery Patient Separate Dishes.' 'Air Your Home Frequently.' An entry light went on over the door, the blond man groaned softly, patted his pockets, and crossed the threshold. Pathetic, pathetic, miserable man! I'm just like him. Time passed. Ignatiev squirmed, sniffed the medicated air, went to look at the pedagogical lanterns; Gleb's story interested him. A bad tooth tormented Gleb, but then let up; and Gleb, cheerier, in a track suit, played chess with a school friend. But you can't escape your fate. Gleb suffered great torments, and bound up his face with a cloth, and his day turned to night, and he went

153

to the wise, stern doctor, and the doctor did ease his suffering: he did pull out Gleb's tooth and cast it out; and Gleb, transfigured, smiled happily in the final, bottom illuminated window, while the doctor raised his finger in admonition, bequeathing his time-honoured wisdom to new generations.

Behind him came the rattle of a trolley and stifled moans, and two elderly women in white coats pushed a writhing, nameless body, wrapped in dried-up bloody bandages – face and chest – only the mouth was a black hole. Could it be the blond? . . . Impossible . . . After them came a nurse with a drip, frowning, who stopped when she noticed Ignatiev's desperate signals. Ignatiev made an effort and remembered the language of humans:

'The blond?'

'What did you say? I didn't understand.'

'The blond, Ivanov? . . . He had it, too? . . . Had it extracted, right?'

The nurse laughed grimly.

'No, they transplanted it into him. They'll take yours out and put it in someone else. Don't worry. He's an inpatient.'

'You mean they do the reverse, too? Why such. . . '

'He's doomed. They don't survive it. We make them sign a disclaimer before the surgery. It's useless. They don't live.'

'Rejection? Immune system?'

'Heart attack.'

'Why?'

'They can't take it. They were born that way, lived their whole lives that way, never knowing what *it* is. And then they go and have a transplant. It must be a fad or something. There's a waiting list; we do one a month. Not enough donors.'

'So, I'm a donor?'

The nurse laughed, picked up the drip, and left. Ignatiev thought. So that's how they do it here. An experimental institute, that's for sure. . . Ivanov's office door opened, and a golden-haired someone strode out, haughty, pushy; Ignatiev jumped out of the way, then watched him go . . . the blond. . . A superman, dream, ideal, athlete, victor! The sign over the

154

door was blinking impatiently, and Ignatiev crossed the threshold and Life rang like a bell in his trembling chest.

'Please sit there for a minute.'

The doctor, Professor Ivanov, was writing something on a card. They were always like that: call you in, but they're not ready. Ignatiev sat down and licked his lips. He looked around the office. A chair like a dentist's, anaesthesia equipment with two silvery tanks, and a manometer. Over there, a polished cupboard with small gifts from patients, harmless, innocent trifles: plastic model cars, porcelain birds. It was funny to have porcelain birds in an office where such things were done. The doctor wrote and wrote, and the uncomfortable silence thickened, the only sounds the squeal of the pen, the jangle of the lone black camel's bridle, the stiffened rider, and the frozen plain. . . Ignatiev squeezed his hands to control the trembling and looked around: everything was ordinary; the shutters of the old window were open and beyond the white window frame was summer.

The warm, already dusty leaves of the luxurious linden splashed, whispered, conspired about something, huddling in a tangled green mass, giggling, prompting one another, plotting: let's do it this way; or how about like this? Good idea: well then, we're agreed, but it's our secret, right? Don't give it away! And suddenly, quivering as one heady, scented crowd, excited by the secret that united them – a wonderful, happy, warm summer secret – with a rustle, they lunged towards their neighbouring, murmuring poplar: Guess, just guess. It's your turn to guess. And the poplar swayed in embarrassment, caught unawares; and muttered, recoiling: easy, easy, not all at once; calm down, I'm old, you're all so naughty. They laughed and exchanged glances, the linden's green inhabitants: we knew it! And some fell down to the ground, laughing, into the warm dust, and others clapped their hands, and still others didn't even notice, and once more they whispered, inventing a new game. Play, boys; play, girls! Laugh, kiss, live, you short-lived little green town. The summer is still dancing, its colourful flower skirts still fresh, it's only noon by the clock: the hands triumphantly pointing upwards. But the sentence has been read, the permission

155

granted, the papers signed. The indifferent executioner – the north wind – has put on his white mask, packed his cold pole-axe, is ready to start. Old age, bankruptcy, destruction are inexorable. And the hour is nigh when there will be only a handful of frozen, contorted, uncomprehending old husks here and there on the bare branches, thousand-year-old furrows on their earthy, suffering faces. . . A gust of wind, a wave of the pole-axe, and they too will fall. . . *I don't want to, I don't want to, I don't want to, I don't want to*, thought Ignatiev. I can't hold on to summer with my weak hands, I can't stop the decay, the pyramids are collapsing, the crack has sundered my trembling heart and the horror of the witnesses' useless suffering. . . No. I'm dropping out of the game. With magic scissors I will cut the enchanted ring and go outside. The shackles will fall, the dry paper cocoon will burst, and astonished by the newness of the blue and gold purity of the world, the lightest, most fragile butterfly will fly out and grow more beautiful. . .

Get out your scalpel, your knife, your sickle, whatever you usually use, doctor; be so kind as to sever the branch that is still blooming but is hopelessly dying and toss it in the purifying flames.

The doctor extended his hand without looking up – and Ignatiev hurried, embarrassed, afraid to do the wrong thing, handed him his pile of test results, references, X-rays, and the envelope with one hundred and fifty roubles – the envelope with an unseasonal Santa Claus in a painted sleigh with presents for the children. Ignatiev began to look, and saw the doctor. On his head sat the backward-tilting cone of a cap – a white tiara with blue stripes, a starched ziggurat. Tanned face, eyes lowered on to the papers; and falling powerfully, waterfall-like, terrifying, from his ears down to his waist, in four layers, in forty spirals: a rough, blue-black Assyrian beard, thick ringlets, black springs, a nocturnal hyacinth. I am the Physician of Physicians, Ivanov.

'He's no Ivanov,' Ignatiev thought in horror. The Assyrian picked up the Santa Claus envelope, lifted it by one corner, and asked, 'What's this?' He looked up.

He had no eyes.

From the empty sockets welled up the black abyss of nothingness, the underground entrance to other worlds, on the edges of the dead seas of darkness. And he had to go there.

There were no eyes, but there was a gaze. He was looking at Ignatiev.

'What is this?' the Assyrian repeated.

'Money,' Ignatiev said, moving the letters.

'What for?'

'I wanted to . . . they said . . . for the operation, I don't know. You take it.' (Ignatiev horrified himself.) 'I was told, I wanted to. I was told, I asked.'

'All right.'

The professor opened a drawer and swept rosy-cheeked Santa with presents for Valerik into it, his tiara shifted on his head.

'Is surgical intervention indicated for you?'

Indicated? It's indicated. Isn't it indicated for everyone? I don't know. There are the test results, lots of figures, all kinds of things. . . The doctor looked down towards the papers, went through the results: good, reliable results, with clear purple stamps: all the projections of a cone – circle and triangle – were there; all the Pythagorean symbols, the cabalistic secrets of medicine, the backstage mysticism of the Order. The professor's clean, surgical nail went down the graphs: thrombocytes . . . erythrocytes . . . Ignatiev watched the nail jealously, mentally pushing it along: don't stop, everything is fine, good numbers, sturdy, clean, roasted nuts. Secretly proud: marvellous, healthy zeros without worms; the fours like excellently built footstools, the eights well-washed eyeglasses; everything suitable, satisfactory. Operation indicated. The Assyrian's finger stopped. What's the matter? Something wrong? Ignatiev craned his neck and looked anxiously. Doctor, is it that two over there that you don't like? Really, you're right, heh-heh, it's not quite . . . a small bruise, I agree, but it's accidental, don't pay any attention, read on, there are all those sixes over there, spilled like Armenian grapes. What, they're no good, either? . . . Wait, wait, let's have a look at this! The Assyrian moved his finger

157

and went down to the bottom of the page, then flipped through the papers, made a neat pile, and clipped it. He took out the chest X-ray and held it up to the light for a long time. He added it to the pile. I think he's willing, thought Ignatiev. But anxiety blew like a draught through his heart, opening doors, moving curtains. But that too would pass. Actually, more precisely, that was exactly what would pass. I'd like to know what it would be like after. My poor heart, your apple orchards still stir. The bees still buzz and burrow into your pink flowers, weighed down by heavy pollen. But the evening sky is darkening, the air is still, the shiny axe is being sharpened. Don't be afraid. Don't look. Shut your eyes. Everything will be fine. Everything will be fine. Everything will be very fine.

I wonder if the doctor had it done, too? Should I ask? Why not, I'll ask. No, I'm afraid. I'm afraid and it's impolite and maybe I'll spoil everything. If you ask, your dry tongue moving meekly; smiling tensely, gazing beseechingly into the nightmarish dark gaping like a black hole between his upper and lower lids, vainly trying to meet his gaze, to find a saving human point, find something, some sort of – well, maybe not a welcome, not a smile, no no, I understand – but even scorn, fastidiousness, even revulsion, *some* answer, *some* glimmer, some sign, somebody stir, wave your hand, do you hear me? . . . Is anyone in there? I feel around in the dark, I feel the dark, it's thick; I see nothing, I'm afraid I'll slip and fall, but where can I fall if there's no path beneath my feet? I am alone here. I am afraid. Life, are you here? . . . Doctor, excuse me please, sorry to bother you, but just one question: tell me, is Life there?

As if in foreboding, something in his chest cringed, scurried, crouched, eyes shut, arms over its head. Be patient. It will be better for everyone.

The Assyrian let him look into his deep starless pits once more.

'Sit in the chair, please.'

And I will, so what, it's no big deal, I'll just go and sit, casually. Ignatiev settled in the leather reclining chair. Rubber straps on his arms and legs. On the side, a hose, tanks, a manometer.

'General anaesthesia?'

The professor was doing something at his desk, with his back to Ignatiev, and he replied reluctantly, after a pause.

'Yes, general anaesthesia. We'll remove it, clean it out, fill the canal.'

'Like a tooth,' thought Ignatiev. He felt a cowardly chill. What unpleasant words. Easy, easy. Be a man. What's the problem? Easy. It's not a tooth. No blood. Nothing.

The doctor selected the proper tray. Something jingled on it. With tweezers he selected and placed on a low table, on to a glass medical slide, a long, thin, disgustingly thin needle, thinner than a mosquito's whine. Ignatiev squinted at it nervously. Knowing what those things were for was horrible, but not knowing was worse.

'What's that?'

'The extractor.'

'So small? I wouldn't have thought.'

'Do you think yours is big?' the Assyrian said irritably. And he stuck the X-ray under his nose, but he could make out nothing but foggy spots. The doctor was already wearing rubber gloves fitted tightly over his hands and wrists, and with bent tweezers he rummaged among the shiny bent needles and vilely narrowing probes and pulled something out: a parody of scissors with a pike's jaws. The Assyrian scratched his beard with a rubber finger. Ignatiev thought that the doctor was ruining the sterility and meekly mentioned it aloud.

'What sterility?' The professor raised his eyelids. 'I wear gloves to protect my hands.'

Ignatiev smiled weakly, understandingly. Of course, you never know, there are people with diseases. . . He suddenly realized that he didn't know how they would drag it out: through his mouth? His nose? Maybe they make an incision on the chest? Or in the hole between collarbones, where day and night the soft throb continues: sometimes hurrying, sometimes slowing its endless run?

'Doctor, how . . . '

'Quiet!' The Assyrian exclaimed. 'Silence! Shut up. Just listen to me. Look at the bridge of my nose. Count to twenty to yourself: one, two . . . '

His nose, mouth, and blue beard were firmly wrapped in white. Between the white mask and the striped tiara the abyss stared from his eyes. Between the two sockets, openings into nowhere, was the bridge of his nose: a tuft of blue hairs on a crumbling mountain range. Ignatiev began looking, turning to ice. The anaesthesia hose was moving towards him from the side. A trunk; and from it, the sweet, sweet smell of death. It hung over his face; Ignatiev struggled, but gave up, tied down by rubber straps, stifled his last, too-late doubts – and they splashed in all directions. Out of the corner of his eye he saw depression, his loyal girlfriend, pressed against the window, bidding him farewell, weeping, blocking the white light, and almost voluntarily inhaled the piercing, sweet smell of blossoming non-existence, once, twice, and more, without moving his eyes from the Assyrian emptiness.

And there, in the depths of the sockets, in the other-worldly crevasses, a light went on, a path appeared, stumps of black, charred branches grew, and with a soft jolt Ignatiev was sucked from the chair, forward and up, and was tossed there, on the path, and hurrying – seven, eight, nine, ten, I'm lost – he ran along the stones with his almost non-existent legs. And Life gasped behind him, and the bars clanged, and Anastasia wailed bitterly, wildly. . .

And I'm sorry, sorry, sorry, sorry for those left behind and I can't stop and I'm running upwards, and huddled low the dacha station flew past, and with Mama and me – a little boy, no, it's Valerik – and they turn, mouths open, shouting; but I can't hear them, Valerik raises his little hand, something in his fist, the wind ruffles their hair. . .

Ringing in the ears, darkness, ringing, oblivion.

Ignatiev – Ignatiev? – slowly floated up from the bottom, his head pushing aside the soft, dark rags – a lake of cloth.

He lay in the chair, the straps undone, his mouth dry, his

160

head spinning. In his chest, a pleasant, calm warmth. It felt good.

The bearded man in the white coat was writing something on a medical chart. Ignatiev remembered why he was there – just a simple outpatient operation, he had to have the whatsit removed; what was that word. The hell with it. General anaesthesia – that took pull. Not bad.

'Well, doc, can I go?' Ignatiev asked.

'Stay five minutes,' the bearded one said drily. 'So pushy all of a sudden.'

'Did you do it all, no tricks?'

'All.'

'Watch it, if you welshed on the deal, I'll shake my money out of you before you know it,' Ignatiev joked.

The doctor looked up from the papers. Well, that was the living end, a real knockout. Holes instead of eyes.

'What's the matter, mate, lose your eyeballs?' Ignatiev laughed. He liked his new laugh – sort of a squealing bark. Turned out smart, hadn't he? 'Well, you're really something, mate! I'm knocked out. Let's hope it doesn't give the girls the greatest fright of their lives, that's all.'

He liked the dull spot in his solar plexus. It was boss.

'Hey, man, I'm off. Let's squeeze yer mitt. *Ciao.*'

He slapped the doctor on the back. He bounded down the worn stairs with sturdy, springy steps, with whiplash turns on the landings. So much to do! And everything would work out. Ignatiev laughed. The sun was shining. Loads of talent on the street. Terrif. First off to Anastasia. Show her what's what! But first, a few jokes, of course. He had made up a few jokes already, his brain was whizzing. 'That'll put lead in your pencil,' 'Gotta keep your shotgun clean,' he'd say. He thought that up. And when he left, he'd say, 'Stay cool, suck ice.' He was so funny now: no joke, seriously, the life of the party.

Should I go home first or what? Home later, now I have to write to the right place and tell the right people that a doctor calling himself Ivanov takes bribes. Write it in full detail, with a lacing of humour: he has no eyes, but all he sees is money. Who's keeping an eye on things, anyway?

And then home. I've had it keeping that cretin home. It's not sanitary, you know. I'll fix a bed in a home for him. If they give me trouble, I'll have to slip them something. That's the way the game is played. Everyone does it.

Ignatiev pushed the post office door.

'What would you like?' the curly-haired girl asked.

'A clean sheet of paper,' Ignatiev said. 'Just a clean sheet.'

HOW I FINALLY LOST MY HEART

DORIS LESSING

IT WOULD BE easy to say that I picked up a knife, slit open my side, took my heart out, and threw it away; but unfortunately it wasn't as easy as that. Not that I, like everyone else, had not often wanted to do it. No, it happened differently, and not as I expected.

It was just after I had had a lunch and a tea with two different men. My lunch partner I had lived with for (more or less) four and seven-twelfths years. When he left me for new pastures, I spent two years, or was it three, half dead, and my heart was a stone, impossible to carry about, considering all the other things weighing on one. Then I slowly, and with difficulty, got free, because my heart cherished a thousand adhesions to my first love – though from another point of view he could be legitimately described as either my second *real* love (my father being the first) or my third (my brother intervening).

As the folk song has it:

> I have loved but three men in my life,
> My father, my brother, and the man that
> took my life.

But if one were going to look at the thing from outside, without insight, he could be seen as (perhaps, I forget) the thirteenth, but to do that means disregarding the inner emotional truth. For all we know that those affairs or

163

entanglements one has between *serious* loves, though they may number dozens and stretch over years, *don't really count*.

This way of looking at things creates a number of unhappy people, for it is well known that what doesn't really count for me might very well count for you. But there is no way of getting over this difficulty, for a *serious* love is the most important business in life, or nearly so. At any rate, most of us are engaged in looking for it. Even when we are in fact being very serious indeed with one person we still have an eighth of an eye cocked in case some stranger unexpectedly encountered might turn out to be even more serious. We are all entirely in agreement that we are in the right to taste, test, sip and sample a thousand people on our way to the *real* one. It is not too much to say that in our circles tasting and sampling is probably the second most important activity, the first being earning money. Or to put it another way, 'If you are serious about this thing, you go on laying everybody that offers until something clicks and you're all set to go.'

I have digressed from an earlier point: that I regarded this man I had lunch with (we will call him A) as my first love; and still do despite the Freudians, who insist on seeing my father as A and possibly my brother as B, making my (real) first love C. And despite, also, those who might ask: What about your two husbands and all those affairs?

What about them? I did not *really* love them, the way I loved A.

I had lunch with him. Then, quite by chance, I had tea with B. When I say B, here, I mean my *second* serious love, not my brother, or the little boys I was in love with between the ages of five and fifteen, if we are going to take fifteen (arbitrarily) as the point of no return ... which last phrase is in itself a pretty brave defiance of the secular arbiters.

In between A and B (my count) there were a good many affairs, or samples, but they didn't score. B and I *clicked*, we went off like a bomb, though not quite as simply as A and I had clicked, because my heart was bruised, sullen, and suspicious because of A's throwing me over. Also there were all those ligaments and adhesions binding me to A still to be loosened, one by one. However, for a time B and I got on like a house on fire, and then we came to grief. My heart was again a ton weight in my side.

> If this were a stone in my side, a stone,
> I could pluck it out and be free . . .

Having lunch with A, then tea with B, two men who between them had consumed a decade of my precious years (I am not counting the test or trial affairs in between) and, it is fair to say, had balanced all the delight (plenty and intense) with misery (oh Lord, Lord) – moving from one to the other, in the course of an afternoon, conversing amiably about this and that, with meanwhile my heart giving no more than slight reminiscent tugs, the fish of memory at the end of a long slack line . . .

To sum up, it was salutary.

Particularly as that evening I was expecting to meet C, or someone who might very well turn out to be C – though I don't want to give too much emphasis to C, the truth is I can hardly remember what he looked like, but one can't be expected to remember the unimportant ones one has sipped or tasted in between. But after all, he might have turned out to be C, we might have *clicked*, and I was in that state of mind (in which we all so often are) of thinking: He might turn out to be the one. (I use a women's magazine phrase deliberately here, instead of saying, as I might: *Perhaps it will be serious.*)

So there I was (I want to get the details and atmosphere right) standing at a window looking into a street (Great Portland Street, as a matter of fact) and thinking that while I would not dream of regretting my affairs, or experiences, with A and B (it is better to have loved and lost than never to have loved at all), my anticipation of the heart because of spending an evening with a possible C had a certain unreality, because there was no doubt that both A and B had caused me unbelievable pain. Why, therefore, was I looking forward to C? I should rather be running away as fast as I could.

It suddenly occurred to me that I was looking at the whole phenomenon quite inaccurately. My (or perhaps I am permitted to say our?) way of looking at it is that one must search for an A, or a B, or a C or a D with a certain combination of desirable or sympathetic qualities so that one may click, or spontaneously combust: or to put it differently, one needs a person who, like a saucer of water, allows one to float off on him/her, like a transfer. But this wasn't so at all. Actually one carries with one a sort of burning spear stuck in one's side, that one waits for someone else to pull out; it is something painful, like a sore or a wound, that one cannot wait to share with someone else.

I saw myself quite plainly in a moment of truth: I was standing at a window (on the third floor) with A and B (to mention only the mountain peaks of my emotional experience) behind me, a rather attractive woman, if I may say so, with a mellowness that I would be the first to admit is the sad harbinger of age, but is attractive by definition, because it is a testament to the amount of sampling and sipping (I nearly wrote simpling and sapping) I have done in my time ... there I stood, brushed, dressed, red-lipped, kohl-eyed, all waiting for an evening with a possible C. And at another window overlooking (I think I am right in saying) Margaret Street, stood C, brushed, washed, shaved, smiling: an attractive man (I think), and *he* was thinking: Perhaps she will turn out to be D (or A or 3 or ? or %, or whatever symbol he used). We stood, separated by space, certainly, in identical conditions of pleasant uncertainty and anticipation, and we both held our hearts in our hands, all pink and palpitating and ready for pleasure and pain, and we were about to throw these hearts in each other's face like snowballs, or cricket balls (How's that?) or, more accurately, like great bleeding wounds: 'Take my wound.' Because the last thing one ever thinks at such moments is that he (or she) will say: Take *my* wound, please remove the spear from *my* side. No, not at all, one simply expects to get rid of one's own.

I decided I must go to the telephone and say C! – You know that joke about the joke-makers who don't trouble to tell each other jokes, but simply say Joke 1, or Joke 2, and everyone roars with laughter, or snickers, or giggles appropriately ... Actually one could reverse the game by guessing whether it was Joke C(b) or Joke A(d) according to what sort of laughter a person made to match the silent thought . . . Well, C (I imagined myself saying), the analogy is for our instruction: Let's take the whole thing as read or said. Let's not lick each other's sores; let's keep our hearts to ourselves. Because just consider it, C, how utterly absurd – here we stand at our respective windows with our palpitating hearts in our hands . . .

At this moment, dear reader, I was forced simply to put down the telephone with an apology. For I felt the fingers of my left hand push outwards around something rather large, light, and slippery – hard to describe this sensation, really. My hand is not large, and my heart was in a state of inflation after having had lunch with A, tea with B, and then looking forward to C . . . Anyway, my fingers were stretching out rather desperately to encompass an unknown, largish, light-ish object, and I said: Excuse me a minute, to C, looked down, and there was my heart, in my hand.

I had to end the conversation there.

For one thing, to find that one has achieved something so often longed for, so easily, is upsetting. It's not as if I had been trying. To get something one wants simply by accident – no, there's no pleasure in it, no feeling of achievement. So to find myself heart-whole, or, more accurately, heart-less, or at any rate, rid of the damned thing, and at such an awkward moment, in the middle of an imaginary telephone call with a man who might possibly turn out to be C, well, it was irritating rather than not.

For another thing, a heart raw and bleeding and fresh from one's side, is not the prettiest sight. I'm not going into that at all. I was appalled, and indeed embarrassed that *that* was what had been loving and beating away all those years, because if I'd had any idea at all – well, enough of that.

My problem was how to get rid of it.

Simple, you'll say, drop it into the waste bucket.

Well, let me tell you, that's what I tried to do. I took a good look at this object, nearly died with embarrassment, and walked over to the rubbish can, where I tried to let it roll off my fingers. It wouldn't. It was stuck. There was my heart, a large red pulsing bleeding repulsive object, stuck to my fingers. What was I going to do? I sat down, lit a cigarette (with one hand, holding the matchbox between my knees), held my hand with the heart stuck on it over the side of the chair so that it could drip into a bucket, and considered.

> If this were a stone in my hand, a stone,
> I could throw it over a tree . . .

When I had finished the cigarette, I carefully unwrapped some tin foil, of the kind used to wrap food in when cooking, and I fitted a sort of cover around my heart. This was absolutely and urgently necessary. First, it was smarting badly. After all, it had spent some forty years protected by flesh and ribs and the air was too much for it. Secondly, I couldn't have any Tom, Dick and Harry walking in and looking at it. Thirdly, I could not look at it for too long myself, it filled me with shame. The tin foil was effective, and indeed rather striking. It is quite pliable and now it seemed as if there were a stylized heart balanced on my palm, like a globe, in glittering, silvery substance. I almost felt I needed a sceptre in the other hand to balance it . . . But the thing was, there is no other word for it, in bad taste. I then wrapped a scarf around hand and tin-foiled heart, and felt safer. Now it was a question of pretending to have hurt my hand until I could think of a way of getting rid of my heart altogether, short of amputating my hand.

Meanwhile I telephoned (really, not in imagination) C, who now would never be C. I could feel my heart, which was stuck so close to my fingers that I could feel every beat or tremor, give a gulp of resigned grief at the idea of this beautiful experience now never to be. I told him some idiotic lie about having flu. Well, he was all stiff and indignant, but concealing it urbanely, as I would have done, making a joke but allowing a tiny barb of sarcasm to rankle in the last well-chosen phrase. Then I sat down again to think out my whole situation.

There I sat.

What was I going to do?

There I sat.

I am going to have to skip about four days here, vital enough in all conscience, because I simply cannot go heartbeat by heartbeat through my memories. A pity, since I suppose this is what this story is about; but in brief: I drew the curtains, I took the telephone off the hook, I turned on the lights, I took the scarf off the glittering shape, then the tin foil, then I examined the heart. There were two-fifths of a century's experience to work through, and before I had even got through the first night, I was in a state hard to describe . . .

> Of if I could pull the nerves from my skin
> A quick red net to drag through a sea for fish . . .

By the end of the fourth day I was worn out. By no act of will, or intention, or desire, could I move that heart by a fraction – on the contrary, it was not only stuck to my fingers, like a sucked boiled sweet, but was actually growing to the flesh of my fingers and my palm.

I wrapped it up again in tin foil and scarf, and turned out the lights and pulled up the blinds and opened the curtains. It was about ten in the morning, an ordinary London day, neither hot nor cold nor clear nor clouded nor wet nor fine. And while the street is interesting, it is not exactly beautiful, so I wasn't looking at it so much as waiting for something to catch my attention while thinking of something else.

Suddenly I heard a tap-tap-tapping that got louder, sharp and clear, and I knew before I saw her that this was the sound of high heels on a pavement though it might just as well have been a hammer against stone. She walked fast opposite my window and her heels hit the pavement so hard that all the noises of the street seemed absorbed into that single tap-tap-clang-clang. As she reached the corner at Great Portland Street two London pigeons swooped diagonally from the sky very fast, as if they were bullets aimed to kill her; and then as they saw her they swooped up and off at an angle. Meanwhile she had turned the corner. All this has taken time to write down, but the thing happening took a couple of seconds: the woman's body hitting the pavement bang-bang through her heels then sharply turning the corner in a right angle; and the pigeons making another acute angle across hers and intersecting it in a fast sweep of displaced air. Nothing to all that, of course, nothing – she had gone off down the street, her heels tip-tapping, and the pigeons landed on my windowsill and began cooing. All gone, all vanished, the marvellous exact co-ordination of sound and movement, but it had happened, it had made me happy and exhilarated, I had no problems in this world, and I realized that the heart stuck to my fingers was quite loose. I couldn't get it off altogether, though I was tugging at it under the scarf and the tin foil, but almost.

I understood that sitting and analysing each movement of my pulse or beat of my heart through forty years was a mistake. I was on the wrong track altogether: this was the way to attach my red, bitter, delighted heart to my flesh for ever and ever . . .

> Ha! So you think I'm done! You think . . .
> Watch, I'll roll my heart in a mesh of rage
> And bounce it like a handball off
> Walls, faces, railings, umbrellas and pigeons' backs . . .

No, all that was no good at all, it just made things worse. What I must do is to take myself by surprise, as it were, the way I was taken by surprise over the woman and the pigeons and the sharp sounds of heels and silk wings.

I put on my coat, held my lumpy scarfed arm across my chest, so that if anyone said: What have you done with your hand? I could say: I've banged my finger in the door. Then I walked down into the street.

It wasn't easy to go among so many people, when I was worried that they were thinking: What has that woman done to her hand? because that made it hard to forget myself. And all the time it tingled and throbbed against my fingers, reminding me.

Now I was out I didn't know what to do. Should I go and have lunch with someone? Or wander in the park? Or buy myself a dress? I decided to go to the Round Pond, and walk around it by myself. I was tired after four days and nights without sleep. I went down into the Underground at Oxford

Circus. Midday. Crowds of people. I felt self-conscious, but of course need not have worried. I swear you could walk naked down the street in London and no one would even turn round.

So I went down the escalator and looked at the faces coming up past me on the other side, as I always do; and wondered, as I always do, how strange it is that those people and I should meet by chance in such a way, and how odd that we would never see each other again, or, if we did, we wouldn't know it. And I went on to the crowded platform and looked at the faces as I always do, and got into the train, which was very full, and found a seat. It wasn't as bad as at rush hour, but all the seats were filled. I leaned back and closed my eyes, deciding to sleep a little, being so tired. I was just beginning to doze off, when I heard a woman's voice muttering, or rather, declaiming:

'A gold cigarette case, well, that's a nice thing, isn't it, I must say, a gold case, yes . . . '

There was something about this voice which made me open my eyes: on the other side of the compartment, about eight persons away, sat a youngish woman, wearing a cheap green cloth coat, gloveless hands, flat brown shoes, and lisle stockings. She must be rather poor – a woman dressed like this is a rare sight, these days. But it was her posture that struck me. She was sitting half twisted in her seat, so that her head was turned over her left shoulder, and she was looking straight at the stomach of an elderly man next to her. But it was clear she was not seeing it: her young staring eyes were sightless, she was looking inwards.

She was so clearly alone, in the crowded compartment, that it was not as embarrassing as it might have been. I looked around, and people were smiling, or exchanging glances, or winking, or ignoring her, according to their natures, but she was oblivious of us all.

She suddenly aroused herself, turned so that she sat straight in her seat, and directed her voice and her gaze to the opposite seat:

171

> 'Well so that's what you think, you think that, you think that
> do you, well, you think I'm just going to wait at home for
> you, but you gave her a gold case and . . . '

And with a clockwork movement of her whole thin person,
she turned her narrow pale-haired head sideways over her
left shoulder, and resumed her stiff empty stare at the man's
stomach. He was grinning uncomfortably. I leaned forward
to look along the line of people in the row of seats I sat in,
and the man opposite her, a young man, had exactly the
same look of discomfort which he was determined to keep
amused. So we all looked at her, the young, thin, pale woman
in her private drama of misery, who was so completely
unconscious of us that she spoke and thought out loud.
And again, without particular warning or reason, in between
stops, so it wasn't that she was disturbed from her dream by
the train stopping at Bond Street, and then jumping forward
again, she twisted her body frontways, and addressed the
seat opposite her (the young man had got off, and a smart
grey-curled matron had got in):

> 'Well I know about it now, don't I, and if you come in all
> smiling and pleased well then I know, don't I, you don't have
> to tell me, I know, and I've said to her, I've said, I know he
> gave you a gold cigarette case . . . '

At which point, with the same clockwork impulse, she
stopped, or was checked, or simply ran out, and turned
herself half around to stare at the stomach – the same
stomach, for the middle-aged man was still there. But we
stopped at Marble Arch and he got out, giving the compartment, rather than the people in it, a tolerant half-smile which
said: I am sure I can trust you to realize that this unfortunate
woman is stark staring mad . . .

His seat remained empty. No people got in at Marble Arch,
and the two people standing waiting for seats did not want
to sit by her to receive her stare.

We all sat, looking gently in front of us, pretending to
ourselves and to each other that we didn't know the poor
woman was mad and that in fact we ought to be doing
something about it. I even wondered what I should say:

Madam, you're mad – shall I escort you to your home? Or: Poor thing, don't go on like that, it doesn't do any good, you know – just leave him, that'll bring him to his senses . . .

And behold, after the interval that was regulated by her inner mechanism had elapsed, she turned back and said to the smart matron who received this statement of accusation with perfect self-command:

> 'Yes, I know! Oh yes! And what about my shoes, what about them, a golden cigarette case is what she got, the filthy bitch, a golden case . . . '

Stop. Twist. Stare. At the empty seat by her.

Extraordinary. Because it was a frozen misery, how shall I put it? A passionless passion – we were seeing unhappiness embodied, we were looking at the essence of some private tragedy – rather, Tragedy. There was no emotion in it. She was like an actress doing Accusation, or Betrayed Love, or Infidelity, when she has only just learned her lines and is not bothering to do more than get them right.

And whether she sat in her half-twisted position, her unblinking eyes staring at the greenish, furry, ugly covering of the train seat, or sat straight, directing her accusation to the smart woman opposite, there was a frightening immobility about her – yes, that was why she frightened us. For it was clear that she might very well (if the inner machine ran down) stay silent, for ever, in either twisted or straight position, or at any point between them – yes, we could all imagine her, frozen perpetually in some arbitrary pose. It was as if we watched the shell of some woman going through certain predetermined motions.

For *she* was simply not there. *What* was there, who she was, it was impossible to tell, though it was easy to imagine her thin, gentle little face breaking into a smile in total forgetfulness of what she was enacting now. She did not know she was in a train between Marble Arch and Queensway, nor that she was publicly accusing her husband or lover, nor that we were looking at her.

And we, looking at her, felt an embarrassment and shame that was not on her account at all . . .

173

Suddenly I felt, under the scarf and the tin foil, a lightening of my fingers, as my heart rolled loose.

I hastily took it off my palm, in case it decided to adhere there again, and I removed the scarf, leaving balanced on my knees a perfect stylized heart, like a silver heart on a Valentine card, though of course it was three-dimensional. This heart was not so much harmless, no that isn't the word, as artistic, but in very bad taste, as I said. I could see that the people in the train, now looking at me and the heart, and not at the poor mad-woman, were pleased with it.

I got up, took the four or so paces to where she was, and laid the tin-foiled heart down on the seat so that it received her stare.

For a moment she did not react, then with a groan or a mutter of relieved and entirely theatrical grief, she leaned forward, picked up the glittering heart, and clutched it in her arms, hugging it and rocking it back and forth, even laying her cheek against it, while staring over its top at her husband as if to say: Look what I've got, I don't care about you and your cigarette case, I've got a silver heart.

I got up, since we were at Notting Hill Gate, and, followed by the pleased congratulatory nods and smiles of the people left behind, I went out on to the platform, up the escalators, into the street, and along to the park.

No heart. No heart at all. What bliss. What freedom . . .

Hear that sound? That's laughter, yes.
That's me laughing, yes, that's me.

THE FISH-SCALE SHIRT

RUTH FAINLIGHT

THE WOODEN TROUGH where she stood was darkened and spongy from a constant flow of water that poured out at an odd twisted angle – like an icicle at the corner of a roof – through a large brass tap fixed onto the wall of the boat shed, and the ground below the trough was always slimy. Moss took hold wherever it could – though there were few places not sealed against its advance by a glistening varnish of fish scales, which gave the whole scene a paradoxical elegance, as if the barrels and buckets, the baskets into which the cleaned fish were packed, the trough and puddled yard and collapsing huts and fences that surrounded it were inlaid with mother-of-pearl. Ann saw and thought about fish scales all day, dreamed of them every night. Her task was to collect enough to cover the shirt she had to make. She tried to imagine how it would look – a glittering shirt of fish-scale sequins, like chain-mail armour.

She had woken one morning on the shore of a small harbour where fishing boats rose and sank at the horizon with the timeless regularity of waves breaking on the stony beach. Someone must have brought her there, but she had no memory of the journey. The contrast with her previous life was so decisive that she might as well have been shot into space and landed on another planet. An old woman had appeared at her side and given the details of the task, adding that when the garment was ready, Ann would discover who it was intended for. She could never find that woman again among the others.

With them, each day she split and gutted the gleaming bodies tumbled from weed-tangled, barnacle-crusted nets onto the cobbled quayside. The skill and speed of her workmates was astonishing. She watched carefully, trying to see how they managed to open and clean a large fish in what seemed one flowing movement. Her chapped hands and fingers, covered with cuts, smarted from the cold air and salt water. These strong-limbed, full-bodied women, and the tall fair sailors in seaboots and oilskins who looked like their brothers and husbands, joked together all day long, shining teeth and glistening lips and tongues in noisy action to speak a dialect she could barely comprehend. But in spite of their energetic, friendly presences, they stayed as unreal to her as she must be to them. Nevertheless, she studied the men's faces and gestures, and listened to the different tones of voice, seeking a sign to indicate that this or that one might become the wearer of the fish-scale shirt. A few had made tentative yet unmistakable approaches, but they soon stopped when she did not respond. None had the special quality that marked a prince in disguise.

The old woman had shown Ann a broken-down lean-to behind the fish sheds, and said that was where she would live. There was a pile of old sacks inside, which she took to the beach and washed in the foam. It was a windy, sunny day and they dried quickly, spread over clumps of seaspurge and marram grass. They would serve as blanket and towel and pillow. She also found a tin plate, a chipped enamel bowl and mug, and a sharp knife. One of the fisherwomen gestured her to come and share their round loaves of bread and cauldron of fish soup. Her basic needs were provided. At the end of a day's hard work and the communal meal, Ann fell onto the bed of sacks as if it were the most luxurious divan and slept more deeply than she could remember ever having done before.

How to gather the fish scales was the first problem. If her hands and arms were wet from fish juices and sea water, they clung to her skin, impossible to detach. They seemed as fragile and easily damaged as the scales on butterflies' wings. If her hands were stiff from gripping the hard bone handle

176

of the knife and the icy bodies of the dying fish, the scales slid through her clumsy fingers. By trial and error she learned that the best way to gather the scales was to let them dry wherever they landed, and then come back and gently scrape them off with the blunt edge of the knife into the lap of her skirt. It was a slow method, but she could not think of a better one. Day by day, the heap of scales in the corner of the hut mounted higher.

Having decided that none of the fishermen was an enchanted prince the fish-scale shirt would release (so that he in turn could rescue her), Ann looked at the women more closely. There was no reason why her hero might not be a heroine. But although each in her own way was amiable, neither did any of them convince her as the destined one.

'When the time comes, your hero will appear,' a voice half-sang and half-intoned inside her head. 'Just go on doing what you must, gathering the fish scales, and thinking about how you can make a shirt to sew them on, and what you will use for needle and thread.' The voice was her companion. There was something familiar and reassuring about it, like a reminder of childhood. But whether the voice was that of mother or father or nurse or someone else, she could not be sure – nor even if it was her own.

Now the problem had been stated, it did not seem so daunting. She could make a needle from a strong straight fishbone, and pierce an eye through its thicker end with the point of her knife. Splitting open the firm cold bodies and scraping them clean, she wondered if she could use the silvery intestines for thread. But the shrivelled, hardened state of some she had put aside overnight eliminated that possibility.

Every day, cold winds beat rain onto the stone quay and high massed clouds moved steadily across the sky. But between the squalls, sunlight lit their edges with vivid silver and flashed from the encrustations of mica-fine fish scales. On certain evenings the sunset melted crimson, orange and purple bands into the horizon. Either the season was softening, or else she was adjusting to the climate's harshness. One morning, picking up a sacking blanket she had thrown off during the night, it became obvious how the shirt could be made and where the thread would come from. Such practical matters left no time to grieve about her past life or this one. She carefully frayed the rough fabric into the shape of a shirt-body and sleeves, then teased out separate threads to stitch seams down the sides and around the edges. 'I hope my hero won't be too tall or broad,' she mused, holding it against herself. The shirt was hardly larger than her own.

The next step was to sew on the scales, one stitch for each, in overlapping rows. Now the days were longer, rays of sunlight struck through the open door of the hut to the far corner where the glittering heap dazzled like tidewater over wet, bright stones along the shoreline. The slightest current of air would lift a few to skid across the floor or fly upwards then settle on her head like snowflakes or appleblossom. Hunched over a dim, but pungent, fish-oil lamp, she continued working until dawn made the lamplight even weaker. The nearer she came to finishing the shirt, the more Ann wondered why she had been set this task.

One day she walked further inland than ever before. Smooth blackish rocks were scattered on the dark ground – isolated boulders or massive stones piled like cairns built by a race of giants. She noticed a wisp of steam at the base of one where an overhanging shelf of rock sloped back into the earth. Between two black stone lips a hot spring bubbled up in sudden irregular gouts like blood being pumped from a deep wound. Grey scum, brilliant green moss and thick white mineral streaks rimmed the outlet in the shape of something being born from the cleft in the rocks.

The sense of another presence and a movement to one side made Ann turn her head, to be confronted by the speckled yellow eyes and unblinking gaze of a large brown toad sheltering there. This must be the one she had been waiting for, she thought excitedly, the one who had waited here for her. Only a creature under a spell would be in this magical place. And the toad was so repulsive that it must surely become the handsomest prince in the world.

She smiled encouragingly and reached out to touch its head, but at the last moment could not make herself do it. She hoped the toad had not noticed this hesitation, and would not be offended or angry or hurt. Walking slowly backwards she chanted, 'Come home with me, dear toad-prince. Come to my hut. Come and see what I am making for you.' And heaving itself forward with an unpleasant movement and a sound like a paper bag full of water being bumped across a wooden floor, the toad followed. Every few steps she turned to make sure it was still there, and each time the toad stared back with a more intense, significant and intelligent expression.

She must be right to believe the toad was an enchanted prince. No ordinary toad would be so delicate, so considerate. All the stories she remembered about princesses forced to be goosegirls or to take a vow of silence and live in a tree spinning thread from nettles or sorting every poppy seed from an enormous heap of lentils and pebbles ended happily in a transformation scene. By comparison to such tasks, hers was not really hard – and she might have made it easier, she realised, by being more friendly with her workmates and the fishermen. But that would have meant abandoning all hope in the redemptive power of her task, and accepting this existence as permanent.

She had been uneasy about what he might expect, but the toad barely stirred from his place in the furthest corner of the hut, opposite the diminishing heap of fish scales. Ann's first thought when she woke was of him, and her first act was to confirm that the squat warty creature was still there, and meet his insistent yellow stare. She began to appreciate the subtle variations of tone on his mottled back. Her life was different now she knew he would be waiting in the hut at the end of each day. She had no idea how he fed himself. The first few evenings she had brought back some soup in an old bowl and put it down in front of him, but the food remained untouched. She supposed that the toad went outside to drink water and catch flies or whatever else toads eat while she was down at the harbour.

She had sewn the final overlapping row of scales, knotted

179

and bitten off the last length of thread, and held the garment out for them both to admire. The toad seemed to examine it with great interest. Ann thought she might faint from excitement. She moved closer and lifted the shirt high above his head, while she imagined a handsome young man uncoiling from the ungainly body and rising up to meet the garment in mid-air as it settled onto his wide, smooth shoulders. But in the instant between her letting-go of the garment and its collapse onto the dirt floor, the toad hopped away into the furthest corner.

She picked up the shirt and shook the creases out. Some of the scales had been bent to one side and a few had fallen off, but it still looked extraordinary – glinting like metal and yet as delicate as soap bubbles. 'Don't hop away, dear prince,' she murmured, carefully taking the shirt by the seam of each shoulder and raising it above him once more. He had already flexed his back legs in preparation for a leap before she moved, so the shirt did not fall onto the ground again. 'Toad, toad, don't you want to be a prince?' she asked, half laughing with vexation. The toad remained as silent as ever.

After several more attempts at investiture and spell-breaking, Ann had to accept either that her prince preferred to remain a toad, or else was and never had been anything except a simple natural creature. She opened the door and the toad hopped out and disappeared into the darkness. She held the shirt up in front of her own eyes and regarded it ruefully.

She was the one who had been enchanted, in thrall. The shirt was beautiful. She remembered that there had only been enough sacking to make a small one and that it should certainly fit. She pulled it over her head and walked through the open door. Perhaps she had felt a comparable joy and freedom years before, but this seemed quite unlike anything she could recall. The fishwives and the fishermen were drinking and laughing on the quay. She smiled and they smiled back and waved as she strode past. Quite soon she came to a broad highway behind the rise of the land. A silvery car, reflecting the moonlight like the fish scales on her shirt, stood waiting – door unlocked, key inside. She sat down behind the wheel and drove south.

BLUE-BEARDED LOVER

JOYCE CAROL OATES

I.

WHEN WE WALKED together he held my hand unnaturally high, at the level of his chest, as no man had done before. In this way he made his claim.

When we stood at night beneath the great winking sky he instructed me gently in its deceit. The stars you see above you, he said, have vanished thousands of millions of years ago; it is precisely the stars you cannot see that exist, and exert their influence upon you.

When we lay together in the tall cold grasses the grasses curled lightly over us as if to hide us.

II.

A man's passion is his triumph, I have learned. And to be the receptacle of a man's passion is a woman's triumph.

III.

He made me his bride and brought me to his great house which smelled of time and death. Passageways and doors and high-ceilinged rooms and tall windows opening out onto nothing. Have you ever loved another man as you now love me? my blue-bearded lover asked. Do you give your life to me?

What is a woman's life that cannot be thrown away!

He told me of the doors I may unlock and the rooms I may enter freely. He told me of the seventh door, the forbidden door, which I may not unlock: for behind it lies a forbidden room which I may not enter. Why may I not enter it? I asked, for I saw that he expected it of me, and he said, kissing my brow, Because I have forbidden it.

And he entrusted me with the key to the door, for he was going away on a long journey.

IV.

Here it is: a small golden key, weighing no more than a feather in the palm of my hand.

It is faintly stained as if with blood. It glistens when I hold it to the light.

Did I not know that my lover's previous brides had been brought to this house to die? – that they had failed him, one by one, and had deserved their fate?

I have slipped the golden key into my bosom, to wear against my heart, as a token of my lover's trust in me.

V.

When my blue-bearded lover returned from his long journey he was gratified to see that the door to the forbidden room remained locked; and when he examined the key, still warm from my bosom, he saw that the stain was an old, old stain, and not of my doing.

And he declared with great passion that I was now truly his wife; and that he loved me above all women.

VI.

Through the opened windows the invisible stars exert their power.

But if it is a power that is known, are the stars invisible?

When I sleep in our sumptuous bed I sleep deeply, and dream dreams that I cannot remember afterward, of extraordinary beauty, I think, and magic, and wonder. Sometimes in the morning my husband will recall them for me, for their marvels are such they invade even his dreams. How is it that you of all persons can dream such dreams, he says, – such curious works of art!

And he kisses me, and seems to forgive me.

And I will be bearing his child soon. The first of his many children.

SECRET OBSERVATIONS ON THE GOAT-GIRL

JOYCE CAROL OATES

AT THE EDGE of my father's property, in an abandoned corncrib, there lives a strange creature – a goat-child – a girl – my age – with no name that we know – and no mother or father or companions. She has a long narrow head and immense slanted eyes, albino-pale, and an expression that seems to be perpetually startled. The veins of her eyes glow a faint warm pulsing pink and the irises are animal-slits, vertical, very black. Sometimes she suns herself in the open doorway, her slender front legs tucked neatly beneath her, her head alert and uplifted. Sometimes she grazes in the back pasture. Though we children are forbidden to know about her we frequently spy on her, and laugh to see her down on all fours, *grazing as animals do* – yet in an awkward improvised posture, as if she were a child playing at being a goat.

But of course she *is* an animal and frightening to see.

Her small body is covered in coarse white hairs, wavy, slightly curly, longest around her temples and at the nape of her neck. Her ears are frankly goatish, pert and oversized and sensitive to the slightest sound. (If we creep up in the underbrush to spy on her, she always hears us – her ears prick up and tremble – though she doesn't seem to see us. Which is why some of us have come to believe that the goat-girl is blind.)

Her nose, like her ears, is goatish: snubbed and flat with wide dark nostrils. But her eyes are human eyes. Thickly lashed and beautiful. Except they are so very pale. The tiny

185

blood vessels are exposed which is why they look pink; I wonder, does the sunshine hurt her? . . . do tears form in her eyes? (Of my eight brothers and sisters it is the older, for some reason, who argue that the goat-girl is blind and should be put out of her misery. One of my sisters has nightmares about her – about her strange staring eyes – though she has seen the goat-girl only once, and then from a distance of at least fifteen feet. Oh the nasty thing, she says, half sobbing, the filthy thing! – Father should have it butchered.)

But we all speak in whispers. Because we are forbidden to know.

Since the goat-girl came to live at the edge of our property my mother rarely leaves the house. In fact she rarely comes downstairs now. Sometimes she wears a robe over her night-gown and doesn't brush out her hair and pin it up the way she used to, sometimes she hurries out of the room if one of us comes in. Her laughter is faint and shrill.

Her fingers are cold to the touch. She doesn't embrace us any longer.

Father doesn't admonish her because, as he says, he loves her too deeply. But he often avoids her. And of course he is very busy with his travels – he is sometimes absent for weeks at a time.

Shame, shame! – the villagers whisper.

But never so that any of us can hear.

The goat-girl cannot speak as human beings do, nor does she make goat noises. For the most part she is silent. But she is capable of a strangulated mew, a bleating whine, and, sometimes at night, a questioning cry that is human in its intonation and rhythm, though of course it is incomprehensible, and disturbing to hear. To some of us it sounds plead-ing, to others angry and accusing. Of course no one ever replies.

The goat-girl eats grass, grain, vegetables the farm workers have tossed into her pen – gnarled and knotted carrots, wormy turnips, blackened potatoes. One day I slipped away from the house to bring her a piece of my birthday cake (angel food with pink frosting and a sprinkling of silver 'stars') – I left it wrapped in a napkin near the corncrib but as far as I knew she never approached it: she is very shy by daylight.

(Except when she believes no one is near. Then you should see how delightful she is, playing in the meadow, trotting and frisking about, kicking up her little hooves! – exactly like any young animal, without a worry in the world.)

The goat-girl has no name, just as she has no mother or father. But she is a girl and so it seems cruel to call her *it*. I will baptize her Astrid because the name makes me think of snow and the goat-girl's hair is snowy white.

The years pass and the goat-girl continues to live in the old corncrib at the edge of our property. No one speaks of her – no one wonders at the fact that she has grown very little since she came to live with us. (When I was nine years old I thought the goat-girl was my age exactly and that she would grow along with me, like a sister. But I must have been mistaken.)

Mother no longer comes downstairs at all. It is possible that people have forgotten her in the village. My brothers and sisters and I would forget her too except for her rapid footsteps overhead and her occasional laughter. Sometimes we hear doors being slammed upstairs – my parents' voices – dim and muffled – the words never audible.

Father asks us to pray for Mother. Which of course we have been doing all along.

By night the goat-girl becomes a nocturnal creature and loses her shyness in a way that is surprising. She leaves the safety of her pen, leaves her little pasture, and prowls anywhere she wishes. Sometimes we hear her outside our windows – her cautious hooves in the grass, her low bleating murmur. I wish I could describe the sound she makes! – it is gentle, it is pleading, it is reproachful, it is trembling with rage – a fluid wordless questioning – like music without words – *Why? How long? Who?* – stirring us from sleep.

Now I see that, by moonlight, the goat-girl is terrifying to

187

watch. Many times I have crept from my bed to look down at her, through my gauzy curtains, protected (I believe) by the dark, and have been frightened by her stiff little body, her defiant posture, her glaring pale eyes. I want to cry out – Please don't hate me! – Please don't wish me harm! – but of course I say nothing, not even a whisper. I draw back from the window and tiptoe to my bed and try to sleep and in the morning it might be that the goat-girl appeared to all my brothers and sisters during the night. . . . But I wasn't asleep, I didn't dream, I try to explain, I saw her myself; but they say mockingly, No, no, you were dreaming too, you are no different from the rest of us, it wouldn't dare come this close to the house.

She isn't *it*. I tell them. Her name is Astrid.

Father dreams of her death but is too weak to order it, so my oldest brother plans to arrange for the butchering as soon as he comes to maturity. Until then the goat-girl lives quietly and happily enough at the edge of our property, sunning herself in good weather, browsing in the pasture, frisking and gamboling about. Singing her plaintive little mew to herself. Trespassing by moonlight. One day soon I will creep as close as possible to look into her eyes, to judge if they are human or not, if they are blind.

She has grown very little over the years but her haunches are muscular, her nearly human shoulders, neck, and head are more defined, sometimes I see her child-soul pushing up out of her goat body like a swimmer emerging from a frothy white sea, about to gasp for air, blink and gape in amazement.

Astrid! I will call. Sister!

But she won't know her name.

188

ANNINA

HELEN DUNMORE

THAT TIME WHEN I was having Annina. The time I had Annina.

No. It doesn't sound right. I can say: *the time when I was having Blaise.* In fact I *have* said it, often. It's my time, my experience, my possession. No-one can contradict me about it.

Long ago in the middle of the night when everyone was sleeping and there was a frost on the ground which killed the last of my geraniums even though they'd lived through the whole of a mild winter, Annina was born.

It doesn't matter what I write, it comes out as lies. And that's very suitable for the story of Annina. Annina's taught me a new language entirely, one of lies and things you leave out. Without it, now, I wouldn't survive. It's more necessary to me than air to breathe.

Annina is my little girl. Annina is my language. I speak Annina. Even in quite ordinary conversations, I pick up scraps of Annina. Out of the fuzz of static which is what ordinary English has become for me, I catch a phrase. Annina.

> My little baby-waby
> My drop of honey
> My own, my secret one.

Quite often I hear lovers speaking a bit of Annina. It may be nauseating, but by God it's recognizable, like one of those tunes you just hear once and it happens that you've got a

189

new dress on and the sun's shining so warmly you can smell both the cotton and your own skin.

But this isn't doing you justice, Annina. Here I am making a mystery out of you when all you ever wanted was to be a secret, and you're that for sure now, because even if I wanted to pick you up and brandish you for the world to see, you've gone. The traces you've left are only those that may be made by any sick-hearted woman whose son has grown up and gone, a woman who's always wanted a little girl, but whose little girl would need to be more a doll than a thing of flesh.

THING. I never called you that. I did Blaise, of course. 'Come here, you bad thing, wait till Mummy catches you.'

None of that with Annina.

'My daughter,' I called her, and 'my girl.' Never *little*. Never *creature*. Never *thing*.

Annina was not quite small enough to sleep inside a walnut-shell. The cracked shell of a hard-boiled egg, for sure, but that would have been quite unnecessary. It was easy enough to make things nice for her, and why shouldn't she have her own bed with pillow and sheets and quilt like any Christian? And she was a Christian, I made sure of that. The big drop of holy water swelling and breaking across her face. Her mouth squaring with anger. And I made the sign of the cross without bruising her forehead. I wasn't sure if I'd done it right, so I went to confession to an old Jesuit in a church in the city centre and told him what I'd done; nothing about the size of Annina, for fear he'd write me off as a madwoman, but everything else. Though maybe I could have told him, for he looked as if nothing in the world would surprise him. I'd done right, it seemed. But as I came out and felt Annina stir in her quilted sling under my blouse, I wondered why it had seemed to matter so much and why I'd gone running to the priest when there was Annina, warm and fragile as a newlaid egg. Already, even though she wasn't yet speaking, a bit of Annina's language had got between me and the priest, and somehow it wasn't the word of Annina I doubted. She was always as warm as any other child. I don't know why that should have surprised me, but it did, almost as if I thought she should have had a slighter heat to match her slight size. Or perhaps it was all the stories I used to read in my Green Fairy Book and my Red Fairy Book, where the fairies were cold and magical and lived under the hills.

But don't mistake me. Annina is no fairy.

Let's go back to *when I had Annina*, since there doesn't seem to be any more accurate way of putting it.

Blaise was eight at the time. He was tall for his age and he'd just had his hair cut short and his freckles were coming on his nose and his cheeks from playing out after school with his friends now the days were growing longer and lighter. He was not my baby any more, but I didn't mind that and I have never wanted to be the sort of woman who stands back bruised and brave to let her young hero make his own way in life. And lets him know that she's always waiting for him back at home. Besides, for the first time since Blaise's birth, I was pregnant again. Not far along, about nine weeks. We'd always wanted more children, but since Blaise it'd been as if we were sitting by one of those rivers you know is full of fish, with juicy bait and a good line but not a single bite the whole afternoon. Not that we were that bothered. We'd enjoyed those afternoons, with the sun on us and the water spreading out and the chance of a little fish under the surface. No, we weren't bothered.

So I was looking at my future in a new way when one afternoon just before Blaise came home I bent down to see if the frost really had got the geraniums or not, and when I straightened up there was something warm and wet running down my legs. My first thought was that I'd wet myself. It was a long time since I'd been pregnant and anything seemed possible. But of course it was red and it was blood and at the same time it began to hurt, very slyly as if it was mocking the period which would have come around that time of the month if I hadn't been pregnant.

And then there were hours of hot panic and fluster, and the doctor coming and being sorry but I'd lost the baby, and Matt coming home seeming to bring the noise and smell of the school-children with him, since he'd come out of class so suddenly. Then Matt went downstairs to cook sausages just for Blaise. Neither of us felt like anything.

There was a little prickle under the sheet. The first stir of that small heat I grew to know better than my own temperature. Annina.

There was a cord like a cotton thread, so I bit through it. She was an inch and a half long and as fast asleep as if she was only half-way through her long journey, and she was damned if she was going to wake up somewhere boring in the middle of it. Not like Blaise, I thought. Blaise was born crying. And that was the first difference between them which occurred to me.

I wiped the blood off her with a corner of my nightgown, then I got up although I was still bleeding and found a box of fancy handkerchiefs in my top left-hand drawer. They were fine lace and the kind of useless thing you get given and keep by you for years without using, but they did for Annina. She looked just like a handkerchief in my hand when Matt came into the room with a cup of tea.

'What in God's name are you doing out of bed?' he asked, and set down my cup of tea in a hurry and helped me back to lie down. All the time I held onto Annina in that light way you do when you've got something in your hand which might break, and I prayed that she wouldn't make a sound, though what kind of noise a baby her size might make, I couldn't imagine.

Of course I found out soon enough. That was the first bit of her language Annina taught me. A lighter, croakier sound than I'd thought. If I breathed in hard and groaned as if in my sleep, I could hide her cries with my own breathing. After a couple of months I couldn't breathe any other way when I lay down to sleep. Matt said to me once, gentle and awkward,

'I always knew you minded more than you let on. That was when you began groaning in your sleep.'

Feeding you, Annina! Well you made it clear right from the start that there was going to be no satisfying *you* on nectar and honey-dew. Cow's milk, boiled and cooled and strained, a drop at a time from an eye-dropper. But it gave you wind and you cried for two hours one night while I shifted about in bed and wheezed and moaned to cover it. So I asked a friend who'd had a baby born at seven months,

192

just marvelling casually at how well she'd managed and how the little thing had thrived, and she told me they'd fed her on goats' milk right from the beginning, on her midwife's advice since her own milk had dried up after a week.

'Right, that's for you, Annina,' I said to myself, and I told Matt that I was going to drink goats' milk from now on, in the hope of curing an itchy rash I'd got between my fingers. How I hated that stuff! But you loved it. I could swear now that I saw the pink flush through your skin when you had your first feed of it, drop by drop, at blood-heat. I could see your right leg kicking as you swallowed it.

You didn't cry much after that. Often you'd be awake, for I'd feel you moving against me in the little pouch I made for you, hung around my neck and hidden by a loose blouse. Poor Matt missed the way we used to sleep together naked, skin to skin, and make love when we were half awake and half sleeping. I think he believed I'd lost heart for making love now I'd lost the baby, even though he must have known that for me that had never been the point of it. So I made a nest for you under my bed and I would tuck you there until I was sure from Matt's breathing that he was asleep. Then I'd bring you into the bed with me, because otherwise I was afraid you'd cry in the night and I wouldn't hear you. And I was afraid of other things for you: wasps and mice and spiders which would be half the size of you or more. When I started to think of dogs and cats I had to close my mind and tell myself to take one step at the time. We had no cat or dog ourselves, only a pair of goldfish which were like dolphins in your eyes. Do you remember how I let you swim in the tank with them when you begged me to let you, and the big goldfish hung quite still in the water with terror before he dived into the weed and lay trembling next to the china diver that had got rooted in there over the years? I told you to keep away from the weed, but as usual you paid little attention and swam in and out of it, peeking at me through the side of the tank and I daresay laughing to yourself as usual for the sheer pleasure you were having. Then afterwards you danced naked on your towel till you were dry, clapping your hands. I can still hear your hands, clapping.

The thing was, you were so beautiful. I was always looking for excuses to be alone so that I could open your pouch and look at you curled up there. Anybody could have pinched your life out with a finger, but you lay there so alive with a life of your own, so much taken up with your own dreams or your full warm stomach or the feel of my skin against your hands that I could never think of you as defenceless. It's not ordinary beauty I'm talking about, anyway. How could you fail to have fine features, even though you took after me with my red cheeks and my black eye-brows that nearly meet over my nose? Nothing frightened you. You hadn't got a chance, really, if you'd only known it, but you got by because you refused to know it, and often I would just burst out laughing for joy at your boldness. What age do babies learn to climb? I suppose they don't climb a lot, in the usual way, but you climbed everywhere. Up my open-work vest. In and out of my front-fastening bra. And my hair! – you couldn't leave it alone. The day I made a plait and you went up it hand-over-hand until you reached my parting and you were so close to my ear I could hear you breathing hard and egging yourself on. I had a hand cupped under you all the time.

All this time you were reaching out, I was closing myself away. There was a job I would have killed for the year before, playing piano for a music therapist in a unit for handicapped children, but I had to turn it down. You were three by then, and I couldn't trust you to keep out of sight. By four you were learning, and at five I could take you anywhere and you'd lie still against me or I'd feel your body vibrating with laughter as you peered out through the gap in my blouse. What a boringly-dressed woman I became! Loose blouses, sensible dresses with collars and plenty of pleats down the front. My sister Claire burst out once:

> 'For God's sake, Teresa, will you look at yourself in the mirror? It's the middle of July, why don't you put on your shorts and sun-top like you used to? You're only thirty-one and anybody would think you were forty!'

She was quite right. I looked older. Men didn't whistle or

call after me in the streets any more as they'd been doing since I was twelve years old. I could wander along with my face up to the sun, and if my lips moved, nobody seemed to pay any attention. I think I must have had that look some women get when they're well on in pregnancy, inward and a bit taken up with something all the time. And that's a look which makes people leave you alone.

Did Matt know about you, or didn't he? Often, again and again, I'd think he'd seen you. I'd think maybe he played with you and talked to you and never let on for fear that once the whole business was out in the open we would have to *do something* about you. People would come to the house and tell us that *arrangements* ought to be made for you. You needed protection; a safe place maybe where you could be kept well away from things which would do you harm. Somewhere light and clean and airy with a spy-hole so that you could be kept an eye on. A little box for you.

You were ten years old and five inches tall. You ran fast, and you jumped high and when you skipped your feet didn't seem to touch the ground. Size for size, I'm sure you were quicker and nimbler than other children. When I looked closely at your feet I saw how strongly-made they were, with high arches and long toes so you could climb and judge a distance and leap without ever making a mistake.

No, of course you made mistakes, Annina. Remember when my worst fear was realized and a cat got into the garden while I had my back turned to you, weeding. And you put out your fist to it and hit it on the nose as hard as you could so that it sprang back and cowered by the bird-table, but not without giving you a slash on your forearm which was like a rip in silk. And it wanted stitching, but I couldn't think of anybody I could trust to do it, so I bound it tightly with the edges of the wound together and dressed it every day until it healed. You were lucky. It healed with only a faint white scar. Though you hated the scar, Annina, however much I told you it was hardly visible.

'You don't see it in the way I do,' you said, and of course you were right.

I thought the cat would have made you more cautious, but

195

it was from then on that you began to go out on your own. You bound waxed thread around the eyelet of a darning-needle, and wore it at your side like a sword. You learned that cats would back off if you screamed at a certain pitch.

Blaise was at college, studying mathematics. When he came home he bent down to me and I kissed his fair prickly cheek with its big pores and splashed freckles and I thought of his sister out there in the jungle with her darning-needle. The bigness of Blaise's hand as he took his cup of coffee. His huge trainers kicked off and lying like mountains on the lino.

Annina, did you love Blaise, your brother? You knew more about him than I ever did. You stayed for hours in his room, listening to tapes with him, watching him study, hearing him talk to his friends. You knew what I didn't know, you heard what only came to me as a drone through the walls. *My brother*, you always said, 'Do you think my brother will be home soon? Are you making those sandwiches for my brother?'

Your light clear voice and your breath at the curve of my ear. You liked best to talk perched up on my shoulder when I was moving about the house, cooking or tidying, or just sitting with a cup of coffee and an unread newspaper in front of me. And I learned to talk very lightly and quietly too, not whispering because that blurred the sounds too much for your ears. And never shouting, for too much noise made you tremble and curl up on yourself. The only thing that always made you afraid.

Annina, you know and I know that I could go on writing to you for ever, just as I could have listened to you for ever as you tucked your right arm round a curl of my hair and leaned yourself comfortably into the shape of my shoulder and told me things I had never seen and would never have been able to imagine. For we didn't really live in the same world, even though we shared house and home and bed and you shared my body as much as you needed it.

You went away and I have no-one else who can talk of you. No-one else knew you, no-one else misses you or grieves for you. No-one else would even believe in you.

You were so sure there were others like you, right from when you were a little girl.

'Have *you* ever told anybody about me?' you demanded. 'Well then! Nobody does! They all keep it secret, just like you do, for fear of what might happen. We need to find each other. How can I stay here knowing that somewhere in the world there are people like me, people of my own?'

You were like me, Annina. You looked like me. I think even our skins and our hair smelled the same. But that was no good to you, and even though I longed for you to stay more than I had ever longed for anything, I made you a pair of trousers and a jacket from buckskin I got from a child's Cowboy and Indian outfit, and I bought thermal silk for your leggings and vests, and you made your own shoes as you had had to learn to do, for I could never get the stitching small enough, and it bruised your feet.

My son went to college with a trunkful of books and a cake I'd made and a letter a week and a telephone in his hall of residence. He went with a bank account and the name of a doctor and his dental records up to date and his term's fees paid. He went with a pair of National Health glasses for reading and vaccination marks on his arm. He went with both of us waving from the station platform and his father slipping him a fiver to get himself something decent to eat on the train.

It was no good giving Annina money. Where and how could she spend it? My daughter went with a backpack on her back which we'd designed together after hours of thought and cutting the silk into the wrong shapes. Light and tough, that was what she wanted. She went with food and drink and I have to say she went with a great gift for stealing which I hoped would stand her in good stead when she grew cold and hungry out in the world. She went with her darning-needle sword at her side, and a sleeping bag filled with the finest down which I'd snipped from duck breast-feathers. My daughter went very quickly, slipping through a hole in the fence, following a map of holes and gaps and secrets and hiding-places which she knew and I did not.

I've learned your language, Annina, and now I've no-one

to speak it with. So I'm still talking to you, wherever you are. It's all right to listen, Annina, for I'm not saying any words that might weaken you. I'm willing you on, Annina, morning and evening. I'll never so much as whisper COME HOME.

One Bear

JOHN BERGER

IF I TELL you about the bear, will you believe me?

The bear was in a room, a large room with links with the past as all rooms which are really living must have.

The bear was a little larger than I and he lived in this room. He belonged there. Perhaps sometimes he was elsewhere but this was where he lived. I was a guest in the house and in the room.

The bear was chained to the wall by a long chain. Apparently he did not suffer by this curtailment. He was as much a part of the room as the fire in the grate, or the table by the wall with the mirror above it. But he was alive. That is important. Although he was chained to the wall, he was like the host of that room. The last thing a visitor could feel was pity for him.

I was conversing with him. Not with words. If I spoke, he understood what I said. But to converse with him, it was necessary to act. I was playing with him, wrestling.

He was a bear. He had a tail, a long busy tail as no bear has. Nevertheless I will call him a bear. And I'll say *he*. Though it might just as well be *she*. Perhaps no pronoun is required. I can always say *bear*.

We were wrestling. Neither bear nor I showed any signs of fear or hostility. Claws withdrawn. At that time it did not occur to me that I could be clawed.

We wrestled and pushed around each other. I can still feel bear's paw. The skin of it, like cooked carp skin, but coarser. And I can see eyes: very dark and opaque. Hiding any expression. It was our wrestling dance that was full of expression. To wrestle is to dance with a bear. And in the well-furnished room in the house which was otherwise silent but not oppressively so, we danced. Bear and I.

Then I noticed something. The chain to the wall was broken. Bear had not realized it. I continued to dance. It was a question of honour. I foresaw the dangers. I thought of disengaging myself and leaving. But I couldn't. Frightened as I was, there was a law stronger than my fear. It was not for me to react first to the chain being broken. It was not my chain. And bear danced the same as before. Bear was still like the fire, a welcome prisoner in the room.

The end of the chain, which had been fixed to an iron ring in the wall, lay on the ground. My eyes kept on coming back to it, as we conversed in wider and wider circles. And although I was still very frightened, I felt something else too. Bear who had been led on a chain during a century or more from village to village, because bear stood on two legs and not four, because bear fur was warm and smelt sweet, because bear had dark intelligent eyes and slow movements, because bear reminded some men of a man, this bear, at last, by breaking the chain, was free.

In every liberation, whatever happens later, there is a beauty. This beauty has a kind of abandon to it. Bear was dancing with more and more abandon. I had been mistaken. Bear knew. Perhaps had known from the beginning.

The beauty was in the knowing as well as in the heavy abandoned swaying from leg to leg. I thought: now I can go: my reaction to the broken chain will not be the first. Still wrestling, still dancing, I steered us towards the door. Previously I had assumed bear was not aware of the new freedom: now I assumed bear would not notice my cunning. For the second time I was wrong.

With one hand I felt behind my back for the door handle. I would be far quicker through the door than bear. I would lock it and leave the house.

Immediately I saw bear with a knife. A knife? Or an extended claw? A blade like a scimitar, curved but very short. Grey-yellow in colour. First one and then several.

The paw was held by my throat: the point of each blade against my skin. I pressed the muzzle of a gun into the bear's stomach. We waited, the two of us.

Then I said: Let us fight without weapons.

Bear threw five knives on the floor. I threw the gun. Before the clatter of these weapons hitting the floor had died away, I was out through the door. I locked it and ran, just as I had planned. Bear, I hoped, was a prisoner again.

During my encounter with the bear, the house had moved, the house and the whole village with it. I turned down a flight of steps off the main street and at the bottom, instead of a road of plane trees, I found the sea. Waves were breaking gently against the walls of the village.

Have I already told you it was night? It was night when I first began conversing with the bear. The sea looked very black except for the spray of the waves. And it was cold. Winter cold. The weather of the bear.

I climbed up the steps and took a passage which led off from the other side of the main street. Again, at the bottom, I came to the sea. During my conversation with the bear, the village had become an island. There was no further question of escape.

Under an empty arcade I went into a café and ordered a hot drink. Nobody in the café looked concerned. The windows were steamed up. I passed between men drinking and clinking glasses. The place had the air of the end of a celebration. All the men were peasants from the village. They knew me – although they considered me a stranger. I could see in none of them a trace of surprise at the fact that their village, so far from the sea, had overnight become an island.

I knew now that the bear would soon be out, at liberty. One locked door would not succeed where a chain and the usage of a century had failed. The bear would find me behind the steamed up windows.

I left the café and walked along the first path by the sea's edge. When I looked up to the top of the flight of steps, I saw bear, descending slowly, wearing clothes. This time no cunning could save me.

Yet in the figure of bear wearing clothes, coming down the

201

steps in the dark and cold, there was still something of the abandon of the moment of liberation. And I felt a pleasure in that, apart from my fear. This pleasure was like the smallest bird in the world – the bee hummingbird – singing underneath the largest cataract.

From my pocket I drew out a book and went to where the only street lamp was attached to the wall of the village, and there began to read.

The book told the story of bear and myself. Hurriedly I turned to the last page to see what was still to happen.

I walked across to the steps. The bear was half way down. I began to climb up towards the bear. The animal made no sign. We were near to each other now, but despite bear's immense weight, each foot descended on to the next step without making a sound. I thought then, whilst ascending and waiting for our meeting, that in that soundlessness we might find a peace.

In the book it said that the bear had forgiven.

The Prospect From The Silver Hill

from CONTINENT

JIM CRACE

THE COMPANY AGENT – friendless, single, far from home
– passed most days alone in a cabin at Ibela-hoy, the Hill
Without a Hat. His work was simple. Equipped with a rudi-
mentary knowledge of mineralogy, neat, laborious hand-
writing, and a skill with ledgers, he had been posted to the
high lands to identify the precious metals, the stones, the
ores, that (everybody said) were buried there.

This was his life: awake at dawn, awake all day, awake
all night. Phrenetic Insomnia was the term. But there were
no friends or doctors to make the diagnosis. The agent simply
– like a swift, a shark – dared not sleep. He kept moving.
He did not close his eyes. At night, at dawn, in the tall heat
of the day, he looked out over the land and, watching the
shades and colours of the hill and its valley accelerate and
reel, he constructed for himself a family and a life less solitary
than the one that he was forced to live. He took pills. He
drank what little spirit arrived each month with his provisions. He exhausted himself with long, aimless walks
amongst the boulders and dry beds. Sometimes he fell forward at work, his nose flattened amongst the gravels on the
table, his papers dampened by saliva, his tongue slack. But
he did not sleep or close his eyes, though he was still troubled
by chimeras, daydreams, which broke his concentration and
(because he was conscious) seemed more substantial and
coherent than sleeping dreams. As the men had already

203

remarked amongst themselves when they saw the sacs of tiredness spreading across his upper cheeks and listened to his conversation, the company agent either had a fever or the devil had swapped sawdust for his brain.

Several times a week one of the survey gangs arrived in a company mobile to deposit drill cores of augered rock and sand, pumice and shale, and provide the company agent with a profile of the world twenty metres below his feet. He sorted clays as milky as nutsap and eggstones as worn and weathered as a saint's bead into sample bags. Each rock, each smudge of soil, was condemned. Nothing. Nothing. Nothing. A trace of tin. Nothing.

Once, when he had been at Ibela-hoy for a few weeks only, one of the survey gangs offered to take him down to the lumber station where the woodsmen had established a good still and an understanding with some local women. He sat in the cab of the mobile drilling rig and talked non-stop. That's the loneliest place, he told them, as the mobile descended from the cabin. There aren't even ghosts. He spoke, too, about the wife and children, the companionable life, which he had concocted in his daydreams. How he wished he had a camera at home, he told the men. Then he could have shown them photographs of his family, of his garden in the city, his car, his wedding day.

The men indulged him. He was still a stranger, they reasoned, and starved of company, missing home. He would quieten down once he had a glass in his hand. But they had been wrong. He became louder with every sip. He spoke in a voice which sent the women back into their homes, which sent the men early to bed. The voice said, My sadness is stronger than your drink. Nothing can relieve it. Nothing. A trace of tin. Nothing.

He daydreamed: a lifetime of finding nothing. He dreamed of prospecting the night sky and locating a planet of diamonds or an old, cooled sun of solid gold. But then the company had no need for diamonds or gold. Find us sand, they instructed. Find us brown mud. Send us a palmful of pebbles. He dreamed again, and produced a twist of earth and stone which contained new colours, a seam of creamy nougat in a funnel of tar. His dream delivered the funnel to his company offices. Soon secretaries typed Ibela-hoy for the first time – and a name was coined for the new mineral which he had unearthed. Then his dream transported friends and family to Ibela-hoy. They walked behind him as he set out to map the creamy seam. Together they charted an area the shape of a toadstool. A toadstool of the newest mineral in the world. His daydream provided a telephone and a line of poles. He telephoned the company with the good news. They referred him to the Agency and then to the Ministry. His calls were bounced and routed between switchboards and operators and his story retold a dozen times – but nobody was found with sufficient authority to accept such momentous information or to order his return to home, to sleep.

Send me a dream, he said aloud, in which my wife and my children are brought to the cabin. When I wake, they are there. When I sleep, they are there. We sit at the same table. The two boys tumble on the bed. The baby stands on my thighs with crescent legs and tugs at my nose and hair. My wife and I sit together slicing vegetables at the table. But when he had finished speaking there was no reply from amongst the rocks, no promises. He spoke again, in whispers. Have pity, he said.

Sometimes he wrapped his arms round boulders, warmed by the sun, and embraced them. My wife, he said. He kissed boulders.

Now the men kept their distance. They were polite but no longer generous. There were no more invitations to visit the lumber station – and they became watchful on those occasions when they brought drill cores to the cabin. Does this man know his business, they asked amongst themselves. Can he be trusted to know marl from marble? They waited awkwardly at his door or stood at his window as their plugs of earth were spread and sorted on his bench, the soils washed and sieved, the stones stunned and cracked, the unusual flakes of rocks matched with the specimens in the mineral trays. His fatigue – the second stage – had hardened his concentration. He was engrossed. He lowered his head and smelled the soil. He sucked the roundest pebbles. He rubbed stones on the thighs of his trousers and held them to the light. No, nothing, he told them. But when they sat in their camps and looked up from the valley late at night, a light still burned in the agent's cabin and they could see him holding their stones to his oil flame and talking to their earth in his skinned and weary voice.

At first the sorted, worthless plugs were dumped each day in a rough pile at the side of the cabin. The clays of the valley consorted with the volcanic earths of Ibela-hoy. Flints jostled sandstones, topsoils ran loose amongst clods, the rounded pebbles of the river bed bubbled in the wasteland shales. He was struck how – held and turned in the daylight – each stone was a landscape. Here was a planet, a globe, with the continents grey and peninsular, the seas cold and smooth to the touch. And here a coastline, one face the beach, four faces cliff, and a rivulet of green where the children and donkeys could make their descent. And here, twisted and smoothed by the survey drill, were the muddied banks of rivers and the barks of trees modelled and reduced in deep, toffee earth. But in the dump, their shapes and colours clashed and were indecent. He remembered how, when he was a child, they had buried his father. The grave was open when the body came. There were clays and flints piled on the yellow grass. The bottom of his father's trench had filled with water. The digger's spade had severed stones. They said that, in ancient times when humankind went naked and twigged for termites and ate raw meat, the dead were left where they fell. What the animals did not eat became topsoil, loam. The company agent had wished for that, had dreamed of his father free of his grave and spread out on the unbroken ground as calm and breathless as frost. But he could not look at that open grave, those wounded flints, without tears. He could not look at road works, either. Or a ploughed field. Or a broken wall. And whenever he had stared at that squinting corner of his room where the ceiling plaster had fallen and the broken roof laths stuck through, his chest (what was the phrase?) shivered like a parched pea and he dare not sleep. The ceiling doesn't leak, his mother said. It's you that leaks, not it.

206

Now he wept when he passed the waste pile, when he was drawn at night to stand before it with a lamp or summoned to salvage one lonely stone for his pocket or his table. Sometimes it seemed that the pile was an open wound or an abattoir of stones. But the longer he stood the more it seemed that a piece of the world had been misplaced and abandoned at his cabin side.

Then he took a spade and dug a pit behind the waste pile. First he gathered the chipped yellow stones which lay on the surface and placed them together in a bucket. And then he removed the thin soil crust and piled it neatly on to a tarpaulin. Each individual layer was dug out and piled separately, until the pit was shoulder deep. The continents and planets, the landscapes and coastlines of the waste dump were shovelled into the pit and one by one, in order, the layers of Ibela-hoy were put back in place. Then he scattered the chipped yellow stones on to the bulging ground.

When the gangs delivered drill cores they noticed that the waste had gone. I buried it, he said. I put it back. He showed them where the swollen ground was settling. Well, they said, that's very neat and tidy. Or, Is that what you're paid to do, fool about with spades? His replies made no sense to them. They continued to talk with him roughly or to humour him with banter. What should we do for him, they asked amongst themselves, to bring him back to earth? Should we write, they wondered, to his wife and children or to the boss? Should we let him be and let the illness pass? Some of the kinder, older men went to talk with him, to offer help, to exchange a word or two about the samples on his bench. Yet he seemed indifferent to them and those funnels of earth and stone which could earn them all a fortune. Was that the yellow of bauxite or the rose of cinnabar or the fire-blue of opal? The company agent did not seem to share their excitement or their interest. But when at last they left him in peace he turned to the samples on his bench and sorted through them with unbroken attention. A stone of apple-green he removed and walked with it into the valley where in a cave there were lichens of the same colour. A fistful of grit he scattered in the grass so that it fell amongst the leaf joints like sleet. A round stone he placed on the river bed with other round stones. A grey landscape in an inch of granite he stood in the shadow of the greyest rock. A chip of pitchblende was reunited with black soil.

Once a month when his provisions were delivered together with letters from home, the company agent presented his report and sent back to the city any minerals or gemstones which were worthy of note. Once he had found a fragment of platinum in a sample from the plateau beyond the hill. He and the gang waited for a month for the company's response. Low quality platinum, they said. No use to us. And once he had identified graphite amongst the native carbons. But, again, the company was unimpressed. Now he wrapped a piece of damp clay and placed it in a sample bag. Its colours were the colours of pomegranate skins. Its odour was potatoes. He sealed the bag and sent it to the company. Urgent, he wrote on the label. Smell this! And, in the second month, he sent them a cube of sandstone and wrote: See the landscape, the beach, the pathway through the rocks. And later they received the palmful of pebbles that they had requested in his dream.

Alarms rang. Secretaries delivered the agent's file to the company bosses. They searched the certificates and testimonials for any criminal past. Was he a radical? Had he been ill? What should they make of clay, sandstone, pebbles? They called his mother to the offices and questioned her. She showed them her son's monthly letters and pointed to those parts where he spoke of insomnia, an abattoir of stones and a family that never was. He misses home, she said. Why would he send worthless soil and cryptic notes in sample bags? She could not say, except that he had always been a good man, quick to tears. If he had only married, found a girl to love, had children perhaps . . . then who can guess what might have been? But worthless soil? Still she could not say.

The bosses sent their man to Ibela-hoy in their air-conditioned jeep to bring the agent home and to discover what went on. The brick and tarmac of the town and villages lasted for a day. The bosses' man passed the night at the Rest

208

House where the valley greens rose to the implacable evening monochromes of the hills. In the morning, early, he drove on to the bouldered track along the valley side. The Hill Without a Hat swung across his windscreen in the distance. On the summit of the ridge the track widened and cairns marked the route down into the valley of Lekadeeb and then up again towards Ibela-hoy. He stood with his binoculars and sought out the company agent's cabin in the hollow of the hill. He saw the company mobile parked at the door and the antics of men who seemed intoxicated with drink or horseplay. A survey team had returned from the far valley bluffs some days ahead of schedule and hurried to the agent's cabin. The men were wild. They had found silver. They had recognized small fragments in their drill cores and had excavated in the area for larger quantities. They placed a half-dozen jagged specimens on the company agent's bench. Tell us it isn't silver, they challenged him. He looked at one piece of silver shaped like a stem of ginger but metallic grey in colour with puddles of milky-white quartz. What he saw was a bare summit of rock in sunshine. But snow in its crevices was too cold to melt. I'll do some tests, he said.

The men sat outside in their drilling mobile and waited for his confirmation that at last their work had produced minerals of great value. There were bonuses to be claimed, fortunes to be made, celebrations, hugging, turbulent reunions with wives and children to anticipate. The company agent turned the snowy summit in his hand and divined its future. And its past. Once the word Silver was spoken in the company offices, Ibela-hoy could count on chaos; there would be mining engineers, labour camps, a village, roads, bars, drink, soldiers. Bulldozers would push back the soil and roots of silver would be grubbed like truffles from the earth. Dynamite, spoil heaps, scars. And he, the company agent, the man who spilled the beans, would have no time to reconcile the stones, the dreams, the family, the fatigue, the sleeplessness which now had reached its final stage. The turmoil had begun already. He heard the smooth engine of the company jeep as it laboured over the final rise before the cabin. He saw the bosses' man climb out with his folder and his suit and pause to talk with the men who waited inside the mobile's cab. Arms were waved and fingers pointed towards the bluffs where silver lay in wait.

I'll put it back, he said.

By the time the bosses' man had walked into the cabin with a string of false and reassuring greetings on his lips, the company agent had pocketed the half-dozen pieces of silver and had slipped away into the rocks behind the cabin. He climbed as high as was possible without breaking cover and crouched in a gulley. He toyed with the stones on the ground, turning them in his palms, and waited for night. He watched as the bosses' man ran from the cabin and the survey gang jumped from their mobile and searched the landscape for the agent. He watched as they showed the bosses' man where he had buried the waste heap, the world misplaced. He watched as the gang brought picks and shovels, and (insensitive to topsoils and chipped yellow stones) dug into the abattoir. He watched the bosses' man crouch and shake his head as he sorted through the debris for the gold, the agate, the topaz which the men promised had been buried, hidden, there. It was, they said, a matter for the madhouse or the militia. They'd watched the agent for a month or two. He had hugged boulders. He had hidden gemstones, their gemstones, company gemstones, throughout the valley. They'd seen him walking, crouching, placing gemstones in the shade of rocks, in the mouth of caves, under leaves.

A bare summit of rock in sunshine was the location of his dream. There were crevices of unbroken snow and pats of spongy moss. He was naked. There were no clothes. He squatted on his haunches and chipped at flints. Someone had caught a hare – but nobody yet knew how to make fire, so its meat was ripped apart and eaten raw. They washed it down with snow. The carcass was left where it fell. The two boys played with twigs. The baby stood on crescent legs and tugged at grass. He and the woman delved in the softer earth for roots to eat and found silver, a plaything for the boys. He conjured in his dream a world where the rocks were hot and moving, where quakes and volcanoes turned shales to

210

schists, granite to gneiss, limestone to marble, sandstone to quartz, where continents sank and rose like kelp on the tide.

When it was light, he unwrapped himself from the embrace of the boulder where he had passed the night and began to traverse the valley towards the high ground and the rocks where snow survived the sun. His aimless walks had made his legs strong and his mind was soaring with a fever of sleeplessness. He walked and talked, his tongue guiding his feet over the rocks, naming what passed beneath. Molten silicates, he said, as his feet cast bouncing shadows over salt and pepper rocks. Pumice, he said to the hollows. Grass.

In two hours the company agent had reached the ridge where the winds seemed to dip and dive and hug the earth. He turned to the south and, looking down into the valley, he saw the men and the trucks at his cabin and the twist of smoke as breakfast was prepared. Bring my wife and children, he said. And one man, standing at the hut with a hot drink resting on the bonnet of the air-conditioned jeep, saw him calling there and waved his arms. Come down, he said. Come back.

But the company agent walked on until he found that the earth had become slippery with ice and the air white like paper. He looked now for grey rocks, metallic grey, and found them at the summit of his walk, his rendezvous. There was no easy path; the boulders there were shoulder height and he was forced to squeeze and climb. But his hands were taking hold of crevices fossilized with snow and soon, at last, he stood upon the landscape that he had sought, glistening, winking grey with puddles of milky-white quartz. He took the six jagged specimens from his pocket. I am standing here, he said, pointing at an ounce of silver. He took the pieces and placed them in a streak of snow where their colours matched the rock and where, two paces distant, they disappeared for good.

In the afternoon he watched the first helicopter as it beat about the hills, its body bulbous-ended like a floating bone. And then, close by, he heard the grinding motors of the jeep as it found a route between the rocks and stalled. He heard voices and then someone calling him by his first name. Was

211

it his son? He walked to the edge of his grey platform and looked down on the heads of the bosses' man, a soldier and two of the survey gang. Climb down, they said. We're going to take you home. A holiday. I have my job to do, he said. Yes, they said, we all have jobs to do. We understand. But it's cold up here and you must be tired and hungry. Climb down and we'll drive you back to the city. No problems. No awkward questions. Your mother's waiting. Just show us what is hidden and you can be with your family.

Bring my family here, he said. Bring my wife and children here. The men looked at each other and then one of the survey gang spoke. You have no wife and children, he said. You lied. The company agent picked up the largest stone and flung it at the men. It landed on the bonnet of the jeep and its echo was as metallic, as full of silver, as the grey hill.

Leave him there, they said. Let hunger bring him down.

It was cold that night above Ibela-hoy. But there was warmth in numbers. The company agent and his wife encircled their children, their breath directed inwards, their backs turned against the moon. And in the morning when the sun came up and the colours of the hill and its valley accelerated from grey and brown, to red and green, to white, the company agent gathered stones for his family and they breakfasted on snow.

AIR RIDE

from IS BEAUTY GOOD

ROSALIND BELBEN

IT ISN'T THE messenger that has to walk, but the message, says Sepp. I understand, clasping his brass one, because I play an instrument, sitting in a gondola swinging high over the rising, falling mountain, I understand a little music, I know then, I know, he says making the gondola swim in the air, why else do we meet once a year on the mountain, whom do you imagine we play to, the faithful, the crowd, we play to the things that hear, things in the mountains, there are things in the mountains that hear, we used to trudge up, three and three quarter hours with a tuba, but we have legs for tuba and cornet alike, we don't leap with a tuba, when we arrive the instrument, that leaps, and all around there are ears.

And suppose those ears do prefer Bach. Well, they listen quite politely to Johann Strauss, they are grateful for anything, those ears are, with cowbells and the breeze and the howling wind for company, and any music sounds strange and beautiful that high, in such a remote place, as rare as the air is, move a space away, out of sight, and the music arrives in a thin stream, a watery noise, isolated, as if borne on a single corridor of the air, a ribbon of music, not Bach, a tiny, dear little stream, and the gondola swings at his pun, most mysterious.

That's the trouble the world over, he says. Nobody listens. Nature listens, but nature is helpless to act, nature is at the mercy. Isn't she! I think, so long as someone bothers to take a tuba to the top of the mountain, so long as, oh! there's my wife, she has to walk, she's frightened of gondola travel, nothing would possess her to ride so easily down. Imagine, she never sees what the tuba sees, sitting in the last of the sun, what an instrument, above the tops of the trees, not every tuba is enabled, to shine in the sun, a wonderful shining that darts off across the mountain-flank.

I'm pretty plump, the tuba and I, we're both plump, and there is more of us to reflect the sun. I'm sure the sun likes us, even if fat is unfashionable, fashions do reach us in the mountains, the same as sun, the sun is stronger and the fashions are weaker, we keep tradition, we've settled for tradition, and fashion sways us little. Sepp clasps his tuba more firmly around the waist. His wife is a speck among other gondola-fearing specks, in bright cotton frocks among the trees, and then hidden from view. That speck is my wife, he says, waving at it. All the specks turn their faces up as the gondola glides over their heads, they look like so many flowers, he says.

You may listen, because you are stuck in a gondola with my tuba and me. But I tell you. Tubas have a satisfying life, being hugged, shining, making sunlight dart. I tell you, whatever it is that the bearer with your password has, it is getting terribly hindered by all these folk with their longing to talk, to chatter, to rabbit on about this and that, whether beauty is good, until the message itself is crying out in a little babyish voice, let me on my journey, let me be transferred to yet another hand, let me smother all the chatterboxes in the world, so I may at last arrive, since that is what I am for, to arrive, to be understood, not held in a clammy hand, but understood, my import fulfilled.

I don't fool myself, he says, squirming to make the tuba comfortable. I adore playing, yet I am not important, we should be listening to our instruments and not to ourselves. Hasn't it always been so? Innumerable messages, throughout history, that never quite arrive. In the mountains we can hear one another, and what do we do? We call back, we are drunk on the sound of our own voices, how they carry, and for practical purposes the carrying is of use. If we speak only of goats, if we pass the time of day, that's fine. In the world, in history, there are bigger messages, and our failing to listen, to understand, makes great nanny-goats of all of us. The dear Lord has enough trouble with his. Passwords are a mistake, they take on an aura and the message whose path they are there to smooth is smothered. These mountains have seen a lot of fighting, undeciphered things pass to and fro.

And tucked beneath the steep drop, my summer hut nestles in the trapped sun, the waterfall is busy, and the breeze tinkling. High above us the lake sits, balanced, precarious, and with the slightest push, it seems, a falling rock, could tip out and run all down the valley, the many valleys, to the plains. That was where the forked stick started, by a hidden lake, a fragile, dark blue water, from there a password is needed, where peace is, farther is not peace, is strife, muddle, and bitterness, and aggrieved parties, hardly a whisper breaks its stillness, the green of the turf, and the blue, the freshness nourishes the heart, I fear there is a thing about a tuba, it makes one lyrical, one sees snow on the peaks, a mountain with a glacier, white snow, blue sky, no clashes, no jealousy, no trampling, no world, not a shred of ugliness, cows and goats, that's all, and one wonders! In winter it is even more beautiful. The first stretch is the wildest. I and my wife and the tuba, we dwell there in the summer, we are being thrust from our home by the conflict. The unfortunate message, how it cries, and weeps, and tears its hair; and no one listens; there are ears in the mountains but they can't reply. The tuba rolls as the gondola bumps home itself. At least we, we at least, have arrived. He says, I don't understand, I don't understand conflict, or life, or my wife, only mountains, music, messages. And we are bound to think that's sad. It's bedtime, he says to his instrument. Good night to you! Good night! I love her, she likes frocks, what is a frock, a piece of bunting, how can a frock speak, she says frocks do a lot of talking, frocks are chatterers, frippery chatterers, and she has no end of time for frocks, the more highly-coloured the better.

215

THE SECRET MIRACLE

JORGE LUIS BORGES

> And God made him die during the course of a hundred
> years and then He revived him and said:
> 'How long have you been here?'
> 'A day, or part of a day,' he replied.
>
> *The Koran*, II, 261

On the night of 4 March 1939, in an apartment on the
Zelternergasse in Prague, Jaromir Hladík, author of the
unfinished tragedy *The Enemies*, of a *Vindication of Eternity*,
and of an inquiry into the indirect Jewish sources of Jakob
Boehme, dreamt a long drawn out chess game. The antagon-
ists were not two individuals, but two illustrious families.
The contest had begun many centuries before. No one could
any longer describe the forgotten prize, but it was rumoured
that it was enormous and perhaps infinite. The pieces and
the chessboard were set up in a secret tower. Jaromir (in his
dream) was the first-born of one of the contending families.
The hour for the next move, which could not be postponed,
struck on all the clocks. The dreamer ran across the sands
of a rainy desert – and he could not remember the chessmen
or the rules of chess. At this point he awoke. The din of the
rain and the clangour of the terrible clocks ceased. A measured unison, sundered by voices of command, arose from
the Zelternergasse. Day had dawned, and the armoured van-
guards of the Third Reich were entering Prague.

On the 19th, the authorities received an accusation against

Jaromir Hladík; on the same day, at dusk, he was arrested. He was taken to a barracks, aseptic and white, on the opposite bank of the Moldau. He was unable to refute a single one of the charges made by the Gestapo: his maternal surname was Jaroslavski, his blood was Jewish, his study of Boehme was Judaizing, his signature had helped to swell the final census of those protesting the *Anschluss*. In 1928, he had translated the *Sepher Yezirah* for the publishing house of Hermann Barsdorf; the effusive catalogue issued by this firm had exaggerated, for commercial reasons, the translator's renown; this catalogue was leafed through by Julius Rothe, one of the officials in whose hands lay Hladík's fate. The man does not exist who, outside his own specialty, is not credulous: two or three adjectives in Gothic script sufficed to convince Julius Rothe of Hladík's pre-eminence, and of the need for the death penalty, *pour encourager les autres*. The execution was set for the 29th of March, at nine in the morning. This delay (whose importance the reader will appreciate later) was due to a desire on the part of the authorities to act slowly and impersonally, in the manner of planets or vegetables.

Hladík's first reaction was simply one of horror. He was sure he would not have been terrified by the gallows, the block, or the knife; but to die before a firing squad was unbearable. In vain he repeated to himself that the pure and general act of dying, not the concrete circumstances, was the dreadful act. He did not grow weary of imagining these circumstances: he absurdly tried to exhaust all the variations. He infinitely anticipated the process, from the sleepless dawn to the mysterious discharge of the rifles. Before the day set by Julius Rothe, he died hundreds of deaths, in courtyards whose shapes and angles defied geometry, shot down by changeable soldiers whose number varied and who sometimes put an end to him from close up and sometimes from far away. He faced these imaginary executions with true terror (perhaps with true courage). Each simulacrum lasted a few seconds. Once the circle was closed, Jaromir returned interminably to the tremulous eve of his death. Then he would reflect that reality does not tend to coincide with forecasts about it. With perverse logic he inferred that to foresee a circumstantial detail is to prevent its happening. Faithful to this feeble magic, he would invent *so that they might not happen*, the most atrocious particulars. Naturally, he finished by fearing that these particulars were prophetic. During his wretched nights he strove to hold fast somehow to the fugitive substance of time. He knew that time was precipitating itself towards the dawn of the 29th. He reasoned aloud: *I am now in the night of the 22nd. While this night lasts (and for six more nights to come) I am invulnerable, immortal*. His nights of sleep seemed to him deep dark pools into which he might submerge. Sometimes he yearned impatiently for the firing squad's definitive volley, which would redeem him, for better or for worse, from the vain compulsion of his imagination. On the 28th, as the final sunset reverberated across the high barred windows, he was distracted from all these abject considerations by thoughts of his drama, *The Enemies*.

Hladík was past forty. Apart from a few friendships and many habits, the problematic practice of literature constituted his life. Like every writer, he measured the virtues of other writers by their performance, and asked that they measure him by what he conjectured or planned. All of the books he had published merely moved him to a complex repentance. His investigation of the work of Boehme, of Ibn Ezra, and of Fludd was essentially a product of mere application; his translation of the *Sepher Yezirah* was characterized by negligence, fatigue, and conjecture. He judged his *Vindication of Eternity* to be perhaps less deficient: the first volume is a history of the diverse eternities devised by man, from the immutable Being of Parmenides to the alterable past of Hinton; the second volume denies (with Francis Bradley) that all the events in the universe make up a temporal series. He argues that the number of experiences possible to man is not infinite, and that a single 'repetition' suffices to demonstrate that time is a fallacy. . . . Unfortunately, the arguments that demonstrate this fallacy are not any less fallacious. Hladík was in the habit of running through these arguments with a certain disdainful perplexity. He had also written a series of

218

expressionist poems; these, to the discomfiture of the author, were included in an anthology in 1924, and there was no anthology of later date which did not inherit them. Hladík was anxious to redeem himself from his equivocal and languid past with his verse drama, *The Enemies*. (He favoured the verse form in the theatre because it prevents the spectators from forgetting unreality, which is the necessary condition of art.)

This opus preserved the dramatic unities (time, place, and action). It transpires in Hradcany, in the library of the Baron Roemerstadt, on one of the last evenings of the nineteenth century. In the first scene of the first act, a stranger pays a visit to Roemerstadt. (A clock strikes seven, the vehemence of a setting sun glorifies the window panes, the air transmits familiar and impassioned Hungarian music.) This visit is followed by others; Roemerstadt does not know the people who come to importune him, but he has the uncomfortable impression that he has seen them before: perhaps in a dream. All the visitors fawn upon him, but it is obvious – first to the spectators of the drama, and then to the Baron himself – that they are secret enemies, sworn to ruin him. Roemerstadt manages to outwit, or evade, their complex intrigues. In the course of the dialogue, mention is made of his betrothed, Julia de Weidenau, and of a certain Jaroslav Kubin, who at one time had been her suitor. Kubin has now lost his mind and thinks he is Roemerstadt. . . The dangers multiply. Roemerstadt, at the end of the second act, is forced to kill one of the conspirators. The third and final act begins. The incongruities gradually mount up: actors who seemed to have been discarded from the play reappear; the man who had been killed by Roemerstadt returns, for an instant. Someone notes that the time of day has not advanced: the clock strikes seven, the western sun reverberates in the high window panes, impassioned Hungarian music is carried on the air. The first speaker in the play reappears and repeats the words he had spoken in the first scene of the first act. Roemerstadt addresses him without the least surprise. The spectator understands that Roemerstadt is the wretched Jaroslav Kubin. The drama has never taken place: it is the circular delirium which Kubin unendingly lives and relives.

Hladík had never asked himself whether this tragicomedy of errors was preposterous or admirable, deliberate or casual. Such a plot, he intuited, was the most appropriate invention to conceal his defects and to manifest his strong points, and it embodied the possibility of redeeming (symbolically) the fundamental meaning of his life. He had already completed the first act and a scene or two of the third. The metrical nature of the work allowed him to go over it continually, rectifying the hexameters, without recourse to the manuscript. He thought of the two acts still to do, and of his coming death. In the darkness, he addressed himself to God. *If I exist at all, if I am not one of Your repetitions and errata, I exist as the author of* The Enemies. *In order to bring this drama, which may serve to justify me, to justify You, I need one more year. Grant me that year, You to whom belong the centuries and all time.* It was the last, the most atrocious night, but ten minutes later sleep swept over him like a dark ocean and drowned him.

Towards dawn, he dreamt he had hidden himself in one of the naves of the Clementine Library. A librarian wearing dark glasses asked him: *What are you looking for?* Hladík answered: *God.* The Librarian told him: *God is in one of the letters on one of the pages of one of the 400,000 volumes of the Clementine. My fathers and the fathers of my fathers have sought after that letter. I've gone blind looking for it.* He removed his glasses, and Hladík saw that his eyes were dead. A reader came in to return an atlas. *This atlas is useless,* he said, and handed it to Hladík, who opened it at random. As if through a haze, he saw a map of India. With a sudden rush of assurance, he touched one of the tiniest letters, an ubiquitous voice said: *The time for your work has been granted.* Hladík awoke.

He remembered that the dreams of men belong to God, and that Maimonides wrote that the words of a dream are divine, when they are all separate and clear and are spoken by someone invisible. He dressed. Two soldiers entered his cell and ordered him to follow them.

From behind the door, Hladík had visualized a labyrinth of passageways, stairs, and connecting blocks. Reality was less rewarding: the party descended to an inner courtyard by a single iron stairway. Some soldiers – uniforms unbuttoned – were testing a motorcycle and disputing their conclusions. The sergeant looked at his watch: it was 8.44. They must wait until nine. Hladík, more insignificant than pitiful, sat down on a pile of firewood. He noticed that the soldiers' eyes avoided his. To make his wait easier, the sergeant offered him a cigarette. Hladík did not smoke. He accepted the cigarette out of politeness or humility. As he lit it, he saw that his hands shook. The day was clouding over. The soldiers spoke in low tones, as though he were already dead. Vainly, he strove to recall the woman of whom Julia de Weidenau was the symbol...

The firing squad fell in and was brought to attention. Hladík, standing against the barracks wall, waited for the volley. Someone expressed fear the wall would be splashed with blood. The condemned man was ordered to step forward a few paces. Hladík recalled, absurdly, the preliminary manoeuvres of a photographer. A heavy drop of rain grazed one of Hladík's temples and slowly rolled down his cheek. The sergeant barked the final command.

The physical universe stood still.

The rifles converged upon Hladík, but the men assigned to pull the triggers were immobile. The sergeant's arm eternalized an inconclusive gesture. Upon a courtyard flagstone a bee cast a stationary shadow. The wind had halted, as in a painted picture. Hladík began a shriek, a syllable, a twist of the hand. He realized he was paralysed. Not a sound reached him from the stricken world.

He thought: *I'm in hell, I'm dead.*

He thought: *I've gone mad.*

He thought: *Time has come to a halt.*

Then he reflected that in that case, his thought, too, would have come to a halt. He was anxious to test this possibility: he repeated (without moving his lips) the mysterious Fourth Eclogue of Virgil. He imagined that the already remote soldiers shared his anxiety; he longed to communicate with

221

them. He was astonished that he felt no fatigue, no vertigo from his protracted immobility. After an indeterminate length of time he fell asleep. On awaking he found the world still motionless and numb. The drop of water still clung to his cheek; the shadow of the bee still did not shift in the courtyard; the smoke from the cigarette he had thrown away did not blow away. Another 'day' passed before Hladík understood.

He had asked God for an entire year in which to finish his work: His omnipotence had granted him the time. For his sake, God projected a secret miracle: German lead would kill him, at the determined hour, but in his mind a year would elapse between the command to fire and its execution. From perplexity he passed to stupor, from stupor to resignation, from resignation to sudden gratitude.

He disposed of no document but his own memory; the mastering of each hexameter as he added it, had imposed upon him a kind of fortunate discipline not imagined by those amateurs who forget their vague, ephemeral, paragraphs. He did not work for posterity, nor even for God, of whose literary preferences he possessed scant knowledge. Meticulous, unmoving, secretive, he wove his lofty invisible labyrinth in time. He worked the third act over twice. He eliminated some rather too obvious symbols: the repeated striking of the hour, the music. There were no circumstances to constrain him. He omitted, condensed, amplified; occasionally, he chose the primitive version. He grew to love the courtyard, the barracks; one of the faces endlessly confronting him made him modify his conception of Roemerstadt's character. He discovered that the hard cacophonies which so distressed Flaubert are mere visual superstitions: debilities and annoyances of the written word, not of the sonorous, the sounding one. . . He brought his drama to a conclusion: he lacked only a single epithet. He found it: the drop of water slid down his cheek. He began a wild cry, moved his face aside. A quadruple blast brought him down.

Jaromir Hladík died on 29 March, at 9.02 in the morning.

1943

THE STONE DOOR

LEONORA CARRINGTON

I

September 15.

Cancer. Illness, New York.
Cancer. Tropic of (Mexico). Cancer, fourth place in the
circle. Water Father. Spider-Crab. Mizte-cacihautl's box, (6)
Scorpion-crab for funeral paraphernalia. Tiger-spider-crab in
dream.

The star follows her strange course in the mountains, in the
round temples, through green, lukewarm woods and penetrating hedges and walls. She lies hard, bright, and cold
under the beds of lovers or under bodies of sleeping cattle.

I never cease spying on the star's course.

Pedro came in drunk again, I made him a screeching sordid
scene and yet I am stuck like a rat in a trap. Will I ever be
free? What secret craving keeps me near him?

Day.
The cuckoo clock is driving me wild. I am always alone, that
is what makes me suffer. Damn that bird.

Words are treacherous because they are incomplete. The
written word hangs in time like a lump of lead. Everything
should move with the ages and the planets.

The time has come for the star to appear once more.
Perhaps I will dress in wolfskin, sitting in a tree watching the
circle, waiting for the next step to be traced in the mud.

223

All these shadows from the unknown. I am ignorant, but soon I shall begin to know.

It is still October.
A clue, October, the scales. The man and woman in the egg. The house of the Sleeping Winds. They hang together like witchstones made into a broken necklace. Clues because they smell of the same sensation, how or why I cannot say.

The ivory box lined with sandalwood which I used to sniff when nobody was in the drawing room. The ivory box awakened unnamed memories.

The last days of October.
Divination is difficult with isolated incidents. Weaving them together into prophecy is an arduous labour. Hazard a word dropped out of the unknown. Several hazards sometimes make a whole sentence. My memory twitches into a sharp image of something never seen, yet remembered and so acutely alive that I am possessed.

A pine forest white with snow in a country where the people are dressed in bright colours. A noise of smashed glass. Little ragged horses as swift and powerful as tigers. Snow, dust, and cinnamon.

Wearing a mask I am on all fours with my nose almost touching the nose of a wolf. Our eyes united in a look, yet I remain hidden behind myself and the wolf hidden behind himself, we are divided by our separate bodies. However deeply we look into each other's eyes a transparent wall divides us from explosion where the looks cross outside our bodies. If by some sage power I could capture that explosion, that mysterious area outside where the wolf and I are one, perhaps then the first door would open and reveal the chamber beyond.

Last night in a dream It returned. A creature wearing a shaggy skin and smelling of dust and cinnamon. Screaming I entered the fur, wool, or hair, crying tears that were dark and sticky like blood. Tears thick with centuries of agony remembered all at once, they matted the furry coat and stank of birth and death. Shamelessly abandoning all that anguish

224

to this man, animal, vegetable, or demon. Then I was in entire possession of the five sensorial powers and their long roots were as visible as the sun. The light of a vision or a dream is united to any given luminous body outside. No longer alone in my own body.

Thoughts and dreams but not a particle of dust to prove their reality. Meanwhile I am wasting each living day in captivity.

All Saints' Day.
Sorcerers and alchemists knew about animal, vegetable, and mineral bodies. To hack away the crust of what we have forgotten and rediscover things we knew before we were born.

November 16.
I rode a white horse through the woods of Capultepec. A grey early morning and few people were about. I galloped around the Palace thinking all the while of my loneliness and of the creature dressed in wool and smelling of cinnamon and dust. Try as I would I could not evoke his real presence and remained a thought. The formula for this evocation is somewhere hidden inside of me, I feel small and ignorant and this pleases me not at all. I cannot accept this, I want to feel enormous and powerful. (I secretly believe that I am a goddess with very short moments of incarnation.) At the moment Pedro and I loathe each other. We scream ourselves to sleep like fishwives. This is a terrible waste of good energy. Yet I dare not go. Return, ghost, animal, or man. I cannot bear this loneliness, I am sick of being alone with myself.

November 20.
Several nights ago I was alone, Pedro being absent as usual. Making a cup of coffee I resolved to be firmly indifferent to his neglect. It is difficult not to feel like an abandoned kitchen maid. Drinking my coffee in my dreary little hole of a kitchen, I pondered about myself.

'I am sitting here alone. I am a fool, a person letting herself starve to death because the odour of food is usually more exquisite than its taste. No philosopher ever told me if one could capture in taste the aroma of roasting coffee.'

While I was busy telling myself this, in a futile attempt to shut out my loneliness, a small white packet on the table caught my eye. Undoing it curiously I found several sticks of cinnamon. I did not remember having bought cinnamon that day.

Cheered, yet afraid, I took myself to bed and placed the cinnamon under my pillow, to give any passing succubus a sporting chance.

When I closed my eyes the following dream, memory, or vision unrolled: I was crossing Mesopotamia on foot and carried a load on my back. It is difficult to say if the load was heavy or light because I already seemed to be accustomed to carrying loads and this had become a function of my body.

My destination was Hungary, which apparently shared a frontier with Mesopotamia. The country in which I travelled was barren, with hardly a tree to be seen. The dusty waste was interrupted here and there by tombs of all shapes and sizes, beautifully decorated and painted like tropical fish. Looking around me I noticed that the people were not entirely human but on the contrary were partially of clay. They glided slowly through the dust, now and then colliding and one or both shattering to smithereens.

The Mesopotamians, thought I, are a savage and lazy race. Approaching what looked like a town or very large cemetery I noticed a person detach himself from the group of human pottery and run to me. Actually it was more of a shuffle than a run, as the tight wrapping which swathed him from head to foot encumbered his movements. As he shuffled one of his feet fell off like a dry leaf from a tree.

As he drew near he started shouting: 'What news, Stranger? What news?'

His appearance was ancient but he was young: the cracked brown face was that of a boy not much older than twelve.

'You are from Baghdad, no doubt?' he asked, panting clouds of dust into my face. I waited to see what I would reply.

'From Baghdad, Master. I have been walking for twenty days.'

'Are you dead?'

'No, I think not. The Lord Mayor of Baghdad paid me three farthings to take this present to the Jewish King who lives on the frontier of Hungary. I pass through here as a shortcut.'

'You are a slave?'

'Why, no,' I replied stiffly. 'I am a beggar.'

'What will you do if you can never get out of the country of the Dead? The stone door of Kecske is jealously guarded.'

'I will shriek till *doomsday*, till my voice is written all over the centre of the Earth like the drawings on the wall of a lavatory.'

'Still, Kecske may never open.'

'Kecske will open.'

He put out his tongue, a mere black thread, and uttered a laugh like the last crow of a decrepit rooster.

'What does the Lord Mayor of Baghdad send to the King of the Jews?'

'A toy, Master.'

'Besides the toy, what is there in your bag?'

I gave him a cunning smile and shook my matted hair.

'That is a secret; there are twelve thousand treasures in my sack.'

Giving another laugh as dry as the wrinkled skin on his young face, he put his head close to my ear and said: 'Tell me a story and I will give you a slice of funeral cake.'

'Must the story be true?' I asked, setting down my burden.

'All stories are true,' he said. 'Begin.'

'One night while passing through the desert by the light of a fat moon I saw a hump on the horizon. Before I was near I could make out more humps, which grew in size and complexity till I could see that it was really the encampment of a large caravan. The tents, embroidered with foreign letters, were grouped about a central pavilion like chicks around a hen.

227

'A hundred slaves armed with musical instruments squatted all around this centre tent, blocking my approach.

'A slave passed near the boulder, and with a quick snatch I imprisoned her ankle in my hand.

' "I am the devil," I said, "and you must do my will."

' "Command," replied the terrified slave.

' "I wish to see your master."

' "That is difficult," replied the slave. "No living being may look at my master, for he is the wise King of all the Jews."

' "If you cannot arrange what I ask I shall release the fire in my fingers and roast you here and now."

' "Then you must climb onto the royal tent and peep through the hole gnawed by the Chancellor's pet rat."

' "How shall I pass through the servants and climb such a height without being noticed?"

' "You must disguise yourself as a bird. The King always travels with a drove of Mexican wild turkeys."

' "Then bring me some feathers."

'When she had gone I lay in the warm earth, which still smelt of the sun. The chill dawn had not yet arrived. Soon the slave returned with a sack of feathers and a jar of honey and I set about disguising myself as a turkey.

'Once I rolled in the honey and the feathers were stuck on, the slave tied a string around my neck and led me through the groups of servants, while I hopped and clucked like an outraged fowl.

' "What have you there?" they asked. "That is a very ugly bird."

' "It's a turkey," replied the Egyptian slave, "a turkey for the King's supper."

'Behind the tent hung a silk ladder. The slave indicated this, saying: "I can help you no more, you must escape as you can when you have seen the King. This was your wish, although you may be cursed to the end of your days for this adventure."

' "I shall perch on the King's tent and crow my triumph," I replied. "The wise King may not pass through the desert till I have seen him."

228

' "That is a great impertinence," said the slave sadly. "Moses was blasted to bits for less."

' "Leave me in peace," I told her.

'I climbed the silk ladder with some tremor. What if I should be discovered? I startled some vultures which had been sitting immobile on top of the tent, like gourds staring vacantly into the night.

'The Chancellor's pet rat gnawed a passably large hole in the roof, and without losing a second I peeped through.

'There stood the King, admiring himself in a sheet of brass. I could well understand the rapt admiration of the King for his own image. Such a beautiful being never stepped out of a female belly. His great curling beard swept the earth at his feet, black as night herself. The Monarch of All Ravens never had such a majestically curved nose, nor any stag a darker or more liquid eye.

'The nightshirt which hung in long folds from his tall body was embroidered with all the secrets of the cabala in scarlet letters.

'Looking deeply into the face reflected in the sheet of brass the King murmured: "I am as bored as I am exquisite. Is it a source of pleasure to possess a beauty which cracks any ordinary mirror? Perhaps I eat too much during dinner, perhaps I am depressed because the talking bronze head from Persia will not talk. . . I have no new toys and no desire to learn more of the Universe. Play and study are devoid of interest. I am bored and sad . . . even fear would be a release."

'Listening to the King I leaned too far through the hole and fell, landing a few paces from his feet.

'The Monarch leapt into the air with the grace of a goat. The ends of his moustache twitched with fright.

' "An angel of God or Satan?" said the King after he recovered his poise.

' "I am an errant angel banished from Heaven with Lucifer. Out of Hell I crept to find the King of Kings they call Solomon."

' "No ordinary being may look at me," replied the King.

"So I must believe you have passed through Heaven and Hell.'

' "I have been feeling a certain soreness in my shoulder blades, which makes me think I'm growing a pair of wings."

' "With what you have learned in Heaven, in Hell, upon and under the Earth, you should possess twelve wings."

'His words shook me. Dreams and nightmares were contained in the King's hermetic smile.

'I was greatly troubled and I asked: "You and I can swim back and forth in time, but are we condemned to remain alone?"

' "It is a great thing to be errant in time and space," said the King. "The frontiers into the unknown are constructed in layers. One layer opens into a fan of other layers, which open new worlds in their turn. It is true that there is an infinite empty space somewhere beyond the Universe. It is equally true that that space is as richly peopled and inhabited as this very Earth. The space is dark, with no beginning and no end. The space is light, it begins, ends, and continues like life."

'The King sat down and I noticed that a brood of small transparent roots grew from the soles of his feet. "Yes, I am also errant. My roots can find no soil and this is why they are visible."

' "You are a prophet," I said. "Tell me, where is the promised land of the Jews?"

' "Far beyond Mesopotamia and Hungary. Those who find the promised land will be few and they must arrive hundreds of years before and after it has been used as a word. The world only recognizes truth after it is dead and gone. . . I should say a million truths, or a particle of reality."

'He curled strands of beard in his fingers as he spoke. I was astounded at the shining texture of his whiskers. He continued: "Words are more useless than the dust of the desert because language has also died, and dead things have movements that are difficult for an eye to perceive."

'He then gave me a small wooden wheel in the centre of which was a spider. "The eight legs of the spider are love

230

and death. The eight spokes of the wheel are triumph, move-ment, and life."

'I was shaken by my encounter, and I moved out of the camp without taking any note of my direction. I was sure that I had a mission but I could not remember what it was. As I racked my brain my feet covered great distances; then I realized with a shock that the bearded King was my mission and that I had left him. It was he I had been seeking in Heaven, on Earth, and in Hell.

'Shouting insults at myself for my stupidity I turned tail and ran till I felt sick back to where the King had pitched his camp.

'All that remained of the sumptuous camp was a little hole in the dust containing a stick of cinnamon, a skein of black wool, and five iron nails.'

When I had ended my story, the creature in tight wrappings laughed till he shook and his body rattled like a dry gourd.

'My heart,' he explained mirthfully, 'is dry as a nut, and rolls about inside me when I laugh.'

He gave me a slice of funeral cake as he had promised, and when his mirth had abated I asked: 'Is there such a black-bearded King in the great cemetery yonder?'

But the only reply was the frantic rattling of his heart.

The dream left a sensation of such bitter loss that I felt life could only be lived in sleep. Occupations like washing, dressing, eating, and talking became so laborious that the sun revolved more slowly on its orbit. Every human creature I saw filled me with repugnance, till I did not dare approach the window to look into the street. When anyone chanced to knock on the door I hid, shuddering with horror in the bathroom. I have never loved my fellow beings but that day the very sight of them became tedious. As long as the light lasted my nerves chattered like parakeets; little by little dark-ness came and the suffering was less acute. When I saw the lamps light in the street I went to bed and shortly found myself back in Mesopotamia.

Standing on a hill and looking back along the road I saw the city of tombs still visible in the distance. Before me the road continued like a dusty ribbon whose borders were marked by heaps of broken sculpture and miscellaneous rubbish such as partially unwrapped mummies in different stages of mutilation, painted tablets in every known and unknown language, books and parchments dried into convulsive gestures, old shoes, sandals, and boots, and any number of pots and casks, urns and dishes in whole or small pieces.

As I walked slowly along the road I examined these rich heaps of rubbish, stopping now and again to root about, putting anything that happened to please me in my sack.

The only tracks in the road leading away from the city were my own. A constant stream of beings passed by, all bent on the same destination. Their appearance was confused and some were transparent. There were animals, vegetables, men and women. Some of them had an individual outline but others were joined like Siamese twins in twos or threes or in greater numbers, forming geometrical shapes and objects such as five-, six-, eight-, nine-, or twelve-sided polygons, triangles, squares, circles, or kitchen utensils and articles of furniture. I saw a five-legged table composed of two fox terriers, a field of daffodils, and three middle-aged women in an embrace. Flapping over them was the carcass of a sea lion.

The motley throng streamed by without noticing me. I supposed they must be ghosts.

After walking some distance putting this and that in my sack I became hungry, and sat down on a Druid's head to eat the funeral cake I had been given in payment for my story. It was hard and dry and difficult to eat. I would have thanked my destiny for a cup of cold water instead, but no liquid was in sight, so I ate what I could and put the rest in my sack for hard times.

Looking back along the road I saw that a vague shape was forming in the distance and advancing in my direction. This gave me some hope for a companion along the lonely road.

232

The thing or person was difficult to define; as it approached it became larger, but it remained a vague form. Only when this fluid and embryonic shape was within a few yards of me could I distinguish a perfect oval containing a moving object within. A light from the centre of the object threw out five rays, forming a star. The oval hopped along like somebody walking on one foot, though it did not lack grace.

'That,' I said aloud, 'is the Egg. The Egg within the Star, the Star within the Egg.'

These words seemed appropriate, for it hesitated a few yards away and hopped nimbly onto a painted tombstone, where it perched.

'Our meeting must explain why I lost the black-bearded King. That I know.'

This produced no effect on the Egg so I realized that I must dive deeper to find the right words. When I could utter these words the reply would follow as day follows night.

Taking a small trowel out of my sack I began to dig in the roadside for the word that would open the secret of the Egg. As I worked I repeated all the long words I knew, such as *federation, conspicuous, anthropology*, and *metamorphosis*. The Egg did not budge an inch. I tried one-syllable words like *am, art, it*, and *off*. The Egg trembled very slightly, without communicating any meaning to me. I then understood that the word to address such a primitive and embryonic body would have to come from a language buried at the back of time. The very moment that I understood this my trowel grated on a hard thing in the earth, and with a cry of joy I pulled a small pipe out of the ground. I put it to my lips and blew some notes, which started low but mounted the scale rapidly till they reached such a high pitch that my ear could scarcely catch the thin sound. An umbilical cord unrolled slowly out of the centre of the Egg and wriggled along the ground towards me. When it reached my left foot I picked up the end and knotted it firmly around my neck. Thus united, the Egg and I started along the road in Indian file. As we advanced I played the pipe. Our movements coincided in a kind of elementary dance, facilitating the journey so much that we travelled far before I felt any fatigue.

A lonely pair we made, the Egg and I, in the great dusty plain of Mesopotamia.

So long as I made my thin tune on the pipe the Egg hopped along behind me willingly, but if I hesitated for a moment it would halt and the umbilical cord would tighten around my neck.

We continued for a long time, until I noticed that the music became slower and the notes lengthened, sounding finally more like shrieks than music. The Egg was drastically affected: the Star stretched and broke the oval contour; each one of the five prongs became a sense and each sense shot out five bright rays, which bit into the earth and up into the air like long sharp teeth. The umbilical cord withered and dried till it hung about my neck like a piece of straw.

The Star and the Egg had become a small white child, who stood frail and luminous in the road. All that remained of the Star was a five-pronged crown of root and bone on the child's head.

The music had not been still for long when the child spoke: 'Be fed by my death; I am half born but my death will be complete. All the colours on Earth have made me white; all the animals under the sky have made my body, but my soul is the rope which hangs from the half circle of light into the half circle of darkness above and below the horizon.' When it had spoken the White Child wrapped its hair around its face and walked on ahead of me. I followed in silence, knowing that our steps would go towards the person that I must find.

The country changed gradually into hills and ravines. Occasionally a wan tree became visible here and there. The painted tombstones thinned out to single dots and were replaced by rocks carved into animals or people or sometimes left in their jagged shapes.

The Child and I were alone. The ghosts had disappeared. As we advanced I began to notice high mountains on the horizon, their peaks white with snow. Then far along the road the dust rose and I could distinguish six horsemen riding hell-for-leather in our direction.

The six men were dressed in coloured rags and metal

jewels, their shaggy horses covered with embroidered blankets haphazardly affixed with chains or rope. As they came they hurled armfuls of Bohemian glass on the road, making a great clatter. The noise of broken glass and the thud of the horses' feet delighted them, and as they ground to a halt in front of the White Child each man shrieked with mirth in six different keys. The foremost of the six men held aloft a wheel. I counted the spokes. They were eight, like a spider's eight legs.

'I am Calabas Kö,' said the man who held the wheel. 'We have come out of Hungary to take the White Child.'

'Then we must move in time,' it piped. 'I am afraid.'

Whereupon one of the men grabbed the Child and tied it to his horse's girth by its hair and they whirled around to gallop back towards the snow-topped mountains.

The morning has been tedious. I have not been able to move away from the window, watching the street, waiting for some sign outside my dreams.

The street is empty and foreign except at night. Outside everything is tainted.

How shall I ever get to the market to buy lunch?

The sign can only appear when I have ceased to need my will. I lurk around the mystery murmuring maledictions on the feebleness of my words.

Hardly daring to touch what I want to say, yet knowing that if I had enough space around me it would be a piercing shriek. White, long, sharp as the crack of a whip.

This is a love letter to a nightmare.

For centuries they dressed up love for easy digestion in the body of a fat little boy with wings, pale blue bows, and anaemic-looking flowers. Behind this bland decoration Love snarled its rictus through the ages. With shrieks of adoration it flung itself on human breasts, 'to crush you, to suck your life away. I cannot drag my own weight over the crust of the Earth so you must carry me on your back so that in time you will be crippled with my weight.' These words are in every heart in the mating season.

Is this the result of loving a fellow creature? Somewhere I

am frightened of my loneliness and feel incomplete with myself.

Love, goat, tiger . . .

Blind Jug, tell the future?

A time, a date, when?

'Midnight,' replies the Blind Jug.

Under what sign, Blind Jug?

'Under the sign of Fire and of Air, Ivory and Milk.'

How many will see the Sign?

'Four, the Moon.'

And how shall we know?

'Urin, the microscopic ocean.'

In some mysterious way these words will enter life.

The air was rare and chill so I thought that I was already amongst the highest mountains. Heavy snow burdened the branches of the fir trees. Streaming grey clouds crept along the Earth and about the rocks, leaving icy teeth where they passed.

Built into the mountainside a few yards from me was a great stone door, on which was crucified an immense black parrot. As I approached I could see that the bird was still alive, though a long iron nail pierced its heart and the blood oozed out in a scarlet rope. The heavy head hung motionless between its shoulders and the hard yellow eye gave an occasional blink.

'This is the frontier of Hungary,' said my thought. 'I must walk, swim, creep, or sail through the Mountain Kecske to the source of the Danube, which flows into Hungary from a subterranean ocean.'

The parrot screamed. It began to speak in a rapid nasal voice, but I could see in its eye that it did not understand what was said.

'Anybody who knows may enter but time begins to harness your memory.'

It repeated this phrase six times and died.

Try as I would I could find no way to open the door. I kicked and knocked and shouted: 'Let me in, Let me in.'

The pipe which had enchanted the Egg into motion had

236

disappeared. I was bitterly alone in the land of the Dead, on the wrong side of the great stone door.

Several days have passed. I have only slept a few hours, an empty black sleep.

Since the death of the black parrot I have remained alone outside the stone door in the mountain, kicking and knocking and shouting: 'Let me in, Let me in.'

All through the night I try to get back; to no avail, I can find no means of opening the stone door.

In the daytime I wander about the marketplace thinking, but the Indians keep their world tight and closed over a secret they have probably forgotten for centuries.

The long tentacles of vision and understanding have withdrawn and all that is left to me is the ragged black hole of my loss. Loss and the world around. A noisy puzzle whose solution is another puzzle noisier and more stupid. The circle widens towards nothing.

An answer is hiding somewhere, if I could only read.

A green shawl has fallen on the arm of a chair. It draws the contours of a horse, a green silk horse, a horse hiding under my shawl.

Lovers get drunk on bitter milk; I am a hermaphrodite in love with one of my own dreams. Beast fed with the shade of a dry funeral cake.

Oh Satan, let me love myself again, loving the nightmare of a dead King has made me hate life.

Good night, good night, I am lost forever in the country of the Dead.

II

'Always be dignified, remember to be polite. You are going to study and learn many things which will help you in the world. Now you must blow your nose, so . . . '

Rebecca demonstrated the adult method of blowing a nose in a huge white handkerchief, rubbing her streaming eyes impatiently as she did so. They were already red and sore.

'Remember that you are a Jew and always remember this with pride and dignity, no matter what the world outside may do or say.'

237

She was kneeling before her little boy, putting on his socks. He was passive and soft with sleep and watched her face with wide black eyes.

'My fingers fumble so with the cold. Stretch your foot, Zacharias.'

Grandmother came in and placed a brown paper parcel in the child's hands. He clutched it to his bosom like a doll.

'It's seven o'clock, Daughter, you must hurry. They will be waiting. Is he ready?'

Rebecca nodded and scrambled heavily to her feet. 'I will get my shawl. Aaron, Aaron, are you dressed?'

'Yes, Mother.' The other boy appeared in the doorway and stared in awe at his brother. Rebecca hurried out.

'Will he ever come back, Grandmother?'

'Yes, of course, child. He will return a great learned man.'

'Is he going far away from Budapest?'

'Hold your tongue, Aaron.'

There was silence for a while as she bustled about the room making small packages.

'Grandmother?'

'Are you a child or a parrot? Always talk, talk, talk.'

Aaron was startled and relapsed into silence. They hurried along on the slippery pavement. A horse drawing a sledge trotted past, tinkling agitated little bells. Aaron wished that they could be riding behind the horse and its gay bells, but he did not dare speak for he was frightened of the terrible stranger his mother had become. She strode along, dragging the children at her side with her cold hands, her face almost invisible inside the black shawl.

The sun was up as they arrived at a square building whose large doors stood open to a crowd of Jewish women and their children. Some were in rags and some, like Rebecca, were dressed in threadbare but respectable clothes, held together precariously by much diligent mending.

Two long benches in the bare entrance hall accommodated the women, while an attendant hustled the children through a stained-glass door.

When he came to Rebecca she clutched her son roughly and kissed him once between the eyes. Then looking up at

238

the attendant she asked: 'Shall I wait?' He was a young man with a forlorn moustache and empty blue eyes.

'As you please.' He seemed impatient and stood with a hand on the boy's shoulder as if wishing to be gone.

'Name?' He scribbled in a shiny little red book. 'Address?' And after a short hesitation he asked: 'Are you a widow?'

Rebecca had hardly time to nod before her son was hustled through the stained-glass door and disappeared after the other little boys.

They went down a passage which smelt acridly of poverty and some strong disinfectant. The walls, distempered green, were occasionally decorated with brown and white prints of the largest monuments in Budapest.

About a hundred and fifty boys were seated on wooden chairs in a long chilly room. Five men with shears and white aprons passed with surprising rapidity from child to child, shaving each small head to a grey stubble. The floor was covered with dark curly hair, as if a flock of black sheep had been shorn to their skins. When the haircutting had finished they hurried the children to the baths. Each child made a small packet of his home clothes, which were afterwards given back to their parent or relations.

Because he was only four, the youngest of all the children, Zacharias was dressed after the bath by the forlorn attendant. He was put into long striped trousers of a harsh material and a jacket buttoned up to the chin with the number 105 sewn on the left sleeve in the same place where people wear the black band of mourning. Each foot was folded in a square of navy blue calico and pushed into a pair of brand-new boots made of rigid black leather. When he stood on his feet he looked like some oddly dressed puppet made by a mad doll maker.

Once the shearing, bathing, and dressing were over the children streamed back through the stained-glass doors. Some clattered to their parents' sides while others stood about self-consciously in their new stiff clothes, stamping their shiny boots.

Rebecca took her child in her arms and kissed his face and hands.

'Be a good boy, be a good boy.' She could think of nothing else to say. 'I'll come and visit you soon. Be a good boy.'

Then taking Aaron by the shoulders she pushed him into the street and they hurried away as they had come.

He tried to run after her, but his new boots slipped on the stone flags and he fell on his face. He was picked up, crying bitterly. At that time he did not mind that others saw him cry and the tears came easily.

An hour later when they were on the train bound for the Northern mountains, he vomited all the breakfast Grandmother had given him over his new trousers and shiny black boots.

105 sat up in bed and screamed. A hundred and forty-nine children stirred, murmured, or sat up, then sank back to sleep as they understood that it was only another of 105's frequent nightmares.

105, however, did not follow their example. He could not go back to sleep. He lay sweating in his narrow bed, pinching his thighs through the coarse nightshirt. He knew it was against regulations to put one's arm under the cover: the offence was severely punished.

The long dormitory did not offer a rich field of contemplation. Beds in two rows against either wall were divided by a strip of linoleum which was worn thin down to the middle. The oblong windows, placed much too high to look out, let in a pale light when there was a moon. Then the linoleum glistened and 105 pretended that it was the Danube and his bed was a boat that would sail him back to Budapest. Tonight however, there was no boat. The horror was too near, it was inside him, all around and over the bed.

Once at a local fair he had crawled unobserved into the chamber of horrors; he had been attracted by a serious-looking black-and-white printed card which said: ADULTS ONLY. The boys had been strictly forbidden to enter. For once in his life 105 regretted having broken one of the rules of the Institution.

Inside was an orgy of horror. A beautiful lady lay in her

nightdress on a silk bed. She was made of wax and looked so much alive that 105 turned back several times to see if she had moved. In her long golden hair sat a demon, a dwarf, a monkey, and a serpent. He whispered temptations into her pale pink ear. After this came coloured photographs of people eaten away by syphilis, unborn foetuses in different stages, and finally a scene from the Spanish Inquisition which had haunted him ever since: at night he was constantly apprehensive that it should return.

As his memory of this scene became older it gathered in detail and richness, finally far surpassing the original in fantasy and horror. It usually began with a vaulted cellar furnished with a somewhat confused assembly of giant meat mincers, iron armchairs with adjustable spikes in the seat and back, long man-shaped boxes, and a thing which looked like a monster sewing machine with a needle as long as a man's body and stained with clots of blood. This object awoke the painful memory of his mother's sewing machine; she earned their living as a dressmaker. From early morning to late night during the short holidays she pedalled away on expensive yards of soft material belonging to somebody else. 105 went stiff with hate when he thought of the monotonous chuffing of the sewing machine. His mother seemed to pedal away on a long painful journey, leaving him when he wanted to tell her so many important things and the time was so short. She pedalled away to Poland, where his father lay dead under the snow.

Somewhere in the thick mobile shadows a door clicked so audibly that he jumped. Eight pale-faced priests scampered lightly about the terrible vaulted chamber, pressing buttons and twirling handles; they were trying out the machines. They were going to sew him into a bloody pair of combinations for a little cream-faced Spanish Prince.

105 screamed and the vision disappeared abruptly, leaving him weak with terror and determined not to fall asleep till dawn. Then for hours he fought not to see the picture lurking in the back of his mind. He tried to evoke the Danube at midday, or another more powerful spell against the moon-faced priests.

Walking up a long avenue of trees towards a castle whose windows were glittering orange squares. Walking: but if all went well he would be wafted off his feet at the fifth tree. Counting them as he passed: one, two, three, four, five; then deliciously wafted off his feet a short distance from the ground. It was not really flying because he used no effort at all. It was being lifted by some power not his own.

The doors of the castle opened as he approached and in the vague interior stood a bright pink damsel. Her high colouring resembled that of a rose-coloured sweet called krumplicukor made out of sugar and potatoes, which 105 had eaten on several memorable occasions. The bright pink sweetmeat quality of the lady was mixed with something else no less fascinating and which he dimly recognized as being female. Trembling with a strange warmth which began in his cheeks and which crept heavily downwards, 105 drifted into her arms. The caress was unlike anything that he had ever known; this, he imagined, was woman, the faraway skirted creature who held the unique power over loneliness, nightmares, and warmth.

As he lay with tightly closed eyes trying to evoke the pink lady something touched his arm and said: 'Shhhh.' He kept his eyes closed and waited. Something sat on the bed, it bent and kissed his cheek.

'You had another,' whispered the voice. 'I know you are not asleep, so don't pretend.'

99 sat shivering beside him.

'You'll catch cold,' said 105, relieved and disappointed. 'And if the Lurcher takes a midnight stroll, you'll get a beating.'

'Let me get in your bed,' said 99. 'I'm cold.'

'No,' said 105. 'There isn't room. I can't even turn over myself without nearly falling on the floor.'

'All right then I'll stand, even if I do catch pneumonia. Let's talk.'

'The Lurcher will catch us. It isn't worthwhile.'

'I feel cold inside too and I can't feel my feet anymore.'

'Then go back to bed.'

'Look, I've got a present for you,' said 99, pressing five

iron nails into 105's hand. 'They're the heavy kind and hardly rusted at all. I traded them with 62 for my green toothbrush. He wanted it to clean machinery.'

Iron nails were used for a game called boki, which consisted of throwing nails into the air and catching them with various methods. Horseshoe nails were the most prized – and these were the kind 99 gave to 105. He tied them cautiously into the corner of his nightshirt and thanked 99.

'Now please go to bed, tomorrow I'll let you see my compass.'

The little boy crept silently back to his own bed and soon afterwards 105 fell asleep.

He dreamt that he was walking up a drive bordered with tufted green trees. The place was quite different from the residence of the Pink Lady and the flowering shrubs along each side of the avenue were a kind he had never seen. Hearing the sound of hoofs beating on the gravel, he hid behind a bush and waited. A little girl rode into view on a fat Shetland pony. She joggled up and down on the saddle chanting: 'Gee up, Bessie! Gee up!' The pony suddenly broke into a gallop and rushed past 105 at an astonishing pace for such a beast.

'She never galloped before,' he heard the little girl say. 'She's too fat even to trot properly.'

When they had disappeared around a bend in the drive, 105 stepped out of his hiding place and followed the direction taken by the girl and pony.

He met them returning rather slowly. The girl looked surprised, and her mouth hung open.

'Who are you?' she said. 'I hadn't counted you in and there you are, uninvited like Tomey.'

105 felt embarrassed and his head seemed full of numbers. 'She is younger than I,' he said to himself.

'Who are you?' asked the girl again. 'I knew I was going to dream of Black Bess but I hadn't counted in anyone else. It's rude. I don't know you, do I?'

'Yes, you do!' shouted 105. 'You know you do, how could you have forgotten? Remember the five horseshoe nails you gave me?'

She frowned and looked puzzled, then after a while she said: 'No, you left them for me and I never could give them back.' She began to cry for no reason, and wiped away her tears with her hair.

'Who are you? Who are you? I can't remember you, you must tell me.'

'Who are you then?' replied 105. 'And why do we go on asking all the time when we know?'

'We know but we can't remember,' said the little girl. 'What else did you give me? There were two things, I know.'

105 shook his head. 'It's too far away to remember precisely. . .'

Then she jumped off the pony and hopped around chanting: 'If you can't guess you'll have to go away, it's a game.'

'The nails were enough for today,' said 105. 'Is this your garden?'

'It's my father's garden. We use it all the time but he hardly ever does, he works.'

'Where are we?' asked 105. 'I mean what country?'

The little girl rolled about cackling with mirth: 'Ha ha ha, he doesn't even know where he is, ha ha ha, what an ignoramus!'

'Stop that or I'll twist your arm till you plead for mercy.'

She stopped obediently and put her lips to his ear – 'We're in England, of course, SILLY!' – suddenly jumping away after shouting the last word into his eardrum.

'England?' said 105, turning the word over in his mind. 'Of course, you are in England now, and I am in Hungary.'

'Of course,' said the girl and stopped suddenly, staring at him. 'In Hungary, in Hungary, now I seem to remember something. How old are you?'

105 was going to say that he was twelve but different words came out of his mouth: 'Very old.'

'I'm six,' she said. 'But I'm in my seventh year.'

The pony had disappeared and they had turned off the drive into a wood.

'We are going to the Big Pond.' She ran in front of him, leading the way. 'They don't allow us to go when we're awake, but in dreams you do what you want unless they're

244

nightmares. Jim Gardner says the Big Pond has no bottom.'
They were pushing through rhododendrons to a small lake
covered with floating green weed: 'Nanny says they're called
rodidandrums, Jackie had some in the garden in Ireland and
my sister-in-law had blue ones. There aren't any blue rodidandrums in England.'

They sat together near the water on the moss.

'This is a dangerous place,' said the girl. 'It's haunted.
That's why Gerard and I love to come here. Gerard is my
younger brother.'

'So you are not alone.' 105 felt cheated.

'Yes I am!' she said violently. 'They all hate me because
I'm a girl. Little girls can't do the same things as little boys,
they say. It isn't true. I can kick harder than Gerard and I
don't allow him to draw horses. Mummy told me I have such
a bad temper that I'll be an old witch before I'm twenty. I
don't care if I do wrinkle up before I'm twenty. I'll still climb
trees and come to the Big Pond whenever I like.'

The stagnant coat of weed seemed to shift, but the girl
took no notice: 'I have three brothers, one mother, and one
father. They all do whatever they like because they are boys.
It isn't fair. When I grow up I'll shave and put hair oil on
my face to grow a beard. Pat has a moustache and at school
he says they call him Bobby whiskers. He says he kicks
them whenever they call him that. Once I called him Bobby
whiskers and he kicked me. I'm the only one that has to
practise the piano for hours, wash all day, and say thank you
for everything. You should see the clothes they make me
wear.'

105 started to laugh. He couldn't stop, and the tears rolled
down his cheeks till he didn't know if he was laughing or
crying. The little girl stared at him horrified, then scrambled
to her feet and ran away. 105 was panic-stricken. He leapt
to his feet and followed her as fast as he could. When he
caught her she was crying and struggling in his arms: 'Let
me go you Damn Pig!'

'Shut up,' said 105. 'You're nothing more than a silly baby.
Why waste all our time complaining? Don't you realize we
have to wake up?'

She became suddenly quiet and afraid. 'We won't go back, we'll refuse. Can't we escape now that we're together?'

'Come on back to the Big Pond,' said 105. 'Something was going to happen when you started babbling all that nonsense.' They walked back together hand in hand to the Big Pond and sat down once more near the water. 'Jim Gardner calls it mucky. Mummy says its vulgar to say "Mucky," but we use it in secret.'

They watched the stirring weed expectantly. 'Soon we shall know,' said the little girl. 'Now do you remember what you gave me?'

'Five Iron Nails, a Stick of Cinnamon, and a Skein of Black Wool.'

The water was parting. Two curved horns, then the head and neck of a black ram emerged. In its mouth hung a pair of golden scales.

The little girl drew a circle on the ground and filled it with different polygons, then pointing first to the left and then to the right, she exclaimed: 'Fire and Air, you and I, Little Brother; our mother is Earth and our father is Water. In twelve houses we lived, through twelve houses we will pass. When we hold hands across the circle, yours is Air, mine is Fire.'

The black ram picked its way daintily out of the Big Pond and stood in the centre of the circle.

The girl handed the boy a sharp triangular stone, which he took in his left hand. Kneeling before the ram he caught its spiral horn in his right hand, twisting back its head and exposing the beating pulses of its neck. He cut its throat with the triangular stone. The girl caught the blood in her cupped hands, saying: 'Drink the scarlet milk of Paradise, Little Brother, it is ours.'

He bent his head and drank the blood out of her cupped hands. When he had also drunk he said: 'The Old Gods are our food, the New Gods will be revealed to us in time and out of time. The Old Gods are dead; Earth, the Goat will renew the lifeblood of the Myth and will violate the Garden of Paradise. The Goat will deliver us the New Myth and she will be clothed with animal, vegetable, and mineral; nothing dead, alive, or unborn will she lack and nothing on this Earth or in the Nine Planets around will remain untouched by her or she by them.'

The girl took the triangular stone and cut two meshes of wool from the head of the dead ram; one she entwined around the boy's neck, and the other she hid inside her nightdress. 'This is a jewel and also a weapon: black wool rope into the centre of the Earth, where our roots were entwined at the beginning of life.

'Black wool, Black hair, Air roots for the night. Our roots into the Air, our roots into the Earth. We shall knit a ladder of Black hair and climb into the centre of the Earth to our roots and when these long strands join again we will Hear, Taste, See, Smell, and Touch.'

They joined hands over the carcass of the ram and sang a song to the music of an old tune: *'Buj buj zöldag, zöld levelecske. . .* Open, open, little green leaf, Open, open, great stone door, You are the black ram, I am the black ram, It is dead so I am no longer I but you are I and I am you. Secret Enemy, we have quit the first house and have entered the fifth in the dark water.'

'Water the place, we have met in Time.'

When 105 awoke he was horrified to find that he had wet his bed. The dawn had already made the windows pallid and in an hour's time the waking bell would ring. He rolled around trying to dry the wet patch with the warmth of his body. Afterwards he would try and smooth out the telltale wrinkles in the sheet. They would find out, he thought, feeling his heart shrink to the size of a hazelnut. He would be humiliated and punished; they would make him sleep in the youngest children's dormitory, there would be no water for three days, everybody would know. Even humble 99 would despise him. They would whisper behind his back in class and in the Synagogue, he would be branded forever as the twelve-year-old boy who still wet his bed. He lay there miserably, imagining the consequences till the sharp peals of the morning bell brought him rudely out of bed and into the day's work.

The clubfooted monitor preceded 105 up the strip of linoleum to his bed. He stopped suddenly with a clump of his shoe and indicated the damp wrinkled patch on the sheet. The bed was the only one now uncovered in the dormitory; 105 thought it looked white and guilty.

'What's that, Boy?' he asked, still pointing at the patch of the sheet with a thick and rather dirty finger. 105 was dripping chilly sweat inside his striped coat, but he looked the monitor in the eye and did not reply. 'Well then, I'm speaking aren't I? Are you deaf? You've got a tongue in your head, speak up!'

105 remained silent and the monitor's voice started to sharpen dangerously. 'Come on, Boy, I am asking you a question. I want you to explain just exactly what that is. Come along!'

Something in the persistent question suddenly stabbed 105 into a great rage. He felt the blood beating like a hammer behind his eyes. From without they looked like two hard black stones.

'I will give you five seconds to speak,' said the monitor. He began to count out loud, still pointing at the patch on the sheet: 'One, two, three, four ... now one more chance ... *five*!' He grabbed 105's thin arm on the last word and slapped him hard on the face.

105 did not move. He stared straight in front of him with one side of his face red and the other white. The monitor released his arm and limped away: something in the boy's face frightened him.

Once he was alone again, 105's teeth began to chatter and his body shook convulsively with dry sobs. When the tears began to fall he took refuge in the latrine. He let himself cry and rubbed his face on the grimy walls.

Far away in the building he heard the bell ring for morning lessons. Hurriedly dabbing cold water on his face to remove the tearstains, he ran to class, arriving a few seconds after the history master, who gave him an unpleasant stare.

'Well, Number 105, so we've become a gentleman and arrive for class at the hour we please? I suppose one would say we are one of nature's gentlemen? Ha ha.'

105 tried to shift into his seat beside the fat boy, 20, but

the history master had not finished his little joke. 'Take the chalk, Boy, and write.' He had already detected the signs of tears on 105's pale face. 'And what do we see here?' His voice sounded damp and unctuous. 'The gentleman of the class has been crying? At your age, 105, I am surprised! At age twelve tears are for females, or are we becoming girlish in our old age?'

One or two boys sniggered, but most of the class kept stolid cold faces. They hated the teacher, and 105 was generally popular because he was brave and modest.

'Very well, Boy, take the chalk and write in even clear letters the exact date and description of the coronation of Szent István.'

When 105 turned towards the blackboard he had a clear picture of the date and circumstances of István's coronation, but when the chalk touched the smooth black surface he drew a large perfect circle with a sweep of his left arm. The boys drew in their breath with a hiss, but 105 went on drawing as if oblivious to everything apart from his strange occupation. He filled the circle with polygons placed in different positions. Their points touched the circumference of the circle in twelve places. The diagram was mathematically correct. He could not have said how long he had been drawing when the click of the opening door made him turn his head; he found himself face to face with the Director of the Institution. The wrinkled countenance behind the old man's long grey beard was impassive. They stared at each other for a long time.

'Zacharias,' said the Director, 'seems to have mistaken Szent István's coronation for higher mathematical calculations. Zacharias, you have never shown an aptitude for mathematics up till now and the least I can say is that the time and place are ill chosen. Follow me.'

105 wondered how he knew his name. Following the old man with some misgiving down the corridor, he turned over in his mind different plausible explanations for his exploit on the blackboard.

They entered the Director's study, which seemed luxurious and awesome to the twelve-year-old boy. True, the carpet was somewhat thin in places. Still it was a carpet and nearly covered the entire floor. Well-filled bookcases reached to the ceiling, giving the whole room a sober atmosphere which was not disagreeable. The ceiling was painted dark cream and had decorative moulds in each of the four corners.

The Director made a sign indicating that 105 should take a chair while he sat himself behind a very large desk.

'Zacharias,' he began, joining his fingers just under his large nose, 'reports lately on your behaviour have been far from good; your teachers complain of a continuously rebellious attitude and a refusal to apply yourself to study. This cannot continue, Zacharias. Boys in your situation may not allow themselves the luxury of wasting their time. You are dependent on the State for your education and this is an eminently important factor for your future life. Moreover, remember that we are Jews and our lot is hazardous and difficult, not only in Hungary but unhappily in many parts of the world. Your life, like the lives of thousands of other Jews and Gentiles, will not be easy. Lives are seldom easy, but a good foundation of knowledge is a strong weapon against the stones in the path of life; an aid in earning your bread – and let it be an honest bread! – and in preserving your dignity amongst your fellow men.'

He paused and scrutinized the boy, who was impressed by the measured tones of his voice. They looked into each other's eyes with a certain understanding and mutual respect.

'Now, Zacharias,' continued the old man, 'you are not a stupid boy, I might even say the contrary. But you are proud and wilful, and these faults will be the source of great suffering when you take your place in the world. Pride is a form of blindness and therefore a kind of stupidity. The sage sees himself with such lucidity that the word *pride* ceases to have any meaning. He sees himself as a phenomenon amongst thousands of other mysteries great and small. A humble and dignified attitude is therefore the logical inheritance of his vision. A strong will is sometimes an asset in his life, Zacharias, but beware, for that element we call strength is often a mere assertion of a personality which blinds itself to reality and only seeks to obtain power and domination over its fellow men. Domination, Zacharias, is not only a great sin but also a great waste of time because one becomes a slave of power, and life degenerates into a continuous struggle to maintain something which is no more than a conventional abstraction or word which men have made in a futile attempt to glorify their own ignorance and weakness. In learning the true nature of your faults you will have made the first step towards knowledge, and knowledge, my child, is the doorstep of Paradise. Someday you will understand my words if you grow in the direction I suspect; you shall see what an immense and varied thing is real wisdom, how many and how strange are her faces. Never tire of seeking her, and do not despise her humble costumes.'

He stopped speaking, apparently occupied with his own thoughts. The boy was embarrassed and pretended to find something on the toe of his boot. The old man took a piece of paper and made some diagrams, then he called 105 to his side.

'Can you tell me what this is, Zacharias?'

'Yes, sir, it is similar to the drawing I made on the blackboard in the history class.'

'Quite so. Do you know what it signifies?'

Zacharias went red and hesitated before he replied. 'No, sir, not exactly, sir.'

'But where did you learn such a thing?'

There was a long pause, during which 105 shifted his weight from one foot to the other.

'I cannot say, sir. I don't exactly know.'

'Zacharias,' said the Director sternly, 'you must not lie to me.'

'I cannot say, sir.'

The old man examined his face and finally told him to be seated.

'I believe you, Zacharias, though it is most remarkable. Most remarkable.'

He pulled his watch as the bell rang, ending the first lesson.

'You may retire now, my child, do not keep your teacher waiting. You may say that I detained you in my study. Go

251

now, Zacharias; we will continue this conversation at another opportunity.'

105 saluted the Director and left the world of learning.

At eleven the boys were allowed ten minutes' recreation before returning to their lessons. Black bread was served on a long wooden table in the school yard.

105 was no sooner outside than he was joined by 99, who wore a worried frown. 'What happened, Zed?' he asked, taking his friend by the arm. 'Did the Old Geezer jaw?'

'Not exactly,' said 105, who was reluctant to disclose the details of the interview with the Director. 'The usual stuff about work, behaviour, and manners. He was quite nice really.'

'Quatch! You had guts to pull Dung Heap's leg like that! When you left he was shaking like a leaf.'

105 gave a forced laugh. 'Do him good, the old stinker. He's had his knife into me the whole term.'

'What was it?' asked 99. 'It looked like some sort of geometry.'

105 walked along whistling and throwing the five iron nails into the air and catching them again deftly. 'Oh, something like that,' he replied indifferently. 'It just came into my head, any old thing.'

'Well, it certainly made him waxy; better look out next time, he'll have you out if he can.'

The bell summoned them back to class.

When night came, 105 waited in vain for the little girl and pony; perhaps his fear of repeating the previous night's accident kept her away. Many months passed, during which he was obliged to evoke the Pink Lady to keep away dreams of the Inquisition and the scampering, moon-faced priests. The Pink Lady was still able to exorcize nightmares, but she herself grew evasive and unreal. Her castle thinned to a flimsy structure like a painted theatrical backcloth. It had lost two of its dimensions.

105 passed the winter yearning; a yearning which became acute and anguished towards spring. He strove to ease his nostalgia by taking violent physical exercise and concentrating his affection upon 99.

The evenings grew longer and became warm. Sometimes the boys were permitted to take short excursions to the banks of the Danube, where some of them bathed and others sat around inventing stories of drowned strangers and beautiful female suicides, stories of the Danube ...

During one of those excursions 105 and 99 discovered a huge orchard near the river. The exuberant display of half-ripe fruit tempted them. The orchard was guarded by vigilant keepers and wide dykes, but this only served to make the fruit more desirable to the two boys.

'Who could own such a big orchard?' asked 99. 'And what a large family he must have to eat all that fruit.'

105 was pensively eating the tender stalks of young grass. When he had them chewed to shreds he spat them as far as he could.

'It belongs to a Patriarch,' he explained, 'who has six wives and ten children to each wife. The only meat he gives them is cow's ears, and they eat the fruit so as not to starve to death.'

'You're talking through your hat,' said 99. 'It belongs to a General who only eats meat and all that fruit is for the pigs. He has millions and trillions of jet black pigs.'

105 spat a piece of chewed grass at least a yard. 'Well I don't see why all that good fruit should go to the General's pigs or to the Patriarch's wives. After all we're as good as pigs, or nearly as good because we're probably not edible after the food we've been absorbing for the past ten years. . . Why not pay them a visit? A friendly visit of course, merely to leave our cards.'

'At night,' said 99 excitedly. 'We could muster a gang under oath. . .'

'Entire secrecy,' replied 105, 'is demanded; under pain of Chinese torture.'

The expedition was arranged for the following night and was to include 19, 60, and 38 among others. The boys were to meet at the stroke of midnight in the school latrine and make their exit by the narrow window obscured by shrubbery and conveniently situated on the ground floor. Once outside the Institution they would take off their clothes and rub themselves with the grease 60 would obtain from the kitchen. Capture would be almost impossible, as anybody knows who has taken part in the greased-pig competition in a fair.

Each member of the expedition was to carry a small book sack. Once in the orchard the boys would divide and obtain as much fruit as possible before the alarm was given, then each would save his skin as best he could. They were to meet again at the end of the drive, where their clothes would be hidden.

The latrine was to be the centre for dividing the spoils. Here 105 would supervise an even distribution of the stolen fruit.

Each detail of the plan was carefully examined and accepted, and on the following night the five boys went to bed in a state of high excitement.

A thin new moon was making her way across the dormitory window. Zacharias knew that when she reached the third pane midnight would strike and he would slip out to the school latrine. Thinking about it he realized that he did not really care for the fruit, but an hour's freedom in the night was as precious as a whole holiday.

The moon, slight and sharp as a knife, gave enough light for them to pick their way into the centre of the orchard. They spread fanwise, each choosing a tree at a different point of the compass. Their pale forms moved as quietly as shadows.

105 pushed his way through the long damp grass with his head bent and alert. Alone, he moved as surely as any nocturnal animal intent on his business. He stiffened to hear a foreign sound winding here and there, approaching him deviously. 105 crouched low and waited. In a short while he saw a small white object moving busily in the grass. On close inspection it proved to be a little dog, which sprang towards him, wagging its tail and giving other signs of welcome and recognition. The animal pranced about like a diminutive white horse cutting capers, but when he bent to stroke it it danced away, waiting till he came near to prance off again. They played a circular game, drawing each time nearer to the oldest apple tree.

'Are you there at last?'

105 crept forward on his hands and knees; he saw somebody or something perched high in the branches of the oldest apple tree.

'Come quickly,' it said. 'I have been waiting so long amongst the tricks of time.'

Afraid and excited, 105 started to climb the tree. Over his head crouched a young woman with long dark hair. She appeared not to see or hear him so he stayed still and listened to her voice, a bodiless sound that seemed to come from far away. Yet he heard it intimately in his ears.

'I need you now. Quetzalcoatl the serpent is sucking me dry. Wise King open the stone door, now I understand the black parrot's dying words. Man must open the door, for alone I am impotent. Alone I am a pitiful and incomplete creature.'

Looking down the young woman saw him. She spoke to herself: 'Who is this? Is it the White Child of Mesopotamia?'

He answered without knowing the source of his words: 'I am the White Child, the wise King, the Jew, the Black Ram, and the scales.'

She stretched her hands out, willing. 'I cannot touch you. We are separated by time. Let me in! Let me in!'

He cried out in anguish and tried to climb to her side, but the twisted branches held him like a fish in a net. The young woman turned her face towards the moon and he saw that she was blindfolded.

'The Bohemian is surrounded by shadows. If my eyes weren't covered I could read his past. The Bohemian was there when you were King on the frontier of Mesopotamia, the land where people are crockery. Mesopotamia faces Hungary across a mountain and a deep ravine, each spying on the other.

'Mesopotamia, huge arid cemetery, whose cities are tombs, whose trees are shaped lions and astrological artifacts. Holy, Holy Land, so holy that it is infested with prayers in the form of black butterflies swelling to the size of turkeys' eggs and forged with the life of the Mesopotamians; for seven decades their vitality has been sucked down the gullets of black butterflies. Even the wind is dead, leaving the prayer wheels motionless; the prayer wheels which once spun like tops. Facing this embalmed country across the mountain and ravine you lived, My Love, in a country of trees and snow.

'The stone door is closed against me, let me in, Oh my Love, let me in.'

She shook the tree so violently that the fruit fell thumping to the earth in abundance.

105 lost his footing and fell amongst the apples. When he looked up the young woman had entirely disappeared. As he bent to pick up the fruit and fill his sack he heard somebody whistling in the distance, but the sound was so far and faint that he thought that it only existed in his mind's ear.

III

He made a dejected figure against the snow-crusted street; haggard and dirty, his clothes ragged and torn, a mixture between a young scarecrow and the crows it was supposed to scare. The sole of his boot hung loose and the piece of newspaper inside soaked up the water and made a filthy pulp under his foot.

'My feet are so cold now I can't feel them anymore. So much the better, perhaps they'll drop off with frostbite.'

'Zed! Zed!' He stopped at the sound of his name but did not turn.

'Zed!' Elias, Number 99, caught him by the shoulder and looked deeply into his face. 'Did you hear me call you?'

'Hello, El.'

'Where have you been, Zed? I've looked for you all over Budapest for months.'

Zacharias smiled bitterly and started to walk as the cold slunk back under his clothes. 'I came out of prison last week,' he said. 'There are so many jobs in Budapest I haven't been able to make up my mind.'

El directed him into a café and they took a small table near the wall.

'Drink?'

'Offer me a bun and some coffee,' said Zacharias. 'Rubber dropped a pengö this morning on the stock exchange.'

'Zed, you must tell me what happened. I might be able to help.'

They ordered coffee and szamorodni. El left a packet of cigarettes on the table: whole cigarettes, not damp butts picked out of the gutter and dried surreptitiously on the chestnut man's fire.

'Tell me all about it, you know I'm your friend, Zed.'

'There's nothing to tell.' Zacharias sipped his coffee, warming his fingers on the hot cup. 'There's nothing to tell. I would much rather you tell me your own adventures; stories only make good telling once they've ended. My story hasn't begun yet. I'm still mere offal among the extinct ungulate mammals, waiting to learn slow movement. When the stone age begins – it seems to be a long way off – when it begins, come ask about my past. Till then I'll confine myself to asking for bread and insulting policemen.'

El gave him a cigarette and sighed. 'You haven't changed a great deal, Zed. Still the same old petrified Zed so stuffed with humility and pride that he prefers to starve rather than ask for the help he needs.

'Never mind, if you prefer I'll tell you my own adventures.

'Old Aunt Sari died five months ago. With her went the pension. Having sold the little we had, paid for the funeral and the debts she left, I found myself on the street with five pengö in my pocket. A few hard and dirty jobs here and there, you know the type, then as luck would have it I was drunk one night in a café over by Hokay Ter and I got talking with a barmy Chinese. He wound up offering me a job and to my great astonishment the next day he remembered me and kept his word. I've been working for him ever since. He pays pretty well, he's not over exigent, and even if he is a bit cracked I'm thankful for his pay.'

'What does he make? Sell? Steal? Cook? Grow or knit?' asked Zacharias, who felt revived by the hot coffee. 'And where does he live?'

'Precisely near Hokay Ter, on a side street called O Ucca. The Chinese always seem to live on side streets, however wealthy they are. Perhaps because they're a secretive people, or we imagine them to be.

'In any case, this particular Chinaman is a queer case. He makes dolls, toys, music boxes, cheap paper fans, and what not. He can make almost anything go with a sort of clockwork that he invented himself. There's nothing in the way of toy trains, soldiers, dolls that he can't make go in any way he pleases. He's a nice fellow though in his own way. I haven't quarrelled with him yet, and on thinking it over I don't think I should like to.'

'You are lucky,' said Zacharias. 'Employers are always swine; either that or insidious stinking dogs. There's no happy medium. I'd be content with just a slightly dirty swine, but they don't seem to exist.'

'Well you don't have to starve. I have a small room in Lovag Ucca and earn enough to keep body and soul together. We will share and share alike. Remember the sour apples in the school latrine? What bellyaches we all had! It's funny to think we're the product of an orphan asylum.'

'Yes, I suppose we are,' said Zacharias, 'though I always thought of an asylum as a place where people with unkempt hair, wild eyes, and long nails gibber through iron bars. I suppose our institution wasn't so far off . . . Twelve years locked up in a place like that is enough to give anyone a start in life. Quatch! What a start!'

'You remember the night don't you? Remember the General's orchard?'

Zacharias suddenly became sad and silent. How empty his nights had been since he'd crouched in the oldest apple tree. He had tried to sift that painful hope out of his blood, but it had clung to him through the years.

'Yes,' he replied at last, 'I remember very well. Are we supposed to forget just because we're what they call grown up?'

'You will never grow up.'

'I've had plenty of opportunity. Tell me, El, have you got a girl?'

'No,' said El. 'No, I haven't got a girl, and you?'

'Girls, yes, I have girls when I have money. No money, no girl. There's not many who want to go bed with a scarecrow. Not that I'm fastidious, but between hunger and a brothel I usually choose my stomach. It's not a question of principle but necessity. When the fat days come along again, I shall pick a nice blonde and put her in a bed-sitting room which I shall visit at my will. I always had a fancy for plump blondes. There's lots to catch hold of and they wear well.'

'Women are a poor use for our hard-earned money,' said El. 'Give me a nice bottle of szamorodni any day.'

He paid the bill and they walked out into the street laughing. It was snowing again.

'Come to my place and I'll cook some supper. The bun you ate wasn't enough to fill a canary. I've become a good cook since my café days, you'll see.'

Zacharias followed him with his bitter smile. The day was darkening and it was deadly cold; the snow capped his head and shoulders. Under the cold crown his raven's face was still and indifferent.

Chung Ming Lo used a basement in O Ucca as his workshop. During the winter days when the snow piled high outside, a long twilight reigned in the shop, but at night the petrol lamps gave off a warm yellow light. At eight o'clock every evening Ming Lo pulled down the red blind to the disappointment of the children outside, who loved to gather and spy on his workshop. Between six and eight however they could feast their eyes on piles of cheap toys, musical boxes, wooden soldiers, and a long carpenter's table furnished with saws, chisels, hammers, paint pots, and sharp wheels spitting chips of wood.

Zacharias went to fetch his friend El at the workshop the evening after their encounter. He paused outside and peered in along with the children. He felt slightly guilty peeping into the workshop unseen. El was sitting at a side table painting half a dozen wooden trains bright red. A cigarette on the edge of the table sent up a thin line of smoke.

If I lived alone on top of the highest tree in the world, thought Zacharias, I could not be more outside the lives of human beings. Though if anyone ever asked me where I am, I doubt I could reply. He felt rather heroic, then depressed. It was cold.

'Let me in, let me in.'

259

The nostalgia always returned monotonously when the sun went down.

'Won't you come in?'

Zacharias stiffened at the sudden words. Looking around, he saw the Chinaman at his elbow, a brick-red scarf wrapped around the lower part of his face.

'Come in,' said the Chinaman. 'I was expecting you. The cold is intense out there. It's not difficult to come in. . .'

'I'm a beggar,' said Zacharias.

'Begging is a profession like any other, it takes a certain skill. Even living is a form of commerce: we absorb the fruit of the Earth and pay energy back into the Earth. Work or art merely apes the natural order. You are a Jew, are you not?'

'Yes, I am a Jew.'

'Then you understand me. That which is called forgetfulness in others is to a Jew a long shriek traversing his race from the beginning of Time. Among the Jews are those who can read the spoor of the road, hieroglyphs along the wayside containing the footprints and the knowledge of errant Jews. The Stars too can be read by man.'

The Chinaman took a key out of his pocket and opened the door. Zacharias followed him after a short hesitation.

They were in a small poorly lit hall furnished with ornate furniture on fragile legs. Bric-a-brac clung to every possible space, leaving the walls invisible.

The Chinaman continued talking as he hung up his coat on a brass hook protruding from the jaws of a tiger.

'When a tiger kills his prey,' he said, pointing to the hook, 'he first tears out the liver and devours it. That liver is the best nourishment for the tiger. But how many other elements are contained in the body of an antelope?'

'Most enlightening,' said Zacharias, who did not remove his coat, 'but I should appreciate it if you offered me dinner rather than philosophy. Philosophy is an after-dinner game. Perhaps I am rude, but then I have nothing to lose if I never see you again.'

'Frankly, if not altogether tactfully spoken,' said the Chinaman. 'Though you may gain more from me than you think.

You will eat dinner here; we might interest each other. I am neither proud nor stupid, as you will see.'

'Then you have my respect,' replied Zacharias. 'Real dignity cannot be affronted.'

'You shall join your friend in my workshop,' said the Chinaman, making for a curtain at the far end of the hall. 'I am my own cook, slave and master. Please excuse me.'

As the small man disappeared, Zacharias walked thoughtfully down the stairs to the workshop.

'Any luck?' asked El as Zacharias sat down on a wooden stool beside him.

'I haven't eaten since breakfast. There's no work, no hope of work. I'm cold and tired.'

El looked up from his painting with a sly smile. 'The Chinaman needs another assistant to catalogue the knick-knacks upstairs.'

'He seems to like me,' said Zacharias thoughtfully.

'I'm not surprised. He's a garrulous sort, and you did pretty well at school on the type of thing that amuses him.'

'What type of thing amuses him?'

'Just talking.'

'Well, I would sooner be paid for talking than for shovelling coal, washing dishes, or doing arithmetic. We must fill our stomachs somehow. With our high-class education I suppose it's best not to be too delicate.'

'You're difficult to please,' said El. 'I took anything I could get.'

'And what have I got?' asked Zacharias. 'A cold in the head and an old suit of clothes.'

'Look at my department upstairs.' It was the Chinaman speaking. They did not know how long he had been standing in the doorway watching them.

'Upstairs I have toys for adults. Please follow me.'

They mounted three flights of stairs and finally arrived in a dusty attic packed with junk or precious objects.

'Some I made myself,' said the Chinaman, holding a candle aloft, 'some are presents, and some are objects found or bought. Should you enter my employment it would be to

261

catalogue and sort out the saleable items from the rubbish and to clean the former.'

'You need only look at me to know that I need work,' replied Zacharias. 'But how do you know I'm honest?'

The Chinaman smiled. 'Yes, I think you are honest, though my judgment could be in error.' He lit an oil lamp. 'Have a look around while I finish dinner. I shall be with you shortly.'

When he was gone Zacharias crossed the room to a dusty convex mirror which hung on the opposite wall. Zacharias could not decide whether the mirror was black or so dirty that it appeared black. As he looked at his distorted reflection a sudden star-shaped crack burst in the centre of the mirror where he had seen his face.

Frightened, Zacharias looked about for a place to hide the cracked mirror. On second thought, he realized that a gap on the wall would be even more conspicuous.

He turned away and hunted among the nearest knick-knacks for something to divert his thoughts. He found an old musical box which was made in the form of a coach-and-four; he wound it up to see if it still worked.

'*Buj buj zöldag*,' sang the box in its creaky little voice. '*Zöld levelecske nyitva van az aranykapy. Kapuljatok rajta nyistd ki rózsam Kaputat kaputat hadd öleljem valadat, szita, szita peutek, szerelmes csütörtok bab szerda...* Open, little green leaf, Come in through the golden doors, For I miss the shoulders of my love. Wooden sieve, Friday, Thursday, green leaves, Wednesday, my love...'

The song has more words, thought Zacharias, yet try as he could he could not remember the second verse. Winding and rewinding the music box, he played '*Buj buj zöldag*' a half dozen times. The thin tune evoked a nostalgic pain. He went back to stare at himself in the black mirror.

'You look like a scarecrow, I hate you. One cannot be astonished that such a jackdaw's face cracks mirrors. Ah, my soul and heart have withered up so small that both would fit inside the skin of a fried bean. You are a particle in a senseless malady called life: a puzzle made by a lunatic, the winding circles lead to another puzzle sillier and more puzzling yet.'

262

He turned around and felt foolish: Ming Lo had entered the room.

He thinks I was admiring myself, thought Zacharias. I wish I could feel happier.

'Strange what a puzzle one's own face is,' said the China-man, who did not appear to notice the crack in the mirror. 'How detached we are from our own faces.'

'When I looked it cracked.' After a rapid calculation Zach-arias had decided that the truth would be prudent. 'I am sorry, you will take it out of my wages.'

'It is not a wilful fault,' said Ming Lo. 'Perhaps you have been accustomed to see your reflection on another surface?'

'I don't think my face merits a great deal of attention.'

'I wonder if you always thought so. Opinion is infectious when we are young, either high or low depending on the outside world's opinion.'

'Perhaps one must be loved to love oneself.'

'To be loved is a necessity while we drink our mother's milk. During adolescence when our virility is unformed we need to be admired, when that virility is formed but not satisfied, to hate. Later all these things fall into their right place, little tools hacking out one's form before our fellow men.'

'As a matter of fact,' said Zacharias, 'I do not agree with you. Dreams, thought, love, virility, and hate are too inti-mately entwined. To say one can exist without the other is like saying the perfume of roast coffee exists independently of the coffee.'

'In which case,' said Ming Lo, 'you are destined to a great misery.'

He took Zacharias by the arm and led him below; they were greeted with the pleasing odour of a roasting animal. At that moment Zacharias felt the kitchen was the most delightful place in the world.

On a sunless Wednesday morning Zacharias began to work in O Ucca. Furnished with a small black book and a pencil he set about sorting the varied, dust-ridden possessions of Ming Lo. While scrabbling around in an ornate tin trunk, he came upon a triangular box covered with black feathers fixed

263

one upon the other as cunningly as if they grew on a bird. With some difficulty he opened the box and saw that it contained a stone key of Mexican workmanship.

Zacharias listened to the box, which chanted: 'Let me in, let me in. Open the stone door.' He hid the box in his breast pocket.

Towards midday Ming Lo visited the attic, accompanied by a small man with a foreign accent.

'Monsieur Mangues,' he explained, 'is the secretary of Docteur le Fauvenoir, a French gentleman who is a collector. He wishes you to show him some objects of value which might interest the Docteur. You have not had a great deal of time yet to catalogue our possessions, but if you have happened upon any boxes, mirrors, or keys please show them to Monsieur Mangues; Docteur le Fauvenoir is especially interested in keys.'

Zacharias showed them a few small boxes he had found; they were in bronze, ebony, or ivory, and of various origins. While Monsieur Mangues examined them, Zacharias could feel in his pocket the weight of the box and the stone key.

'You're sure that is all you have found?' asked Ming Lo. Zacharias nodded, without speaking. 'There are nothing but empty boxes.'

'I do have other objects which you could show to the Docteur,' said Ming Lo. 'Is he in Budapest?'

'Monsieur le Docteur is not in town at present,' replied Mangues. 'He is taking a rest cure in his country house. I am here on a small business transaction and intend to return to the country this evening. Whenever I visit town I have the habit of bringing a small present to the Docteur.'

Ming Lo unlocked a mahogany cabinet and showed the Frenchman several objects in jade.

'You could take these pieces of jade to the Docteur. If they do not please him I will change them for something else.'

When they had gone Zacharias went to the black mirror and smiled at his reflection.

'Locked doors,' he said to his face in the black mirror, 'are opened by keys. Stone door, stone key.'

Towards seven o'clock the same evening Ming Lo joined

Zacharias, who was still sorting dusty treasures; he was holding a small package. 'Stupidly I overlooked this this morning when Monsieur Mangues was here. It is a small ivory of ancient workmanship and I think it would please Docteur le Fauvenoir very much; I know he has no such piece in his collection. Would you be so good as to run out to Duna Palota Salloda and see if Monsieur Mangues has not already left? If he is still there give him this note and packet: I recommend this as entirely after the Docteur's taste.'

When Zacharias was outside in the street he stopped under a lamp to read the note: *The other is not presently in our possesion; the enclosed is hermetically sealed, there is no cause to worry. Further particulars later. Do not be impatient, I shall join you within three weeks at Kentaur.*

Zacharias broke open the seal on the packet and found a small ivory doll. It was obviously ancient. He wrapped the doll in its cloth and put it in his trouser pocket, then he walked about for a half hour whistling. He returned slowly to O Ucca and was surprised to find the Chinaman waiting in the street. 'Well?' he asked with unusual impatience. 'Was Monsieur Mangues at the Hotel?'

'He had left,' said Zacharias. 'The clerk said he had checked out at five o'clock.'

Ming Lo considered this news in silence and finally shook his head. 'That is very strange. I particularly wished Docteur le Fauvenoir to see that piece. I must ask you to do me a favour.'

'What do you want?'

'I want you to take a small journey. I would like Docteur le Fauvenoir to receive the packet this evening. There is a train which goes as far as Pilisvörösvár and from there you will find a sledge to the residence of the Docteur. The journey will take several hours and if you agree to leave this evening you could return tomorrow. The train leaves Budapest at nine-fifteen.'

Zacharias was pleased to oblige; a journey outside Budapest was always an adventure. So at 8:45 that evening he pulled his fur cap down over his ears and set out for the station with the packet carefully buttoned into his pocket. At 9:20 the train clanked painfully out of the station.

Zacharias shared a carriage with a man who wore a black suit and dark glasses. He held a small leather book defensively before his face. His hands were pallid and unsteady. He must be a foreigner, thought Zacharias, because his clothes are cut in a narrow and unfamiliar manner. And how can he read through those spectacles? wondered Zacharias. A plain, elegant leather suitcase sat on the rack over the foreigner's head.

Something seemed to go wrong with the lighting in the compartment, and it became so dim that the white world moving outside was visible through the windows. The stranger lowered his book and looked outside. In the half-light, the lower part of the man's face seemed to be featureless. Zacharias could not distinguish his mouth, even when he spoke in a mumbling, broken Hungarian.

'Do you mind if I open the window?' he asked. 'The carriage is rather stuffy.'

He is English, thought Zacharias, rising and opening the window. Where is his mouth? . . .

'Are you travelling in Hungary?' he asked, politely offering him a cigarette. If he takes it then I shall see, thought Zacharias.

The Englishman refused. 'I never smoke, thank you. I suffer from chronic bronchitis. I find this climate very trying for the bronchial tubes.'

'I believe you are an Englishman?' continued Zacharias. 'You are visiting Hungary on a pleasure trip?'

'Yes, I am English. I am here not entirely for pleasure, but I am a great believer in mixing business with enjoyment.'

'Are you going to Pilisvörösvár?'

'Thereabouts. They say it is a mining district.'

'Are you interested in mining?' asked Zacharias, to make conversation. He still could not see an opening in the stranger's face.

'No, I can't say that I am. Old mines are of course interesting to me, as I am an archaeologist.'

He handed Zacharias a neatly engraved card: PETER STONE. STONEHENGE.

'I am employed by the British Museum.'

'I have never been out of Hungary,' said Zacharias, 'but I always wanted to travel. London, Paris, Madrid . . . they are like magic words to me. Someday I shall go to Paris.'

'Well, do not miss the train. They say anybody who misses a love tryst or a journey to Paris dies without knowing they ever lived.'

'I am sure that is true,' said Zacharias. The train dived into a tunnel and above the clattering darkness he thought he heard the Englishman shout something.

'I beg your pardon?' said Zacharias, as the train clanked into the open night. 'Did you say something?'

'I used to be frightened of tunnels,' replied the Englishman. 'When I was a child. They still have a disagreeable effect on my nerves.'

'I was horribly frightened of the dark.' Zacharias thought about his school days. 'Frightened and fascinated. I saw things in the dark which were more terrible and more beautiful than anything I have ever known.'

'Most children are frightened of the dark because they have a more acute vision than grown-up people. Sometimes I think that a person who kept a child's sensibility as he aged would die of fright when the sun went down.'

The wheels of the train squealed and drew to a noisy halt. The Englishman let down the window and leaned out to see what had happened. Somebody was shouting.

'We're in a snowdrift,' he told Zacharias. 'They are going to shovel it away. We may be stuck for some time. What a nuisance. I was anxious to reach Pilisvörösvár this evening.'

Five horsemen rode past the compartment window, looking into the train.

'Travelling in Hungary during winter is always rather hazardous,' said Zacharias. 'In England I suppose you don't get so much snow?'

'Fortunately we do not. A French poet once said: "*Pour ne pas que ça se perd, je vais vous dire mon opinion sur la neige: c'est de la merde qui fait sa première communion.*" I must admit I share his point of view. The only merit of snow is it is white.'

The five horsemen returned and stopped at the window of their carriage. 'Hey you!' called one of them. 'Give us a cigarette.' Zacharias tossed him what he had left in his packet. The man caught it deftly.

'Got a light too?'

'I wouldn't talk to them if I were you,' mumbled the Englishman. 'They might be bandits.'

'What happened?' Zacharias asked the first horseman. 'Are we snowed in?'

'Like a pig in a poke.'

The Englishman was pulling at his arm, trying to drag him away from the window. 'Be careful, don't talk to them. You never know, they might be gypsies.'

Zacharias shook him off impatiently and continued talking to the horsemen: 'Will it be long?'

'It'll take them three hours or more. Maybe you'll see Pilisvörösvár by morning!' He let out a great hooting laugh and the horse tossed its shaggy head.

'If you let me get up and ride behind you I'd get there quicker.'

'Jump up!' bellowed the horseman. 'I'll give you a run for your money.' One of the others had pulled a zither off his back and was plucking tunelessly on the strings.

'What did I say?' hissed the Englishman. 'Gypsies.'

'Give us a tune,' called Zacharias. 'You with the zither.' Five wild voices broke into song together: '*Buj buj zöldag, zöld ... levelecske....* Let her in through the stone door. White Child. Wouldn't you kiss the shoulders of your love?'

'Come back! You can't do that!' yelled the Englishman, plucking at the disappearing tail of Zacharias's coat. But he had landed unhurt on the snow. The horseman stretched out a dark hand and helped him mount. Whirling about, they took to the forest at a gallop.

'Fool!' screamed the Englishman in the distance. 'The penalty for opening the door is ... '

'Freedom!' yelled the horseman over his shoulder.

They lost the stopped train behind the trees and galloped

along a winding track. Later they stopped to rest the horses and light a fire.

'My name is Calabas Kö,' said the first horseman. 'My four companions, are Ivor, Tej, Fa, and Vas. They can only speak to music, otherwise they are dumb.'

At these words the four men put out their tongues, which were cloven and coloured like blackberries. The wagging black tongues made them look like cobras.

'Ivor, play the zither,' commanded Calabas Kö. 'Tej, Fa, and Vas, sing what you see.'

'We see the sky, a spangled skin stretched domelike over the world and her companions. The world is a fur ball. The moon is a nest of feathers.'

'Enough astronomy!' shrieked Calabas Kö, flinging snow into Ivor's impassive face. 'They're always talking about astronomy. It makes me sick.'

The four men dangled their dark tongues stupidly. Ivor continued plucking at his zither.

'Calabas Kö,' he sang, 'you are an imbecile. Someday you will give up your soul like a belch of boiled cabbage. Your destiny is not even written in the sky.'

'You'll pay for that!' screamed Calabas Kö, spitting in the singer's face. 'I'd kill and roast him if the fire was big enough.'

The four men in turn spat into the fire and started to sing once more.

'Hungary shares a frontier with Mesopotamia.'

'There they go again,' said Calabas Kö with disgust. 'Geography.'

But Zacharias leaned forward to catch each word they sang. 'Leave them alone.' To his surprise Calabas Kö held his peace.

'Hungary and Mesopotamia are divided by a deep ravine. Facing the desert you lived, my Love, in the mountains. Your palace on the highest peak in Hungary was surrounded by trees. Three kilometres from the Mesopotamian frontier. In your land the snow is your only cloak now, dear Love, but mine is my own wrinkled skin. *Buj buj zöldag, zöld levelecske.* Open, open, little green leaf, Open, open, stone door.'

Tej and Fa stood up and danced around the fire, clapping

their hands to the rhythm of Ivor's zither. When they had danced around three times, they sat down abruptly and Vas rose to his great height and sang along in a penetrating treble voice: 'Sweet Love, Dear Love, Eternal Love, listen to my rhyme. *Buj buj zöldag, zöld levelecske*. Hungary's hairy men on their shaggy tiger-horses. Calabas Kö! Igen! Ivor! Igen! Tej, Fa, and Vas. Igen! Igen! Igen! Stone, ivory, milk, wood and iron, but where, My Love, are Fire and Air?'

He sat down abruptly. Ivor twanged his zither for a while before they started singing again: 'White horse, red horse, black horse, Motion is the horse, there is no motion without the horse. The Moon is my love and my love is a horse. Five horsemen, Calabas Kö, Ivor, Tej, Fa, Vas, to whom do you come to do homage?' Each man touched his lips, eyes, ears, nose, and fingertips while his voice rose to a shrill treble: 'We come for the Böles Kilary. To salute him we throw armfuls of glass on his path. The road is written with characters from the feet of errant Jews.'

They threw pieces of glass into the fire and leapt to and fro over the flames without stopping their song: 'His city is the forest. They burn whole fir trees for the Böles Kilary. But who lives in a bier covered with wolfskin? The Old Böles Kilary! Old Böles Kilary.'

The five men circled around Zacharias and the fire, spinning together like a wheel. They called out like night birds: 'Who are you? Who are you?'

'Zacharias, a Jew.'

'No more?'

'I am Zacharias, a Jew.'

'Then marry Fire, for she is yours. Take her, take the Fire.'

Zacharias bent over the blazing logs and stretched out his hands; the flames leapt up to meet his fingers and disappeared into his hands, leaving nothing but cinders and black charred wood on the ground.

Calabas Kö took a decagonal stone from his bosom and handed it to Zacharias singing: 'Jew, this is your heritage from Solomon.' Zacharias placed the stone in the pocket over his left breast. They mounted the horses again and took the road East.

270

They climbed a steep slope and the air grew rare and thin. The snow-ridden trees in the waning moonlight resembled script. Wolves' cries echoed over the steady beat of the horses' gallop.

Sweating, the five horses at last halted of their own accord before a solitary lighted tavern at a crossroads. As they dismounted Zacharias could hear a voice inside the tavern chanting, and the slow clapping of hands to the long wail of a mourner.

'Hey there, János!' yelled Calabas Kö. 'Come out, you limping spotted tyke!'

A man with a wooden leg hopped out of the tavern, his head and shoulders obscured by a black-and-scarlet hood. He addressed himself to Calabas Kö. 'We have been waiting for three days, and the embalmers have not yet arrived.'

'You stink like a corpse, Jancsi.'

'I tell you the embalmers are three days late and Sari insists on keeping him warm with big fires. . .'

'Take the horses, feed and stable them, and get out of my sight.'

János gathered the horses' reins without a word and led them around the corner of the tavern.

'You are the Young Böles Kilary,' said Calabas Kö, placing his hand on the head of Zacharias. 'Beyond a doubt.'

When they opened the door a large black ram charged past them.

They entered a large kitchen lit bv six candles. On a sexagonal bier lay the enormous corpse of a bearded king. The great recumbent body was clad in a long black shirt exquisitely embroidered with scarlet letters, circles, and polygons. His curling black beard reached as far as his feet.

The five men stood back as Zacharias walked slowly to the bier. He slapped his hands over his face: the dead King's features were identical to his own.

A red-headed woman who piled wood ceaselessly on the fire started to chant, keeping rhythm by striking the poker against the stone flags. 'Böles Kilary, Böles Kilary, *Buj buj zöldag, zöld levelecske.* Die Old Böles Kilary, for the stone door cannot open till Young Böles Kilary lets you into the country of the Dead. Open, open, little green leaf, for when you open the Earth must open too.'

She peeped through her hair at Zacharias with pale inquisitive eyes.

Calabas Kö and his four companions stepped forward and squatted around the corpse with closed eyes. The woman rose, took five red handkerchiefs out of the pocket of her skirt, and blindfolded them. Then, sticking their fingers in their ears and spitting, they prophesied war.

'And when the massacre is done, the juice will germinate in the centre of the Earth and split her crust and leap up on Land, in Water, in Fire, and in Air. The old powers will seek to suppress it.'

When they fell silent, the red-haired woman gave them warm water from a large jar, then wine from a stone jar, and finally milk from an ivory goblet. Taking her place once more by the fire, she lit a pipe. As she puffed a thin music issued with the smoke.

Zacharias was so moved by this music that tears ran out of his eyes and with them went twenty years of bitterness. The red-haired woman watched him weep with a sly smile. When she had stopped smoking the music she put the pipe in his hands. 'It is yours,' she said. 'Use it well.'

Zacharias put the singing pipe to his lips and blew, but the only sound that came out was his own breath. The woman let out a peal of laughter. 'Ah, no! You cannot use it to charm yourself! Young Böles Kilary, you must grow up! For you it has other uses.'

She went back to the fire laughing and Zacharias, annoyed, hid the pipe in his pocket.

Having fed the flames with more pine logs, the woman walked over to the dead King and covered his closed eyes with her hands. 'Böles Kilary, your old body must return amongst the dead. Your castle, which was vomited out of the mountain, will sink back from whence it came. The house of shadows: in the light between twilight and dawn, imprisoned in your castle, walk the bodiless shadows you loved and tamed. Remember your castle, Böles Kilary. Listen . . . constructed of black-and-red stones spat from the crater of live volcanoes through the Earth's shell. The stones were as huge as seven camels, three elephants, and two horses squashed into a great cube.

'The stones that built your house contained old mineral knowledge from the nine planets. The walls of your house were wise, covered with presents, stolen objects, and lost property. From the ceilings hung embalmed yaks from Tibet stuffed with preserved fruit, as well as piñatas and country sausages. So many things hung from those ceilings, Böles Kilary! You could see all the animal, mineral, and vegetable kingdoms in the Universe looking up at your ceiling, Böles Kilary.

'Your furniture of precious woods, prehistoric bones, mammoths' ivory, and fur covered with lunatic drawings; the tables of turquoise glass with all the tints and reflections of the lake. Bouquets of Egyptian mummies stood like dry flowers in Syrian and Greek vases. Metals and jewels, heaps of jewels as high as the garbage dump outside the walls of Baghdad. This was your house, Böles Kilary, Wise King.

'At night you combed your beard before nine trees burning in the grate, and you jumped a little when a wandering shadow tickled the nape of your neck. The shadows threaded softly through your hair, lost shadows. . .

'Coming and going from the hall were slaves laden with wine, rich cakes, milk, honey, and succulent little birds. You gorged yourself, sometimes you threw whole cakes to your creatures. Animals sat in every corner and followed the slaves distractedly. Wolves and hyenas and exotic dogs from China, naked and no larger than a grown lizard; giant white poodles from France, with ears like huge rose-coloured butterflies; dogs of every race and kind. Abundant cats and small black pigs, a mandrill and his female, three does and a stag, an Assyrian bull with a human head, owls as big as lions; ducks, turkeys, and geese as fat as priests. All these creatures wandered near you because of your wisdom and tenderness.

'Sometimes you watched your beautiful face in a polished sheet of steel. You looked into your eyes for hours on end, Böles Kilary, but they said nothing. Still you talked to yourself: "Gorgeous creature, Fascinating Wise King, Exquisite

Jew, Savoury Body, what does she say, my lover, the Moon?"
You laughed and your creatures gathered around you.

'One of those silent nights, when the snow fell outside, you looked deeply into your steel mirror and your image said: "I hear."

'Let me in, let me in, Stone Door.'

The red-haired woman lifted her hands from the king's closed eyes and covered her own face.

'Böles Kilary, may these ten fingers suck up the perfume of your great wisdom.'

A six-toned bell rang out; Janos limped through the kitchen to the door. They heard him call: 'The embalmers have arrived!'

Everybody stood away from the corpse and the eight embalmers trooped into the room. Each bore a jar on his head containing sweet elixirs for preserving the dead; each man carried a Theodolite and a twig sprouting nine little green leaves. They wore masks and long yellow shirts girdled with swines' tails sewn into a rope.

The woman pointed over her head to the granary and the eight embalmers picked up the bier and followed her upstairs.

Calabas Kö and his companions let out a long sigh and lit their pipes. Zacharias sat down near the fire and fell into a reverie which eventually deepened into sleep.

Dawn had scarcely arrived when Zacharias was awakened by a black cat who rubbed itself against his ear.

Hearing sounds overhead, he guessed that the embalmers were still at work, though he had slept for several hours. The five horsemen snored soundly in their mantles. On the fire a pot of milk started to rise and froth. He leaned forward to pull it off the fire. No sooner had he moved than Sari ran down the stairs.

'He's hanging by the feet from the rafter,' she told Zacharias. 'He looks like a dead stag, his beard reaches the floor!'

She took the milk off the fire and scooped up a gobletful, which she handed to the Jew. 'Drink, Little Brother. The goat yielded a full bucket at three o'clock this morning.'

'When will they be done?' asked Zacharias, drinking the milk gratefully. 'Will it be long now?'

'They will have done at sunrise, when men are hanged. Listen, Young Böles Kilary. Millions of dead have passed through here and I have seen them lose their past and future. I would not have you do likewise. Now hear me, when the sun rises I shall call the eight embalmers down to the kitchen and feed them milk and bread. While they are still eating you must say to me: "Sari, I hear a rat in the attic, let us hope he is not gnawing at the Wise King." I will then reply: "Why yes, I also hear something in the attic, take this broom and frighten it away." Upon these words you will gather your cloak and run upstairs, where you must cut down the Wise King and escape with him as fast as you can: the quickest way out is through the window.'

'Very well,' said Zacharias, 'but where should I go?'

'If all is well a black ram will be waiting under the window; as soon as you jump he will take to his heels and you may follow him, for he was bred where you are going.'

She wrapped up a piece of cake and gave it to Zacharias saying: 'A piece of cake the mourners overlooked. How I cannot say, they nearly ate me out of house and home. Six geese and two sheep; seventy-five kegs of wine; most of them crawled home drunk as swatted cockroaches.'

Suddenly she ran to the window and pulled aside the curtain. 'Hey! The Sun is about to rise! Gather your wits, Young Böles Kilary, soon you will have to set them loose again.'

With her hands she formed a horn in front of her mouth and bellowed: 'Come, Master Embalmers, the Sun will be risen in an instant and I have prepared you milk and bread.'

A few minutes later there was a shuffling overhead and the eight embalmers came down the stairs. They brought with them a peculiar, sickly-sweet odour. Their long yellow shirts were stained. Without uttering a word they squatted on the floor in a rough circle and Sari served them mugs of milk and chunks of bread.

Calabas Kö stirred in his sleep and muttered: 'Hyenas and tuberoses! Stinking beasts!'

'Sari,' said Zacharias nervously, 'I hear a rat in the attic, let us hope he is not gnawing at the Wise King.'

275

She shook her head and replied: 'Then take this broom and frighten it away.'

Zacharias snatched the broom and his cloak and ran upstairs, stumbling. He found himself in a large granary. It had been tidied but still reeked of embalming fluids. The floor was stained and had been roughly swept. A great stone jar in the corner contained the King's entrails. Zacharias looked about for the King, but all he could see was a small object, about the size of an otter, hanging from the ceiling. Looking closer he saw that it was indeed Böles Kilary, shrunken to the dimensions of a newborn babe. He took a stool and cut him down, then, cradling him in his arms, he climbed through the little window and leapt into the air. He almost landed on the woolly back of a black ram, who trumpeting with rage, galloped off down the road East.

Zacharias followed as swiftly as he could, holding the tiny bearded King in his arms like a baby. Zacharias soon found it less cumbersome to clutch the King by his beard and swing him in one hand, which, if not altogether respectful, was a good deal more practical and allowed him to run faster. He still held Sari's broom in his left hand, thinking it might be useful.

The twinkling black buttocks of the ram cut forked tracks in the crusted snow ahead of him. The early morning was beautiful with a gaudy sky and the glittering white hide of the Earth.

Without looking at the country, Zacharias became conscious of the road rising; the forest had already thinned to an occasional tree. He seemed to be gaining the summit of a mountain. A hundred yards ahead the black ram disappeared around a bend in the road; when Zacharias got to that point the ram had disappeared, but his tracks led up to a small plot of ground which seemed to dominate the whole world. The mountains rolled away to the sky; below, in a ravine between the two highest mountains, lay the Danube, frozen and still.

Zacharias looked around, recovering his breath. He let his eyes follow the course of the Danube, which seemed to eat a huge portal between the two mountains.

'The Danube emerges from a subterranean ocean,' he said to himself.

He searched awhile in the snow and finally found the ram's tracks, which led downwards towards the ravine. He started off at a trot along the same course. The narrow, twisting path led down between trees and boulders. By dangling the Wise King from his fingers and using Sari's broom as a staff, Zacharias managed to descend swiftly without breaking his neck.

The mountains leaned over him as he descended to the Danube. The path threaded its way along the banks of the river to the gorge ahead, but the tracks of the black ram ceased suddenly. Here the snow was beaten hard by the different footprints of man and beast; the tracks of claws, hoofs, and boots were entangled along the way. After gazing awhile at his feet, Zacharias continued towards the opening in the rocks.

Far along the path he saw a huge man walking towards him. The creature was naked except for a black skin slung over his shoulders, which dripped blood down his torso and legs to his feet. As he drew near Zacharias recognized the skin of a newly slain ram. The man's face was disfigured by a harelip. He had the pointed features of a dog.

'What-ho, young man, where are you going?' The words whistled through his harelip. He had blocked the path with his huge body. Zacharias rapidly hid the Wise King under his cloak and held up Sari's broom like a weapon.

'Where are you going?'

'What's it to you, brother?'

'My business. Where are you going?'

'I am free to go where I wish.'

'Free until something stops you,' whistled the harelip giant. 'I can stop you if I wish.'

'How?' asked Zacharias, trying to edge past.

'Not so fast.' The giant blocked the way. 'If I skinned you I could have the pair of pants I lack.'

Zacharias realized the giant meant what he said. 'They would be too small,' he suggested nervously. 'Besides, I haven't any fur.'

'True,' said Harelip, 'but leather suits me just as well.'

'You need two cart horses to make you a pair of pants. My skin wouldn't make you much more than a truss.'

'There's no reason you should go on living. You're more useful as a truss, a handbag, or even stuffed on my chimney place. So why should I let you live?'

'Several reasons,' said Zacharias, thinking rapidly. 'First, because in my own quaint way I like living; second, because I must find somebody before I die; and third, because even to you I am more use alive than dead.'

'What use are you to me?' asked Harelip. 'Because that seems your only valid reason for living.'

'With my hands I could make you trousers, sing you songs, and cook you dinners more delicious than you ever tasted in your life. Also, I would bring you luck.'

Harelip considered Zacharias for some time and eventually nodded his head several times. 'Very well then, let us see if what you say is true.'

'Hurry,' said Zacharias, 'if you want the pants by nightfall.'

Harelip turned and led the way towards the portal in the mountains. Every now and then he looked back over his shoulder to make sure Zacharias was following.

As they drew near Zacharias could see through the gorge. Beyond the rocks he saw a frozen loch hemmed in on all sides by mountains; the light fell indirectly from the sky, which now seemed infinitely far away. In the distance on the opposite mountain he saw a castle.

Harelip stopped and pointed at the castle. 'He's dead and they took him away.' His voice whistled sadly. 'But he will return.'

On the near side of the gorge they came upon a construction resembling a cromlech. The low opening was covered with a sack, which was frozen stiff. Harelip pulled this aside and, crawling in on his hands and knees, beckoned Zacharias to follow. The gloomy dwelling cut into the rock contained nothing but bones and rotted skins strewn about the floor. A heap of dirty straw in the corner evidently served the giant as a bed. The air in the cavern was heavy and fetid. Harelip collected some wood and, striking a flint with some dexterity, lit a fire in the middle of the floor.

'Now,' he said, 'I want my trousers.'

'As you please,' replied Zacharias, wondering desperately how he would make a pair of trousers amongst so much garbage. 'But remember that trousers are the first rung down the ladder of degeneration.'

'I want a pair of pants,' said Harelip firmly, 'and if you cannot or will not produce them I shall have to make them myself, and you know how.'

'All right,' Zacharias fumbled, 'but if I had such beautifully shaped legs as you I would not hide them under an ugly pair of trousers.' He looked around the dwelling at the rotted skins and realized they were unfit to make clothes. Then the beard of Böles Kilary tickled his hand and a terrible idea came into his head. He remembered the dimensions of the King's body before it had been embalmed; if it had once been so large perhaps it could grow again. The least he could do was try. In its present condition however, he thought in despair, it would hardly cover the haunches of a decent-sized tomcat. He looked again at the expectant giant and decided he would try the experiment.

'Listen to me,' said Zacharias. 'I will make you a pair of trousers, but I must be alone for this and I shall need a cauldron full of snow. You must give me your word not to enter till I give you permission.'

'How long will it take?' asked Harelip suspiciously. 'You already promised they will be done by nightfall.'

'Get me the cauldron full of snow and you will soon see,' insisted Zacharias. 'And bring another armful of wood.'

The giant pulled a large iron pot out of a recess in the wall and carried it outside. He soon returned with a pot full of snow. Zacharias told him to set it on the fire.

'Now,' said Zacharias, 'get out and do not return till I call.'

When the snow had turned to water and the steam began to rise, Zacharias cut a thong of leather from his jacket and hung the Wise King over the pot.

Humidity, he thought, will make him swell.

The pot boiled, and in the humidity and warmth of the steam the Wise King began to swell. Zacharias could hear Harelip stamping about outside. Like a plant growing before his eyes, the body of Böles Kilary filled the space above the pot. His nails and hair grew as rapidly as his body. Then with a sudden loud pop the Wise King burst: a cascade of spiced juices poured into the boiling pot. The whole cavern stank of musk, cinnamon, and other spices. The Wise King's empty skin flapped huge and feeble over the fire.

Now, thought Zacharias, I can begin to make the trousers.

He took down the skin and with his pocketknife fashioned it into the rough form of a pair of trousers: cutting it in two at the waist and joining an arm and a leg as the trouser leg, the head and buttocks serving as the joining piece in the fork. He wove the King's beard into thread and, piercing holes with his knife in the skin, he sewed the pieces together into a creditable pair of pants.

Now and then Harelip called out: 'Have you done yet? The sun is already low in the sky. Remember what you promised.' And Zacharias replied: 'They will be ready at nightfall. Be patient till the first star appears.'

As the sun finally set Zacharias put the last stitch in Harelip's trousers and called out to the impatient giant: 'Come in, Harelip, you have a pair of Royal breeches!'

Within a few seconds Harelip had entered the cavern and, grunting and swearing, wrapped his limbs in the Monarch's skin. He walked slowly around the cavern before making any remark, then he went up to Zacharias and embraced him, spraying him with fetid breath, and said: 'You are my brother and my friend.' Then, almost dipping his face into the boiling pot he exclaimed: 'Ah, soup! And spiced like the King's own dinner!' He walloped Zacharias on the back. 'You're a wizard, let us celebrate!'

Dipping a colossal mug into the mixture, he swallowed the boiling liquid at one gulp. 'Delicious! Fit for a King! Help yourself, my friend.' Zacharias explained that he was not hungry and that he had already eaten. Harelip rapidly tossed off five mugs full of the embalming broth. Then, belching loudly, he sat himself down on the straw. Zacharias waited with interest to see the result of the giant's repast. He continued, however, in apparent health and even seemed disposed to talk. 'Brother, you have shown yourself a superior creature. I surmise therefore that your mission must be of great importance, you are . . . ' He stopped suddenly and stared at Zacharias in sudden recognition. He covered his face with his hands and muttered: 'It had to be. Salamander's double has returned among us.'

'The Danube is born across the loch, isn't it?' asked Zacharias.

Harelip raised his head as if it bore a great weight. 'That is correct; the subterranean ocean lies under the mountain Kecske. Beyond Kecske is Mesopotamia, the country of the Dead.'

'Between Kecske and Mesopotamia, is there a stone door?'

'Yes,' he replied heavily. 'But the stone door only admits the dead into Mesopotamia.'

'Just suppose,' said Zacharias, 'that a wanderer should wish to come out of the land of the Dead to the land of the living through the stone door. . .

Harelip's great body trembled. 'It would be disastrous, the Masters would never permit such a thing.'

'I recognize no master,' said Zacharias.

'That is what they wish. They govern without being recognized, nobody knows who they are. That is the secret of their great power.'

'Do you know who they are, Brother Harelip?'

The giant fingered his mouth, still viscous with the broth. 'I know and I do not know.'

'And where did you get such knowledge?'

'Across the loch, in the castle you can see from the doorway of my cavern, lived a Böles Kilary. This king was a prisoner because he escaped through the door, Kecske, from the dead. Those who return forget nothing, and so he was full of dangerous wisdom. The Masters set me to guard him; that was my work till he died.'

'Once dead,' said Zacharias cunningly, 'they feared him no more?'

'Some say that when he passed through the door he was a twice born. They still fear the Böles Kilary.'

'And do the twice born possess the wisdom of memory?'

'They possess a half wisdom buried in dreams and omens.'

'A whole could have two bodies,' said Zacharias.

'The Masters would never permit that,' answered Harelip. 'They would arrange such a terrible fight between the two bodies that knowledge would always be obscured by hate. One would destroy the other, so only one half would be truly alive.'

'These masters are powerful,' said Zacharias. 'Their power lies in the unit. The belief is one.'

'You will be destroyed for knowing that.'

'Why?'

'Because as long as man thinks that he is whole in his one body he can never achieve the wisdom which would endanger the Plan. Believing that he is one keeps him in perpetual combat with another half of himself. Once he could see and accept that other half without combat, the Plan would totter like a ninepin.'

'That,' remarked Zacharias, 'would not meet with the Masters' approval?'

'It would not be permitted.'

'Why do you tell me all this?'

'Because you already know and because I know who you are.'

'Then why don't you kill me?'

Harelip stretched out his arms. As the ram's skin fell away, Zacharias saw that he had many luminous moles on each arm, which twinkled like a constellation.

'You are Air seeking Fire. To find her you must ride your Mother Earth over your Father, Water. The sacrifice of the ram is over; Ram must become woman and Air must become man. Then crossing hands in the centre of the Egg and alternately touching Fire and Air, their feet will be joined under Water.'

So saying, he rose and went outside. Zacharias heard him playing a shepherd's pipe. This was followed by the bleating of a goat. At that moment a gust of cold night air blew the

282

sacking away from the doorway; the fire reddened and sprang into flame, and Harelip stepped into the cave leading a white-bearded goat.

'She is the Earth, your Mother, and she is also a goat.'

Harelip released the goat, which stood bleating and emitting white drops of milk from her full teats.

Zacharias knelt down and was suckled by the goat. When he had drunk his fill she started to walk around the fire in ever-smaller circles, till her feet were in the flames. Then she threw back her head and screamed from the centre of the fire.

'Time is,' said Harelip. 'You must cut her throat and drink her blood.'

Zacharias took the decagonal stone, the gift of Calabas Kö, from his pocket and cut the exposed throat of the goat, who offered no resistance. Then cupping his hands he caught the blood and drank it. Harelip pulled the dead goat out of the fire and flayed her with a knife shaped like a gnomon. He put the carcass whole in the cauldron and set it to boil.

'She will be your boat, Brother,' he told Zacharias. 'In her you will cross the subterranean ocean to Kecske, the stone door.'

After some boiling the goat's flesh dropped off the bones. Harelip lifted the skeleton out of the broth and stretched the hide over it, forming a light boat.

'You must take to the water at moonrise,' he told Zacharias. 'Her skeleton is Saturn and will ride farther across the water at that hour.'

Harelip then slowly stripped off his breeches and handed them to Zacharias, saying: 'Brother, your boat must have a sail to catch the subterranean wind. Take my most prized possession and use them well.'

They fixed Sari's broom as a mast and the skin of Ancient Böles Kilary as a sail. The little brig stood ready for her journey.

The moon rose. Harelip and Zacharias dragged the goatship through the gorge and onto the ice of the loch. They trudged toward Mount Kecske, which loomed before them like a pale featureless head.

Harelip drew the small vessel behind him, the ram's skin flapping around his shoulders and his great arms twinkling with luminous moles.

When they had almost reached the foot of Kecske, Zacharias saw the mouth of the cavern which led inside the mountain. The ice around the opening was hacked into chunks, creating a passage on the water.

'I shall wait till you return, Brother,' said Harelip.

He pushed the boat off the brink of the ice and handed Zacharias aboard. The boat floated like a leaf. Taking a huge breath, Harelip blew powerfully into the skin of Böles Kilary. It billowed and the ship skimmed over the water and into the cavern.

Here darkness was different from night: it seemed full of the movement of water. Then as the boat penetrated farther inside the mountain, subterranean bodies became luminous. Lights appeared around the goat-ship and slowly began to move before Zacharias. He saw the bodies shudder and shift; a sound moved through the mountain. It was the echo of a voice.

Somewhere in the recesses of the Earth a light wind struggled free and tugged at the sail. The boat skidded easily over the water with a soft lapping.

The echo freed other sounds; muffled shrieks and screeches, hoots and crashes followed upon one another. Light and sound bounced off the cavern walls.

The wind dropped as suddenly as it had started and the boat, after trailing a few yards slowly, lay still on the water.

Zacharias sat and waited. As time lengthened he began to worry, then worry turned into fear. The boat heaved slightly on the water. It was the only movement as the luminous bodies petrified around him.

The space around seemed square. To his panic, Zacharias repeated over and over: 'North, South, East, West. The four corners of the Earth.'

The slight heaving of the boat became almost imperceptible, then it ceased altogether; the panic inside Zacharias became a hard solid knot. He thought he was hanging in eternity with no beginning or end, where life and movement no longer existed. He sat powerless and immobile with his panic, waiting for nothing.

A rigid and mortal battle was taking place amongst the subterranean forces: they were so finely matched that they did not move a hair's breath.

The scales quivered. Like a finger passing through a tree of hair, a gentle sound began in the head of Sari's broom; the gentle sound turned into a rustle and the rustle into a thread of smoke. Tiny sparks as small as insects' eyes appeared in the tuft of the broom and dropped into the water. Then little tongues of flame like agitated leaves on a tree: Sari's broom was on fire.

With a shriek Zacharias plucked the mast off the boat and dipped it into the water. It sizzled. He paddled forward, softly crying warm salt tears of release.

With the first movement of the boat light, darkness, and sound vibrated with a quality Zacharias had known but never seen.

The Earth itself seemed to yield up its own life.

He heard the roots of trees over his head suck their life from the minerals and putrid vegetation. He felt the struggle of death becoming life. He tasted acrid fear in the darkness. He smelt the stench of all beasts' desire. He saw all gradations of light, even those that vibrate in pitch darkness. And among all these things the voice continued calling: 'Let me in!' It echoed a thousand times in the far recesses of the Earth until it traced itself as a fossil in the stone.

Zacharias did not need to row anymore; the voice's magnetic power pulled the boat towards its source. He sat still, holding the broom on his knees.

They came in sight of a great stone door feebly lit by a large luminous egg hung lamplike on a pole.

The goat-ship reached the edge of the subterranean ocean. It ground against a rough wharf hewn in the rock. It was made of jasperite and as red as blood. Zacharias leapt ashore and tied up the boat to an iron ring.

By the light of the luminous egg he searched for the keyhole. But he could find no keyhole, no opening of any kind in the smooth red face of the rock. The stone key hung impotent in his hand.

'I am here,' he shouted. 'We are only divided by the stone door.' A long silence followed his words. Then with a sigh the voice replied: 'Who are you? Have you come for me?'

'I have come out of snow, through the Earth, and over the Water to find you. Our roots were linked before Time began. I am Air, the Scales. Who are you?'

'I am Woman, Fire, and Ram. Where are you, Dear Love?'

'I am in the mountain, Kecske, in the subterranean ocean which fills the Danube.'

'I must be with you.'

Zacharias searched the surface of the rock again, but there was no keyhole.

'How can I open the door,' he shouted, 'when there is no keyhole?'

'Break through it with words, blows, prayers, or music. I've been waiting too long and it is breaking my heart.'

These words were followed by a cry which ended in a bleat. Still holding the broom he thought of Sari and remembered the musical pipe and Ivor's zither; the tune echoed through his head: '*Buj buj zöldag, zöld levelecske.* Open, open, little green leaf, Open, open, great stone door.'

He took the pipe from his breast pocket and put it to his lips. With the first breath the pipe uttered a long high shriek and burst along the stem into nine little green leaves. A great creaking, the sound of stone rending, sent shivers into the marrow of the Earth. The goat-ship heaved and curled up like burning paper. Before his eyes a string of light opened; the stone door wheezed inwards as if pressed by a great weight. Then the air shuddered and vibrated with the bleating of five hundred white sheep, which poured into the Earth like a deluge of curdled milk. Zacharias was swept aside by the stampede. He clutched a piece of rock which jutted out over his head.

The white flock took straight to the water and swam west. Zacharias recovered the goat-ship and hastened after the sheep, paddling swiftly with the broom.

A hot wind charged with dust, cinnamon, and musk blew

behind him from the country of the Dead. The great stone door, Kecske, swung rumbling on the wind and closed with a crash.

Zacharias, rowing with all his might, followed the sheep west.

Author Notes

MARGARET ATWOOD (1939–), novelist, poet and critic, is one of Canada's leading writers. Two of her novels, *The Handmaid's Tale*, 1986, and *Cat's Eye*, 1989, have been shortlisted for the Booker Prize. In addition to nine volumes of poetry, she has published three collections of short stories, of which the most recent is *Wilderness Tips*, 1991.

ROSALIND BELBEN (1941–). Born in Dorset, Rosalind Belben is the author of *Bogies*, 1972; *Reuben, Little Hero*, 1973; *The Limit*, 1974; and *Dreaming of Dead People*, 1979. Our extract, Air Ride, comes from her latest novel, *Is Beauty Good*, 1989.

JOHN BERGER (1926–) was born in London and has had a varied career as a painter, teacher, art critic and writer. His work spans many genres, including poetry, documentary writing and fiction. His novel, *G*, was awarded both the Booker Prize for 1972 and the James Tait Black Memorial Prize, 1973. John Berger now lives in a village in the French Alps, the inspiration for his trilogy of short stories, *Into Their Labours*.

JORGE LUIS BORGES (1899–1986), the renowned South American fabulist, was born in Buenos Aires. Throughout an illustrious career, he was the recipient of numerous awards: in 1961 he shared the International Publishers' Prize with Samuel Beckett and in 1966 received the Ingram Merrill Foundation's Annual Literary award for his 'outstanding contribution to literature'. A poet and novelist, he is best known for his short stories, notably the collections, *A Universal History of Infamy*, 1935; *Fictions*, 1945; and *Labyrinths*, 1953.

MICHAEL BRACEWELL (1958–), was educated at Epsom College and Nottingham University. His first two novellas, *The Crypto-Amnesia Club* and *Missing Margate* brought him critical acclaim in 1988 and he consolidated his reputation as a rising young novelist with his third title, *Divine Concepts of Physical Beauty*, 1989. He is also a journalist and reviewer and now lives in Surrey.

ANTONIA BYATT (1936–) was the 1990 winner of the Booker Prize with her novel, *Possession*. Born in Sheffield and educated at Cambridge, she is the author of four earlier novels, *The Shadow of the Sun*, 1964; *The Game*, 1967; *The Virgin in the Garden*, 1978, and *Still Life*, 1980, and has also published a collection of stories, *Sugar and Other Stories*. She has had a distinguished career as a lecturer, critic and broadcaster and was awarded the C.B.E. in the New Year's Honours List 1990.

LEONORA CARRINGTON (1917–) grew up in Lancashire, but later lived in France as the companion of the Surrealist artist, Max Ernst. She is a painter in her own right and both her pictures and writing were influenced by the Surrealist movement. The novella, *The Stone Door*, comes from her anthology of fantastical tales, *The Seventh Horse and Other Tales*, 1988, which brings together many previously uncollected tales, some of them published here for the first time. Other stories have been collected recently under the title, *The House of Fear: Notes From Down Under*, 1989.

JULIO CORTAZAR (1914–1984) was born in Brussels, but later gained dual citizenship of Argentina and France. His early work is characterised by playful fantasy and surrealism, but in later years his preoccupation with political oppression in Argentina was increasingly reflected in his novels and stories. His collections include: *End of the Game and Other Stories*, 1967, *All Fires the Fire and Other Stories* and *A Change of Light and Other Stories*, 1977.

JIM CRACE (1946–) was born at Brocket Hall and grew up in North London. He gained immediate recognition with his first collection of linked 'narratives', *Continent*, 1986, for which he won three awards, the 1986 Guardian Fiction Prize, the Whitbread Book of the Year First Novel Prize, and the David Higham Prize for Fiction. His reputation was confirmed with his second novel, *The Gift of Stones*, 1988.

ANNIE DILLARD (1945–) won the Pulitzer Prize for general non-fiction with Pilgrim at Tinker Creek, 1974, an autobiographical account of a solitary year in the countryside of Virginia. Born in Pittsburg, Pa., she has worked as a journalist, contributing to a wide range of magazines, including Chicago Review and Harper's, as well as a creative writing teacher at Western Washington State University. Her books include *Holy the Firm*, 1978 and *Tickets for a Prayer Wheel* (poems), 1974.

HELEN DUNMORE (1952–). Born in Yorkshire, she has published four collections of poetry, *The Apple Fall* 1983; *The Sea Skater* 1986; *The Raw Garden* 1988; and *Short Days, Long Nights, New and Selected Poems* (1991). Her short stories have appeared in a number of magazines, including Writing Women and Stand. She is currently Writer-in-Residence at the Polytechnic of Wales.

RUTH FAINLIGHT (1931–), poet, writer and translator, was born in New York, but now lives in London. She has published numerous poetry collections, including *A Forecast, a Fable*, 1958; *Cages*, 1967; *The Region's Violence*, 1973; *Sybils and Others*, 1980 and *Fifteen to Infinity*, 1983. Her selected poems appeared in 1983. She published a collection of stories, *Daylife and Nightlife*, 1971, and was a contributor to the anthologies, Penguin Modern Stories, Volume IX, 1971, Bananas, 1977 and the Arts Council series, New Stories 4, 1979.

GABRIEL JOSIPOVICI (1940–), is the Professor of English at Sussex University, whose writings have won him international acclaim. Born in Nice, he lived in Egypt for much of his childhood, later moving to England to read English at Oxford. He is both a distinguished critic and novelist. His fiction includes *The Inventory*, 1968; *The Present*, 1975; *The Air We Breathe*, 1981, and *Contre-Jour: A Triptych after Pierre Bonnard*, 1984. *The Book of God*, 1988, about the Bible, was much praised. He is a contributor to Adam International Review, Critical Quarterly, European Judaism and the New York Review of Books, among other titles.

DORIS LESSING (1919–), novelist and non-fiction writer, was born in Persia of British parents, but grew up in South Africa, which provided the setting for her first novel, *The Grass is Singing*, 1950, as for her later short story collections, *This Was the Old Chief's Country*, 1952 and *African Stories*, 1964. Her wide-ranging fiction embraces realism, polemic and allegory. Her experimental novel, *The Golden Notebook*, 1962, which explored the personal and political concerns of a woman in the fifties, both generated controversy and won her a devoted following. Her later books, which include the mythic series, *Canopus in Argos Archives*, continue to break new ground. Her most recent novel is *The Fifth Child*, 1988. Her many awards include the Shakespeare prize, 1982, and the Premio Internazionale Mondello, 1987.

CLARICE LISPECTOR (1924–1977), is one of Brazil's foremost writers. She was born in the Ukraine, but spent her childhood in Recife and Rio de Janeiro. A Law graduate, her first novel, *Close to the Savage Heart*, was published in 1943 to critical acclaim. Two short story collections followed: *Some Stories* in 1952 and *Family Ties* in 1959. Her novels, *The Apple in the Dark*, 1961 and *The Passion According to G.H.*, 1964, further established her reputation. Her fiction often has a surface realism, but this is usually the gateway to profoundly philosophical and psychological meditations.

PÉTER NÁDAS (1942–) is a contemporary Hungarian writer, born in Budapest, who originally trained as a chemical engineer and worked as a photo-journalist. His work, which includes stories, plays and essays, is widely appreciated in Europe, but has only recently been introduced to England. An extract from his novel, *Book of Memoirs*, to be published in English translation by Pantheon, appeared in the first issue of the new quarterly, Storm, 1991.

JOYCE CAROL OATES (1938–), represented here by two short fictions, is a prolific writer, whose work includes plays, novels, stories, poetry and literary criticism. Her first short story collection, *By the North Gate*, 1963, was published when she was 25 years old and, at 31, she was one of the youngest ever writers to receive the National Book Award for Fiction. In addition to her numerous novels, her story collections include: *The Lamb of Abyssalia*, 1980; *A Sentimental Education*, 1981; *Last Days: Stories*, 1984 and *Raven's Wing: Stories*, 1986.

BEN OKRI (1959–), was born in Nigeria and was educated both there and in London. He studied Comparative Literature at the University of Essex. He published two early novels, *Flowers and Shadows* in 1980 and *The Landscapes Within* in 1982. After working as a broadcaster for the BBC World Service and as poetry editor of West Africa magazine, he published two short story collections, *Incidents at the Shrine*, shortlisted for the Commonwealth Prize in 1987 and *Stars of the New Curfew*, shortlisted for the Guardian Fiction Prize, 1988. His third novel, *The Famished Road*, won the Booker Prize in 1991.

TATYANA TOLSTAYA (1951–), was born in Leningrad and studied at the Philological Faculty of Leningrad University. She worked for the publishing house, Nauka, in the Oriental Literature department and has twice been a Writer-in-Residence at American Universities: at the University of Richmond, 1988, and Texas Tech University, Lubbock, 1990. Her first collection of stories, *On a Golden Porch*, sold out within an hour of publication in Russia and was rapturously received in the West. Among her inspirations, she cites ' . . . Russian and European folklore, the Old Testament, and crazy contemporary life.' Her second collection, *Sleepwalker in a Fog*, will be published in London in 1992.

MICHEL TOURNIER (1924–), respected French novelist, originally studied philosophy and is an expert German linguist. He worked variously as a broadcaster in French radio and television and in publishing, before turning to writing full time. He won the prestigious Grand Prix du Roman of the Académie Française with his first novel, *Friday or the Other Island* in 1967 and the Prix Goncourt for his second, *The Erl King*, 1970. He has published one collection of short stories, *The Fetishist*, and our extracts come from his latest collection of fabulous tales, *The Midnight Love Feast*, 1991.

ACKNOWLEDGEMENTS

The following stories were specially commissioned for this collection:

THE OTHER BOHEMIA © Michael Bracewell 1991

THE STORY OF THE ELDEST PRINCESS © A.S. Byatt 1991

ANNINA © Helen Dunmore 1991

THE FISH-SCALE SHIRT © Ruth Fainlight 1991

A MODERN FAIRYTALE © Gabriel Josipovici 1991

Acknowledgements are due to the following for permission to include the stories which appear in this book:

Isis in Darkness. Reprinted by permission of Margaret Atwood © 1990. From the short story collection *Wilderness Tips* as published by Bloomsbury Press in the United Kingdom, McClelland and Stewart in Canada and Bantam Doubleday Dell in the United States; *Air Ride*, an extract from *Is Beauty Good*, Serpent's Tail, 1989. Copyright © Rosalind Belben 1989; One Bear © 1991 by John Berger, published in a collection of texts: *Keeping a Rendezvous* by Granta Books, 1992; *The Secret Miracle* from *Fictions*, published as a Calder Jupiter Book in 1965 by John Calder Publishers Ltd, 1965 and reprinted in 1974 by Calder & Boyars Ltd., © Emecé Editores S.A., Buenos Aires 1956, © this translation Grove Press Inc, New York 1962, 1965, 1974, 1985. First published in Great Britain as *Ficciones* by Weidenfeld & Nicolson Ltd, 1962; *The Stone Door*, copyright © 1988 by Leonora Carrington, translation. Original French translation © 1976 by Editions Flammarion, from *The*

material acknowledged above were obtained. In the event any inadvertent omission has occurred, full acknowledgement will be made in future editions of this book.